DANGEROUS HEAT

Justin knew he would never forget the way Emily looked, standing alone on the stretch of beach where he had first found her. She was as rare and exotic as a wild English rose blooming in the desert. The wind tousled her curls and whipped at her skirt. Her chin tilted in defiance even as she twisted her hands together for courage.

As he angled toward her, he could feel his face hardening in ruthless lines of desperation. "I don't like you," he said.

"I don't like you either."

Each weighted step through the damp sand carried him nearer to his destruction. "I'm too old for you."

"Much."

He tangled his hand in her curls, drawing her head back until her mouth was a scant breath from his own. "I won't marry you."

Her hand crept around his nape. "I wouldn't have you."

"Oh, you'll have me."

She shivered at his husky promise. His mouth closed on hers, tracing its shape, its softness with a patience and delicacy he was far from feeling. He wanted to make her ache deep inside, as he was aching. He rubbed his lips across hers, nibbling and coaxing with an expertise he'd almost forgotten he possessed. He was determined to stoke the flame of her need with exquisite stealth until she burned for only him.

Her lips parted shyly beneath the tantalizing pressure, burning his restraint to cinders. . . .

BANTAM BOOKS BY TERESA MEDEIROS

ONCE an ANGEL

Teresa Medeiros

BANTAM BOOKS
New York Toronto London
Sydney Auckland

ONCE AN ANGEL

A Bantam Book / April 1993

ISBN 0-553-29409-1

Published simultaneously in the United States and Canada

Bantam Books are published by Bantam Books, a division of Random House, Inc. Its
trademark, consisting of the words "Bantam Books" and the portrayal of a rooster, is
Registered in U.S. Patent and Trademark Office and in other countries. Marca Registrada.
Bantam Books, 1540 Broadway, New York, New York 10036.

PRINTED IN THE UNITED STATES OF AMERICA

OPM   19   18

I remember clinging to Mama's hand and watching you walk away in your uniform to fight for your country in Vietnam. You were the most handsome man in the world to me. But nothing could top the sight of you coming home again. You'll always be my hero, Daddy, and this one's for you.

For Barbara Caldwell and Anne Hall Eiseman, the finest two sisters I never had.

And for Michael, who proved to me that angels do exist.

ONCE
an
ANGEL

Prologue

❖

Justin Connor's numb fingers uncurled. The smoking pistol fell from his hand. Frightened by the blast, the natives had fled, leaving him alone with the primeval roar of the waves and the dark shape crumpled a few feet away.

He bit off a savage curse.

Dread flooded him as he moved toward the motionless figure sprawled like a broken doll in the sand.

The moonlight caressed David's face, a face handsome in its good-natured ordinariness, a face one might pass on the London streets without giving it a second glance. A thin trickle of blood eased from the corner of his mouth.

His eyes fluttered open. "I do say, lad, could you move a bit to the left? You're blocking the breeze." His voice was such a matter-of-fact comfort that Justin wanted to weep.

He sank to his knees and caught David in his arms. "Damn you, Scarborough. Don't you dare die on me now!"

Blood soaked the front of David's shirt. Justin had seen

too many fatal wounds in the taming of this brutal land. Even as he struggled to stanch the bleeding with his palm, he knew this man who had been friend, brother, and father to him was going to die. He brushed a wayward curl from David's pallid brow.

David lifted his hand. A gold chain was tangled around his fingers. "Claire," he whispered hoarsely.

As he pressed the chain into Justin's bloody hand, Justin knew why David had fled back to their tent instead of to the waiting boat. He hadn't gone to fetch a weapon as Justin had supposed, but the precious miniature of his daughter that he carried in his watch case.

David's voice was waning. "Go to her. Tell her I'm sorry. Tell her I loved her. Take care of my little angel, Justin. Swear you will."

Justin couldn't speak. A lump welled up in his throat. He stared down at the watch in his hand, afraid to open it. How could he face that gamin smile, those gentle brown eyes, and be forced someday to tell her how her father had died in his arms on a lonely shore? If he didn't say the words, perhaps David would not die.

With a last burst of strength David's fingers dug like claws into his arms. His words were driven through clenched teeth. "By God, Justin! Swear it. You must!"

Justin bowed his head, refusing to meet David's fevered gaze. His tears washed over David's face. "I swear it," he whispered.

David slumped across his lap. "That's my boy." A shadow of a smile creased his mouth. "I shan't be needing a gold mine where I'm going," he murmured. "The streets are paved with nothing but gold."

Justin managed to smile through his tears. "The eternal optimist, aren't you?"

But there was no one to answer his question.

He cradled his friend's lifeless body to his chest, rocking back and forth as guilt and desolation washed over him as pounding and relentless as the waves against the sand.

When he finally rose, his stiff legs trembled. He hefted David in his arms like a child. His limp head dangled over Justin's arm, the auburn tangle of his hair gilded by moonlight. Justin laid him in the bottom of the curricle, arranging his limbs with the utmost tenderness. Using a long pole, he shoved off from the shore, then sank down beside David's body, frozen with numbing anguish.

His hand throbbed. He looked down to discover he had been clutching David's watch case so hard that the imprint was embedded in his palm. He slowly opened it.

A moppet's face, framed in unruly curls, gazed up at him, her eyes trusting and merry. David's eyes, sparkling with life. Justin snapped the watch shut. All their dreams were done now. All of it gone—the gold mine, Nicholas, little Claire's inheritance. He leaned his head against the rim of the boat, drifting, endlessly drifting as the mocking glitter of the stars blurred before his eyes.

London, England
1865

Miss Amelia Winters stole a look over the rim of her spectacles as the child slipped into the library. Only a few months ago Claire would have come pounding through the door, ribbons flying, boot buttons unhooked, chattering a merry stream. It was a pity it had taken her father's disappearance to tame her exuberance and make a proper young lady of her.

Except for that hair. The headmistress sniffed in disdain. All the brushing in the world couldn't subdue those absurd curls. Even garbed in somber colors, the child more resembled a disheveled cherub than a Foxworth girl. At least her pinafore was clean for a change. There was none of the coal dust that revealed she'd been romping with the maids again and none of the hairs that warned she'd sneaked out to the stables to feed the mewling litter of kittens rescued without Amelia's approval from a neighbor's well.

As the girl bobbed a perfunctory curtsy, her breath wafted out on a chill cloud. It wouldn't do to waste coal when it was nearly February, thought Amelia, snuggling deeper into her heavy tweeds.

Claire perched on the edge of the upholstered cushion as if afraid the rosewood armchair would swallow her. Amelia suppressed her shock. Where had the girl's childish plumpness gone? The black dress made her look gaunt and leggy, all enormous dark eyes in a face as pale as milk. Those eyes, so solemn and unflinching, rested on her now with an expression far older than Claire's eleven years. Only the child's hands betrayed her restlessness, crumpling the yellowed paper that was to be her last letter from her father.

A thread of pity stirred in Amelia. Better to be brisk and kill the child's hopes with one swift, clean blow.

She rattled the crisp sheaf of paper on her desk and cleared her throat. "I regret to inform you—"

"Do you?" Claire interrupted.

She lifted her gaze from the paper. "Do I what?"

"Regret it?"

Miss Winters blinked. Their gazes locked for a moment. The child did not look insolent, merely curious, which only infuriated Amelia more.

She adjusted her spectacles, dismayed to discover her hands were shaking more in fear than anger. "I must remind you to curb your impertinence, young lady. I have before me a letter from Sir George Grey, the governor of New Zealand. He regrets to inform you that your father, one David Scarborough, is dead."

The word fell flat in the still room. Claire went a shade paler. Her small fist convulsed around her father's letter. She knew, Amelia thought. My God, she already knew.

Regretting her sharpness, Amelia blundered on. "Your father made no provisions for you, but you shall be welcome to stay at Foxworth Seminary until satisfactory arrangements can be made."

What was she saying? She could hardly tolerate the precocious little creature. All those shocking years of living unchaperoned with her father had given her a self-confidence bordering on arrogance. Hardly a proper demeanor for a Foxworth girl. She must pack her off to the orphanage without delay.

But caught in the web of the girl's unnerving calm, Amelia droned on. "You will have to give up your sitting room, of course, as the paying students will—"

"That won't be necessary."

Amelia winced. The girl was interrupting again. Had her doting father taught her no manners?

"I shall have no need of your charity," Claire continued, her manner as cool and regal as that of a recently deposed princess. "My father's dear friend and partner in the gold mine will be coming for me very soon. Mr. Connor is heir to the present Duke of Winthrop and a rich and powerful man. My father promised he would take care of me should anything untoward happen to him."

A hint of a sneer curled Amelia's lips, showing Claire what she thought of her father's extravagant promises. She, too, had been taken in by David Scarborough's winning smile. She had been so confident that he would pay the tuition that she had made several purchases for both the school and herself credited only to his charm. Who would pay her debts now? His ghost?

He promised to come back for you as well, didn't he, dear?

Amelia bit back the cruel words, forcing a smile. "We don't feel you should harbor any childish hopes, Claire."

"Don't call me that!" Suddenly the girl was looming over the desk, her eyes seething with fierce emotion, her hands clenched into fists. "Don't ever call me that again. Only my daddy called me Claire. My name is Emily."

Amelia shrank back in her chair without realizing it. Her hand fluttered at her lace collar.

The girl fled for the door. She flung it open, almost tripping over the aproned child kneeling at the portal. By the time Miss Winters reached the door, she was gone. The pounding of her footsteps echoed through the listening silence. A flash of white dimity through a far door warned the headmistress that the maid had not been their only audience.

Amelia clung to the door frame, her breath coming in short, hard gasps. The maid straightened, weeping too hard to pretend she'd been doing anything but eavesdropping.

"Oh, mum, the poor dear," she wailed. She swiped at her reddened nose with her apron, leaving a smudge of coal dust on its tip. "Only this mornin' she gave me the sweetmeat off 'er plate to take to me consumptive brother Freddie."

Amelia straightened, giving the girl a quelling look. "If I'd wanted your opinion on Miss Scarborough's charitable activities, Tansy, I'd have asked for it."

The maid snatched up her cloth and dabbed at the face of the hall clock as the headmistress jerked her jacket straight and marched back into the library. The slam of her door thundered through the school.

The little maid rolled her eyes heavenward, her hands clasped around the rag. "'Elp the dear child, Lord," she whispered fervently. "If ever ya sent an angel to this earth, I knowed me sweet Emily Claire to be the one."

"Damn it! Damn it to bloody hell!" Emily stamped her stockinged foot on the Aubusson rug.

A porcelain doll stared back at her from a lace-trimmed pillow, her round blue eyes glazed with apathy. A delicate thread of gold circled her tiny wrist. Emily shuddered. Only the allure of gold had been strong enough to drag her father away from her. Somewhere in New Zealand there was a mine full of gold. What good was it, though, when her daddy slept beneath the earth, bound by its shining chains? Emily's hand lashed out, knocking the doll across the elegant bedroom.

She dropped to her knees and stuffed the hem of the satin coverlet into her mouth so the whole school wouldn't hear her scream. Tears scalded her cheeks. Her sobs had faded to choked whimpers before she dared to open her eyes to the lonely extravagance of the suite.

The doll lay in a pitiful heap before the window, her petticoats tossed over her face.

"Oh, Annabel," Emily whispered. She crawled to the doll and turned her over.

A thin crack gashed her china temple. Emily hugged her, feeling the jagged fissure that ran from the doll's hairline to her own shattered heart.

"I'm so very sorry, Annabel." She smoothed the doll's velvet skirt and gently kissed the crack. "We have to be very brave now, dear. Daddy said we must be very brave." Her laugh came out as a feeble hiccup. "All we have to do is wait."

She climbed into the window seat, clutching the doll to her breast. A lamplighter wound his solitary path down the cobbled street below, nursing the gaslights to flickering life. Their misty halos pierced the twilight with a greenish tint. Annabel's reflection gazed back at her from the window, her rosy cheeks and blond ringlets a startling contrast to her own tousled, dark curls and wan face. She tucked the doll beneath her chin. A shiver wracked her slender body.

"We'll wait like good girls, Annabel," she whispered. "Daddy can't come for us now, but Mr. Connor will. Daddy promised he would come."

As she rocked back and forth in the gathering darkness, a tear splashed from her chin and trickled slowly down Annabel's porcelain cheek.

PART I

And yet, as angels in some
brighter dreams
Call to the soul when man doth
sleep . . .

—HENRY VAUGHAN

What angel wakes me from my
flowery bed?

—WILLIAM SHAKESPEARE

Chapter 1

· 🐚 ·

My darling daughter,
I pray this letter finds you well. . . .

New Zealand,
the North Island
1872

"*If* ever a brat needed a beatin', it's Emily Claire Scarborough!"

Barney's snarled refrain almost made Emily smile. She turned, bracing her back against the prow of the small steamer. He glared at her, his pockmarked face twisted with hatred.

Flexing his wiry hands on the boat's rail, he muttered, "And I'm just the lad to give it to 'er."

Doreen grabbed her brother's ear, twisting it with one of the pinches that had made her the terror of every classroom at Foxworth's Seminary for Young Ladies.

"Ow, sis!" he howled. "Turn loose. I 'aven't laid a fist on 'er. Not yet, anyway."

"It's more than a fist I'm thinkin' you'd like to be layin' on 'er. I saw yer eyes when we was stuffin' 'er into that fancy frock."

Emily did smile then, and Doreen twisted harder, her lapse into cockney enraging her further. They all knew it was only her ability to mock the genteel speech of the upper classes that had earned her a position at the school. That and Miss Winters's rapidly failing finances.

Barney knocked her hand away. "Between you two buggers, I'm like to be blind *and* deaf before we ever see New Zealand. Women!" he spat out, reluctantly including his sister in that scathing epithet.

Rabid ferrets, Emily mused.

She had been dragged halfway across the world by two rabid ferrets. They walked upright and wore bonnets and caps, but even draping them in silk and diamonds wouldn't have cloaked their true . . . ferretness. She rubbed her arms. They were black and blue from Doreen's pinches. She supposed the woman would bite her if she didn't fear the captain would find it uncivilized. Or that Emily just might bite her back.

She sighed. The tiny mail packet chugged through the water, churning an aqua swath through the indigo sea.

Barney clawed at his collar. The wool suit Miss Winters had bought him before their departure would be well suited for the brisk autumn winds now whipping through London, but not for the balmy breezes of New Zealand. The suit had obviously been tailored for a man two sizes smaller than he.

He mopped sweat from his brow. "This country ain't natural. It's like bein' in 'ell before me time." He narrowed his one good eye at Emily. "And if this is 'ell, that wench is the devil's own imp. Look at 'er. You'd think she owned the bloody steamer and the Tasman Sea with it."

His sister glanced not at Emily, but back at the bridge. The elderly captain was slumped over the wheel, half dozing.

"She might own it after we dump her in the lap of her rich guardian," Doreen said. "The highfalutin duke's heir is to pay us all the money he owes poor Miss Winters for looking after the evil little bitch all these years. And a tenth of it's ours to keep."

"Ought to be 'alf," Barney muttered, fingering the shiny bruise beneath his eye.

Emily was tempted to agree with him.

Monday she had smothered all of their rations with salt.

Tuesday she had poured out Barney's whiskey and replaced it with the contents of his sister's privy pot.

Wednesday she had tossed his only suit overboard. He had been forced to dive after it buck naked while Emily sliced her finger and cheerfully dripped blood into the sea in hopes of attracting sharks. It had taken both Doreen and the burly engine stoker to restrain him from throwing her overboard.

Only this morning she had blackened his eye with her flailing fist as he and Doreen had stripped off her simple pinafore and crammed her into a skirt and bustle.

"She ain't even got the decency to wear a bonnet," Barney growled.

While his face blistered and Doreen grew more sallow with each day of the journey, Emily had the sheer audacity to turn her face to the sun and brown like a little butternut.

"At least we finally got a proper frock on the boyish little fiend," Doreen snapped.

Barney's gaze roamed up and down Emily's figure, making her shudder. Emily knew he found her less than boyish, much as he loathed to admit it. Her breasts still ached from the horrid press of his bony chest as he had held her down for Doreen to tie the bustle tapes. She edged as far down the rail from him as the deck would allow. Leering at her, he adjusted his trousers. Emily hoped he was strangulating.

Doreen boxed his ears. "Keep yer bloody hands where I can see 'em. We can't muck this up now. We got this job only because Miss Amelia couldn't afford to send another detective."

Barney's answering whine was interrupted by the captain's drowsy cry: "Land ho!"

Emily's pulse quickened.

The steamer slowed. A green flush appeared on the horizon. Doreen gripped the rail, her drawn features made almost pretty by anticipation. When they drew closer, Barney fumbled at the ropes on the small lifeboat that would carry him ashore. He was determined to find the elusive Mr. Connor himself before he risked Emily running away again on dry land. She had run away once in Sydney and twice in Melbourne. But Barney was as dogged as a bloodhound. He'd simply thrown her over his shoulder and carted her back.

Doreen sucked in an excited breath through her pinched nostrils. "Shall I go with you? Do you think you can find him alone?"

"If this bloke is as fine and uppity as Miss Winters said 'e was, I'll march straight up to 'is fancy 'ouse and fetch 'im. Then we'll be rid of the brat and rich to boot."

Emily waited until Barney had hoisted the little boat into the bucking waves before leaning over the side and waving her handkerchief at him. "Do take care, Barney. One of Mr. Connor's partners is dead. The other disappeared without a trace." She smiled sweetly. "I should so hate for the same thing to happen to you."

Barney's complexion paled to green. Shooting her a nasty look, he steered around and began rowing for shore.

A gull circled the dingy steamer, then soared into the sky. Emily's gaze followed its flight toward the silvery rim of the island.

"Never forget," she whispered to herself. "Justin Connor is a very dangerous man."

"The devil take that blasted Winters woman!"

As his soft-spoken master exploded in a burst of temper, Penfeld jumped, rattling the teacups on his tray. The sea gull marching across the windowsill cocked his head in curious reproach.

Justin Connor threw down the crumpled letter and paced the hut, ruffling his dark hair into wild disarray. "Am I never to be left in peace?"

Penfeld set the tray on the stained tablecloth, fearing for his precious china with Justin's long limbs at such odds with his gait. "It must have been the gum digger, sir. I told you the man was asking too many questions."

Justin turned with a sweeping gesture that made Penfeld thankful he had eased his sturdy bulk in front of the tea service. "What makes you think the tenacious Miss Winters would require a mere mortal for her endeavors? She probably spotted me in her crystal ball." He flapped his arms. "I'm only surprised she posted a letter instead of flying straight over on her broom to fetch me."

Penfeld's lips twitched, but he hid it behind a somber cough.

Justin stabbed an accusing finger at the gull. "Are you one of her familiars, too? No black cats for our indomitable Miss Winters."

The gull tucked his head shyly beneath his wing.

Justin growled. "Ought to wring your scrawny little neck. Put you in the pot for supper." He started for the bird, hands outstretched.

Penfeld cleared his throat meaningfully.

Justin swept up the letter that had been posted from London over five months before and had arrived per a native runner only that afternoon. "The sheer arrogance of the woman! She insists I retrieve the girl immediately. She's concocted some fabulous hints about her being involved in a scandal. What could the child have done? Spilled her milk at supper? Pilfered the sugar bowl?"

Penfeld patted his rotund belly fondly. "I was once caned myself for a similar crime."

"The grasping creature. I've sent every halfpenny I could scrape together for the girl's education."

Penfeld already knew that. He had been the one to post the slim envelopes devoid of a return address.

Justin sank down on an upended rum barrel. His shoulders slumped. "She must want more money. But I've nothing left to sell. What am I to do?"

Penfeld directed all of his attention to polishing the immaculate spout of the teapot with his sleeve. "The Winters woman might not be the only one to learn of your whereabouts. Perhaps your family, sir . . ."

Justin lifted his head and looked at him with amber eyes that were dusted with flecks of ruthless gold. He spoke with the level enunciation that had been known to freeze the staunchest Maori warrior in his tracks. "I have no family."

For a moment the only sound was the clink of one cup against another. Justin's gaze slowly melted from furious to imploring. "I'm a bachelor. Doesn't that woman understand? I can't be responsible for a child. It's quite impossible. She's far better off staying in England, where she can get a proper education."

Penfeld blew an imaginary speck of dust from the cream pitcher. "And when she's of an age to marry?"

Justin's laughter had a wild edge to it. "We've years to worry about that. She was only three when David died. She can't be more than ten or eleven now." Fueled by purpose, he donned his gold-rimmed spectacles and began to scribble furiously on the back of the paper. "I'm sending a letter back with the runner. The girl stays in the school her father chose for her. It's in her best interest. I'll send more money when I'm able."

"Have you ever thought the child might want a home? A family?"

Justin's pen hung poised over the paper. As he lifted his naked gaze, Penfeld wished he could bite back the words.

His master's sweeping gesture encompassed the dusty hut, the crude dirt floor, the books heaped in every inch of available space. "Does this look like a home?" He touched his stubbled chin, his shirtless chest, the jagged hole worn in the knee of his calico dungarees. "Do I look like a family?"

Penfeld stared at the floor. Justin folded the letter in a neat square, scrawled a new address on the envelope, and held it out. Penfeld took it.

He paused at the door, glancing back to find Justin still slumped on the barrel, his hand cupped around the gold watch he wore on a chain around his neck. In their years together, Penfeld had rarely seen him without it. As Justin snapped open the cover, a distant mist haunted his amber eyes.

Sighing with regret, Penfeld turned away and plodded toward the native village.

He caressed the worn envelope between his fingers, fearing it was not the poor little girl who needed his master, but his poor master who needed the girl.

Emily shifted her bustle with both hands, watching with amused interest the battle taking place at the stern of the steamer. Three hours had passed with no sign of Barney's boat. Doreen alternated between searching the horizon with a rusty spyglass and threatening the half-deaf, and, Emily suspected, half-daft steamer captain into drifting for one more hour. The captain's little mail packet ran only once a month from Melbourne to Auckland, and he was determined to sail.

While Doreen squawked and the captain bellowed, Emily turned back to the water, preferring the soothing lap of the waves against the hull. The balmy wind tore at her curls. The sun drifted like a golden feather into the sea. How ironic that after all those years of waiting, she had spent her last ounce of energy trying to abort this trip. They would never have gotten her aboard the ship from England if they hadn't laced her coffee with a dose of belladonna that had almost killed her.

They were determined to deliver her to the one man in the world she loathed more than them—Justin Connor.

The roar of the steamer's engines shook the deck. Emily clutched the rail, feeling the pistons throb to life like her hatred for her guardian.

Rumors had flown through London society when the only son of the wealthy duke had failed to return from his New Zealand expedition. Girls Emily had once called friends brought her the murmured tales from their parents' drawing rooms, their malice masked by well-meaning sighs of pity and pointed glances at her shabby frocks and scuffed boots.

In the best London circles Justin Connor's very name came to embody danger and romance. At the school it was whispered in tones of naughty reverence. Emily wasn't the only girl who drifted into sleep with his image swashbuckling through her dreams.

Most believed him a dashing adventurer, a speculator who had made his fortune gambling in land and gold and human lives. They swore he had cast aside his own family and had scoffed at their written pleas to come home and take his rightful place as heir to the Winthrop shipping fortune.

Emily narrowed her eyes. She could well imagine him ensconced on the fertile New Zealand coast, living in the handsome Victorian mansion he had built with her father's gold . . . and her father's blood. Perhaps he had his own daughter by now—a golden-haired little doll-child swathed in love and lace. In seven years he had sent her not one personal note, not one word of kindness. Miss Winters had taken great pains to show her the stilted messages, the pathetic handfuls of pound notes and shillings.

After a few weeks of such obvious neglect, they had given her spacious sitting room to Cecille du Pardieu, a china-faced brat who was rumored to be the illegitimate daughter of an Austrian prince. It was only Miss Winters's fear of Emily's mysterious guardian that stopped her from casting her into the streets. It was decided she would earn her bread by teaching the younger girls who had once been her adoring equals.

In her tiny attic box-room, Emily had crawled beneath the gables and rubbed a clean spot on the sooty glass with her sleeve. She had gazed for hours across the grimy ocean of roofs and chimneys and waited for Mr. Connor to come and take her away.

Groaning, the steamer jolted into motion. Doreen screeched a protest. As the island melted into the horizon, Emily's nails dug into the rail.

"We won't meet today, Mr. Connor," she whispered. "Not today. Not ever." He would never have the chance to laugh in her face for daring to believe he might want her in his life.

But as the steamer chugged into its tidy rhythm, Doreen's moan of despair careened into a whoop of joy. Emily's gaze followed the stretch of her outflung arm.

Barney's tiny boat cut through the waves. Emily's breath caught in her throat. She took two dazed steps toward the rail and watched as Doreen and Barney struggled to hoist the boat up the side.

Before Barney could climb out, Doreen was poking him in the ribs. "What did he say? Didn't you bring him back with you?" She craned her scrawny neck to peer into the boat as if her brother might be hiding someone under the narrow seat. "Is he coming? Is he sending a fancy boat for us?"

Barney slowly raised his head, his eyes flat peridots in his sallow face. "He ain't there. Ain't no one there but a pack o' bleedin' savages and some old 'ermit named Pooka livin' in a hut. There ain't no fancy 'ouse and there ain't no fancy gentleman either."

"It can't be. He has to be there. Our Miss Amelia said so."

Barney's gaze came to rest on Emily with pure malevolence. "You 'eard me. 'E ain't there."

Doreen's shoulders slumped. "Miss Amelia was afraid of this. She didn't even tell him we were bringing the brat in the letter she sent."

"Then 'e must o' found out some other way and moved on. Wouldn't you?"

A bolt of raw pain shot through Emily, shocking her with its intensity. She hated Doreen. She hated Barney. She hated the whole world. But most of all she hated the tiny corner of her heart that had dared to hope.

Tears sheened her vision. She threw back her head and burst into laughter, speaking for the first time in that long, sullen afternoon. "I'm sure Miss Winters will be receiving an explanation very soon. 'Dear Miss Winters, I regret to inform you my present situation is not suited for the care of a child. Enclosed within is my generous offering of three pounds and five shillings for the continuance of her education, her board, her dowry, and an extra halfpenny to buy her a sweetmeat.' "

Barney and Doreen gaped at her; their pointed jaws dropped to their throats.

"Christ, the two of you are so pathetic! You trot halfway around the world at the bidding of some grasping, senile old woman on an idiot's mission. You with your hideous bonnet and you with your short, ugly suit. You're both clowns! We're all clowns in Miss Amelia Winters's bloody traveling circus!"

Emily spun around. She was gulping back tears now and she would be damned to eternal hell before those two leeches would see her cry.

She heard them whispering behind her and wondered if she had gone too far. She doubted if any of Miss Winters's genteel pupils had ever dared address the prickly Miss Dobbins in such a manner.

The creak of a plank warned Emily. She turned around. Barney and Doreen slunk toward her, shoulders hunched like two alley cats. Emily cast a frantic glance at the bridge. The captain was draped over the wheel, snoring with his eyes open.

"You were poor Miss Amelia's last hope," Doreen said, her voice as oddly flat as her eyes.

"Ungrateful little witch," Barney muttered.

Emily pressed herself to the rail. The rough wood dug into her back. "Stay away from me. I'm warning you."

"Why?" Doreen taunted. "Is the great and mighty Mr. Connor going to swoop down from the sky to save you? He don't want you. Nobody does."

The words should have lost their power to sting. But Emily discovered they hadn't. Silently cursing the weight of her heavy skirts, she gauged her chances of dashing past them on the narrow deck.

Barney cocked his head. "What was it Miss Amelia said about bringin' 'er back?"

Doreen lapsed into pure cockney. "Said she was a disgrace to the school. Drivin' 'er finest pupils away. Said if I brought 'er back, I'd be lookin' fer a new position meself."

Barney nodded smugly. The twilight wind blew cooler as brother and sister gazed at each other in a moment of silent accord. With a resourcefulness born of surviving a motherless childhood in the East End of London, they rushed her.

Barney caught one leg, Doreen the other. Emily balled up her fist and smashed it into Barney's face. Blood spewed, and she knew she had broken his nose. She enjoyed a fierce second of triumph. Then the sky and water swapped places as they heaved her up and over the rail of the steamer into the darkening sea.

*C*hapter 2

· ❀ ·

You haunt my thoughts both day and night. . . .

*E*mily sank like a stone. The narrow double skirts twined around her legs in serpentine cords, cutting off her feeble kicks. The weight of the whalebone bustle dragged her down, deep into the murky depths until the shimmer of the sunset on the water faded to black.

God? Her voice was shy and hesitant, as it had been when her father was alive before she learned that swearing and stomping got more attention than tugging politely on someone's skirt.

No answer.

God? Are you there? Louder this time, more strident. The crushing pressure in her chest worsened. *I know I haven't been very nice the past few years. Miss Winters says I'm quite a naughty girl, especially after that sordid incident with the gardener's son.*

Her skirt wrapped around her face in choking folds. Perhaps this was an inopportune moment to be reminding God of her sins.

She clawed the skirt from her face. *I guess what I'm trying to say is that I'd be very grateful if you would let me live. Not really for myself, sir. Just to spite Barney and Doreen.*

And Justin Connor, that dirty, no-good, thieving wretch who stole my daddy's gold mine.

The familiar litany was a prayer all its own. She had breathed it, dreamed it, and feasted on its bitterness for seven years. Her legs pummeled the water with new ferocity. She tore at the buttons of her bodice, wrenched the bustle's tape from its mooring. Her head pounded. Tiny dots of light danced before her eyes. Still she clawed at the heavy garments, shedding each layer like musty skins. Finally, she was able to shoot toward the surface, strong and lithe in the simple cotton chemise issued each of the girls at the seminary.

Her hands pressed on with a life of their own, ripping the chemise as if they could somehow tear asunder not only the garment, but all the drab, lonely, soot-stained years since she had sat in Miss Winters's library and been told her daddy was never coming back.

The buoyant water bore her upward. Her head split the surface with a splash. She sucked in a shuddering breath. Life and air tingled through her blood all the way to the tips of her toes. The brilliant orb of the sun lay flat on the water, and for a dazzling instant Emily couldn't tell where the exploding rainbow of the sunset ended and she began. She dove beneath the waves and turned an exultant flip.

She emerged from the water, shaking sun-gilded drops from her hair. "Thank you, God," she whispered fiercely. "I shall try to be nicer. I swear I will."

At that moment she saw the steamer chugging toward the far horizon. A faint cry floated on the wind. Barney waved his arms and Emily knew he had spotted her.

Noble intentions forgotten, Emily thumbed her nose and wiggled her fingers at him in a gesture seldom practiced at the seminary. Blowing him a final taunting kiss, she kicked herself around, rolling and bobbing like a sleek seal. The silvery curve of the shoreline beckoned. She quenched a flare of trepidation. Before he'd gone off on his quest for gold, she and her father had rented a modest cottage at Brighton each summer. She'd become a strong swimmer. It couldn't be as far to land as it looked. Could it?

The cool water caressed her bare skin. A wave of heady delight coursed through her. She drew in a deep breath and struck for the shore with long, graceful strokes, free at last.

As Justin prowled the deserted beach, the bloated moon laved the peak of each swell in molten silver. The waves broke on the sand and rushed over his feet in a swirl of foam before the sea could suck them back. He felt the inexorable tug against his bare soles as if the sea held the power to melt the very shore beneath his feet.

He thrust his hands deep in his pockets. The breeze whispered of a respite from his aching restlessness, but for Justin it was a taunting refrain. He couldn't even still his thoughts long enough to hear the night's music calling to him. The only thing more elusive than sleep was peace.

Damn the tenacious Miss Winters and her letters! It had been months since he had been jolted from sleep by the bright, merry edge of a child's laughter. Tonight the mocking echo had driven him stumbling and groaning from his pallet to seek the brighter darkness of night.

He paused, rocking back and forth on his heels, and stared blindly out to sea. Cool spray misted his skin. It had been seven years since he, Nicholas, and David had come to New Zealand to seek their fortunes. Seven years since Trini had dragged his boat ashore and pried David's stiffening body from his grip. But when Justin closed his eyes, time melted like the sand beneath his feet.

If the smooth-talking Nicky had been their wit and Justin their brains, it was David who had been their heart.

After weeks of fruitless panning for gold in the cold shadow of the Southern Alps, it had been David's relentless optimism that had given them the cheer to continue. David had hope enough for all of them; David had dreams for the future; David had Claire.

Claire. Long after Nicky was snoring, Justin would lie awake in the dark and listen hungrily as David talked of his baby daughter. As he would drift into sleep, it was almost as if the scent of her tousled curls and the echo of her irrepressible giggle would warm their lonely camp. He had even dreamed of her once. She had toddled from the sea, her plump arms outstretched, the lilting timbre of her voice crying for her father. In the dream it had not been David but Justin himself who soothed her puckered brow against his shoulder.

The stringent cry of a kiwi shattered his memories. Justin sucked in a breath, half expecting the beach to erupt in a welter of Maori natives, their tattooed faces twisted in frenzied cries for *utu,* their sun-browned hands twined around the deadly hilts of their *taiaha*s. From behind him came only the flurry of wings as a startled gannet took to the sky.

Justin opened his eyes. He stood on a different shore now. The salt-tinged breeze of the North Island was kinder and balmier than the stiff winds of the South Island. The palms swayed in lulling rhythms and the sea sang instead of roaring. He had created a life for himself here. A small and simple life stripped of snarls and entanglements. But the stench of gunpowder and blood still haunted his nostrils, mingling with the rich, sweet scent of the crimson-flowered pohutukawas.

It had been Trini, with his innocent wisdom, who had told him he still carried with him the body of his friend.

Justin kicked at the waves and started down the moon-drenched ribbon of beach. If he didn't return soon, Penfeld would come searching for him. His valet believed him too absentminded and too immersed in his music to find the hut once he wandered far from it.

He turned his face to the wind, abandoning his senses to the seductive beauty of the night. Stars misted the smudged charcoal of the northern sky. His hair danced against his shoulders like a dark cloak as he ambled along, lost in the pounding symphony of sand and surf.

A cloud darted across the moon; Justin spotted a dark shape against the sand. Seaweed, he thought. Or driftwood. The cloud sped away. Moonlight spilled over the beach, illuminating the shape in a pool of riveting clarity.

Justin's heart slammed into an uneven drumbeat; he glided forward as if in a trance.

A woman lay on the sand, half curled into herself, half exposed to his piercing gaze. No, not a woman, but a gossamer creature woven of moonlight and dreams. Justin blinked, expecting her to vanish. But she remained—mysterious, provocative—and wearing not a single stitch of clothing.

He crept nearer. Her cheek was pillowed on folded hands. Her breasts rose and fell gently with each breath. Justin's dazed mind absorbed details with dizzying lucidity: a cherub's face—a dash of freckles across the bridge of a snub nose, a rosebud mouth, lashes of stubby velvet, an unruly mass of chestnut curls. Before he could stop it, his gaze drifted lower, where a nest of darker curls glistened with sea drops. His toes curled into the wet sand.

The sun had kissed her face and arms, but the rest of her was polished to creamy pearl. Sand sparkled against her skin like ground diamonds. Luminous coral tipped her breasts. He was tempted to look around for the giant shell that must have birthed her.

His gaze flicked upward to the mocking wink of the stars. "For me?" he whispered.

He sank down cross-legged in the sand beside her. He ought to be rousing her, checking her for injuries, covering her. But he had worn only his tattered dungarees. Even with the best of intentions, one of them was going to be naked. And he wasn't yet sure his intentions were the best.

He rested his chin on steepled fingers, unable to drag his gaze away from the rosy little nymph. He couldn't fathom the effect she had on him. He felt as if someone had punched him low in the gut, driving out all the breath with one blow. His rising desire was a foreign heat that bore no relation to the rare fumble in the dark he might share with some generous Maori woman or Auckland whore.

He felt he might sit forever, afraid of not touching her, more afraid of touching her, locked in her strange spell until someone dragged him away. The breeze whispered encouragement even as the waves chanted a warning. They might have been the only two alive. For the first time Justin understood Zeus's temptation to turn himself into a swan to mate with Leda in the forest. He knew the hunger of the fierce knight Huldbrand groaning for the siren song of his sea witch Undine.

A primitive enchantment beckoned him. It had nothing to do with the civilized constraints of his time, but hearkened back to another era, when a man had knelt between a woman's thighs with no need for polite small-talk to woo her heart.

Justin buried his face in his hands. Sweet Lord, his morals were becoming as muddled as his dreams. Perhaps he should return to England, where he wouldn't be tempted to ravish a girl just because she'd had the ill luck to wash up naked on his beach.

He shoved his hands through his hair, determined to take some action. He would have to carry her back to the hut. Unless he wanted to drag her by the hair, that would mean touching her.

He sat up on his knees. The feathery fingers of his shadow fell over her, brushing all the plump swells and lush hollows his hands burned to touch. Dragging in a breath that was more a groan, he eased an arm beneath her shoulders. The coral petals of her mouth parted in sleepy surrender. Justin's tongue darted out to moisten his lips.

What could one kiss hurt? Even Sleeping Beauty's prince had stolen that much. He leaned forward, taking painstaking care that no less-principled part of his body should meet with hers. He touched her mouth softly with his own. Her lips were salty-sweet. Justin licked the salt away, glazing her lips with liquid moonlight. He couldn't remember the last time he had kissed a woman. His head reeled. Only minutes ago he had been walking alone on the beach. Now he was kissing a goddess.

A mistake. As her lips parted beneath the subtle, hungry pressure of his own, Justin knew kissing her had been a terrible mistake. But it was too late to extricate himself. He could only slide his tongue between her parted lips, making hot, slippery love to her mouth with all the tender ferocity his body craved. Her taste was magic and he couldn't have pulled himself away if she had wrapped her legs around him and dragged him to her kingdom deep beneath the sea.

He buried his face in her damp curls. The faintest aroma of vanilla clung to her hair, rendered erotic by its very purity. Just one touch, he promised himself. Just to rake his fingers across her sand-sugared skin, to cup the gentle swell of her breast in his palm . . .

He was already reaching for her when the husky whisper came, so close to his ear it had the intimacy of his own thoughts. "I stabbed the last man who stuck his tongue in my mouth."

Justin slowly lifted his head. He hung there, caught dead in the sights of her sparkling brown eyes.

"What's wrong? I didn't swallow it, did I?" Her pert nose crinkled as she laughed. Justin thought it was the most endearing thing he had ever seen.

Her merry eyes went somber. She lifted her hand. Justin couldn't move, couldn't breathe. Her fingers caught a stray lock of his hair, brushed it gently from his brow. "You have the most extraordinary eyes," she whispered.

Then she rolled over, snuggled her face against the warmth of his lap, and went back to sleep.

Time stopped. Justin couldn't have said how long he knelt there, brushing the sand from her tangled curls and enduring the exquisite torture of her warm sigh breaching the threadbare calico of his dungarees.

He didn't even hear Penfeld approach, huffing and puffing as if he'd trotted all the way from England. "There you are, sir. I was just out for a stroll—" His gaze dropped to Justin's lap. He threw a hand over his eyes. "Good Lord!"

"What?" Justin gazed dumbly up at him, still lost in the throes of his reverie.

Penfeld peeped between his round little fingers. "If I've come at an inopportune moment, sir . . . ?"

Justin blinked as if coming awake after a long sleep. The sleep of a lifetime. He reluctantly untangled his fingers from the skein of curls. "No, no. You've come at the perfect time. Give me your coat."

Justin had to admire his valet's aplomb. Penfeld turned his back and peeled off his coat as if finding his master cuddled on the beach with a nude, insensible woman were a normal occurrence. He started to fold it. Justin tugged it out of his hand. If he hadn't stopped him, Justin knew he would have washed and pressed it before handing it over.

Penfeld rubbed his arms, shivering in his crisp linen shirt as if he were the one naked. "I do say, is it a mermaid, sir?"

"Do you see any gills?"

Penfeld chanced a tentative glance over his shoulder. What he did see was a voluptuous young woman being tenderly enveloped in the folds of his coat.

Justin stood, gathering her like a child in his arms. Her head lolled warm and damp against his shoulder. His gaze traced her features—the elfin tilt of her nose, the pout that made no apology for its sensual promise.

Penfeld dared to turn around. "Wherever did she come from, sir? Could she be the victim of a shipwreck perhaps? Or a stowaway?"

Grinning, Justin lifted his head. "No stowaway, Penfeld, but a gift. A gift from the sea."

Penfeld couldn't remember the last time he'd seen his master truly smile. Justin was already striding down the beach, his steps no longer weighted, but as light as if he carried not a woman, but a blithe spirit fashioned of sea foam and stardust. As Penfeld watched, Justin did the most extraordinary thing. He lowered his head and pressed a kiss to the tip of the woman's nose.

Penfeld mopped his forehead, wondering if they'd both been struck with the moon madness so coveted and feared by the natives.

Emily burrowed into the thin mattress, her mind tugging greedily at the blurred edges of sleep. She despised waking up. Despised the sleet tapping at the tiny attic window, the wash water frozen in her basin, the prospect of crawling down the steep stairs to teach French to wealthy little brats who didn't know their *demitasses* from their *derrières* and who teased her mercilessly because her dress was two years too small. Groaning, she fumbled for a pillow to pull over her head. Perhaps if she hid long enough, Tansy would come tapping on the door with a mug of steaming black coffee smuggled out from under Cook's bulbous nose.

Her groping search yielded no pillow. A new sensation crept over her, a feeling utterly delicious and so foreign to her gloomy attic that she wanted to weep at its beauty.

Warmth.

She slowly opened her eyes. The sun fanned tingling fingers across her face. She lay there, stunned, basking in its heat, enveloped in its healing rays. She closed her eyes against the dazzling shaft of light. When she opened them again, a twisted green face hung only an inch above her own, its pointed teeth bared in a ferocious grimace.

She shrieked and scrambled backward, groping for a weapon. Her fingers curled around the first blunt object they could find. As her back slammed into a wall, dust exploded, setting her off on a quaking chain of sneezes.

"Now look what you've done, Trini. You've frightened the poor girl. I dare say she's never seen a savage before."

Emily wiped her streaming eyes. Now two faces were peering at her. One was still green, but the other was round and decidedly English. It was clicking its tongue and shaking its side-whiskers like a great overgrown hamster.

The fierce green face loomed nearer. "How do you do, miss? The sheer luminosity of your countenance beguiles me. I take extreme delight in welcoming you, our most charming breast."

The round face pinkened. Emily gaped. The savage's words had come rolling out in deep, resonant tones as if he'd just strolled from the hallowed corridors of Cambridge, his feathered cloak swinging around his shoulders. Emily realized his teeth were bared not in a snarl, but in a beaming smile. Nor was he entirely green. Deep furrows of jade had been tattooed in his honey-colored skin in elaborate curls and soaring wings.

A soft groan came out of the shadows. "Not breast, Trini. *Guest.*"

She squinted into the corner, but the sunlight had blinded her. She could make out only a vague shape.

The tattooed man stretched out a hand. She recoiled and smacked it away. "I'll keep my breast to myself, thank you. I'm not a simpering ninny for some native Lothario to ravish."

The savage threw back his head. His musical laughter rocked the small hut.

"Did I say something amusing?" she asked the hamster. Her head was starting to pound and she was wishing even more desperately for that coffee.

"Oh, dear, I'm afraid so. You see—the Maori don't ravish their victims." He leaned forward and whispered, "They eat them."

Emily felt herself go the same color as the snorting native. She pressed herself to the wall. "Stay away from me. I'm warning the both of you. I wasn't kicked out of every girls' school in England for nothing." Emily disliked lying. She much preferred to embellish the truth.

She attacked the air with her makeshift weapon. The native danced backward. Narrowing her eyes in what she hoped was a menacing fashion, she said, "That's right. I know how to use this thing."

"What a comfort," came a dry voice from the corner. "If Penfeld ever decides to stop serving tea long enough to dust, you'll be of great service."

Emily glanced down to discover she was threatening a cannibal with a feather duster. Her cheeks burned.

A man unfolded himself from the shadows with lanky grace. He stepped into a beam of sunlight, tilting back a battered panama hat with one finger.

Their eyes met and Emily remembered everything. She remembered swimming until her arms and legs had turned leaden and her head bobbed under the water with each stroke. She remembered crawling onto the beach and collapsing in the warm sand. Then her memories hazed—a man's mouth melted tenderly into hers, his dark-lashed eyes the color of sunlight on honey.

Emily gazed up into those eyes. Their depths were a little sad, a trifle mocking. She couldn't tell if they mocked her or himself. She forced her gaze down from his, then wished she hadn't.

Her throat constricted. His physical presence was as daunting as a blow. She had never seen quite so much man. The sheer volume of his sun-bronzed skin both shocked and fascinated her. In London the men swathed themselves in layers of clothing from the points of their high starched collars to the tips of their polished shoes. Shaggy whiskers shielded any patch of skin that risked exposure.

But this man wore nothing but sheared-off dungarees that clung low on his narrow hips. The chiseled muscles of his chest and calves drank in the sunlight. To Emily's shocked eyes, he might as well have been naked.

Another unwelcome memory returned—damp sand clinging to her own bare skin. The pulse in her throat throbbed to mortified life. She glanced down to find herself wrapped in the voluminous folds of a man's frock coat. The sleeves hung far below her hands, nearly enveloping the duster.

"My man Penfeld was kind enough to lend you his coat."

The husky scratch of the stranger's voice sent shivers down her spine. An endearing lilt had been layered over his clipped English, flavoring it with an exotic cadence. She had heard similar accents in Melbourne.

Disconcerted to find her thoughts read so neatly, she shot him a nasty look. A dazzling smile split the somber black of his stubbled chin. Dear Lord, the amiable wretch had kissed her! What other liberties had he taken while she lay in his embrace? Dropping the offensive duster, Emily buried her fists in the coat and hugged herself, fighting a sudden chill.

Penfeld-the-Hamster leaned forward in his shirtsleeves and suspenders and peered into her face with concern. "You look a trifle pale, miss. Would you care for some tea?"

"Coffee, please. Very strong and very black."

Penfeld looked as dismayed as if she'd asked for a straight shot of arsenic. His whiskers quivered.

"You'll have to forgive him," said the man. "He's been waiting years for the opportunity to serve a lady tea."

"He'll have to wait a bit longer, then, won't he?" she snapped.

She couldn't tell if it was laughter or reproach that kinked the corner of the stranger's well-shaped mouth. While Penfeld retreated to the cast-iron stove, shaking his head sadly, the native squatted and grinned at her. To Emily he still looked hungry.

"Fix some for him, too," she commanded. "Or does he prefer blood?"

The stranger crossed his muscular arms over his chest. "Only the blood of virgins."

Emily pasted on her cockiest smile, determined to boast her way past these half-naked rogues. "Then I've nothing to worry about, have I?"

A shadow flitted over his face but was gone before she could define it. Her mind raced feverishly. She was not in London, but halfway across the world in New Zealand. What if the dim-witted Barney had been wrong? If Justin Connor *was* living somewhere on this isolated stretch of coast, she would have to flee as soon as possible. No body of land was big enough to hold the two of them.

A silver tray wielded by a pristine white glove slid into her vision. A dainty china cup perched on its gleaming surface. Penfeld held one hand behind his back with painstaking care. "Do forgive me, miss. I lost my other glove in a thermal geyser."

"My condolences." She snatched the steaming cup. As she brought it to her lips, her sleeve threatened to swallow it before she could.

The stranger knelt beside her and deftly rolled the cumbersome sleeves past her wrists. Emily gazed at the top of his head. Threads of sun-burnished silver webbed his silky, dark hair. She brushed a riot of tangled curls from her own eyes, shied by his nearness.

"Thank you," she said softly.

"My pleasure, Miss . . . ?"

"Scar—" the word was halfway out before Emily could

stop it. She took a deep swig of the coffee, scalding her throat "—let," she finished. "Miss Emily Scarlet."

If Justin Connor was somewhere nearby, she couldn't afford to have her name bandied about the island. Her guardian did not want her. He'd made that painfully clear by never retrieving her from the seminary. If she showed up on his doorstep demanding her share of the gold mine, she might meet the same fate as her father's other partner, Nicholas Saleri. She might disappear. For good.

The man straightened. "Well, hello, Miss Emily Scarlet. I'm"—Emily noticed his hesitation as he exchanged a wary glance with Penfeld—"delighted to meet you. Would you care to tell us how you stumbled upon our humble shore?"

"I fell off a boat." That much was true anyway. She hoped God was smiling down on her. From the skeptical gleam in the man's crystalline eyes, she had a feeling she'd be needing all the heavenly help she could get.

"Shall we send a message to Auckland for you? Perhaps we could locate this boat. Find your family."

Wonderful, she thought. Just what she needed. Another chance for the darling Dobbinses to sink their claws into her.

She shook her head violently. Coffee sloshed onto Penfeld's coat, eliciting a soft moan from the valet. "That won't be necessary. I have no family. I'm an orphan."

She couldn't help feeling rather pleased with herself. That was the second time she'd told the truth today. And it wasn't even noon yet.

Her confession seemed to disturb her host. He rose and paced the hut, raking a hand through the scandalous length of his hair.

Emily sipped her coffee, studying him from beneath her lashes. Tansy would love to dig her pearly little teeth into this one. She had to admit he was handsome in an unpolished sort of way. Tall, broad-shouldered, and just a shade too thin. The kind of man any woman would love to fatten up. She tucked her toes beneath the coat, wondering where that last treacherous thought had come from.

A gold chain gleamed on his chest. The sun glinted off a single earring as he turned.

Pirates! Emily thought. They must all be pirates! That would explain his reticence in introducing himself. His name and face must be plastered on wanted posters all over the South Pacific. Perhaps he would sail her off the island before Justin Connor found her. Emily's imagination soared. Why, she wouldn't mind turning a hand to pirating herself! She and Tansy had often sneaked off to play at Jean Laffite until Miss Winters had discovered them dueling with two of her finest parasols while Cecille du Pardieu, squealing like a piglet, prepared to walk the plank. Miss Winters might have forgiven them if they hadn't balanced the plank on the roof—forty feet above the street.

A little pirating and she would be powerful enough to win back her daddy's gold and send old Justin Connor himself to a watery grave.

Emily gulped the last of the coffee, immensely cheered at the thought. "You're so very kind to let me stay. I promise to be very little trouble."

"Stay? Stay here?" The man turned so fast that his knee dislodged a stack of books. They toppled to the floor, sending up a new cloud of dust. Penfeld wheezed.

Emily reclined against the wall with what she hoped was convincing frailty. "I don't wish to impose on your hospitality, of course, but I do feel dreadfully weak. You'd be very generous to show mercy to a homeless orphan." She pursed her lips in a beguiling pout that had been known to drop grown men to their knees.

But this man only rested his hands on his slim hips. A muscle clenched in his jaw, and suddenly Emily was afraid. Wasn't it Tansy who had warned her that someday she would cajole the wrong man?

The native slipped soundlessly to his feet. As Emily's

bravado wilted beneath the heat of the stranger's gaze, she rather wished the savage would eat her.

But he only bowed with a flourish, then slipped a sprig of greenery from behind his ear and laid it at her feet. "Trini Te Wana welcomes you to our humble abode with the most celebratory of congratulations." He backed away, still bowing.

The stranger's sun-flecked eyes challenged her. "It seems Trini has made his wishes known. Go on. Take it. It's a Maori sign of welcome." When Emily frowned skeptically, he squatted beside her, lifted her curls, and whispered, "It means he doesn't intend to eat you."

His warm hand lingered against her nape. At the flash of his wolfish grin Emily wondered if it was Trini's appetites she ought to be concerned about.

She took the sprig of shiny leaves with trembling fingers. A warbling cry sounded from outside the hut. The man leaned one elbow on his knee and snapped open the watch case dangling from his chain.

"Trini, Penfeld, could you see to that?" he asked. "I'll be along shortly."

As Trini and Penfeld left, the watch spun on its golden chain, sending a blinding dart of sunlight across Emily's eyes. She stared at it, hypnotized.

"Miss Scarlet? Are you all right?" he said gently. When she didn't answer, he nudged her chin up with his knuckle.

"I'm fine," she whispered, studying his features with a fresh mixture of wonder and horror.

He gazed down at her; a frown deepened the tiny sun creases around his eyes.

She forced a smile. "Really. It's nothing a fresh cup of coffee won't cure." She held out her cup.

As he sauntered to the stove, whistling under his breath, Emily stared at his broad back through a fractured prism of tears. She had lied. Heaven had stopped smiling, and she wasn't sure if she'd ever be fine again.

She had caught only a glimpse of the tiny tintype mounted in the watch case. An angelic moppet smiled out at her, her brown eyes twinkling with hope. Emily knew that child had died long ago with her father. And no matter how hard she tried, she could think of only one reason why the gentle pirate with the stunning eyes would be wearing Claire Scarborough's portrait around his neck.

Her hand closed in a convulsive fist, crumpling Trini's friendly offering to shreds.

Chapter 3

*The memory of your tender smile brightens
even my drearest day. . . .*

*E*mily silently whispered frantic words of hope to herself.

Perhaps the handsome pirate had kidnapped Justin Connor, tossed his fat corpse overboard, and kept her father's watch as booty.

"Here you go. Careful, it's hot." The man's husky voice interrupted her reverie.

She took the cup he offered and watched him settle his lean hips against the windowsill. The breadth of his shoulders blocked the sunlight, leaving him in silhouette. At least she was to be spared the temptation of gawking openly at his face. She took a swig of the coffee, but its bitter warmth failed to ease her chill.

Maybe the cannibal had eaten Justin Connor but been unable to digest the watch.

Her spirits lifted at the thought. She tilted the cup to hide her grin. Ending up as an English delicacy at some native feast was more than equal to the various tortures and lingering deaths she had devised for the scoundrel over the years. This man simply couldn't be Justin Connor, she assured herself. If he were, he'd be living in a mansion, not a ramshackle hut with only a prim valet and an overeducated cannibal for company. She opened her mouth to ask him his name, then closed it again, part of her quailing from what he might answer.

"I could hardly sleep last night, wondering about one thing," he said. Suspicion shaded his voice and Emily sensed he was a man who did not trust easily. They had that much in common.

She set down the cup, embarrassed to discover how badly her hands were shaking. "I should hate to be the cause of your insomnia. Do satisfy your curiosity."

Pulling off his hat, he fixed her with a gaze of disarming candor. "Were you naked before or after you fell off the boat?"

A fierce heat burned her cheeks. She resisted the urge to tug the coat down over her pale calves. "After," she croaked dutifully. "My dress was pulling me under the water, so I tore it off."

Justin knit his hands at the small of his back, struggling not to smile at her bold ingenuity. "Most of the women I once knew would have gracefully drowned before shedding their precious petticoats and corsets."

Anger surged through Emily. This scowling stranger suddenly represented all the narrow-minded prigs she'd left behind in London. "Forgive me if I offended your delicate sensibilities. Better dead than immodest. Wasn't it our noble Victoria who said that?"

Except for a faint quirk of his eyebrow, he ignored her sarcasm. "So you're English."

"No. I'm Chinese," she snapped.

She knotted her hands in Penfeld's coat, struggling to control her temper. Miss Winters always said it would be her downfall, along with her profanity, her ardor for green apples, and her penchant for sliding down the banister in her Sunday pinafore.

"Why were you expelled from boarding school?"

Damn. Could the man read her very thoughts? she wondered. "Which time?" she replied innocently.

The question took him aback. "The most recent?" he offered.

She crossed her arms over her chest, mentally arming both barrels. She liked to see how well a man stood up under fire.

Drawing in a deep breath, she recited, "I ate a bucket of green apples and threw up on the headmistress's best cloak. I put a snake in Cecille du Pardieu's bed. I substituted firecrackers for the candles on last year's Christmas tree. I cut off the buttons on the teacher's boots . . . while she was teaching. I sawed off the newel post at the end of the banister. I replaced all the pepper in the kitchen with saltpeter, and I called the neighborhood curate a pompous, lily-livered, Satan-spawned, son-of-a—"

"Enough!" he shouted. "Thank you very much. That will be quite enough. There's really no need for further explanation."

She ducked her head modestly and cast him a shy look from beneath her lashes. "Oh," she added as if in afterthought. "And the headmistress caught the gardener's son and me in a rather . . . um . . . compromising position."

Justin gazed down at her, thinking that a man could become intoxicated from the wicked sparkle of her eyes. Her grin slashed an impish dimple in one cheek and crinkled her nose. What manner of girl was she? She had tossed the torrid facts of a ruinous scandal in his face with the naughty aplomb of a fallen angel. Thank God he had a few more years of reprieve before David's little Claire was faced with temptations so grave.

He was forced to turn away, the image of Emily rolling in the leaves with some pimpled gardener's lad filling him with unexpected fury. Did they rendezvous in the gazebo? he wondered. Behind the toolshed? Did he bring her roses? Weave chains of daisies to crown her chestnut curls?

He found himself at the stove, fiddling aimlessly with the tin coffeepot. She'd been kicked out of other schools, had she? Had there been other boys? Grocery lads? Lamplighter's nephews? Chimney sweeps? A series of visions, erotic and vivid, raged through his mind, obliterating all his hard-earned sanity in their path. Because in those visions it wasn't some boy who took her, but he himself who knelt between her thighs and showed her how it felt to be loved by a man.

His knuckles whitened on the warm edge of the stove as he struggled to remind himself how fast a desire this hot could scar.

He stole a glance at her. With her tousled curls and flushed cheeks, she looked to be no more than a child, a little girl playing dress-up in her father's coat.

Perhaps he should be locked away for even entertaining such notions about her. "How old are you, Miss Scarlet?" he choked out.

She lifted her cup in a mocking toast. "Grown."

Taking a deep breath, he turned. His voice came out with the cool detachment of a stranger's. "I am terribly sorry, but I fear it's impossible for you to remain here unchaperoned. There are missionaries in Auckland who can help you."

"The curate suggested an exorcist."

Justin suspected she needed an exorcist less than a sound spanking. He lowered his voice to a hollow whisper. "I could call on Trini's *tohunga,* the high priest. I'm sure he'd know some way to get those nasty spirits out of you."

"Oh, no, you don't." She shook her head violently. "I'll not be an hors d'oeuvre for some leering skull shaker."

"Why, Emily, you insult the Maori! They're quite civilized, you know. They never eat their friends. Only their enemies."

"How benevolent." Emily blew a stray curl out of her

eyes. She had no intention of being frightened off so easily. Not until she'd quenched her burgeoning suspicions. "Very well, then. If you want to be rid of me, then rid of me you shall be."

Justin thought he had won until she began to briskly unbutton Penfeld's coat. His mouth fell open as the ebony folds parted to reveal the creamy swell of her breasts.

He leaped across the hut and grabbed her wrists. "What in heaven's name do you think you're doing?"

She blinked up at him. "Returning your valet's coat. I'm not blind. I can see he cherishes it."

"I'll buy him another in Auckland," Justin growled. He released her, ashamed to find his fingers had dug red marks into her creamy flesh. "Come on," he said gruffly. "We'll borrow a wagon from Trini."

He pulled her up. Before she could take a step, her leg collapsed. Justin caught her in the circle of his arms.

Moaning, she clung to him. "Oh, my ankle. I must have twisted it when I crawled ashore."

Her curls tickled his nose, maddening him with their softness. He was tempted to drop her, but forced himself to lower her gently. He knelt to examine her ankle. No swelling. No bruising. Not so much as a freckle marred the smooth satin of her skin. He pressed the bone with his fingertips. She winced and clenched her teeth.

"Terrible pain, eh?" He cocked a skeptical eyebrow.

"Dreadful." Tears welled in her luminous eyes. "Do you think it might be broken?"

Her face was next to his, her lower lip soft and trembling. Justin wanted to bite it. He trailed his fingers up her calf to the hem of Penfeld's coat, helpless to keep from envisioning what she wore beneath it—nothing. She gave him one of those melting glances—her eyes all sparkling coffee innocence. He was tempted to give her what she was so unwittingly asking for. Tempted to continue the slow glide of his fingers up her thigh toward a dark and sensual destruction. But whose destruction? Hers or his own?

He snatched back his hand and stood, his spirits sinking. Unless he wanted to carry her all the way to Auckland, the girl was staying for a few days. He suspected she was faking her injury, but other than setting fire to the hut and hoping she'd run out, he had no way to prove it. A thread of relief ran through his irritation. Auckland would swallow a girl like her without a qualm. If it *was* a hint of purity shining in her eyes, he didn't care to see it destroyed. New Zealand took little mercy on innocents. He was living proof of that.

"It seems you'll be staying until you're well enough to travel." He shook a finger at her. "But if you've any thoughts about slipping a snake into Penfeld's pallet, be warned. There are no snakes in New Zealand."

Her cheek dimpled. "I shall endeavor to put forth my best behavior."

He sensed her best behavior might be more than he could handle. He strode to the door, then paused. He wanted desperately to question her further, but to do so would violate the unwritten creed of this land. Too many ships had dumped their secrets, their scandals, and their unwanted convicts on these shores. It had resulted in a privacy hard won and so jealously guarded that a man might honorably defend it to the death. At least his past would die with him. So Justin bit back his questions, knowing he, too, might die or kill before he let someone rake open his own raw scars.

"You've no need to fear discovery here, Miss Scarlet. There are many who come to New Zealand to elude the past."

She inclined her head. A fall of curls veiled her expression. "And there are some, sir, who come to find it."

He realized he had become so accustomed to the island's code of suspicion that he hadn't even offered this small, bedraggled young woman his name. She hardly looked the sort of spy the efficient Miss Winters or his rigid father would dispatch.

"You may call me Justin. Justin Connor." He closed the door behind him, never seeing the bitter, triumphant twist of Emily's lips.

Justin couldn't seem to put enough distance between himself and the hut. He strode through the cornfield, his long strides eating up the turf. Penfeld trotted along behind him.

"Hell and damnation!" he finally exploded. "A girl simply shouldn't go around looking at a man like that."

Penfeld plucked at his suspenders, more worried about being outdoors without a coat than about his master's consternation. "Like what, sir? I hadn't noticed anything unusual about her looks. A bit on the boyish side, perhaps."

Justin spun around, his voice rising on a note of disbelief. "Boyish? Compared to whom—Helen of Troy? Cleopatra? Besides, I wasn't referring to her looks in particular. I was referring to the way she *looks* at me. That ridiculous sparkle in her eyes. That clever little trick she does with her bottom lip."

Justin tugged on his lip to illustrate, but Penfeld only blinked at him dumbly. A trickle of sweat snaked between Justin's shoulder blades at the mere thought of it. As the sun beat down on his bare head, he realized he'd forgotten his hat.

"Blast her anyway! She had no way of knowing what sort of men we were. What if she had given that look to some of those whalers or timbermen in Auckland? They'd have slapped her in a whorehouse so fast, it would have made her curly little head spin."

The valet paled. He became as nervous as a rabbit when anyone mentioned Auckland. Justin had found him in the teeming harbor town four years earlier, wandering the streets in a daze, his handsome suit in rags, a shattered teacup his only possession.

Justin plucked a corn silk from Penfeld's thinning hair. "Now *you're* doing it. Don't stick out your lip and go all quivery on me, because Auckland's exactly where I'm taking her. She must think I'm a blithering idiot to have fallen for that old twisted-ankle ploy."

"I've never known you to blither without cause, sir." Penfeld looked as downcast as if his master had announced he was taking the girl to Sodom with a side picnic to Gomorrah.

Snorting with determination, Justin spun on his heel. "I'm going to march right back to that hut, make her gather her things—"

"She has no things."

Penfeld's quiet words halted him at the edge of the field. A hill studded with tussock grasses rolled down to the beach. The warm breeze teased the golden clumps into waving fingers.

Penfeld was right, he realized. The girl had nothing. Not even the coat on her back. She had come into his world as bare and unfettered as on the day she had come into God's.

He was a grown man. Surely he could temper his lust with common decency for a few days. If she refused to leave by the end of the week, he would ignore Penfeld's sulks and insist on escorting her to Auckland. Until then he would spend the long days working in the fields so he could collapse on his pallet at night, too exhausted to even dream of—

He drove his fingers through his hair. It was hardly her fault that every time he looked at her he saw her as she had been in the moonlight, that each time he touched her he wanted to bury his fingers in her silky curls. All of them. Justin groaned.

His agonized musings were interrupted by a joyous cry. *"Pakeha! Pakeha!"*

A line of naked honey-skinned children streamed up the hill with Trini in tow. Justin squatted and a wiry little boy barreled into him with the force of a muscular cannonball.

He faked a stagger. "Ho, there, Kawiri! You're too strong for an old chap like me."

The children swarmed around him, chattering in Maori. A little girl with almond-shaped eyes crawled between Kawiri's legs and held Justin's hand. His face relaxed in a smile as their musical tones soothed his troubled spirit.

"You can come out, Penfeld," he called over his shoulder. "They won't eat you."

Penfeld crept out from behind a cornstalk and gave the children a shy bow. Trini beamed proudly as several of the children bowed back. Justin knew his unflappable valet wasn't afraid of cannibals, but children terrified him.

I have no family.

Emily's words came back to haunt Justin without warning, echoing what he had said to Penfeld only yesterday. He hadn't been completely truthful. The Maori were his family now. They had adopted him as their beloved Pakeha, sharing with him both their land and their trust, giving him the right and power to negotiate even the most delicate trade with other natives and whites. Justin ruffled Kawiri's black hair. Perhaps they were all orphans beneath the stark blue bowl of God's sky.

The little girl tapped the watch case resting against his chest, muttering beneath her breath in Maori.

"English, Dani," he commanded. If he could teach more of the children English, perhaps someday they would have no need of a stranger such as he living in their midst.

She popped her thumb in her mouth, then uncorked it and bellowed, "Claire!"

Justin winced.

Dancing around him, the other children took up the chant. "Claire! Claire! Claire!"

"Oh, dear," Penfeld murmured.

Justin leveled a lethal gaze at Trini. "Have you been letting them play with my watch again?"

The native lifted his palms in a universal gesture of

apology, choosing in his chagrin simple English words rather than the longer ones he delighted in. "They'd never seen a white little girl before. They believe her to be a lost angel whose spirit is trapped in time."

Justin dropped his head in defeat. Was he to be haunted by orphans today? In his preoccupation with the girl, he had almost forgotten that other child. He made no protest when the tiny Dani reached up and slipped the chain over his head.

Kawiri brushed the gold with reverent fingers, letting out a soft "Oooooh."

Justin knew he didn't have to worry about the safety of his watch. Dani cupped it in her plump hands as if it were the most holy of relics.

As the children trailed after her, he stood, absently flattening his palm against his chest. If Claire Scarborough was his cross to bear, why did he feel so naked without her image resting next to his heart?

That night Emily kicked restlessly at her blankets. The island breeze had turned cool, but an icy fire burned in her veins, stoked by both disdain and fury. Her guardian lay on a pallet a few feet away. She pillowed her chin on folded arms and studied his sleeping features with hungry fascination.

He was nothing as she had imagined him. Somehow she had always expected him to be blond with a neatly clipped beard and side-whiskers. A cap of shining gold hair complemented a suit of armor, did it not? Self-contempt at her own naïveté flooded her.

"Wouldn't have been able to cram his horns under the helm, would he?" she muttered.

From his pallet beneath the window, Penfeld emitted a lumbering snore. Emily shifted to her elbow.

Justin Connor more resembled a dark satyr than a noble knight. His lashes were too long, his lower lip too full. He hadn't one perfect feature, but in combination they were devastating, giving his face a flawed male beauty that made her unwilling heart beat like the wings of a captive bird. She fought an absurd desire to crawl over to his pallet and run her fingers over him, to commit each feature to her memory in the fear she might awake in the morning to find him gone—just another elusive creature of her dreams.

She had spent years clutching her dreams of a noble savior to her child's breast. But her dreams had been only phantoms, disappearing like smoke in the cold light of day. Reality lay on that pallet—six feet of reality, all refined sinew and muscle. She could reach out and touch it just as she had touched a stranger's face in the moonlight.

The light from the low-burning lantern gilded the chiseled planes of his face. She had expected him to be older, but he couldn't be far over thirty. The same age her father had been when he died.

Her eyes narrowed. Justin stirred, groaning low in his throat as if sensing her enmity. The lines etched around his eyes deepened. He twitched as if in pain. Pain? Emily wondered. Or guilt? Her guardian did not sleep the untroubled sleep of the innocent.

She wanted to shake him out of his dream and demand he look at her. She had lived in his shadow for seven years. Every prank, each profanity, all the wasted fury of her tantrums had been played to an invisible audience of one —the man who had abandoned her then dared to hold her in his arms without showing even the scantest hint of recognition. His apathy touched an old pain in her, a pain she'd thought shoved to the farthest reaches of her heart. She could tolerate many things, but being ignored was not one of them.

She flung herself to her side, forcing her gaze away from him. Questions buzzed through her mind like angry gnats. Why was he living in this dusty hut, and where were the riches her father had written of? Had he hidden the gold somewhere? Was he a smuggler using the pristine solitude of the beach to escape the stiff port taxes of the harbors? Perhaps he was still just a dirty swindler taking advantage of his reputation as the son of one of the richest dukes in England to bilk decent men of their inheritances, as he had done to her father.

Against her will, fate had delivered Justin Connor into her hands. He didn't realize who she was, but she knew him only too well. Surely somewhere in these musty stacks of books and papers she could find the sordid story of his life.

Her ruse of an injured leg had given her time. Time to probe his secrets and discover the truth about the missing gold and her father's untimely death. Time to make him sorry. Let him enjoy his dreams for now, because once she had gathered enough evidence of his foul play, he would come face-to-face with his worst nightmare.

Drawn like a moth to a sizzling flame, she rolled back over and glared at the dark purity of his features until her weighted lids dragged her into a dreamless sleep.

Chapter 4

·🐚·

In your absence, God has sent me solace in that
most precious of his gifts—a true friend. . . .

"More tea, Penfeld?" Emily gazed wanly into the delicate china cup the valet offered. "What a delightful surprise. You must have read my mind."

"A fine New Delhi brew," he pronounced, beaming proudly. "Justin procured it from the Bay of Islands for my last birthday."

"How dear of him," she murmured.

She waited until he had bustled back to the stove before tossing the contents of the cup over her shoulder and out the window. She'd trade all the fine teas in the world for one coffee bean to suck on. The mannerly valet had been very vocal in his opinion that coffee was simply too crude a drink to pass her dainty lips. Emily was beginning to wonder if the sly Mr. Connor was smuggling not gold, but tea.

She smacked her lips on the cup's rim, pretending to drain it. "Marvelous flavor. I've never tasted anything quite like it."

Penfeld clapped his plump hands. "It warms my heart to see a young lady enjoying tea." He swept the cup from her hand. "If you like it so well, I'll pour you another."

Groaning silently, Emily buried her face in her hands. The portly valet was killing her with kindness. Every time she'd wiggled in the past three days, he had been there—fluffing the blankets beneath her ankle and pouring tea down her throat as if it were the elixir of life. She would almost swear her wary host had sicced him on her out of spite.

The mysterious Mr. Connor disappeared each day at dawn and did not return until sunset. After wolfing down some flat biscuits and a hot pasty stew consisting mostly of canned beans, he would collapse on his pallet with little more than a grunted good night.

As attentive as always, Emily thought grimly.

A cooling breeze wafted through the window, stirring the curls at the nape of her neck. Her nose twitched at the salty tang of the sea. A twilight paradise beckoned to her with a whisper of sunlight and surf, but thanks to her own lie, she was trapped in this musty hut, watching Penfeld polish his teapot. She ached to sink her toes into the warm sand, to feel the ocean spray mist her skin. She eyed the stacks of books longingly. She was also dying for a moment of privacy to dig through the hut for some hint of the treachery her guardian had worked on her father.

Her wish was granted when Penfeld pulled a wicker basket off a peg and trotted out the door, mumbling something about a "tidy pinch of mint." Praying mint did not grow in this hemisphere, Emily jumped to her feet and whirled in a giddy circle. A teetering stack of books blocked her way. She steadied them with her heel, torn between the books and the window. The warm breeze was too strong a temptation. She thrust her head out the window, savoring the salty bite of the sea air.

The wicker hut crouched at the very edge of a sun-dappled forest, huddled beneath the sweeping boughs of two trees that resembled gigantic ferns. The murmur of the sea was a distant sigh, luring her toward freedom. She ought to climb out that window and never look back. But how far could she get before the truth would catch up with her? She'd spent far too long eluding it.

She tightened her jaw in determination and turned back to the books. Her daddy had always said you could divine a man's soul by reading his books. Somewhere among them might be a deed, a map, or a journal holding clues to the whereabouts of her father's gold.

She picked up a leather-bound volume and blew the dust off its cover. *"Mozart: The Master and His Music,"* she read aloud. She thumbed through the pages, then tossed it aside and plucked out another. *"The Polyphonic Symphonies of Beethoven?"*

Emily frowned. She had been hoping for Machiavelli's *The Prince* or perhaps the Marquis de Sade's *Les 120 Journées de Sodome.* She examined book after book, only to discover weighty biographies of Mendelssohn and Rossini, fifteen volumes describing the rhythms and meters of the world's greatest operas, and a mildewed treatise pleading the case of the viola against the violin. She pawed through the stacks, swearing under her breath as the precious minutes ticked away.

A hefty libretto of Wagner's *Tristan und Isolde* slowed her progress. She gave it a vicious yank. The entire heap weaved dangerously. She threw her arms around it, bracing the books with her chest. Dust tickled her nose. She swallowed a sneeze. All she needed was for Penfeld to return and find her buried beneath a pile of musty tomes, her skull crushed by *The Encyclopedia of West Indian Dance Rhythms.*

The shift had revealed a tiny cavity between two larger books. Emily drew out a slim volume bound in morocco. Although the leather had worn well, the gilt-edged pages had tarnished with age. It was almost as if the book had been tossed aside and forgotten. Or carefully hidden.

Emily's hands began to tremble as she stroked the unmarked cover. Perhaps now she would learn her guardian's dark secrets.

She sank down cross-legged on the floor and opened the book. Inscribed across the frontpiece, not in the strong, measured script of a man, but in the clumsy scrawl of a child were the words: *This book is the property of Justin Marcus Homer Lloyd Farnsworth Connor III. (Peek at your own peril.)*

"Homer?" Emily whispered, smiling in spite of herself.

Her finger traced the ominous skull and crossbones sketched beneath the warning. She turned the page, already suspecting what she would find. But instead of hasty jottings about how many frogs he'd caught or plum puddings he'd pilfered, she found wavering lines connected into grids and splotched with ink.

She held the book up to her nose. "Why, the clever little brat was already writing his nasty secrets in code!"

Her vision blurred; the lines danced, then steadied into a recognizable pattern. Her mouth fell open as she fanned the pages, turning them faster than her eyes could follow. Not a code after all, but wavering bars connected by blots of ink. Music. Bar after bar, note after note, transcribed with a patience that should not have belonged to any child.

Baffled and oddly touched, Emily let the little book fall shut. She almost didn't hear the warning creak of the door.

She made a diving roll for the pallet, praying Penfeld's coat would follow. Losing it could have dire consequences. Apparently no one had thought of offering her the valet's long underdrawers.

As Justin ducked beneath the lintel, Emily realized with horror that she was still clutching his journal. She shoved it under the blankets, faking a tremendous yawn.

"Hello, Emily," he said, his voice notably devoid of warmth.

She bit her tongue to keep from blurting out *Hello, Homer.* "Good evening, Mr. Connor."

He gazed around the hut. "Where's Penfeld?"

She folded her hands in her lap. "He went out to pick some mint."

Justin lifted an edge of the stained linen tablecloth and peered beneath. "You sure you don't have him trussed up somewhere?"

She flashed a deliberate dimple. "Why, Mr. Connor, you flatter me."

He drew off the watch and laid it on the table.

"Beautiful workmanship," she murmured, hoping his face might betray something.

"Pity I don't have a waistcoat pocket to keep it in. I have to wear it around my neck like a woman."

One would have to be blind, deaf, and comatose to mistake him for a member of that fairer sex, Emily thought as he dipped into the wash bucket and poured handfuls of water over his flushed face. Sparkling drops caught in the dark filaments of hair along his forearms. An errant trickle eased down his muscled abdomen and disappeared into the low-slung waistband of his dungarees.

She swallowed, wishing for even a drop of tea to wet her throat.

He turned toward the door. "Tell Penfeld I went down to the beach."

It was all Emily could do to keep from scrambling to her feet. She would have gone to the beach with Lucifer himself to escape the stifling confines of the hut.

"Take me," she blurted out.

Her innocent plea stopped Justin in his tracks. She would be gone in a few days, he reminded himself, and then he could resume the orderly tempo of his life. All he had to do was turn around and tell her he wasn't interested in her company.

He turned around. Her ardent brown eyes sparkled up at him. "Penfeld's coat is due for a washing. We might as well wash it with me in it."

Justin ruffled his hair. She lowered her lashes, obviously bracing herself for his refusal.

"I have only one question, young lady," he said sternly, bending over her.

"What?" Emily replied, biting her lower lip. To her embarrassment, genuine tears of disappointment stung her eyes.

She gasped as he caught her under the knees and shoulders and swept her into his arms, bringing her nose to nose with him. "What if Penfeld should decide to *iron* the coat with you in it?"

She giggled. "It wouldn't be the first time I'd been ironed. My teachers used to sit on me and iron my hair."

His gaze softened. He raked his fingers through her mop of curls, mesmerizing her with his tenderness. "What a crime."

As they started down the short, sandy path to the beach, Emily threw an arm around Justin's neck. They burst onto the beach and her senses exploded in drunken abandon. The warmth of the setting sun branded her skin; the wind dragged soothing fingers through her hair. Moaning with delight, she tilted her face back and closed her eyes.

When she opened them, Justin's face was very close to hers. She could see each stubbled hair along his jawline and was seized with a strange urge to rub her cheek across it and see if it felt as prickly as it looked. Her face flushed with more than the heat of the sun.

"You may put me down," she said primly.

Mischief glinted in his golden eyes. "Oh, no. You wanted a bath, and it's a bath you'll be having."

Before she could even squeal, he strode through the damp sand into the waves. She buried her face in the haven of his chest, clinging as he waded deeper into the swirling surf. Cool water licked her thighs. Penfeld's coat ballooned around her hips. She pressed it down with frantic fingers.

"There now, isn't that pleasant?"

"No." Her teeth chattered against his chest. "It's bloody cold."

"I'm afraid there's only one cure for that."

He dropped her.

Emily thrashed wildly. Salty water rushed into her mouth. Good Lord, the lunatic was trying to kill her! She should have suspected as much. He must have recognized her from the photograph. Her toes churned up a mass of sand and she realized the water was only a few feet deep. She also realized the muffled sound above her was not the pounding of the surf, but the infuriating rumble of a man's laughter.

Her fingers dug into Justin's thigh, and she shot from the waves, climbing him like a tree monkey. She shook water from her stinging eyes. "You ill-mannered, wretched—" She sputtered to a halt, trying to remember some of the viler names Barney had called her on the journey from England.

"Would you like to sit on my shoulders?" he suggested dryly. "The view is much better."

Justin knew a brief moment of panic when it looked as if she might take him up on his offer. The prospect of being cradled between her shapely thighs for such a benign purpose was too torturous to contemplate.

He caught her hips to stop her panicked ascent. "I was only trying to help."

Emily opened her mouth to argue, but realized the water now swirled around her hips in currents of delicious warmth. Even worse, most of the warmth seemed to be centered at the juncture of her thighs, where the faded V of Justin's dungarees was pressed with alarming intimacy. By flinging her legs around him, she had put herself in a more precarious position than she dared to admit. She'd lost track of Penfeld's coat during her writhing, and most of it was trapped around her waist. She stilled, terrified Justin would discover only a fragile weave of calico bound her nakedness from his own.

He already knew. He betrayed himself by the downward flicker of his gaze, the faintest shift of his hips, the barely perceptible wince of his chiseled mouth. A buoyant wave rocked against his back, and her body cradled his with an artless skill as primal as the sea itself. She had never been more aware of a man's strength or a woman's vulnerability. Heat stung her cheeks.

Justin gazed down at her, already beginning to regret his brief lapse into kindness. He should have let Penfeld bring her to the beach. His own peace of mind was too hard won to surrender without a fight. Half wishing he were a more ruthless sort of man, he rested his hands against her ribs, his thumbs a ticklish inch from her breasts.

Emily's heart rocked into a shuddering slam as Justin's palms rode to her hips, easing the coat down to cover her. He slipped an arm around her shoulders and turned her away from him, cradling her back against his chest.

"Relax, Emily," he commanded in that husky lilt of his.

He guided them past the place where the waves crested and broke. Emily poked her toe toward the sea floor but met only a chill current of deeper water. Damp hairs clung to the bronze skin of Justin's forearm. How easy it would be for him to push her under, she thought. To hold her head beneath the water with exquisite gentleness until her struggles ceased.

She shivered, and Justin wrapped his other arm around her. "Don't be afraid. I won't let you go."

The shiver that rocked her at those words was so deep, he never felt it. It filled her with both a terrible fear and an insatiable longing that sharpened her loneliness to an unbearable edge. Her eyes stung. She blinked, swearing it was only the salt.

His breath warmed her ear. "Close your eyes, Em, and let the water take you."

She couldn't fight the sensation that she was being taken by something far more potent than the water. She let her eyes drift shut, surrendering to its seductive pull. Her head fell back against his shoulder. Her feet drifted up until her lower body was floating, rocked in the rhythmic cradle of the sea. The sunset faded to a warm spatter of gold against her eyelids. The water caressed her with liquid fingers, deliciously cool against the heat of his chest.

"Why would anyone live in London when there's such a place as this?" she murmured, licking the salt from her lips.

He guided her around to face the shore. "Some say New Zealand is God's own paradise, that after He created the rest of the world, He made this Eden for His own pleasure, then destroyed all the land bridges so it could belong to only the boldest adventurers."

Emily wondered if he, like her, was thinking of three bold young men who had dared the sea to come here.

He rested his chin on top of her head. "Look at it, Emily. Can you really see it?"

Her gaze swept the shore. She wanted desperately to see it through his eyes. Glittering stars punched holes in the fading fabric of day. Night shadows melted across the swaying palms. The plaintive cry of a bellbird lifted the tiny hairs at her nape.

His long, elegant fingers curled over her collarbone. She studied them, dazed by their grace. They were saved from effeminacy by their tensile strength and the dusting of dark hair along their knuckles. "God banished every deadly creature here. There are no dangerous animals, no poisonous bugs, no snakes. He molded the mountains with His fists and blew roaring blizzards down the slopes. He sculpted icy fjords and smoothed the pristine beaches with His loving fingers." His voice grew soft, wistful. "Then He sprinkled the hills and streams with gold."

His love for this country was palpable, but Emily sensed that running through it like a thread of gold through a gurgling stream was a deep sadness. What had his love cost him? New Zealand might be a paradise, but for him it had become a paradise lost. Her heart ached.

Before she realized it she was cupping his hand and bringing it toward the comfort of her lips. She gently kissed his fingertips. He drew in a ragged breath and Emily stiffened, horrified by what she had done. How could she have fallen so quickly beneath the sway of his charms. Had her father succumbed as easily?

"Let me go," she whispered, pleading for far more than her physical release.

His grip tightened for an implacable instant. "Who are you, Emily? What are you running from?"

"You!" She began to struggle, afraid panic might force her to blurt out more than she intended. She worked her fingers up between them and shoved at his arms with all her strength. "I've met men like you in London. You take a girl out in the moonlight, relax her guard with soft words, then play your little game of seduction."

Before she could wiggle away, he caught her arm in a steely grasp and jerked her around to face him, his eyes dark-lashed orbs of brandy fire. "Is that what you think this is about? Seduction?"

Emily hung in his grip, accusing him with her silence and the sullen set of her jaw.

"I might remind you, *Miss* Scarlet, that *you* were the one who just kissed me. I live on a bloody island, for Christ's sake. I'm surrounded by hundreds of miles of coastline." His voice rose to a roar. "And *you* had the sheer audacity to wash up on *my* beach stark raving naked." He pulled her tight against him, molding her like a wet glove to the lean curves of his body. His voice softened to a dangerous purr. "I'm warning you now—this isn't England. We don't deal in seduction here. If I decide I want you, I won't need any flowery words or moonlight swims."

Braced in the powerful cradle of his thighs, Emily knew his words to be true. A helpless shudder rocked her.

He shoved her away from him. She didn't dare look at him. A little thrashing and a few awkward strokes and she felt sand beneath her feet. She lurched forward until she could crawl up on the shore. She wanted to run, to flee far away, where his mocking anger could not find her, but her ruse of an injured ankle forced her to sprawl in the sand like some wounded fish. If she jumped to her feet and sprinted for the shelter of the bush, would he follow?

A furious splashing came from behind her. She looked over her shoulder to see Justin emerge from the waves—a smoldering Poseidon, magnificent in his fury. Water streamed from his chest, plastering his dungarees to his hips and thighs like a second skin. Emily lowered her shocked gaze.

She needn't have worried. Justin strode past her as if she were no more significant than a sand crab.

"Justin?" she said tentatively.

He moved down the shore, slowing only long enough to scoop up a shell and hurl it into the sea.

"Mr. Connor?" she said louder.

He was rapidly fading into the darkness. Emily cupped a hand around her mouth and yelled, "You lied! You said you wouldn't let me go!"

She flopped to her back and let her fist fall over her eyes. "Damn," she whispered. "Damn. Damn. Damn."

He had opened up to her, given her a glimpse of the ticking works of his mind, spoken of New Zealand and adventurers and gold. And what had she done? Behaved like a galloping ninny.

The surf tickled her toes. She crossed her arms over her chest and watched the moon drift like a weightless pearl over the horizon. The night wind caressed her cheeks. She wondered how long it would take to crawl back to the hut. Justin was probably lurking somewhere in the brush, laughing at her. She considered limping up the path, sprinkling her performance with a pathetic stumble or two. But maybe it was time she taught him that no one could be as stubborn as Emily Claire Scarborough when she set her mind to it.

She was still glaring at the stars when Penfeld marched down to the beach, threw her over his stalwart shoulder, and carried her back to the hut.

Justin cringed as another sneeze rocked the hut. He jerked the blanket over his ears.

"There, there, dear, just tuck this around your shoulders and have another sip of tea. I put a lovely sprig of mint in it just for you."

Muttering under his breath, Justin flopped over on his back. He wasn't sure what was more annoying—Emily's infernal sniffing or Penfeld's motherly clucking. He stole a reluctant glance at the other side of the hut.

There was nothing visible of Emily but a mop of damp curls and two huge, accusing eyes. She was swathed in a woolen blanket all the way to the tip of her pinkened nose. Even through the folds of blanket Justin could hear her teeth chattering. Penfeld loosened the blanket and held a steaming cup to her lips, but she freed an arm and waved it away. The valet watched in horrified fascination as she snuffled into his coat sleeve.

"Thank you, Penfeld, but I'm sure I'll be all right. I just caught a tiny chill lying in those icy waves." The entire blanket shuddered.

Penfeld swiveled to skewer Justin with a reproachful stare.

"For Christ's sake!" Justin threw back the blanket. "She wasn't out there twenty minutes."

"It seemed like hours," she said earnestly.

"I dare say it did, miss," Penfeld agreed, tucking the blanket around her toes. "I can't imagine what possessed my master to be so thoughtless. Why, he rescued me from the clutches of Auckland's slums when my own employer sailed back to England and deserted me! He's usually a very caring fellow."

Emily's snort might have been a sneeze, but Justin doubted it.

He sat up on his elbow, narrowing his eyes. "Take a good look at her, Penfeld. She doesn't have a cold. She's the very picture of good health. I suppose you're going to tell me those roses in her chubby little cheeks are the ravages of some gruesome fever."

Penfeld reached to feel her brow, but Emily stopped him. "No. Justin's right. I don't have a cold." Her pale hand fluttered at her breast. "I do believe it might be consumption." Wheezing, she doubled over.

Justin smoothed his voice to liquid honey, addressing Emily directly for the first time since Penfeld had carried her in. "Perhaps Penfeld should take the rifle and put you out of your misery. That's what we do to lame horses here."

Emily paused in the middle of a hacking cough. Her eyes widened in chiding accusation. "Why, Mr. Connor, your lack of compassion makes me feel faint." Her lashes drifted down, but not quick enough to veil the malicious sparkle of her eyes.

Penfeld bustled off for his smelling salts. Growling, Justin pulled the blanket over his head. He hadn't had a decent night's sleep since he'd found the brat. His nightmares had worsened and all his efforts to work himself into exhaustion had failed. Only last night he had bolted straight off the pallet, a child's merry giggle still spinning through his head. He had jerked around, frantically seeking its source, but all he had seen was Emily curled in the blankets, her chest rising and falling in the sweet rhythm of sleep, her face lax in angelic repose.

Angelic, hell, Justin thought, shifting restlessly. The curate should have summoned that exorcist. The girl seemed to be possessed by at least five different spirits. She'd play the temptress in one breath, and in the next entertain Penfeld with stories of the Regent zoo, chattering of lions and baboons with all the guileless enthusiasm of a child.

But it hadn't been a child he had held in his arms, Justin reminded himself. She had brought his fingers to the softness of her lips with all the empathy of a woman, willing to absorb an anguish he'd never even dared to name. Even now the memory of her tenderness riveted him.

He threw himself over. She was like a ceaseless melody pounding at the back of his brain. There had to be a way to break the skein of enchantment she had cast over him, a way to get her out of his hut and out of his life before she drove him mad. He kicked the blankets, praying that once she was gone, the ache in his groin would become more tolerable than the one in his heart.

As soon as the door shut behind Penfeld and Justin the next morning, Emily bounded off the pallet and kicked up her heels in a fling of freedom. She didn't care if Justin brooded forever. At least he had dragged Penfeld along on his mysterious chores, to deprive her of his devoted attentions.

She hefted the blankets, holding her breath while she shook out the pepper she'd hoarded to enhance her sneezes. Justin's little blue journal thumped to the floor.

She knelt and picked it up, turning it over thoughtfully. She was still no closer to unraveling the enigma of the man. She surveyed the crowded stacks of books despairingly. There could be a hundred hiding places within their dusty ranks.

Tapping the book against her thigh, she straightened. The books in the rear should be the oldest. She wiggled between two stacks and squatted to peruse the titles.

A rush of warm wind teased her curls, then stilled abruptly as if a door had been slammed. Emily pivoted on her heel to peer behind her. The thatched door was still closed.

Shaking her head, she bent back to her task. Tiny claws clicked across the floor. The hair on Emily's nape tingled to life. Justin's book slid from her fingers.

Holding her breath, she turned. The dirt floor was empty.

She blew out a shaky breath. What had Justin said? There were no snakes in New Zealand, no dangerous animals? The musty stacks suddenly seemed ominous, blocking the cobwebbed corners from the morning sunlight. Something blunt thumped to the floor. Emily snapped to attention. From the corner of her eye she saw a shadow scuttle behind the table.

She rose, measuring each step as if it would be her last. Her trembling fingers closed around the handle of Penfeld's broom. She eyed the rifle hanging over the door longingly, but she would have to cross in front of the table to get it. Clutching the broom like a shield, she tiptoed toward the table.

"Probably just a cat," she whispered, soothed by the sound of her own voice. "Justin forgot to tell me he had a sweet little cat."

She got down on her knees and pinched the edge of the tablecloth between two fingers. "Nice kitty," she crooned, easing the cloth up. "Come out and meet your auntie Emily."

As she lowered her head, a fat green monster galloped out of the shadows, charging straight for her nose.

Chapter 5

·❦·

*I long to hear your
dulcet tones bringing me cheer. . . .*

A bloodcurdling scream fractured the serenity of the morning, startling a gull into soaring flight across the azure sky.

Completely unruffled, Justin leaned back in the sand, resting his head on his folded arm. If his plan worked, the scheming little orphan would be out of his life and on her way to Auckland by nightfall.

"Look at those clouds, won't you, Penfeld? Magnificent, aren't they?"

Penfeld eyed the hut a few yards away, expecting Emily to come bursting from the door, newly healed of her affliction, as his master had promised she would. A ringing crash was followed by the thunder of wildly running feet. He would almost swear the hut was rocking.

He took out a handkerchief and mopped beads of sweat from his upper lip. "She really should have come out by now. Perhaps I should go back and—"

"Back in London you can't even see the sky for the

soot." Justin tucked a blade of tussock grass between his lips, the very picture of indolent ease.

From the hut a shrill squeal was followed by a string of colorful profanities. Clouds of dust billowed from the windows. An ominous silence fell.

"But, sir . . . what if she uses the rifle?" Penfeld's voice lowered to a horrified whisper. "Or stomps it to death?"

Justin uncurled his fingers to reveal a handful of rifle shells. "Not loaded. Trust me. He'll outrun her. I'd wager he'll outlive all of us." A smile teased his lips. "Why, it might even be snowing in London right now! Do you fancy snow, Penfeld? Doesn't that cloud over there to the left favor a giant snowflake?"

Sighing, Penfeld sank back into the sand. "No, I do believe it more resembles a giant teapot." Pottery crashed. He winced. "A broken teapot, sir."

Emily was chasing a dragon. She slammed the broom into the floor, wishing the horrid creature would sprout wings and fly out the window. With an insolent flick of its spiked tail it darted behind the nearest stack of books. She crept nearer, picking her way over toppled books and shattered earthenware, muttering under her breath. Sweat trickled down her brow.

She swung the broom in a whistling arc. It caught the books broadside and sent them crashing to the floor. Pepper shot up her nose; a chain of sneezes blinded her. As she stabbed wildly into the dust, she heard the *thump-thump* of fleeing little monster feet behind her.

She threw herself after the sound and tripped over her own blankets. She swung the broom, swiping tin pots off the stove. They crashed to the floor in a ringing symphony. Her coat caught on the edge of the stove, bringing her up short. She knuckled her eyes and peered into the musty gloom. The beast was gone again, always one step ahead of her. Perhaps it wasn't a dragon. Perhaps it was a very clever alligator.

The swing of the tablecloth caught her eye. She felt a wicked grin curve her lips. Not so clever after all. Stupid enough to return to its original hiding place.

Lifting the broom, she inched toward the table.

"Come out, you darling little thing. Emily won't hurt you." Her fingers dug into the broom handle.

A beam of sunlight pierced the dust, caressing the porcelain beauty of Penfeld's tea service. It was the only thing in the hut left intact. Emily hesitated, formulating her plan. She would calmly coax the beast out of hiding, *then* obliterate it from the face of the earth.

The monster poked its head out from beneath the cloth, taunting her with a flick of its little red tongue.

Emily's control snapped. A fierce battle cry tore from her throat. She charged, swinging the broom like an enraged samurai. The bristles whisked past the tea tray without so much as rattling a cup, then skimmed beneath the table. The broom handle caught in the hem of the linen cloth, jerking it askew. The tray started to slide, but it was too late for Emily to stop the momentum of her swing. She could only watch, horrified, as the tray teetered on the edge of the table for a timeless moment, then flipped. The crash seemed to echo forever. A single unbroken cup rolled across the floor, coming to rest against her toes.

Emily cringed. She gazed at the scattered carnage, then down at herself in the deafening silence. Penfeld's coat was furred with dust. One tattered sleeve hung by a few threads. She blew a curl from her eyes, her shoulders slumping in defeat.

Behind her someone cleared his throat.

She whirled around, dropping the broom.

Through a curtain of glittering dust motes she saw Justin leaning against the door frame, his arms crossed over his chest. Beneath the slanted brim of his hat his eyes crinkled in a lazy smile. He had never looked more handsome. Or more infuriating.

She sat down abruptly on the floor, clutching her ankle. Something scuttled out of the shadows, darting straight for Justin.

"Watch out!" she shrieked, snatching up the broom.

Before she could swing, Justin reached down and scooped up the creature. He dangled it above his head like a fat, scaly baby.

"There now, my pet," he crooned, giving Emily a reproachful look. "Did the wicked little girl frighten you?"

Her jaw dropped. "That thing is a pet?"

He cradled the beast to his chest. "This *thing* is a tuatara lizard, a veritable living fossil. They can survive for more than a century, although I dare say you've taken a few decades off this poor fellow's life."

"Then we're even. He's taken a few decades off mine."

The lizard's spiked tail waved near the waistband of Justin's dungarees. Emily felt an absurd flare of jealousy as he tickled it under its beaked chin. "Poor, sweet Fluffy."

"Fluffy?" she echoed.

"What would you have me call him? Scaly? Ugly?"

"It would seem more appropriate."

"Ah, but your parents didn't name you Brat, did they?"

She snapped her mouth shut, tempted to whack *him* with the broom. The lizard flicked its tongue out at her. She poked out her own in return. "You might have told me you had a two-foot dinosaur for a pet."

He smiled with maddening sweetness. "You never asked." He held the lizard up, examining it in the sunlight. "She didn't hurt you, did she?" As Justin kissed its scaly head, Emily would have sworn its beady little eyes flickered in demure triumph.

"Poor Fluffy, indeed," she muttered. "Poor Fluffy gets all the sympathy." She knuckled the corner of her lip, tasting blood. "What about poor Emily? I could have been killed, but nobody cares enough to fuss over me or lick my wounds."

Justin slanted an unfathomable look at her. Her heart thumped into an off-key rhythm.

He gently deposited Fluffy outside the door, then shut it with deliberate care. "We wouldn't want you to feel neglected, now, would we?"

Emily's eyes widened as he closed the space between them and hauled her to her feet. His hands were rough, but his mouth as it found hers was achingly tender. His tongue glided with silky ease over the contours of her lips, lingering and soothing until a yearning ache replaced the sting. He didn't stop then, but tangled his hand in her hair and tilted her head back. He swept his tongue across hers, branding her with his taste and heat. Her hand curled helplessly around his nape, winding in the textured silk of his hair. A moan rose from deep in her throat.

He released her.

Emily was so shocked she forgot to fall down. She just stood there in the middle of the floor, stunned by the knowledge that with one kiss he had shattered all her defenses, all the independence she had fought so hard to win. She was the sort of woman who could be had by her worst enemy for only the subtle eroticism of a kiss. Dazed, she touched two fingers to the tingling pillow of her bottom lip. Miss Winters must be right. She must be a very bad girl indeed.

Justin took a step backward, unprepared for Emily's trembling vulnerability. He had expected an enraged shriek, perhaps a slap, but not the lost expression that darkened her pretty eyes. She looked as if he had struck her, not kissed her, and it made him feel both cruel and ashamed. If she started to cry, he feared Penfeld might return to find them both on the floor, bawling like babies. He ached to touch her, but satisfied himself by plucking a dust ball from her curls.

She sank down on an overturned bucket, wrapping her

dignity around her like the shreds of Penfeld's coat. "I fear the joke's on me this time. I lied about my leg." She met his gaze with aching candor. "I didn't have anywhere else to go."

Justin's heart lurched. He had the odd feeling that those were the truest words she'd ever spoken to him. A wave of unexpected anger surged through him, driving him to break his own precious code of privacy. "Where is your family? Is there no one to take care of you? What is society coming to when a girl like you can roam halfway across the world without a soul to protect her?"

"I don't need protecting. I cherish my independence." She lowered her eyes. "I've been too long dependent on the fickle whims of men."

He cupped her cheek in his palm, forcing her to meet his gaze. "Perhaps you've only chosen the wrong men."

"A mistake I don't care to repeat," she said with forced lightness, drawing away from him. "You were kind to let me stay. You knew better than anyone that I had nothing to pay you with."

Nothing but the cheering warmth of her chatter, the clean scent of her curls, and more laughter than the dusty old hut had heard in years. He opened his mouth, then closed it again, afraid he might beg her to stay not for another week, but for another month.

"You can pay me," he said abruptly.

Her fingers knotted in her lap. She rolled her foot over Penfeld's remaining cup, tension written in the curve of every toe. "I know such arrangements are common in a land such as this, but I don't believe I could—"

Justin bit off one of Nicky's favorite oaths. Emily's eyes widened in shock. He snatched off his hat and turned away to pace, not wanting her to see him bleed from her careless cut.

His foot scattered a pile of books. "Is that what a *kind* man would do, Emily? Force you to share his blankets for a thatched roof and a plate of beans? Is that what you're worth?" He whirled to face her. "What manner of man do you think me?"

Justin didn't think she could hurt him any more than she had, but when she lowered her gaze to her lap without answering, he discovered he was wrong. Dust motes drifted down to halo her disheveled curls. His throat tightened with a temptation sharper than pain.

What if he allowed Emily to barter her tender young body as the price for his protection? Would he be a monster for wanting to blunt the sharp edges of night with the pleasure of her charms?

"Come here."

An unbidden shiver raced through Emily at the smoky timbre of Justin's voice. She untangled her fingers and smoothed the remnants of Penfeld's coat over her thighs. She rose and glided toward him, mesmerized by the clarity of his golden eyes. How could such crystalline eyes hide such dark secrets? she wondered.

She tilted her face to his, meeting his gaze boldly despite the faint quiver of her lower lip.

"You can repay me . . ." he said, brushing a strand of hair from her brow.

His shadow fell over her; Emily's eyes fluttered shut in unwitting invitation.

". . . by cooking dinner tonight."

Emily snapped open her eyes. Justin was already striding toward the door, stepping over broken bits of china with the lazy grace she found so unnerving.

"You've piqued my curiosity about one thing," he said. "Why didn't you just run outside when I put Fluffy in the hut?"

"Run?" she echoed, still dazed by his abrupt mood change. "I never considered it."

Grudging admiration touched his voice. "No, I suppose you wouldn't, would you?"

Justin watched his words sink in; Emily's eyes slowly widened to vengeful saucers. "When you *put* Fluffy in?

When you put Fluffy . . . do you mean you deliberately
. . . why, you miserable wretch!"

She fumbled at the floor. Justin slammed the hut door
just as the last unbroken cup crashed into it and shattered.
Grinning, he slapped on his hat at a cocky angle. "Now,
that's my girl."

He strode toward the fields, the music of Emily's
curses still ringing in his ears.

Penfeld was moping. Even the creases in his trousers
looked droopy. Emily fussed over him with unrelenting
cheer, bringing him conch shell after conch shell of tea
heavily sweetened with precious treacle. In the course of a
day, their roles had oddly reversed. The valet reclined on
his pallet, his hands folded over his belly in plump wings.
He hadn't made a single remark about Emily's miraculous
recovery. Even in tragic defeat he remained tactful.

Emily clucked into his untouched shell of tea. "This
won't do at all. If I didn't know better, I'd swear you were
sulking."

"A good valet never sulks, miss. He mourns."

"I am terribly sorry about your tea service. It wasn't
entirely my fault, you know." She shot Justin's back a dark
look.

Her host stood at the stove, flipping the sweet potato
pancakes she had molded earlier. He had the good grace to
turn around at her pointed words, but she almost wished
he hadn't. There was something hopelessly compelling
about a man as virile as Justin wearing an apron. Her toes
started to feel sticky, and she realized she was pouring the
lukewarm tea over her feet. She dried them with the hem
of Penfeld's coat.

"Emily's right. It wasn't entirely her fault." Justin
pointed his spatula at the impassive lizard perched on a
stack of books. "Fluffy must have been dipping into the
rum again. You know how clumsy he gets on one of his
drunken rampages."

Emily, Penfeld, and the maligned lizard all glared at him.

Justin threw up his arms. "I confess! I murdered those innocent cups and sugar bowls with my own ruthless hands. But I've promised you new ones the very first chance I get. Even if I have to swim all the way to Fleet Street to find them."

Penfeld's long-suffering sigh was enough to make Emily weep. "You can't afford it, sir. Your every halfpenny is promised to Miss—"

Justin flashed a warning glance toward Emily. If Fluffy had been blessed with visible ears, she was sure they would have perked up.

Penfeld snapped his mouth shut and began toying with his suspenders. Miss who? Emily wondered. Miss Auckland Strumpet? Miss Greedy Mistress with Soft Blue Eyes and Not a Freckle on Her Body? Justin obviously wasn't channeling his fortune to his ward. Was some New Zealand beauty bleeding him dry? Did he have a shrewish paramour and five mewling brats tucked away somewhere? She supposed it would serve him right after what he had done to her father. So why had she suddenly lost her appetite?

Their meager supply of plates had been broken, so Emily began slamming pancakes on palm fronds.

Justin crouched beside the pallet. "Picture it in your mind, Penfeld. A gleaming vista of Waterford goblets and Wedgwood jasperware. Linen napkins heaped like snowy Alps beside each plate."

The valet only sniffed. "How arrogant of me to think I could preserve a tiny corner of civilization in this wilderness, a small fragment of the mighty dignity of the British Empire in this wasteland of . . ."

He droned on. Justin shrugged at Emily over his head, indicating it best to let him ramble. As they sat, picking the sand out of their pancakes, a trilling cry interrupted Penfeld's recitation.

A long, tanned leg jutted over the windowsill, followed by a tattooed arm waving a bottle of rum. "Greetings, most noble companions. I come bearing liquid sustenance for your delectable banquet."

"Doesn't Trini know any words under six syllables?" she hissed at Justin. She was still cranky from envisioning him adrift in a welter of milk-skinned, golden-eyed babies.

"Of course he does, but he prefers the ones I taught him."

"That explains why he's so pompous."

Justin slanted her a dark look, but she was already taking a dainty bite of her pancake. He caught the bottle Trini tossed and splashed rum into his tea. Emily reached for the bottle, but Justin slyly eased it out of her reach. He was afraid rum and Emily might not mix. He could too easily imagine them igniting with a lethal flash, burning his lean, hungry body to cinders.

Trini squatted in their circle and Emily hastened to offer him a pancake. Penfeld's pancake. She ignored the valet's protests, more concerned with soothing the native's hunger. She didn't have to worry about Penfeld eating her. Trini gulped down the crisp treat, then licked his fingers and grinned at her. Emily looked around frantically.

"Oh, no, you don't." Justin slid his own food out of her reach. "Give him yours."

"But I'm hungry," she wailed.

Justin grabbed her foot and ran his thumb over the sleek curve of her instep. A decadent heat tingled up her calf. "Have I ever mentioned what succulent little toes you have?"

She caught her breath, so paralyzed by the wicked sparkle of his eyes that she absently handed her pancake to Trini. When Justin freed her foot, it felt even more bereft than her empty stomach.

Trini's voice boomed out. "You benevolent gentlefolk have shared your sumptuous repast with me. Now I beg for the privilege of repaying the favor."

He vaulted out the window, returning with a platter of glazed meat. The exotic aromas of honey, cinnamon, and passion fruit wafted from the steaming dish, making Emily's mouth water.

She clutched Justin's arm. "Please tell me it's not—"

"Good old-fashioned English pork, my dear. A favored delicacy of the Maori."

She slumped in relief. Even Penfeld perked up as bottle and platter were passed around. The shadows of dusk lengthened across the hut, but the gathering darkness did not pierce their warm glow of laughter and conversation.

As Penfeld rose to light the lanterns, Emily leaned against the wall, content to watch the emotions dance across Justin's face and hands. She'd found most Englishmen to be stilted in both speech and manner, but Justin's fingers were eloquent extensions of his voice. He spoke briefly to Trini in Maori, the foreign words rolling like song from his tongue. Trini rose and disappeared out the window again.

"His comings and goings are enough to make a kiwi dizzy," Penfeld said, splashing a healthy dose of rum into his tea as Trini bounced back into the hut.

The native knelt in front of Emily and offered her a calico-wrapped package.

"For me?"

Trini nodded. "For that most elegant of womankind, the veritable apex of feminine pulchritude—"

"Did he just insult me?" she asked Justin.

His shoulders shook with suppressed laughter. "No. He said you were lovely." The warm glow in his eyes made Emily wonder if he shared that opinion.

She tugged open the package. Nestled within the worn folds were a skirt of woven flax and a thin scarf of flowered calico.

She held the skirt up to the light, admiring the exquisite workmanship. "It's stunning, Trini, but I mustn't accept it. Look what I've done to poor Penfeld's coat."

Penfeld offered a toast to that, sloshing rum on his immaculate trousers.

Trini spoke rapidly to Justin in Maori. He grunted a reply. The native took the skirt and laid it across her hands once again, saying simply, "Not for Trini. For Em."

For Em. Not borrowed from a befuddled valet. Not outgrown by some snobbish teacher. For Em. Virgin flax woven to hug the curves of her body. She looked around at their expectant faces, wondering how she could have allowed them to become so familiar and so dear in such a short time. Her gaze stopped at Justin. A wistful hunger touched his smile.

She offered Trini her hand, hiding a flinch when he brought it toward his teeth. "My most marvelous gratitude, Trini Te Wana," she said.

He kissed her palm with the suave charm of any London swell. Emily gathered her gift and withdrew to the other side of the hut, terrified Justin might hear the tiny cracks shooting through her frozen heart.

Justin reclined on one elbow and tipped the rum bottle to his lips. The liquor spread its warm haze through his veins. Behind him Penfeld was snoring. The valet had forgotten to put any tea at all in his last conch shell. Trini had confiscated Justin's watch and was twirling it over the lantern, watching darts of light dance across the hut in drunken fascination. Conversation had long ago declined, as it tended to do when stomachs were full and bottles empty.

Sighing, Justin allowed his gaze to lead him to the same hopeless place it had all night. To Emily.

She sat, hugging one leg, her chin pillowed against the satiny curve of her knee. A jagged tear in Penfeld's coat exposed a creamy shoulder burnished with freckles. The lantern light tipped her chestnut curls with flame, haloing a profile as fragile and inscrutable as porcelain. Her eyes followed the spin of his watch as if hypnotized.

He closed his own eyes for a weary moment, wondering if they'd somehow wounded her with their kindness.

When he opened them, Emily was staring at him, her pensive expression hardened to something more feral. For a chilling instant he would have sworn she hated him.

Then the lantern flickered, Trini began to hum softly, and the moment was gone.

Too much rum, Justin assured himself uneasily as he tipped his hat over his eyes and eased into stupor.

Justin awoke to darkness. His head throbbed and his mouth tasted as if Fluffy had been tramping through it. No nightmares though. The thought gave him little comfort. He had learned long ago the seductive danger of drowning his dreams in rum.

Penfeld's rumbling snores assured him it was still night. He stumbled to his feet, hoping a trip into the moonlight would relieve more than his aching bladder. His eyes adjusted poorly, and he stubbed his toe on Trini's prone form. A sliver of moonlight beckoned him into the night. He was already fumbling at his dungarees when he hit the door.

He stumbled a few feet away, then stopped, his back to the hut. His shoulders slowly relaxed in relief.

"Feel better?"

A rich note of humor tinged the feminine voice. An icy heat knifed between Justin's shoulder blades and crawled all the way to his hairline. *Dear God, don't let her see me blush,* he prayed.

"Quite," he said gruffly, making crucial adjustments with frantic hands. He hitched his thumbs in his waistband and swaggered back to the hut as if he had known she was there all the time.

Emily sat in the sand, staring glumly at the fragments of china gathered in the circle of her legs. An elfin frown crinkled her brow.

She swept a floppy curl out of her eyes, leaving a pale

smudge of flour on her cheek, and held up a teacup with no handle. "I made some paste for Penfeld's tea set."

Justin wondered how long she had been sitting out there alone. Shadows stained the fragile skin beneath her eyes. Her efforts seemed to have yielded little more than sticky fingers and sandy china. As they watched, a gaping fissure split the cup she was holding.

Her bereft sigh was more than Justin could bear. He ducked into the hut and returned with a small jar. "Kauri gum. Hand me that teapot and we'll give it a try."

Emily's grin swept away the last of the rum's stale fog. Their fingers brushed and lingered as he knelt and took the spoutless teapot from her hand.

Penfeld threw open the door, inviting the brisk morning air into his lungs. He had awakened to an empty hut and was mortified to have outslept Justin. It wasn't that his master required any assistance wiggling into his dungarees, but a proper valet should always rise first.

He balled his hands and stretched, shading his tender eyes against the sunlight. He lifted his foot but mercifully glanced down before lowering it, realizing he was about to tread directly on someone's fingers. He hopped backward. His eyes widened as he took in the spectacle before him.

Justin and Emily lay in a heap, entwined like a pile of sleeping kittens, her arm looped across his stomach, his head pillowed on her thigh. Emily's cheeks were flushed. Justin's dark hair stirred in the morning wind. Beside them in the sand lay one of the sweetest sights Penfeld had ever seen.

The sun gleamed across the silver tray, kissing the sleek curves of the porcelain. They had rescued a handful of cups, the teapot, and the sugar bowl. What did it matter that the china was webbed with thick brown gum and crusted with sand? Or that the spout of the teapot now hung upside down like the trunk of some morose elephant? Penfeld thought it all unbearably lovely.

He drew out his starched handkerchief and dabbed at his cheeks. "Silly sand," he muttered. "Always blowing in my eyes."

Later that same morning Emily danced around the hut, delighting in the musical sway of the flaxen skirt. It hugged her hips, then flared around her legs in a graceful bell, granting her giddy freedom of movement. After nearly lynching herself, she had even managed to tie the calico scarf around her breasts in a makeshift bandeau. She wished Miss Winters could see her now. The flowered material bared enough skin to send the poky old headmistress past death into rigor mortis.

She folded Penfeld's ragged coat with tender hands. She was worse at sewing than she was at pasting together teapots and wouldn't have inflicted her seamstress skills on her worst enemy.

Not even on Justin.

Her hands paused in their motion. Her worst enemy, she thought. The man who had sat with her until dawn, using his exquisite patience to piece together shards of broken porcelain to cheer his friend. The man she had vowed to somehow destroy.

She tossed the coat on Penfeld's pallet. Today was to be her first taste of real freedom, and she refused to dwell on such dark thoughts. The slant of the sun warned her she had slept past noon. Such decadence made her shiver with delight. She started for the door, but could not resist one last peek at Penfeld's tea tray. She had awoken alone on her pallet to find it displayed proudly beneath the window.

The sun illumined bulbous cracks patched with amber gum, but Emily had to admit it was a valiant effort. She leaned forward, lured by a hint of her reflection in an unbroken stretch of silver. She tugged at one of her curls. It popped back like a coiled spring. She sighed. Why couldn't she have been born with a straight fall of ice-blond hair like Cecille du Pardieu?

The door swung open, and she thrust her hands behind her back, embarrassed to be caught primping. Miss Winters would never have tolerated such vanity.

Justin ducked beneath the lintel. "Thought I'd come back and see if Sleeping Beauty had decided to rise. I was beginning to wonder if you were ever—" As his gaze lit on her, he stopped.

Emily held her breath as he reached up and slowly pulled off his hat. An odd tingle swept up her body in the smoldering path of his gaze. Their easy banter of the previous night perished in its flame.

Laughing shakily, she spread her arms and spun around for his perusal. "Do I look like a native? Would Trini be pleased? Of course Trini wouldn't be pleased. He would be exultant. Or rhapsodic. Or—"

"You look fine." Justin's tone bordered on surliness.

She caught a tantalizing glimpse of something pained, almost stricken, in his eyes. Then he donned his hat, tilting it forward as an effective veil.

She flitted around the hut, gathering a towel and a wicker basket. "I thought I'd go down to the beach and dig some clams for supper. I'm weary to death of this dusty old hut." She started for the door.

"No!"

His yell startled her so badly, she dropped the basket.

She felt her jaw drop as he threw his body across the door. "You can't go out there! I absolutely forbid it."

Chapter 6

· 🐚 ·

Like you, Claire, my friend has been blessed with
the ability of keeping a cool head under fire. . . .

Justin knew he was behaving like a madman, but he was helpless to stop. The same impish demon who had driven him to return to the hut at midday had taken his little pitchfork and twisted it deep into Justin's heart.

He had opened the door, expecting to find the bedraggled waif he had carried to the pallet after Penfeld had awakened him that morning. But the fairies had come while he was in the fields, leaving in her place one of their own—an ethereal vision of womanhood. Her loveliness pained him, opened up a raw chasm of hunger in his heart and in his arms. He wanted to cover her shy smile with his lips, to ease her back down on the pallet and beg her to adore him with both her woman's body and her child's heart.

She had tried to tell him she was grown, but he had refused to heed her warning. Until he had heard the teasing whisper of flax against her thighs and traced the exquisite cling of the fabric across her full breasts, it had been less painful to pretend she was just a funny little moppet, a minor annoyance to his well-ordered existence.

But when he walked through that door, his neat existence had crumbled like sand before an irresistible tide, and he had ended up flung across the doorway like a pagan sacrifice.

"You can't go out there," he repeated. "I won't have it."

Emily's brow folded in a stormy frown. Justin knew he had made a mistake. Forbidding Emily anything was like tossing a haunch of beef to a starving lioness.

She crossed her arms and tapped her foot on the dirt floor. "I beg your pardon."

"I'm sorry, but I simply cannot allow it."

"Why not?"

"It's not safe. There are too many—uh—um—"

"Tigers? Cobras? Bears?" she offered.

Bears? He wanted to reply that there were too many other men out there. Maori warriors, undeniably handsome even by English standards. Virile Polynesians whose bronze muscles gleamed with sweat and whose bones never ached, not even after long, hot hours in the sun. Strutting young heroes in the first flush of manhood with not a gray hair among them. Justin searched his mind frantically.

"Cannibals!" he almost shouted. "Too many cannibals. I'm disappointed in you, Emily. How could you have forgotten?"

"And you think they might want to gobble me up?" She swept her tongue across her pearly little teeth.

Justin wadded his hat into a ball. His body was strumming like a piano wire strung to reckless limits. God, she was luscious. She was in far more danger of being gobbled up in here than out there.

"They might," he replied, refusing to commit himself.

"How odd. I distinctly remember Trini telling me the surrounding tribes were all friendly to whites. He said they even fought side by side in the recent land wars against the hostile natives."

Luscious and gifted with a good memory, Justin thought. A lethal combination. "There are still hostile Maori to the east of us in Rotorua who have been known to send out marauding parties." Her lower lip inched out, and Justin groaned. "I'm simply asking you not to go out alone. I'll come back and take you out later." Much later. Preferably after it was pitch dark and there was no one to ogle her but him.

She tossed back her curls and struck a long-suffering pose. "So until then I'm to remain your prisoner in this hut?"

Justin was torn between laughter and painful desire. Her words summoned up some very naughty images of fur rugs and silken chains. Once again he thanked God she had fallen into his hands instead of some less scrupulous man's. His own scruples were wearing thin faster than he cared to admit.

She had worked herself up to a full pout now. Justin decided it best to go before she started throwing things. She was standing dangerously near the skillet, and he didn't want to spend another sleepless night gluing together teacups. He donned his hat, wondering how it had gotten so misshapen. He dared a last glance from beneath the shelter of its brim and caught Emily's expression in a moment of rare honesty. She wasn't angry. She was hurt. As she watched him go, it had become impossible for her to hide the forlorn tilt of her lips.

He crossed to her and nudged her face up with one finger. "I'll be back for you. I promise."

Unable to deny himself, he touched his lips to hers in a brief caress. Her shiver of response rocked his soul. As he turned to go, the look in her fathomless dark eyes made him wonder which of them was truly the prisoner.

·　·　·

Justin's words haunted the lonely hut.

I'll be back for you. I promise.

Those were the last words Emily's father had ever spoken to her.

They had faced each other in Miss Winters's elegant parlor, awkward and at a loss for words for the first time in Emily's memory. The fawning headmistress had offered them the room for their farewells. She had assured him she would spare no expense for her cherished new pupil and her doting father, a man they all knew had a healthy investment in the booming New Zealand gold rush. Frost had webbed the windows, but a cheery fire had crackled on the hearth.

Eleven years before, when he'd been only twenty himself, David Scarborough's lovely Irish bride had died, leaving a squalling red-faced infant in her place. He delighted in telling his friends that he and Emily had grown up together. He was more than father and mother to her. He was her dearest friend. They'd never been separated, not even for a night, and now he was going away.

Emily was afraid to look at him. Snowflakes melted on the cape of his greatcoat. His own unruly curls had been tamed by a top hat of polished beaver. She thought he had never looked taller or more handsome. Or less like her daddy. She comforted herself by studying his leather shoes, memorizing each familiar knick and scuff, ignoring the trickle of the tears down her cheeks.

He folded her face in his kid gloves, his voice choked with a helpless agony that mirrored her own. "Claire. My sweet, my darling . . ."

She had buried her nose in his waistcoat, savoring the scent of pipe tobacco that always clung to him. He had touched his lips to her hair and whispered, "I'll be back for you. I promise."

Then he had turned and gone, leaving her standing alone in a blast of icy air.

"He would have come back, too," Emily whispered to the silent hut. "If it hadn't been for you."

She curled her lip in a snarl. How dare Justin make a mockery of her father's words! How dare his lips caress hers as if she were still a child to be pacified with a kiss and a promise! Promises were only as good as the men who made them.

She wiped her mouth with the back of her hand. "As if your words mean spit to me, Justin Connor!"

She snatched up the basket and threw the towel over her shoulder. Justin had been lying to her. The furtive dart of his eyes had given him away. Being a skilled kisser did not preclude being a bad liar. He probably wanted her safely closeted in the hut so she couldn't discover what dark deeds he accomplished in the glaring light of day. She marched across the hut, fully intending to tell him where both he and his mythical cannibals could go.

She threw open the door. A half-naked savage sprang into her path, swinging his club in a whistling arc. Emily froze. He shoved his face into hers. She recoiled from the fishy stench of his breath. The sunlight shining through her hair seemed to mesmerize him. Muttering under his breath, he wrapped one of her curls around his grubby finger, baring his yellowed teeth in a fearful grimace.

When he released the curl, it sprang back and hit her in the nose. Nodding as if satisfied, his chant swelled to a wail and he began to roll his eyes and wag his tongue in time to the wild gyration of his hips. Emily didn't know if he wanted to kill her or marry her. A churning throng of natives milled behind him, their gleaming teeth sharpened to menacing points.

Emily slammed the door in their tattooed faces and threw her back against it.

Cannibals! Oh, dear Lord, Justin had been telling the truth! Moaning under her breath, she pressed her eyes shut, feeling sick. Perhaps they'd go looking for fatter prey. Where was Penfeld when she needed him? She eased the door open and peeped through the narrow crack. A bulbous brown eye peered back at her.

Muffling a shriek, she slammed the door and backed away from it. Miss Winters had always warned her that disobedience would lead to a dire fate, but Emily thought being eaten by cannibals a trifle too dire. She could well imagine the superior smirk on Justin's face as he toasted her demise with Penfeld. *I tried to warn her,* he would say, shaking his head sadly. *The obstinate little vixen just wouldn't listen.* Mock tears would well in his golden eyes. Penfeld would snort into his own starched handkerchief and pour him another cup of tea.

Anger stiffened Emily's spine. She forced her frantic hiccups into slow, deep breaths. Damn Justin. Damn them all. She'd never met fate gracefully, and she wasn't about to start now. A beam of sunlight caressed the sleek stock of the rifle hanging over the door.

She dragged herself over the rum barrel and climbed on top of it. It teetered beneath her weight as she drew the rifle from its hook. She'd never held a gun before. Running her hand over the cool barrel gave her a heady sense of power.

Her gaze darted between the door and the window. She had little advantage except the element of surprise. If the natives had surrounded the hut, she was done for.

She tiptoed across the hut and poked her head out the window. Bushy fronds waved in the breeze. She might be able to slip out undetected and run for the beach. But what glory was there in running to Justin's arms, screaming like a hysterical chicken? Wouldn't he be far more impressed if she captured an entire band of hostile marauders alone? If she proved she could look after herself, he might grant her the freedom to roam the beach undisturbed.

Emboldened by that thought, she heaved herself out the window and slunk toward the front of the hut, the rifle cradled awkwardly in the crook of her arm. Sheltered by a fat bush, she peeped around the corner.

The savages' attention was focused on the door. The one who had threatened her with his club had melted back into the crowd. They jabbered among themselves in low musical cadences. Almost every man carried some sort of weapon, except for two who bore an iron pot between them. Emily flared her nostrils indignantly. The arrogant wretches, she thought. What were they going to do? Boil her on her own doorstep?

Her finger curled around the cold trigger. Before she could move, a burly warrior wearing dangling jade ear pendants had a heated exchange with an older man whose shock of white hair contrasted sharply with the green furrows dug into his wizened skin. The muscled cannibal made a dismissive gesture toward the door. They argued briefly, then the old man demurred, baring his yellowed teeth in a smile that conveyed respect without obeisance.

As they turned toward the hill, Emily plunged out of the bush, waving the rifle wildly. A vine tangled around her foot.

The Maori gaped at her as she came to a hopping halt. She realized how ridiculously pathetic she must look. Bracing the stock of the rifle against her shoulder, she swaggered forward. The natives rewarded her with several nervous glances toward the weapon.

"Don't take another step," she barked. "I know how to use this thing."

At least she knew which end to point at them. The gun was definitely inspiring more fear than Penfeld's feather duster.

The tall warrior crossed his arms over his chest and glared down his nose at her. His broad nostrils flared with contempt, but the older man lay a restraining hand on his arm and made frantic signs in the air. The men holding the pot dropped it in the sand. Several of the natives covered their eyes and made whistling sounds through their teeth. The whites of their eyes swelled with fear. Emily bit back a giggle, finding it all rather gratifying. But when the old man flattened his knuckles against his skull and wiggled his fingers like snakes, obviously indicating the state of her hair, she was less than amused.

The massive warrior took a menacing step toward her.

She swung the rifle in a dangerous arc. "Halt, you carnivorous fellow. You won't be putting me in your pot today. Down on your bellies! All of you."

Her command might have eluded them, but they understood the language of the rifle as she swept it across the sand. They flopped to their bellies like beached fish. The muscular warrior was the last to fall. His growling snarl made the hair on Emily's nape tingle.

An awkward silence descended over the clearing, broken only by the cheerful chirp of a cricket. Emily chewed on her lower lip. Now that she'd captured the cannibals, she hadn't the faintest idea what to do with them. She searched the cloudless sky, wondering how long it would be before Justin returned. She considered firing a shot in the air, then realized she'd never checked to see if the rifle was loaded. A hollow click at an inopportune moment might see her well on her way to martyrdom.

She knew of only one sure way to get Justin's attention. Ignoring his grunt of protest, she rested her foot on the curve of the warrior's back in what she hoped was a noble pose, threw back her head, and screamed at the top of her lungs.

Chapter 7

· 🐚 ·

*I fear Justin uses his cool head to shelter a heart
more tender than he'd care to admit. . . .*

𝒯he scream echoed across the amber hills. The hoe
slipped from Justin's hands, smashing his toes. The pain
was only a nagging reflection of a sharper agony as he
whipped his head around.

"Good Lord, sir, what manner of hellish creature could
have—"

Before Penfeld could finish, Justin was gone, his path
marked by a wild crashing through the dense brush.

Justin could not have explained how he knew the unearthly cry had come from Emily, only that the timbre of
her voice had somehow become as familiar to him as his
own. An icy sweat broke out on his body as he careened
down a hill, scraping his back on the serrated trunk of a
totara tree. Ferny boughs whipped his face, blinding him,
but still he pressed on, driven by the stark terror that by
his absence he had allowed something terrible to happen
to her. Time spilled back to the night when he had rushed
to another beach, clutching Nicky's bloody coat like a

talisman against the darkness, only to arrive a moment too late.

He tripped over a trailing creeper and went sprawling. His cheek struck the warm, rich earth with a thud. He shook damp tendrils of hair from his eyes and flung himself to his feet, catching a tantalizing glimpse of wicker through the trees. He hurtled into the clearing and stumbled to a halt, his heart slamming against his ribs, his breath dragged from his lungs in raw rasps.

Emily favored him with her sweetest smile. "What took you so long? I thought you'd never come."

Nothing could have prepared Justin for the sight of Emily holding court over a throng of prostrate Maori warriors like some triumphant Amazon queen. She cradled the rifle in her arms. Her little foot rested daintily on the spine of one of the largest and most irate warriors Justin had ever seen. Even his ears were pink with fury.

Justin doubled over, flattening his palms on his knees, before she could begin to guess at the depth or bitter sweetness of his relief. Its intensity terrified him. He took a deep breath as a hard-edged fury born of thwarted fear flooded his veins.

He jerked his head up. "What in the bloody hell do you think you're doing?"

Emily recoiled. Why didn't Justin look more pleased with her? She shrugged. "It's obvious, isn't it? Capturing cannibals."

Contempt iced his voice. "You, my dear, have just captured our neighboring tribe of Maori. A tribe, I might mention, that has been quite friendly to me, at least before they made *your* acquaintance."

"I don't understand," she said faintly. The rifle slipped a notch in her hands. "That horrid creature waved his club at me. They were all armed. They even brought their own pot. I only assumed—"

"That 'horrid creature' was performing the *te wero*, a ceremonial dance to welcome you to his country." Justin

picked his way over several inert Maori and grabbed a
long-handled tool topped by an innocuous blade. "What
were they going to do? Hoe you to death?" He pulled an
orangy-brown object out of the overturned pot and waved
it at her. "A *kumara.* Sweet potatoes. Their gift to you."

"Oh, dear." Emily mopped her brow, feeling suddenly
sicker than she had before.

Justin glided toward her with such lethal grace that
she started to point the rifle at him. He plucked the
weapon out of her arms, handling it with two fingers as if
it were a deadly serpent, and tossed it in the sand.

"I'd like to introduce you to Witi Ahamera, their
ariki, their chief."

She squared her chin, mustering her fading pluck. "I'd
like to meet him, too. I've got a few things to say about
his tribe running about, terrorizing unsuspecting young
Englishwomen."

"You're standing on him."

A brilliant heat flooded her cheeks. She followed Justin's mocking gaze down her calf to the foot braced against
the bronze muscles of the Maori warrior. Her toes twitched
nervously.

She looked to Justin for help, hoping he'd provide a
graceful dismount, but he only smirked at her.

"Well, so I am," she said. "Who would have thought
it?" She hopped off the man and tugged at his arm. He
rose slowly, towering over her. She reached above her head
to brush sand from his chest, avoiding his stony glare. "If
Mr. Witi would have bothered to tell me he was the chief,
I'd never have trod upon him in such a thoughtless manner."

Biting off what sounded like a distinctly Anglo-Saxon
oath, the chief shoved her hand away. She shrank against
Justin without realizing it. His arm slipped around her
waist, molding her to his lean frame. She felt as if she'd
flopped literally from stew pot to fire.

Taking their cue from their chief, the natives rose,

shaking sand out of their raw flax skirts. An admiring murmur of "Pakeha, Pakeha" rose from their ranks. Emily looked around, but could see nothing or no one who might inspire such deference.

The chief jutted out his hand. All murmuring ceased. A fierce intelligence burned in his bright, dark eyes. His nostrils flared as he pointed at Emily and bit off a string of guttural words that made her thankful she did not understand Maori.

She pressed herself to Justin, basking in his strength. "What is he saying?" she whispered.

His lips touched her ear. "You have offended his *mana*."

"His mama?"

Justin gave her a hard squeeze. "His *mana*. His honor. His pride. *Mana* is all-important to the Maori. Every slight, real or imagined, demands retribution. He wants to declare war on you."

She squirmed. "Why, that overgrown, jade-headed bully! Where's my rifle? Of all the arrogant, ridiculous—"

Justin clapped his hand over her mouth. The chief punctuated his newest accusation by leaning forward and poking her in the chest. She gulped.

"Cease!" Oddly enough, Justin's soft-spoken command stilled the irate warrior in mid-poke and threw an unnatural hush over his men.

Justin kept one hand firmly anchored over Emily's mouth, but his other hand took eloquent wing as Maori words spilled from his lips like song. Emily felt her body relax, lulled by the velvety timbre of his voice, hypnotized by the graceful flight of his fingers in the air. The natives hung on every word. Even the chief cocked his head in reluctant attention. Justin's hand slid from her lips and cupped her chin, tilting her face up for their regard.

Several of the men hopped back in fear, making signs in the air. A dreamy assurance melted through Emily's veins. He must be warning them never to trouble her again, telling them that she belonged only to him and he would protect her even at the cost of his own life.

The chief made a disgusted gesture toward the white-haired man. He nodded and they climbed the hill, leading their men into the brush and leaving her and Justin alone in the clearing.

Justin released her. Emily locked her knees, fearful she might melt into a besotted puddle at his feet.

She grabbed his arm. "Thank you, Justin."

He shook her hand off, his lips twisted in scathing dismissal. "Don't mention it. Now, if you don't mind, I'm going to meet with them as I'd planned to do before they were ambushed by Emily Scarlet, the jungle princess."

He started up the hill, brushing dirt off his dungarees with a disgusted motion. Emily's hands clenched into fists.

"What did you tell them?" she cried, refusing to be daunted by the note of desperation in her voice. She had to hear him say he cared. She'd waited to hear the words for almost half her life.

He picked his way over a thorny bush without slowing his pace. "I told them you were crazy. That you'd escaped from Bedlam and stowed away on a banana boat before the attendants could catch you."

He topped the crest of the hill. "I told them insanity ran rampant in your family and one of your ancestors thought he was a kiwi bird and tried to leap from the London Tower, not realizing, of course, that kiwis don't fly."

Emily suddenly knew what it meant to be blinded by rage. Or at least by the glint of the sun off a rifle barrel. She snatched the gun, cocked it, and aimed it at the tree nearest Justin that she thought she might hit without blowing his head off. She didn't want to maim him, just scare the hell out of him.

She squeezed the trigger. The lifeless click seemed to reverberate for miles.

Justin froze, his back rigid. As he came scrambling

down the hill at twice the pace he'd climbed it, Emily tried to shove the rifle behind her skirt. It was a very poor fit indeed.

His eyes blazed as he reached around her and snatched the weapon. He leaned forward until his nose touched hers. "If you think I'd leave you alone with a loaded gun, you're loonier than they think you are."

He hurled the rifle into the hut and turned away, dismissing her with contemptuous swiftness.

"Justin?"

He stopped, his shoulders braced against the sound of her voice.

"You must hate me, don't you?"

He sighed. "I wish I could, Emily. It would make life so much simpler."

An odd glow touched her. As he ducked into the bush she felt a grin steal over her face. In all the confusion he hadn't forbade her to leave the hut. She gathered her skirt to muffle its rustle and slunk up the hill after him.

Emily darted from tree to tree, running to keep Justin in sight. As she threw herself behind the trunk of a kauri tree, her foot came down squarely on a twig. The crack resounded through the forest. The quivering silence warned her Justin had also stopped to listen. She shrank into herself, holding her breath until his crashing path through the underbrush resumed. She poked her head out from behind the tree, looked both ways, then ducked after him. This might be her only chance to discover how he spent the long hours of daylight.

The trees thinned, shrinking into thick clumps of broom fragrant with masses of delicate pink amaryllis. She dropped down, forced to scramble up the slope on hands and knees to avoid being seen.

The hillside ended abruptly in a sprawling fence of stakes, their points whittled to menacing sharpness.

"At least there aren't any shrunken heads on them," she whispered to herself.

Not yet anyway.

Less than comforted by the thought, she followed the curving line of the palisade, still shielded by tangled growth. A yawning gate divided the stakes. Emily parted the fronds of a bush and watched Justin disappear into its maw. Seeing no guards, she dared to follow.

Hugging the palisade, she slipped through the gate to find a small village drowsing in the midday sun. Across the courtyard Justin was entering a round hut thatched with wicker. As Emily picked her way after him, a mangy dog lifted his head from his paws. Instead of barking, he greeted her with a pant and a lazy wag of his tail. These natives must be a trusting lot, she thought. Just as her father had been.

She inched around the walls of the windowless hut. What reasons did Justin have for meeting with the Maori? Was he buying land with her father's gold? She had read of some diabolical white men turning the natives against other whites so they could step into the carnage and steal their land. Her stomach tightened to a nervous knot. A trickle of sweat inched down her cheek.

Her groping fingers found a weak spot in the wicker. She tore it away, then knelt and pressed her eye to the tiny hole.

Her gaze adjusted slowly to the cavernous gloom of the meeting house. Burning torches had been spiked into the dirt floor, casting an amber glow over the gathering. Skirted natives sat cross-legged throughout the hut. A handful of women wearing feathered cloaks were sprinkled among the men. She recognized the stern chief and his white-haired companion. They all gave the center of the hut their rapt attention, their faces glowing with a common serenity. Even the fierce chief had allowed his expression to soften to curiosity, although the skeptical glint never completely left his dark eyes.

A smoke hole had been cut in the domed ceiling and a single shaft of sunlight cut through the gloom, illuminating the finely hewn features of the man sitting cross-legged in their midst. Emily was tempted to believe he had planned it that way, but realized he must need the light to read from the leather-bound book spread across his thighs. Trini sat beside him, translating Justin's English into Maori each time he paused.

Puzzled, Emily strained her ears to hear. She doubted if cannibals would be that enthralled by the life and times of Mozart or Vivaldi.

She didn't have to strain long. Justin's voice carried like the rich, sweet tolling of a cathedral bell.

" '. . . she brought forth her firstborn son, and wrapped him in swaddling clothes, and laid him in a manger because there was no room for them in the inn.' "

He paused so Trini might translate. The glowering chief shook his head as if saddened by the fate of the hapless child.

" '. . . And lo, the angel of the Lord came upon them, and the glory of the Lord shone round them . . .' "

Emily had squirmed through seven interminable Christmas pageants at the seminary. Pageants where Cecille du Pardieu played Mary while she got stuck as the far end of a sheep or donkey. But as she closed her eyes, it was as if she were hearing the power of the old, old words for the first time.

" '. . . And the angel said unto them, Fear not: for, behold, I bring you good tidings of great joy, which shall be to all people . . .' "

She opened her eyes, blinking away the tears caught in her lashes. The hut seemed to reel, pivoting slowly around a man with somber gold eyes caught in a web of sunlight. It sparkled across his hair, glinted off the gold watch case that lay against his breastbone.

Emily shoved herself away from the hut, clapping a hand over her mouth. A hysterical giggle escaped her, then another. The dashing rogue Justin Connor a missionary? Had her father bequeathed both his gold mine and his daughter to a madman? What had he done with the gold? she wondered. Given it to the natives to buy supplies? Or Bibles?

She doubled over, clutching her stomach as helpless laughter crippled her. How could she have let her own suspicions and the gossip of London society blind her to the man's true character? He had opened his life and heart to every stray who wandered past, taking in abandoned valets, reformed cannibals—even ugly lizards.

Everyone but his ward, she realized. There was no room at the inn for Claire Scarborough.

Until she felt the tears streaming down her cheeks, Emily didn't realize she was crying. She backed away from the meeting house. The emotional carousel she'd been on since her guardian had stepped out of the shadows was spinning out of control and, dear God, she had to get off.

The village blurred as she pelted past the gate into the tangled arms of the forest. Behind her a dog barked, the sound hollow against the blood rushing through her ears. She might have heard a man's frantic cry, or it might have been only the careening slam of her heart.. Dappled shadows lured her deeper into the bush, promising escape. Vines swatted her face, but she barely felt their sting.

The land climbed and Emily scrambled upward, digging her nails into a naked root to keep from falling. This narrow finger of land jutted high above the island, giving her a breathtaking view of a slim ribbon of beach below and rolling hills of grain to the west. The shimmering crowns of the fern trees waved over the emerald forest to the east, giving it all the illusion of a tropical paradise. The air was cooler here, sheltered from the sun by a tall stand of trees.

At another time Emily might have delighted in its beauty, but now it only pained her—like gazing at something she wanted desperately but could never have. She claimed the farthest tip of land as her own, flinging her arm around a tree and digging her toes into the cottony moss. A snowy bird hopped off a vine and went dancing into the sky. She stood aching and adrift in a whisper of birdsong as the breeze cooled her flaming cheeks. She had to flee the island, flee Justin before her own defenses were replaced by the tender adoration she had seen on the faces of the natives.

A shrill giggle rang out, mocking her heart's turmoil, only to be followed by the maniacal patter of little feet. Emily whirled around. The hill was shaded, the surrounding trees rife with shadows.

On the other side of the bluff a bush shuddered. Emily moaned. What now? she wondered. Pygmies? Gnomes? She'd been awake only since noon, and the day had been one disaster after another. She was beginning to feel like the little girl who had tumbled down the rabbit hole in Mr. Carroll's novel. She wouldn't have been surprised if a white lizard had bolted out of the trees, pulling her father's watch from his waistcoat pocket.

She scanned the tangled undergrowth. It trembled as if alive. Tiny invisible eyes bored into her like poison darts.

She turned to flee and ran straight into a tree, eliciting a demonic ripple of laughter.

"It's not funny!" she cried, spinning around.

Straight ahead of her a low-slung bush quivered with mirth. Anger surged through her. She narrowed her eyes. "Wouldn't be laughing so hard if I had an ax, would you?"

Gathering her skirt in her fists, she dashed toward the bush. At the last possible second she jumped, clearing it in one leap, catching the barest flash of tanned skin and shocked eyes.

The hunt was on.

The forest erupted in running feet. Emily hurtled through the dense brush, leaping bushes and dodging branches with an agility that surprised even her. She expected an arrow to tear through her tender flesh at any second. The trees thinned, but she didn't dare pause to look behind her.

She burst out of the cool canopy into the warmth of sunlight and an endless vista of aqua sea. There was an instant when she might have stopped, but the stampede of little feet spurred her on. The land tilted beneath her and she went tumbling head over heels down the sandy slope. Flashes of brown and blue spun in her vision. After an eternity of undignified grunting she caught the land and held it still beneath her stomach.

Eyes closed, she turned her face to the side, gasping for breath. Her fingers curled in the warm sand. A breeze stiff with salt caressed her aching legs. A curious silence assailed her.

She eased her eyes open to find herself surrounded by toes—dozens of plump little toes browned like raisins by the sun.

She lifted her head. Her eyes widened in shock to find a little boy wearing nothing but a necklace of shells and an impudent grin.

Naked children ringed her. Emily had never seen so much baby fat in one place.

These children had never been swaddled in corsets and crinolines. They'd never been stuffed into stockings or endured the torture of hooking a dozen buttons on high black boots that pinched their toes. They stared at her, and Emily stared back, shocked but fascinated by their freedom.

A solemn little girl gazed shyly at her from behind a fall of dark hair. Her belly pooched out in the swayback posture of a toddler. She popped her thumb in her mouth, sucking it noisily.

Groaning, Emily flopped to her back in the sand. "Why couldn't you have been Pygmies? I hate children."

The little boy offered her his hand. "Isn't it a bit intolerant of you to condemn an entire echelon of society based only on their collective ages?"

She jerked her head up. She hadn't expected him to understand her, much less answer in anything more than childish jabber.

She warily took his hand and climbed to her feet. "Let me guess. Justin must have taught you English."

"Justin?" he repeated.

The little girl spat out her thumb and squealed, "Pakeha!"

The children's faces lit up as they joined in her joyful trilling.

"Oh, for heaven's sake. Stop that, won't you? You're making my head ache." Emily backed away from them, throwing out her arms in a helpless gesture. "Of course. It only makes sense that Justin would be the almighty, magnificent, all-holy Pakeha!"

They lapsed into silence. The boy stared at her vacantly. Apparently, his tutor had yet to teach him the sting of sarcasm. The little girl gazed up at her with something akin to awe.

"Must she stare so? It makes me fidget."

The boy gathered the toddler to his side. "She is my sister, Dani. They call me Kawiri."

Emily bobbed a reluctant curtsy. "They call me Emily." She rested her hands on her hips. "Why were you chasing me?"

"We weren't chasing you. We were following you. We had no idea you'd be asinine enough to fall off the hill."

Emily couldn't find an argument for such evenhanded logic. "Neither did I," she muttered. "Asinine. Now, there's a good word. Did your mighty Pakeha begin with the *A*'s?"

Dani opened her mouth to chirp. Emily didn't think she could bear another hymn to Justin's goodness, so she squatted and plugged the child's thumb back in. While the other children experimented with Emily's name, the little girl pulled a crimson flower from behind her ear.

She tucked the bloom in Emily's hair, weaving it among the curls. Emily felt a hesitant smile touch her lips.

As a new excitement rippled through the children, she straightened. A plump boy pointed toward the waves, yelling in Maori.

"High tide," Kawiri explained.

"High tide?"

At Emily's blank look, he added, "A natural phenomenon initiated by the waxing and waning of lunar forces which in turn—"

"I know what a tide is," she interrupted.

He shrugged and jogged after the others. They pounded across the beach toward the waves, whooping in sounds that needed no language.

Emily watched, envying them their freedom and fighting a wistful sense of abandonment.

She felt a shy tug on her hand. Dani gazed up at her, grinning toothlessly. "Emmy," she said.

Her heart contracted.

Kawiri had spun around to jog backward. "Make haste, Emily. The day won't last forever."

"For a while it seemed like it might," she said softly.

Clinging to Dani's hand, she pelted after him, scattering sand in her wake.

Justin sat high atop the sandy bluff overlooking the beach. The wind raked his hair from his eyes, but not even the ocean breeze could cool his fevered musings. His gaze was locked on the beach below, drawn like the tide to the enchanting child-woman dancing through the waves.

Who the hell was she?

Had women changed so much since he'd left England? Emily was so little like those he had known in London that she seemed to be some exotic species, both irresistible and mysterious. Her mercurial moods both compelled and exhausted him. She was nothing like his addle-witted mother and even less like his vapid sisters. Their only concerns in life had been which gentlemen were going to sign their dance cards for the next ball. His stunning fiancée, Suzanne, had slapped his face in the lobby of the Theatre Royal when he'd informed her he'd rejected his inheritance, but at least he had understood her motive—healthy greed.

As Justin watched, Emily lifted her skirts and frolicked through the shallow waves, tossing her head with laughter as the children splashed her. Droplets of water caught in her hair, sparkled on her skin. A flower nestled in her hair, a crimson splash against her chestnut locks.

Had some man wounded her? Justin wondered. His hands clenched into fists. He'd like to get his hands on the wretch. The image of her being ill used at the hands of some scoundrel filled him with both jealousy and rage. And grief—a wistful longing that he could have known her before the shadow touched her smile.

She knelt in the wet sand, cupping her hands around a castle tower while Kawiri dug a moat with his toe.

Had some wealthy rake seduced her? He knew only too well the morals of his London. Propriety and upright thinking were the false gods of society. What went on behind closed doors was another matter. A man could do what he liked to a woman as long as he wasn't caught doing it. The sinking sun dipped behind a cloud, and Justin shivered. David's wealth had given him and Nicholas the means to escape London's stifling confines, but what means had Emily been forced to use? If left alone without the guidance of her guardian, would David's daughter be forced into similar straits?

The children took their leave in laughing clusters, leaving Emily alone on the beach. Justin stood, hoping to slip away before she caught him spying on her. But at that moment the sun clipped away the edge of the cloud; its rays struck his chest with a fiery warmth. Emily shaded her eyes and he knew she had seen the sun glint off his watch case.

Their gazes locked and held for a long time before she turned her face away and stared out to sea.

Justin scrambled down the bluff, but the proud curve of her back warned him to silence. He was beset by a terrible urge to touch her there. To lay his palm against the warm satin of her bare skin and draw her into his arms. His breath caught in his throat, trapped by an unbearable wave of longing.

He swallowed his questions, hesitant to shatter anything as fragile as her pride. "I saw you in the village."

"Forgive me for intruding. I hope I didn't stop you from healing any lepers or raising any natives from the dead." Her voice was as brittle as her stance as she swung around to face him. "Where are your followers? I expected you'd be trailed by a veritable parade of blind men and paralytics."

Her mocking tone stung him less than the depth of her emotion. It was not a child's petulance he read in her darkened eyes, but the anguish of a woman.

He stretched out his hand, no longer able to keep from touching her. She recoiled visibly and his fingers slowly curled into his palm.

He fought to keep his voice steady. "You're not the only woman to flee to this country to escape an intolerable past. If someone has hurt you . . . if a man has hurt you . . . ?"

Justin's compassion stabbed Emily like a blade. She wanted to scream, "You! You've hurt me!" but the words were locked inside some dark, secret place.

Her gaze raked him with all the cool contempt she could muster. "I'm not like them. You're not my savior. I'm not compelled to spill my sins to the mighty Pakeha."

He stepped back, and she suddenly knew what made his face so compelling. His features came alive with every emotion. Even pain. A desperate need to comfort him flooded her. Fighting it, she struck out like a wounded animal.

"What is it, Mr. Connor? Haven't I put you high enough on my pedestal?" She stalked him, spurred by some dangerous need to move him, to elicit some reaction that would prove he was no marble saint, but only a flawed creature like herself. "You enjoy their adoration, don't you? It must be very gratifying for a man like you."

A moment earlier she wouldn't have thought it possible, but his face had closed now, gone as immobile as a Maori totem. His words were clipped. "What sort of man might that be, Emily?"

"Patron to valets. Friend to lizards." She drew the crimson flower from her hair and ran it up his muscular arm, tracing teasing swirls on his sun-heated skin. "Is that what you want from me? Blind adoration?"

His body was rigid with tension, but the uneven rhythm of his breathing warned her she had affected him.

Tilting her face to his, she rubbed against him with a boldness that would have shamed a feline. "Shall I fall on my knees and wash your feet with my tears?"

Emily was mocking him. Mocking his faith and his life. And all Justin could think of was the kittenish softness of her breasts pressed against his chest. He wanted to free them from their thin band of calico, to feel their lush curves brand his skin with their naked splendor, to stroke their coral tips to aching fruition with his fingertips. The velvety petals of the bloom opened against his skin just as her lips might open to his tongue's invasion, her body to his fierce possession.

She must be truly mad to taunt him in such isolation. His senses sang with the relentless rhythm of the sea. How easy it would be to push her down on the bed of sand and take her without any of the niceties society demanded.

He wrapped one arm around her and pulled her crudely and deliberately into the cradle of his thighs.

Emily hung in his embrace, her courage melting in the heat of his wary, smoldering gaze. Somehow he had seized the moment and made it his own. She trembled with a primitive fever, but still she met his gaze squarely, refusing to lower her lashes, refusing to shy away from his blatant need.

He pressed against her, moving, seeking, showing her without words how easy it would be for the contours of their bodies to mold into one. He was marble, yes, but molten marble, not cool and distant, but hot and seething. He was not a saint, but a man. All man.

"Which of your foolish lads taught you to play such a dangerous game?" he asked.

"You don't like danger, do you, Mr. Connor?"

"I don't like games."

As she gazed deep into his eyes, his pupils seemed to swirl in a sea of amber. Her need. His power. Her temptation. His challenge. Emily dropped her head back, going light-headed with fear.

He caught her by the shoulders, his face darkened with emotion. "I never asked you to worship me, Emily. All I wanted from you was a little common courtesy."

He thrust her away from him and strode down the beach. Emily knew he was lying. He wanted her. Badly. And that was one weapon she'd never thought to hold. Shaken, she sank down in the sand and watched the encroaching tide crumble her castle.

Chapter 8

Despite the similarity in our ages, he has been more son to me than brother. . . .

Justin had walked the twisted corridors of the Victorian mansion hundreds of times, first in childhood, then in dreams. The plush burgundy carpet unrolled at his feet. He was a boy again, hurrying past dim passages drenched in the shadows of flickering gaslight. Tall doors flanked the hallway, dwarfing him with their mahogany splendor. He was late again, always late, and he knew his father would be displeased.

His thin legs would not carry him fast enough. The corridor stretched into infinity. He began to try doors, afraid they'd be locked, but more afraid they wouldn't be. He rattled each crystal knob with shaking fingers. If he made too much noise, his father would lock away the piano and send him back to his room without supper. His stomach knotted with hunger.

Light blazed at the end of the corridor. His steps slowed, mired in some unspeakable dread. Now the carpet was unrolling faster, dragging him into the widening arc

of light against his will. As the light engulfed him, he
swallowed a scream.

Thank God he had. There was nothing to be afraid of.
He was standing inside the dining room, where his family
had gathered around the long oak table. He scooted into
his seat, perplexed by the empty chair at his side. They
were all there. His mother. His three sisters, demure in
their ruffled frocks. His ancient grandmother, nodding in
her pudding.

Glowering, his father lifted a carving knife and pulled
the covered warming tray toward him. The light from the
gasolier burnished the keen blade. Justin glanced again at
the chair beside him, haunted by its emptiness.

His father's fingers curled around the handle of
the silver lid. Justin's stomach spun. He slammed his
chair back, overturning it. He had to warn his father, to
somehow stop him from lifting that lid before it was too
late.

His father shook his head. His mouth didn't move,
but the unspoken words pounded through the room in
bass counterpart to his sisters' soprano giggles. *Don't be so
sensitive, boy. You're too damned sensitive for your own
good.*

With a terrible grin his father lifted the lid of the
warming tray. Justin screamed. Then he was alone in the
dining room, alone with the shadowy figure in the chair
next to him. The figure turned, basking in the glow of the
gaslight.

Nicky.

Nicholas in all of his dark beauty, his hair slicked back
at the temples, his teeth flashing white against his swarthy
skin.

He pointed a tapered finger at Justin. "Your father was
right, my boy. You always were too goddamned sensitive
for your own good."

He threw back his head in a burst of baritone laughter.
Justin clapped his hands over his ears and backed into the

corner until his own screams faded into the bright, tinkling notes of a child's laughter.

Emily sat straight up as a hoarse whimper arrowed
through the darkness. She rubbed her eyes, disoriented.
How late was it? she wondered. Exhausted by the playful
beating her body had taken from sea and sun, and unable
to endure either the false cheer of Penfeld's prattling or the
sight of Justin's empty pallet, she had crawled to her own
blankets after dinner and collapsed in a dreamless heap.

Her eyes adjusted slowly. Pale wisps of moonlight
drifted through the window. Penfeld's comforting bulk
was humped under his blankets. A low moan shuddered
the silence.

Emily sat up on her knees, her heart hammering in her
throat. Justin was only a vague shape in the shadows. She
crept toward him, dragging one of her blankets behind her
like a lifeline.

A shallow beam of moonlight caressed his face. His
waking defenses had fled, leaving him as helpless as a child
in sleep. Sweat beaded his upper lip. Emily wanted to
touch him, to smooth away the grooves of pain around his
mouth, to wipe the shadows from beneath his eyes. He
flung out an arm, startling her, and she jerked back her
hand.

He had thrashed his way out of the blankets, and the
first two buttons of his dungarees had come undone. There
was something touching about the untanned swath of skin
beneath the folded flap of calico, a beguiling reminder of
the pale, proper young Englishman he had once been. He
muttered a name between clenched teeth. Emily leaned
over, torn between curiosity and empathy.

His body twitched. His face crumpled in a spasm of
horror. She reached for him, despising herself for her hesitation.

His eyes flew open. With dizzying speed and no more

than a grunt of exertion he caught her wrists and rolled over, pinning her beneath the hard length of his body.

A single word, fraught with meaning, hoarse with accusation, flew from his lips.

"*Claire.*"

Chapter 9

· 🐚 ·

Someday, God willing, the two of
you shall meet. . . .

*E*mily's heart stopped.

A jolt of recognition blazed like a comet through Justin's eyes, then skimmed away, leaving her straddled by a bewildered stranger. She didn't know whether to laugh with relief or weep with disappointment.

"Emily? What in the hell . . . ?"

She chose her words with care. "You were dreaming. Having a nightmare."

"Dreaming?"

Justin's gaze traced Emily's features in confusion. The moonlight had softened her gamin edges, given her brown eyes a glow hauntingly familiar in its tenderness. Why did it hurt so bloody much to look at her? There was something there. Something he ought to remember flirting with the edges of his consciousness. His gaze traveled downward, held captive by the pliant sprawl of her limbs beneath him, her unspoken acceptance of his weight and will. Her slender wrists hung limp in his harsh grip.

Consternation flooded him along with the waking memory of his nightmare. He shoved himself off her and stumbled out the door.

Refusing to be abandoned yet again, Emily trailed after him. He stood in the sand a few feet away, his back to her, his shoulders heaving. She was afraid for a moment that he was going to be ill, but he straightened, dragging the back of his hand across his lips, shivering despite the heat.

"I'm sorry," he said. "I could have hurt you."

"Could you?"

Only the forest answered, creaking and sighing around them in a midnight symphony.

She touched his shoulder. His skin felt like warm marble to her fingertips. He flinched, but did not pull away.

"Tell me about Nicky," she whispered.

He swung around, and their faces almost collided. His tension had returned, as palpable as his suspicion.

"The nightmare," she said swiftly. "You cried out his name."

He bent to scoop up a stone and cast it into the darkness. "Nicholas was my partner."

"What happened to him?"

"He died. His vanity killed him."

Emily was very still. If vanity had killed Nicholas Saleri, what had killed her father? she wondered. His generosity? His loving nature?

A humorless laugh bubbled out of Justin's throat. "Even the wilds of New Zealand couldn't rob Nicholas of his precious vanity. He used to preen for the natives in his fine coat of English broadcloth. He even deigned to let the high priest run his shriveled hands down his silk lapels."

"He must have been quite the swell."

"He was." Justin tugged his ear. "The earrings were his idea. He fancied us Gypsy rogues—daring exiles from society. He pierced our ears himself with Maori needles that seemed as long and sharp as spears. I bled for days."

Emily bit back a small, sad smile as she tried to imagine her bewhiskered father sporting a dashing earring.

Justin's eyes clouded. "Sometimes I can still see him in the firelight, swilling beer with the natives. I believe he thought himself immortal."

"He was wrong?"

"Dead wrong."

A night bird echoed a haunting refrain. Emily shivered, remembering something her father had said in his last letter. "Did you trust this Nicky?"

His eyes narrowed thoughtfully. "He was my friend. He was penniless himself, but took me in when everyone else turned their backs on me. I suppose I loved him. But, no, I knew him too well to trust him." He stared unseeing into the shadows. "When the land wars broke out and the Maori turned against us, he insisted on going to talk to them alone. He honestly believed his old drinking companions wouldn't hurt him." Justin met her gaze, his jaw set at a grim angle. "We never saw him alive again."

Emily swallowed. Justin had been only too clear on how the Maori dispensed with their enemies. Had her father met with such a fate? Why did Justin never mention his name? Was David Scarborough haunting yet another of his twisted nightmares?

Her vision blurred. She swayed on her feet. Then Justin was there, his strong arms wrapping her in a cocoon of warmth. She buried her face in his chest, too shaken to apologize.

He rubbed his cheek against her curls. "God, girl, you're as pale as milk. I'm bloody sorry. You're so damned brave about everything. I wasn't even thinking how such a story would affect you." He tilted her chin up, running a thumb over her trembling lips. "Where's my courageous Em? The one who fought the deadly dragon, routed savage cannibals, and even faced the dreaded scourge of naked toddlers."

She laughed weakly. "I left her snoozing on my pallet."

"Let's go find her, then, shall we?"

He carried her into the dim hut and lowered her to the blankets. Penfeld was still snoring blissfully.

"Dreaming of winged teapots, no doubt," Justin whispered.

She giggled, but his own eyes sobered as he gave the valet a furtive glance. Emily knew what he was thinking. How much noise could they make without disturbing Penfeld's slumber? Would he hear the whisper of their lips in the darkness?

Like a thief in the night, he leaned down and kissed her with a fierce sweetness that left her breathless.

He smoothed the tangled curls away from her face. "Don't worry about what I told you. What's in the past is done."

He touched his lips to her brow before slipping back into the shadows. Was he comforting her or warning her? Emily wondered. She licked the bittersweet taste of him from her lips, wondering what he would do if he only knew how wrong he was.

Emily awoke the next morning to a deserted hut and the patter of a gentle rain against the thatched roof. She felt a pang of disappointment as she crawled out of the blankets. She had hoped to continue her exploration of the beach that day and had promised Kawiri she'd teach him how to swear in English.

Wrapping a blanket around her shoulders, she shambled to the window. A sky frosted in pewter gleamed between dripping fronds. The rain showed no sign of abating. Was Justin safe and warm, crouched before a Maori fire, or was he out there somewhere, shivering in the cool, damp air?

Sighing, she turned away from the window. Should she once again paw through his belongings for some clue to his past? A dull weight settled in her throat. If Justin's nightmare was only the tip of his anguish, what new agony might her search uncover?

She dropped to her knees and reluctantly began to sort through a pile of books and papers. It seemed a waste of time to simply move books from one pile to another, so she began to dust them with a corner of the blanket and separate them according to subject and author. As exertion warmed her, the blanket slid unheeded from her shoulders. Lulled by the cozy drumbeat of the rain, she had fashioned several tidy stacks of books and whiled away half the morning before she realized it. Without books blocking every path, the hut had swelled to twice its size. It was actually beginning to look homey.

Seized by this alarming spirit of tidiness, Emily folded their blankets and decided to drag the table into the center of the room. Fluffy watched her efforts from his perch on the stove without blinking.

"You might help me, you lazy lizard," she berated him. "I ought to light a fire under you." His tongue darted out in disdain.

She tugged at the table. The heavy oak resisted her. Grunting, she gave it another pull. A narrow drawer snapped out, striking her hard across the thighs.

Emily's curse faded in the silence. Was this the secret cubbyhole she had been searching for? She reached slowly into the shadowy recess as if afraid she might find a nesting adder.

Her hand trembled as she drew forth a sheaf of papers rolled into a fat tube. Fearful her knees would betray her, she sank cross-legged to the floor. She sat for a long time, staring at nothing. Claire Scarborough's bright, loving spirit had died with her father. Why couldn't Emily let her go? Why couldn't she accept Justin for what he was? A kind man who had welcomed a naked stranger into his life without knowing if she was a thief, a murderer, or a pox-ridden doxy from the London wharfs. He might not have wanted her as a child, but the fierce hunger of his kiss promised he wanted her now. Her fingers toyed with the frayed ribbon that bound the heavy scroll.

She tugged the ribbon. The pages flopped open in her lap. She clapped a hand over her mouth to muffle a sob of relief. Neat bars had been etched in black from margin to margin on the long sheets. These musical notes were drawn not in the painstaking scrawl of a child, but in the thick, measured strokes of a man. She flipped through the pages, marveling at their sheer volume.

The enormity of what she was holding struck her like a blow. Justin's life work. He had been holed up in New Zealand for the past seven years, pouring his soul into this music. She ran her hand over a page, caressing the blots of ink with her fingertips. A tremendous sadness touched her as she imagined him hunched over the table, scratching away in the feeble glow of the lantern until his eyes burned and his vision blurred. Music written in silence and hidden from the world, symphonies that would never know the joyous strains of violin or piano. A world of uncaring ears deaf to their peculiar magic.

She turned the page with reverent fingers. Music had been one of her more tolerable classes at Foxworth's. Every girl had been taught to bang out "God Save the Queen" on the scarred piano in the music room. She squinted at the notes, forcing them to unite in a pattern she could understand.

A smile touched her lips as she began to hum softly. She picked out the melody, bright, simple, and wistful. She was haunted by its beauty, seduced by its innocent genius. Almost of its own volition her voice warbled into full-throated song, weaving a shining thread of sound through the tapestry of the falling rain.

Justin shook the sparkling drops out of his eyes. He loved the New Zealand rain. In London it had fallen in a dull curtain, heavy with soot, but here it shimmered from the sky, misting the world in radiant defiance of its ordinary colors. It sharpened the greens to a minty gloss and deepened the browns to mahogany. Tramping through the bush on a rainy day almost made him believe the stains of the world could be washed clean. Almost.

He ducked beneath the shaggy branch of a punga tree, chagrined to realize he had made yet another loop past the hut. Thank God Penfeld had stayed behind in the Maori meeting house to nurse a cup of steaming clam soup. He couldn't bear another roll of the valet's expressive eyes.

Why shouldn't he wish to check on Emily? It was nearly midday. With her penchant for mischief, she'd had ample time to sell the hut to passing natives or set her skirt ablaze.

He crouched beneath the shelter of a bush. Rain poured from his hat brim and dripped off his nose, but he paid it no heed. His hungry gaze was locked on the window, on the cozy halo of lantern light that warmed him simply by its existence. He imagined Emily within, her chestnut curls inclined toward a book or some gentle feminine task.

Like skinning Fluffy to make a pair of boots.

Justin lowered his forehead to his hand, chuckling at his own whimsy. At some point he would have to learn to trust the girl. How else was he to teach her to trust him?

He forced himself to rise and turn away. A lilting whisper of angel song drifted to his ears. At first he thought the melody was in his head, as haunting and familiar as the rhythmic rush of blood through his veins. Then a spasm of pain crushed his chest.

Emily.

Her husky contralto toyed with his creation, gifting it with an artless charm and an innocence he had been able to envision only in the maddened inspiration of his dreams. It cut through his sophistication like a blade, peeling away the pretentious layers of oboes and French horns he had labored over for days. Without even trying she had stolen his song and made it her own. He knew that for the rest of his life, even if that song resounded through every concert hall in Europe, he would hear only the resonant purity of her voice.

Justin felt violated. He felt as if someone had stroked the most intimate heart of him and left it quivering, too easily shattered by the next careless touch.

Burning with fury, he strode across the clearing and threw open the door.

Emily lifted her head. Her soft trilling died in her throat. "Why, Justin, it's so beautiful."

Her cheeks were flushed, her lips parted. Her eyes shone with trust and tenderness. He had seen that look before, and being unable to remember where or when only stoked the fires of his anger.

He pulled off his hat. "Who gave you the right to rifle through my private things? Who the hell do you think you are?"

Emily's smile faded. She gazed up at him, wondering what he would do if she told him. Rain pelted the back of his oilcloth coat. Damp hanks of hair curled across his brow, shadowing his eyes. He smoothed them back and she swallowed a flinch. She had seen that look of embittered ire often enough in her life.

"Nobody gave me the right." She dragged her knee closer to her body, cradling his symphony to her chest. "Are you angry?"

He slammed the door. A handful of thatch spiraled down from the ceiling.

"Miffed, eh?"

He crossed the hut and jerked his music out of her hands. Still glowering, he rolled the sheets into a tube, giving her the distinct impression he wished it were her neck he was throttling.

She climbed to her feet, brushing dust from her skirt. "Are you ever going to speak to me again?"

He slapped the scroll against his palm. "Not if you're lucky."

"Luck was never my strong suit."

"Nor mine," he shot back. "At least not since I met you."

She clasped her hands behind her back. "You didn't actually *meet* me. You sort of found me. Like a stray pup or a—"

"Bad apple?"

She looked down at her feet, but not before Justin saw her lips twist with a wry pain. Guilt shot through him. She hadn't helped his temper by reminding him of the night he had found her. The nubile curves of her moon-drenched body still haunted him. A gift from the sea, he had so foolishly called her. A gift from hell, more likely. Poseidon had probably laughed himself off his underwater throne to be rid of her. For a savage moment Justin wished he could recall that night, wished he had thrust apart her silky thighs and ravished her before she'd ever opened her impudent mouth.

"Why are you looking at me like that?" Emily asked, alarmed by the open voracity of his gaze.

"Like what?" His dangerous purr folded an aching knot in the pit of her stomach.

She pressed her fist there. "Like I'm a French pastry and you haven't eaten in a month."

"Oh, it's been far longer than a month, my dear." He stalked toward her, backing her up with each silky word. "I wish I had gobbled you up that night on the beach. Because then at least I would have had a moment's peace in the afterglow . . . which is more than I've had since then." He stroked her cheek in the tenderest of caresses. "Did you know you are an ungrateful, deceitful, rude, ill-tempered, nosy little wench?" His voice shot to a roar. "And those are your good points!"

Emily's rear struck the table. She tilted her chin in wounded dignity. "I'm quite aware of my shortcomings, but if it makes you feel better, do continue your assassination of my character."

Growling under his breath, Justin spun on his heel. It didn't take him more than three strides to realize he was pacing without having to hop over stacks of books or snarled blankets. Emily folded her hands in a demure knot.

"My books," he muttered. "What the hell has she done to my books? She's trying to drive me mad. I'll never be able to find anything."

"Why, of course you will. I've organized them ever so nicely."

His accusing gaze impaled her. "I knew where every book was. *Before* you moved them."

A spirit of perversity seized Emily. She pulled his boyhood journal off the nearest stack and waved it under his nose. "Even this one, *Homer?*"

Justin snatched it out of her hand and reached around her to jerk open the secret drawer. It slid from its moorings and clattered to the floor, spilling out papers, bottles of ink, several charcoal pencils, a thin pair of gold spectacles, and a yellowing packet tied with string. Muttering under his breath, he squatted and crammed the journal and his symphonies into the cubbyhole.

Emily knelt to gather some papers, prepared to hand them over as a peace offering. She glanced curiously at an official-looking document signed with flourished signatures, but it drifted from her fingers, forgotten, as her gaze fell on the packet of letters. She recognized the bold strokes of Justin's handwriting.

He was still muttering through clenched teeth. "If I'd have wanted an infernal woman pawing through my belongings, I'd have married one, now, wouldn't I? Why can't you stay out of my things? Better yet, why can't you just stay out of my life?"

His hand closed around the letters, but it was too late.

A tear splashed the envelope, smearing the faded ink. Another pelted his hand like a salty raindrop.

"Oh, Christ, Em, don't go all weepy on me. I get enough of that from Penfeld."

But Emily wasn't looking at him. She was staring at the thick bundle of letters, each one addressed to a Miss Claire Scarborough of 45 Queen Square, Bloomsbury, London, and never posted.

She gazed up at him through a mist of tears. He reached for her, but she was already gone, leaving the door swinging in her wake.

Chapter 10

· ❧ ·

I believe your charm would challenge even his most serious bent of mind. . . .

𝒯he rain melted to a fine mist against Emily's skin, mingling with her tears. The wind tore at her curls and whipped the sea into foaming whitecaps. She hugged her knees to her chest, lulled by the sibilant hiss of the waves against the shore.

It didn't take Justin long to find her. She looked up to find him silhouetted against a curtain of gray, hatless, his hands clenched into fists, empty and beseeching. Rain misted his hair and caught like crystal beads in the stubble of his beard.

She turned her face to the sea, dashing her tears away. How could she explain it wasn't sadness making her weep, but a fierce joy?

He had never forgotten her, she realized. In all of those long, lonely years he had never once forgotten her. The thick packet of letters bound by a frayed string was proof of that. But why had he never posted them? Why had he robbed a bereft child of the solace his words might have given? She had slipped downstairs each morning at the school when the mail was delivered only to creep back to her attic empty-handed, praying the others girls hadn't seen her. She could only imagine the joy and pride she might have felt had Miss Winters laid one of those crisp brown envelopes in her hands. She would have flown up the stairs then, torn open the letter, and savored every word from the guardian she had never met.

Confusion buffeted her like the wind. If Justin had uttered one word, one contrite syllable, it might have all come tumbling out—the questions, the accusations, the pleas. Instead, he offered her his hand.

Emily took it, relieved to find something of warmth and substance in her shifting world. He pulled her to her feet, and they faced each other for a timeless moment, just a man and a woman alone on a barren stretch of sand. He entwined her fingers in his own and led her up a sandy hill to a broad bluff crowned by a rough-hewn cross.

The wind was stronger there. It whipped Justin's hair to a dark froth and battered the purity of his profile as he freed her hand and faced the sea. Suddenly Emily didn't want to know the truth. With a desperation that shocked her, she longed to press her fingertips to his chiseled lips, to silence his mouth with the ravenous heat of her own.

But when he opened his mouth, only these halting words came out. "I hear music in my head all the time. I always have. For as long as I can remember."

Emily sank down in the shallow grass, her knees weakened by relief. "It must be a gift."

His laugh was short and bitter. "A curse perhaps. My family thought me a freak. I was my father's only son, yet I had no interest in his shipping firm or the blasted social obligations that accompanied his wretched title. He couldn't drag me away from the piano." His voice dropped, became as gray and passionless as the sky. "When I was twenty-one he gave me a choice. My music or my inheritance. I chose the music. He tossed me into the streets with nothing but the coat on my back. I ended up at a music hall in a rat-infested rookery playing bawdy tunes for drunken sots who tossed me pennies for pay. That's where I met Nicky. He took me under his wing and taught me how to survive."

He glanced down at the cross. Emily sucked in a breath, suddenly realizing what she was sitting next to.

"Nicholas?" she said softly. "Is he buried here?"

Justin looked up, blinking almost absently. "We never found anything of Nicholas to bury. My other partner rests here." He reached down and ran a hand over the cross. "The dearest friend I ever had."

Emily couldn't move, couldn't breathe. Emotions she'd thought long suppressed welled up in her throat, rendering speech impossible. She was as helpless as a doll in Justin's hands as he cupped her cheek and gently tilted her face to his. He could have hurled her into the sea, and she wouldn't have been able to do so much as whimper a protest.

"I'm trying to say I'm sorry for shouting at you, Emily. I was afraid you'd think me a freak, too."

He leaned down and brushed her lips with his own, leaving his indelible taste. Then he jammed his hands into his pockets and started down the hill, his shoulders braced against the wind.

Emily stared blindly out to sea, far out, where the hazy curve of the horizon met the waves. The rough-hewn cross slowly filled her vision. No marble angels for her father. No elaborate script carved in granite—*David Scarborough, Beloved Father.* Only a simple cross on a windy hill overlooking the sea. A cross, she knew somehow, lovingly carved by Justin's hands.

Tears dimmed her vision as she ran her palm over the sparse grass blanketing her father's grave.

"Oh, Daddy," she whispered. "What am I to do?"

.   .   .

Emily returned to the hut much later. She pushed open the door, expecting to find it deserted in the deepening gloom.

But orange and yellow tongues of flame licked at a handful of brush inside the stove. A pot simmered on top of it, fragrant with cumin and cloves. Penfeld met her at the door with a towel to dry her hair. Touching his finger to his lips in a plea for silence, he cocked his head toward the table.

As Emily saw Justin, she shivered, realizing how chilled she had been. He sat with his long legs sprawled before him, his head inclined toward the table. As she watched, he drew a fresh sheet of paper to him and continued making furious marks, his hand flying across the page. His hair gleamed in the lantern light like damp silk. Emily wanted to wind her fingers through it, to bring it to her lips and dry it with a whisper of her breath.

The towel fell from her fingers as she drifted toward him, remembering his earlier explosion. He pulled off his spectacles to rub his eyes, then glanced up, slanting her a smile that made the fire in the stove cool by comparison.

She dared to peek over his shoulder. His arm curled to shield his work, then relaxed in surrender to her curiosity. His casual posture did not deceive her. Her heart did an unbidden flip at his trust.

She hummed a few shy notes under her breath. "Something new?"

"Very." He shuffled the papers so she could start at the beginning.

Her hair brushed his cheek as she leaned over his shoulder. The wordless melody warbled from her throat, growing in confidence with each enchanting bar. As the notes tapered to an end, a lilting echo hung in the air.

She lifted her head to find Justin's eyes narrowed in a lazy appraisal that could not quite hide their hungry glitter. Emily leaned forward, lured by the irresistible curve of his parted lips.

Penfeld's applause broke the spell. "Bravo, master! One of your finest, I do believe."

"Thank you, Penfeld," Justin replied. Wariness tensed his jaw as he tore his gaze away from hers and began to roll the papers. "What did you think?"

Somehow to Emily it didn't seem enough to murmur "Wonderful" or some other benign praise. She struggled to find words to express her brimming heart. "It began like a gentle rain, all soothing and safe. But then something dangerous happened, something free and joyous like a burst of thunder and lightning. Because of it, nothing will ever be the same again."

Justin's hands stilled.

"Do you have a name for it?" she asked.

A ghost of a smile played around his lips. He swiveled on the barrel to face her and she heard once again the joyous strains of his song. "I call it 'Emily.'"

A new melody began that day, weaving its shy strains through the sunny days and lush tropical nights that followed. It whistled through Emily's head as she splashed in the waves with the children. It danced with elfin feet across her heart as she trailed Justin through the fields, catching his hat in her hands when a gust of wind blew it astray. It haunted her serenity each night as she sipped her rich coffee and beneath her lashes watched him scribble his symphonies in a pool of lantern light.

She found herself standing alone in the hut one morning, Justin's letters to Claire Scarborough clasped in her trembling hands. She'd never had any qualms about reading anyone else's mail, so why was she so reluctant to read her own? She held a letter up to the window. Sunlight filtered through the worn envelope, illuminating the bold strokes of handwriting within. Emily quickly lowered it. The morning was simply too bright to be dimmed by old memories and fears, she thought, tucking the packet tenderly back into its hiding place. For now it was enough to know that Justin had remembered her.

She awoke that moonlit night to the discordant drumbeat of her own heart. A hoarse moan tore through the silence. Justin was dreaming again.

Her blankets fell away as she scrambled across the hut. Her hand brushed his fevered brow. She was helpless to explain even to herself her frantic desire to soothe him. Was Nicky haunting him tonight? Or was it her father, his brilliant smile faded, his merry brown eyes glittering not with laughter but accusation? Pain twitched in the grooves around Justin's mouth, and suddenly it didn't matter who his demons were. She wanted only to banish them.

She lay down and curled into his side. Her palm crept across his bare chest, coming to rest over his heart. His restless thrashing eased, then stilled completely. His groan was one of contentment as he drew her into the shelter of his arms and buried his face in her hair.

Feathers tickled Justin's nose. He wiggled it, sniffing back a sneeze. Aroma filled his nostrils, a scent so rich and pure it was rendered exotic by its sheer simplicity. Vanilla. It assaulted his brain with a longing for an England he barely cared to remember. It made him crave civilized delights like Gracie's cookies hot from the oven and sprinkled with cinnamon. Scones rolled in sugar and wrapped around steaming peaches. Emily dipped in stardust and laved with melted moonlight.

His eyes flew open. Emily?

His nose nested not in feathers, but in her curls. Her body twined around his in drowsy innocence. She was as fervent in sleep as in wakefulness. Her thigh was flung across his leg and her hand lay in a gentle cup over his abdomen. The tempered glow of dawn caressed her face.

The craving in Justin's stomach shot to his groin with merciless swiftness. He shifted his hips. To hell with cookies and scones, he thought. He wanted a taste of Emily. He wanted to gorge himself on her tender body until they were both sated. It was torture enough to rise each morning to find her huddled under her own blankets, her pert rump tilted to the ceiling. But to emerge from the fog of sleep to find her curled around him like some sweet wanton? He felt so hard it might take only one of her artless wiggles to shatter him. Careful not to disturb her, he reached down and freed a button of his dungarees.

She'd become more than a burden to him in the past few days. She'd become an obsession. He struggled to treat her with the same gentle affection he showed the children, but the sharp edge of his desire was only whetted by her merry smile. She'd flourished like a tropical bloom in the wilds of the island. Sunlight had honeyed her skin and tipped her lengthening curls with gold.

His world belonged to Emily. She hovered around him like a gamin angel, lithe and funny. He pressed his eyes shut, battered by images of her bending over a flax plant at his side, wading through the shallow waves at sunset with Maori children dangling from her arms like crabs. He had even glanced up from his Bible Sunday at the meeting house to find her sitting cross-legged on the dirt floor, her expression pensive, her cheek resting against Dani's sleek head. He had stammered through five verses of Matthew, then lost his place entirely. When he had looked up again, she was gone.

He'd had his share of mistresses in London, both false and true, yet none of them could compare to the mischievous charms of the barefoot waif clinging to his side.

Emily stirred. Her lips parted in a delicate snore. A twinge of shame touched him. Here he lay, plotting a seduction so lascivious it would have shamed even Nicky, and she was probably dreaming of starfish and sand castles. He ran his finger down her nose, expecting to find a dusting of cinnamon freckles on his fingertip.

Her eyes fluttered open, then widened in a mixture of

dread and horror that made him wonder if he'd sprouted fangs during the night. He ran his tongue over his teeth. They all felt reassuringly blunt.

Ruefully, he touched his bristled jaw. "I know I haven't shaved in a few days, but I'm not that frightful, am I?"

He must have been, because she struggled to untangle her leg and roll away.

He gathered her tighter into his arms, not willing to let her go without an explanation. "Why the terrible rush? Contrary to my staid reputation, I'm not averse to a little morning cuddle."

She gave a husky squeak. "But Penfeld—"

"—is sleeping."

A sonorous snore from beneath the window proved his words.

"So was I," she blurted out. "Sleeping, that is. Sleep-walking, actually. I must have stumbled and fallen on you. Perhaps I struck my head. I should walk about and see if I'm dizzy."

She was halfway up when his arm snaked around her waist, jerking her back. He winced as her plush rear wedged against the part of his anatomy that at the moment was too prominent to be seemly.

"If you're dizzy, you need rest," he said, hoping she would attribute the croak in his voice to drowsiness. "You know, for a good prankster, you're a terrible liar."

"That's not true! I'm a very good liar. All my teachers said so." She wiggled in protest.

Justin's beleaguered body reached its breaking point. He shoved her off him, then rolled on top of her, stilling her struggles with his weight. He laced his fingers through hers and imprisoned her hands above her head.

He arched his eyebrow in a wicked threat. "Now, suppose you tell me what you were doing on my pallet. Blowing pepper up my nose? Tying my blankets into knots? Planting brambles in my dungarees?"

She lowered her eyes, leaving him gazing at the velvety silk of her lashes. "I had a bad dream. I was afraid."

Her sheepish confession touched his heart. He knew only too well how it felt to awaken trembling in the dark. He imagined her creeping to his side, trusting him to chase away her monsters. He lowered himself, wanting only to kiss away her fears. Before his lips could touch hers, his hips grazed her bare belly. A shock of pleasure electrified him. He realized too late that swapping positions had only worsened matters. The heavy fullness in his dungarees had become impossible to ignore. For both of them.

Emily's mouth fell open in shock.

To his utter horror he felt a blush creep up his jawline. "It's nothing," he said tersely. Her eyes widened in comical disbelief. "A normal phenomenon of the morning, I assure you. It has absolutely nothing to do with you," he lied.

She hesitated, then sniffed in prim sophistication. "I knew that."

Justin sat up, swinging his legs away from her. Of course she knew that, he thought. Her smug little gardener's lad had probably taught her. Or had it been the chimney sweep? His temper burned with a ferocious urge to shove her back on the blankets and teach her a few lessons of his own.

Out of the corner of his eye he saw her sit up. She drew her skirt down to hug her shapely thighs as if she were the shyest of virgins.

He owed her a warning, he reminded himself, nothing more. "Emily?"

"Yes?"

"If you have any more nightmares"—he felt her waiting silence—"go to Penfeld."

"As you wish, Mr. Connor. I shouldn't wish to burden you."

Justin was unprepared for the bitterness of her reply.

He swiveled to face her, but she had already dropped to her pallet and pulled the blankets over her head like a sullen child.

That afternoon Justin stood on the shore and watched the storm roll in with the tide. Black clouds poured from the west, driving the rain before them. Far out at sea it was already falling, melting sky and ocean into a seamless curtain of gray. Lightning crackled and snapped in a broken web above pitching waves tinted green by the eerie light of the approaching squall. Justin braced his legs against the wind and thrust his hands into his pockets. He welcomed the storm, seeking in its savage wildness a kindred spirit to his own mood.

An oppressive heat had hung in the air all day, simmering like the tension in his body since he had awakened to find Emily snuggled in his arms. He recognized it for what it was: desire—hot, potent, and too long denied. She had shattered the fragile peace he had found on the North Island, stirred the hungry beast within him who craved excitement and passion and more than the loyal devotion of a small tribe of natives.

His nostrils flared at the scent of the coming rain. If only the breaking of the storm could ease his own pent-up frustration. His gaze raked the deserted beach. A ripple of saffron caught his eye.

He watched as Emily made her way down the path from the bluff. The wind molded the flaxen skirt to her legs and whipped her curls into a blinding frenzy. Her feet slipped in the soft sand. She slid a few feet and Justin took a step toward the bluff without realizing it. She didn't see him. As the first fat raindrops pelted his back, she ran for the shelter of the forest path and disappeared among the wind-lashed trees.

Justin glared at the bluff, his brow furrowed. This was the third time he had seen Emily descend from the path, always at twilight and always alone. Oblivious to the rain, he strode down the beach and started up the sandy hill, groping for handholds in the tussocks of grass.

As he topped the bluff, a blaze of color brought him up short. Crimson flowers spilled like blood around the base of the cross that guarded David's grave. *Pohutukawas.* Justin dropped to his knees and touched a fragile petal with his fingertip, drowning in the cloying sweetness of their scent. Remembered shame washed over him in waves. He pressed his eyes shut as David's voice whispered through the rain, carrying him back through time.

Take care of my little angel, Justin. Swear you will.

Thunder drummed the air in a sharp cannonade.

Justin flinched, smelling gunpowder on the wind. His eyes flew open. He knelt at the edge of the lonely bluff, gripping David's watch in his hand. He did not dare open it. Even after all these years he dreaded facing the child within. The child who still waited for him in England. The child who wore David's eyes.

Mystified, he lifted one of the flowers. He imagined Emily struggling up the narrow path, her arms laden with the fragrant blooms. Why would she carry flowers to David's grave? Had she somehow sensed how important this place was to him?

He brushed a raindrop from the velvety petal. It melted to his touch like tears against Emily's creamy skin. His fingers unfolded, and a gust of wind tore the flower from his hand, sending it skimming into the sea. As the storm broke hard around him, it bobbed on the water until the inky waves swallowed it without a trace.

Chapter 11

·🐚·

*You must be curious
about the treasure we've found. . . .*

*E*mily trotted through the forest, cradling a basket in the crook of her arm. Despite her burden her steps were as light as the shimmering air washed clean by yesterday's storm. Tomorrow was the day they were to join Trini's tribe in welcoming their neighboring Maori to a magnificent feast. Her own humble offering was a basket of fuzzy green fruit plucked from a rambling gooseberry vine with Kawiri's help.

As she approached the hut, male voices rose in furious argument.

Puzzled, she stopped, then took a step backward. Yes, she thought, she was at the right hut.

Her basket slipped a notch as Penfeld's voice boomed out. "Our dear Lord said it far better than I when he told the Pharisees 'I will have mercy, and not sacrifice.' I fear you're making a tremendous mistake . . . sir." The last word was bitten off in such a tone of insult that Emily broke into a grin. Apparently, Justin's timid hamster had gone rabid.

"Sic him, Penfeld," she whispered under her breath. She would gladly cheer anyone who dared to defy the mighty Pakeha.

"If I wanted your interpretation of scripture, King James, I'd have asked for it," Justin shot back.

She set down her basket. She hadn't learned many of Tansy's more lurid skills, but eavesdropping was one she had mastered. She crept around to the window and dared a peek. Justin's back was to her, but Penfeld's profile was a livid shade of pink. He was definitely in the throes of what Miss Winters would have labeled "a huff." As Justin swung around, she dropped to a crouch.

"The woman has left me no choice," he was saying. "I haven't two halfpennies to rub together. I have to send the old witch something even if it's only a gesture of good faith."

Penfeld sniffed. "Have you considered cutting out your heart? A suitable offering from a man who enjoys martyrdom as much as you do. It has always escaped me why you didn't just throw yourself in your friend's grave when you had the chance."

From the pained silence that followed, Emily knew the valet had gone too far. A tiny vise squeezed her own heart.

Justin's quiet voice finally came. In its passionless tones Emily heard a ringing chord of the duke he might have been. "I could dismiss you for that."

Penfeld's frosty dignity was palpable. "If you prefer, I will seek another position."

To Justin's credit, he didn't point out the ludicrous nature of that offer. What was a valet going to do on this isolated coast? Offer his services to Trini's chief? Iron his flax skirt? Polish his jade earrings?

Justin sighed heavily. "I simply don't trust that Winters woman."

Emily's fingernails dug into her palms as she realized they were talking about her. No, not about her, she corrected herself coolly. About Claire Scarborough.

"If she doesn't have word from me soon," he added, "she might toss the child out in the street."

Or the ocean, Emily thought, quenching a hysterical giggle.

The valet's voice lowered to a fervent plea. "If you don't trust her, why don't you remove the child from her care? The calculating woman may try to sell the knowledge of your location to your family for a profit anyway. Perhaps your father could—"

"I'm dead to my father. He made that painfully clear when I threw my inheritance back in his priggish face."

Penfeld fell into defeated silence. Emily heard the rustle of tissue paper, the clink of metal. She eased her eyes above the windowsill. Justin was drawing her father's watch over his head. It dangled from his graceful fingers, spinning in the sunlight above a tissue-lined box.

She sank back down, pressing her fists to the cool earth. Her thoughts raced in time with her heart. What in God's name had happened to the gold mine? Had Justin lost not only his friends and partners, but his fortune as well, in the Maori uprising? She realized he hadn't sent more money to the school because there had been no money. And now he meant to send her father's precious watch to Miss Winters.

Emily felt sickened by the image of the old woman digging her talons into the fragile tissue, clawing greedily for the heavy gold at the bottom of the box. She would probably send Barney to the goldsmith that very day to have the engraved case melted to a formless lump.

Emily choked back the lump in her own throat. Their words had only confirmed what she had come to suspect. Claire Scarborough's sole inheritance lay in the inscrutable gold of Justin Connor's eyes.

"Gor blimey, ya bloody brat! 'Aul yer arse to the other side of the beach or I'll 'aul it there for ya!"

As the vulgar words spewed out in Kawiri's musical

tones, Justin dropped the basket he was carrying and exchanged a startled look with Penfeld. Children swarmed over the kumaras and passion fruit heaped along the shore for the following day's feast. Kawiri glowered at his sister.

Dani thrust her hands on her hips and stuck out her little pink tongue in a defiant gesture Justin found painfully familiar. "Ya ain't big enough to make me move." Justin cringed at the grating cockney. "An' effin ye try, I'll call my Emmy and she'll box yer damned ol' ears."

Justin spared her the trouble. He threw back his head and bellowed, "Emily!"

She popped up from the newly dug clam pit, brushing sand from her stomach. "You rang?"

She looked so charming that Justin almost forgot his reprimand. Her cheeks were flushed with the afternoon heat. Her hair twined in damp tendrils around her face, framing a smile that was an intoxicating mix of mischief and tenderness. A menacing thud from the direction of the baskets jarred his memory.

He pointed. "Those children. What have you been teaching them?"

She shuffled her feet primly. "The King's English?"

"Guttersnipe English, more likely. They'd do better at an East End brawl than at court. What are you trying to do? Erase all the good I've done?"

She poked her toe in the sand, showing excessive interest in the tiny crab she unearthed. "Have you ever heard Dani speak a complete sentence of English before?"

"That horrid exhibition could hardly be called—" He stopped, scratching his head. "Well, no, I suppose I haven't."

He was spared from further thought by the solid thwack of a kumara striking someone's head. An answering wail followed. Justin winced.

Emily wiggled past him. "I shall endeavor to set a better example," she promised, bending over to box both Kawiri's and Dani's ears in one smooth motion. "Hush your silly selves," she hissed, "or I'll blister both your naked little arses."

A reverent course of "*Aye, mums*" followed.

Justin's lips twitched as he gazed at the delectable curve of her own ripe derriere.

A voice boomed out, unmistakable in its resonant bass. "Move out them torches, laddies! We ain't got all bloomin' day!"

Justin groaned. "Oh, no. You didn't. Not Trini too."

Giving him an innocent shrug, Emily ducked back into the clam pit. Justin's snort of mirth choked him. He dropped his basket and was forced to watch all of his hard-picked kiwi fruit roll gently into the sea.

Emily failed to return to the hut for dinner that night. Justin left Penfeld snoring and went in search of her. Several of the Maori had chosen to camp along the beach rather than return to their fortified *pa.* He drifted from fire to fire, smiling, calling out greetings, and pretending not to be as lost as he felt. From the tangled bracken came the forlorn cry of a foraging kiwi. Justin pitied the bird—it was clumsy, shy, and despite its noblest efforts to fly, forever bound to the earth.

A melody stirred the air, mingling with the lap of the waves against the shore. Justin's melancholy vanished. He quickened his steps toward the sound, crunching the powdery sand between his toes.

At the edge of the shore a crackling fire shot sparks into the crushed velvet of the night sky. Justin squatted in the shadows just outside the circle of light.

Emily had gathered the children around the fire like a snub-nosed angel directing a choir of naked cherubs. Their pure, sweet voices rose in the air, ringing with a clarity that would have been the envy of any St. Paul's boys' choir. A grin touched his lips as he imagined the shocked reaction of a staid London congregation to this ensemble of chubby, nude moppets. Especially since they were lending their lilting tones to a jolly rendition of "Naughty Maud, the Shrewsbury Bawd, by Gawd!"

He dropped his head down, laughing under his breath. He had dreamed his whole life of studying music with the masters in Vienna, but seemed destined to learn of its subtleties on his knees at the feet of a brash young girl.

As he lifted his head he met Emily's gaze over the swaying heads of the children. His breath caught in his throat. The children's song faded, making way for a brighter melody, poignant with longing. A shy invitation sparkled in her eyes. At that moment she was neither angel nor child, but a woman rife with tender promise. Justin's resolve swayed. Did he truly enjoy martyrdom as Penfeld had accused? Would it be so selfish to allow himself some small measure of happiness in Emily's arms? To awaken each morning with her curled against his side? To sleep each night with her taste burning on his lips?

To lose his heart and soul to this fallen angel and perish in the scorching flame of his own desires?

Justin stood abruptly. Penfeld was wrong. He didn't crave martyrdom. He craved solitude. He'd tucked himself in this corner of the world for seven years just to keep anyone from looking at him the way Emily was looking at him then. Steeling his heart against her fading smile, he gave her a cool nod and melted back into the darkness, still haunted by the lonely cry of the kiwi.

The night of the feast fell in a warm explosion of wind and stars. Emily and Justin stood with Trini's tribe and watched as a shimmering line of torches wound its way down the shore.

Justin gently rested his hands on her shoulders. Emily drew in a shuddering breath, afraid to speak for fear of destroying the tender emotion unfolding its wings in her soul. It had been so long absent, she almost didn't recognize it.

Happiness. A chord of joy striking her treacherous

heart like the echo of chimes on the wind, once heard and never forgotten.

A song rose into the night, a melody so pure and harmonious, it seemed to quiver on the air, casting its own light across the somber dark. Justin swayed, pulling her with him in a timeless dance. She leaned the back of her head against his shoulder, feeling at one with the music, with the night, and with him. Their guests filed down the beach, accepting their hosts' song of welcome in reverent silence.

As the last plaintive note died on the air, Justin whispered, "Don't applaud. It could start a war."

Just as he'd predicted, a moment of respectful silence passed before the celebration broke into full flower around them.

No nobles of the English court could have afforded such hospitality as the Maori offered their friends. If Witi Ahamera was their king and his white-haired *tohunga* their royal physician, then Justin was their cherished crown prince, greeting the other tribe with respectful familiarity. Emily tried to shrink into the crowd, but Justin caught her beneath his wing and shielded her with the umbrella of his popularity. Basking in his reflected glow made Emily feel rather like a princess herself.

A short while later she tucked a juicy piece of ham between her lips, entranced by the swirl of motion and color along the beach. Children grasped hands and ducked beneath the arms and legs of the dancers, mocking their motions with clumsy exuberance. Emily's own toes twitched in rhythm with their song.

Trini and Justin flanked her, sitting cross-legged in the sand.

Smiling shyly, a Maori girl offered her a wicker tray heaped with chicken. She groaned and waved it away, rubbing her sated tummy. She'd been so delighted to escape Penfeld's bean stew that she'd fairly gorged herself on morsels of ham, pork, and the precious *toheroa* clams steamed in the sand.

Finding Justin occupied with the toothless old man to his left, she reached for his cup.

His stern hand closed around her wrist. "Tsk, tsk. Are you being a naughty little girl again?"

"I'm not a little girl," she retorted, crossing her eyes at him. "I'm thirsty."

They both knew his cup of icy spring water had been laced with rum, while hers was plain.

He tilted his head thoughtfully, "I suppose one sip wouldn't do you any harm."

"No, but denying me might do you harm."

He held the cup out of her reach. "Patience, love. Allow me the honor."

Emily was so stunned by his chiding endearment that the press of the cool cup against her lips startled her. The noise and confusion seemed to fade, leaving her alone, trapped in the golden heat of Justin's eyes. He tilted the cup and she drank deeply. Liquid fire spilled through her veins, intensifying with each slow throb of the pulse at the base of Justin's throat. He drew the cup away, leaving clear drops of flame pearled on her lips. Her greedy tongue lashed out to extinguish them, and his breath caught in a groan.

The old man tugged on his arm, begging his attention.

Emily summoned a shaky smile. "There. I promise not to be naughty anymore."

She waited until he'd set down the cup, then deftly switched it with her own. She took care to sip, not gulp, knowing the rum was more exotic and far more potent than the cooking sherry she and Tansy used to pilfer from the seminary kitchen.

A line of oil-sheened warriors leaped into the center of the torchlit circle, their wild gyrations telling of battles won and battles still to be fought. Emily swayed to the chant of their mighty war song. They used no drums, but kept the tempo by stamping their feet. The packed sand reverberated with their masculine fervor, churning Emily's blood to a dangerous pitch. She shifted in the sand, feeling acutely the press of Justin's hip against her own.

She was almost relieved when the women of both tribes appeared, weaving a dance to a lilting melody as they twirled balls of plaited flax between their graceful fingers. Her relief vanished as a dusky-eyed stranger broke from their ranks and started for Justin.

Emily slumped with a long-suffering sigh, awaiting the deferent bow, the adoring squeal of "Pakeha!"

"Justin, my darling!" the woman cried, her voice a musical purr.

"Rangimarie! I didn't know you were coming," he answered, breaking into a boyish grin.

Emily sat straight up.

The woman flung herself to her knees, enveloping him in her embrace. He disappeared in the straight fall of her silky black hair. Emily dazedly touched her own coarse curls. The humid air had tightened them into corkscrews.

The lush Polynesian beauty spread her skirt around her, speaking rapidly in Maori. Justin answered in kind, bringing her hand to his lips in a gesture so civilized, so purely English, Emily found it as damning a confession as if he'd laid the woman on the sand at her feet and bedded her. Their intimacy was obvious. The woman shook her hair in a seductive motion. Emily glared at it, wondering what sort of war she would start if she yanked it out by its ebony roots.

She nudged Trini, nearly overturning his cup. "She's rather pretty, isn't she? If you fancy women with tattoos."

In truth, only the woman's chin was tattooed. The etched wings emphasized the pouting tilt of her lips, the exotic slant of her eyes. Reaching across Emily, she plucked a passion fruit from a tray and snapped half of it away with her straight white teeth. Golden juice trickled down her chin.

"Did you see that?" This time Emily did tumble Trini's cup, spilling cold water down his bare chest. "What horrid table manners. The brazen wench wouldn't last through tea at Miss Win—" She bit off the word, casting him a nervous glance. Trini didn't seem to notice her slip. He was too busy sponging off his chest with his feathered cloak.

Her mouth fell open in hopeless shock as the intruder tucked the other half of the passion fruit into Justin's mouth, her tan fingers lingering against his lips as if in memory of past delights and a promise of future ones. A jagged spear of pain plunged into Emily's heart. Feeling small and ugly and freckled, she bowed her head, wishing for hair long enough to hide behind.

The song of the dancers swelled to a new rhythm, hypnotic and sensual. Laughing, the woman pulled away from Justin's hands and rose to join the sultry dance of her native sisters.

Justin leaned toward Emily, forced to yell over the music. "Now you can see why I find the Maori so irresistible. They do nothing without singing."

"Nothing?" she bit off acidly.

He hummed under his breath, blithely unaware of the petite volcano seething at his side. "Rangimarie was one of my best pupils. I taught her English."

"Is that all?"

He missed her lethal look. His admiring gaze was hovering at the opulent bosom of his sloe-eyed friend. Her serpentine twists threatened to shake the golden orbs free. She danced toward him, stamping her feet and swinging her hips in blatant invitation.

The tips of her hair flicked Emily's cheek like tiny eels as she bent over Justin, mouthing Maori words. He grinned and ducked his head. It might have been the torchlight, but Emily would have sworn a flush crept along his cheekbones.

As the woman slithered away, Emily slammed her fist into Trini's arm. "What did she say?"

Trini gave her an infuriating smile and wagged his finger under her nose. "No, no! Not for the hearing appendages of filial progeny."

"Not for the hearing appendanges . . . ?" She muttered the words under her breath before their meaning came to life with furious clarity.

Not for the ears of children.

Justin's own voice, smooth and condescending, echoed through her head. *Are you being a naughty little girl again?*

Her nails dug into the woven flax of her cup. They all seemed to think her some overgrown toddler who needed her fingers slapped to keep her out of mischief. She tilted the cup to her lips, draining it in one swig. Fire raced through her limbs, throbbing in time with the music.

Rum and wavering torch smoke blurred her vision. The exotic features of the dancers melted into the smug faces of Miss Winters's students. She had hovered in the corner during their ballet class as they floated past, wrapped in yards of delicate white organdy. Her feet had itched to join them, but it had been Cecille who drifted to her sylvan death as Giselle at the recital each spring. Emily's own small satisfaction had come last year when Cecille had lifted her head to take her bow only to find her shimmering blond mane pasted to the stage.

The stamp of native feet thundered through Emily's veins, enthralling her with their primal beat. She glanced over at Justin. His rapt attention was still held by the siren song of the dancers.

The empty cup slid from her fingers. She was sick of watching from the wings while others took their bows.

She rose with sinuous grace and slipped among the dancers. She had no need to mock their motions. As she closed her eyes and lifted her hair from her sweltering nape, the rhythm took her in its masterful hands, swaying her like a long-stemmed bloom in the wind.

The wailing song of the dancers soared and the pent-up spirit of a lifetime burst into flower. Emily spun free, caught in the sheer joy of the motion. The stamping swelled until it resonated through her bones and fueled her pumping heart.

One by one the natives left their places in the sand to join the dance, bewitched by the spell of rhythm and song. Kawiri leaped and grimaced, wielding a piece of driftwood as a spear. Trini spun with a graceful swirl of his feathered cloak. The old *tohunga* gummed a smile and rocked in the sand. Dani hopped from one foot to the other, shaking her dark mop of hair.

For one magical moment Emily was no longer alone. She belonged to something larger than herself—a family. She whirled around, coming face-to-face with Justin.

Somehow in the midst of this exuberant crowd Justin had never looked more alone. A quizzical sadness tinged his expression. Emily faltered.

He swept his hair from his eyes and made a courtly bow, giving her a jarring glimpse of how striking a figure he might cut in a London drawing room. "May I have the pleasure of this dance, my lady?"

The native music seemed to fade, merging into the sweet strains of a formal waltz, half imagined and half remembered from a dream.

Emily had trouble finding her voice. "I should be honored, my lord."

He took her into his arms, holding her at arm's length with flawless grace. His big, warm hand pressed against the bare skin of her lower back. The natives faded to faceless blurs as they swept through the sand in an ever-widening circle, both of them too lost in the charm of the moment to recognize its incongruity. They never saw the

Maori step back, yielding their own dance to the exotic cadences of the waltz.

Emily gazed up into his face, marveling anew at the strong line of his jaw beneath its careless whiskers, the somber sparkle of his feline eyes. This was nothing like waltzing with Tansy in the cramped corners of their attic rooms.

She had been dancing for him as long as she could remember. She had always imagined Cecille would twist her ankle and she would be forced to take the lead in the recital. Her guardian would materialize from the fog-shrouded night and slip into the back of the recital room. As she collapsed in a graceful heap of organdy, his beautiful baritone would ring out, crying, "Bravo, bravo! There's my girl!" to the shocked stares of Miss Winters and the other girls.

Tears pricked Emily's eyes. She blinked them away, then wished she hadn't as Justin's face came clearly into focus. Lust and tenderness and hopeless longing warred in his gaze. She closed her eyes, dizzied by his strength and the warm, spicy scent of his skin. The windy beach vanished. They might have been dancing alone in a darkened ballroom beneath the tinkling fingers of a thousand chandeliers.

He folded her deeper into his embrace. She lay her head against his chest, half expecting to feel a crisp waistcoat instead of the warmth of his bare chest.

He rubbed his cheek against her curls. A shuddering breath escaped her. They were merely swaying now, clinging to any excuse to remain entangled in the tender web they'd woven. As the last pure note of the Maori song rang between them, the solution came to Emily, a revenge so simple and so diabolical, it could not fail to destroy him.

Tansy had always said there was only one way to bring a good man to his knees.

The music died and she quivered in the sudden hush.

The silence seemed too harsh, too penetrating. Justin reached to tilt her face upward. She tore herself out of his arms and ran, fleeing both herself and him, yet knowing in her heart that he would follow.

Chapter 12

· ❧ ·

*As rich as our mine may be, it cannot compare to
the wealth I've always found
in your company. . . .*

A laughing mob of dancers streamed around him, but
Justin stood in a daze, staring at the spot where Emily had
been as if he expected her to reappear in a puff of smoke.
Blood rushed through his veins, flooding uninvited to his
loins, his heart, his pounding head. The roaring in his ears
had nothing to do with the sea. It was the same roar he
had heard on the night he found Emily, the same relentless
ebb and flow of warning and desire that had taunted his
waking moments and colored his dreams with madness.

He plunged forward, shoving his way through the
Maori, deaf for the first time to the lilting intricacies of
their song. A woman's hand touched his arm, but he shook
it away, blinded to all else by the lithe shadow growing
smaller in the distance.

The ribbon of beach unfurled beneath his pounding
feet. A shy moon peeked through the sparse clouds, scattering diamonds of light across the sand. Emily stayed just
ahead of him, a whisper of movement between the shallow

dunes. His nostrils twitched. He would almost swear he could scent her on the wind, an alluring blend of vanilla and musk.

As he ran, the lights from the feast faded to a rosy glow in the sky. The echoes of music and laughter were drowned in the crash of the waves. He rounded a high dune and staggered to a halt. Emily stood alone on the stretch of beach where he had first found her.

Justin knew he would never forget the way she looked at that moment. She was as rare and exotic as a wild English rose blooming in the desert. The wind tousled her curls and whipped at her skirt. Her chin tilted in defiance even as she twisted her hands together for courage. He couldn't have said which made her more beautiful to him —her vulnerability or her pride. She might have been a defiant Eve dangling a juicy apple in front of Adam's nose.

As he angled toward her, he could feel his face hardening in ruthless lines of desperation.

"I don't like you," he said.

"I don't like you either."

Each weighted step through the damp sand carried him nearer to his destruction. "I'm too old for you."

"Much."

He was near enough to touch her now. "I have gray hair."

She reached up, wound a silvery strand around her finger, and jerked it out. "Not anymore."

He tangled his hand in her curls, drawing her head back until her mouth was a scant breath from his own. "I won't marry you."

Her hand crept around his nape. "I wouldn't have you."

"Oh, you'll have me."

She shivered at his husky promise. His mouth closed on hers, tracing its shape, its softness, with a patience and delicacy he was far from feeling. He wanted to make her ache deep inside, as he was aching. He rubbed his lips across hers, nibbling and coaxing with an expertise he'd almost forgotten he possessed. He was determined to stoke the flame of her need with exquisite stealth until she burned only for him.

Her lips parted shyly beneath the tantalizing pressure, burning his restraint to cinders. With a will of its own his tongue snaked out, delving deep inside the lush sweetness of her mouth. She met his thrust with a soft swirl of her own. He groaned. She tasted like a hot, luscious berry—succulent and ripe for his picking. With a hunger that made him quake inside, he wanted to taste the rest of her, to feel her sugared heat melt around every throbbing inch of his body.

The knowledge of what Justin wanted to do to her exploded through Emily, both terrifying her and imbuing her with a delicious sense of power. Gasping for a breath of sanity, she tore her mouth away from his. Dear God, what was she doing? It wasn't supposed to happen this way. She was supposed to coolly seduce him, scorn him, and toss the shreds of his broken heart in his face like confetti. Instead, she was clinging to him like a helpless wanton, drowning in the fervor of his kiss. With only a few expert caresses he had become the hunter and she the prey.

His lips flowered hungrily against her dimpled cheek, the curve of her jaw, the tingling skin of her earlobe. His tongue flicked out to taste the damning pulsebeat below her ear. A hoarse whimper escaped her throat. She struggled to remember why she must hate him.

Pressing her burning brow to the hollow of his throat, she whispered, "You always treat me like a child."

"No more," he vowed, sliding his hands down her back. Their callused strength against her bare flesh made her shiver. "You're all woman. Woman enough to take whatever I can give you." His warm, rough tongue plundered her ear, sending ribbons of sensation cascading deep into her womb.

Her knees buckled, but he caught her, dragging her

against him. If he only knew how desperately wrong he was. She was no match for him, she knew. No match at all. She knew that with dread certainty as he angled her thigh upward and pressed his flagrant arousal to the aching cradle between her legs.

She moaned as his mouth took hers again. The slow grind of his hips and his tongue's feverish strokes painted a dark and vivid picture of his desires. She trembled, but his body was too broad, too unrelenting for escape. There was no place for her to flee from the tender assault she had provoked.

The rough satin of his fingertips inched between her breasts, gliding wider with each sensual circle. She gasped as his palm cupped the threadbare calico of her bandeau, molding it to the soft globe of her breast.

He pressed his mouth to her ear. "I'm not like the others, Em. I won't hurt you. I swear it."

How could she tell him he'd already hurt her beyond bearing? Unable to resist his hoarse promise, she clung to his shoulders. His fingertips skimmed her nipple like butterfly wings, igniting tremors of pleasure. Beneath his caress the calico became not a barrier, but silky kindling for a spreading wildfire. She muffled her whimpers in his chest, desperate to hide her agonized blush. She could not still the irrational fear that he might discover not only *what* she was, but *who* she was as well.

His lips brushed her hair. "I've spent the last few nights pouring all of my passions into my music, when all I really wanted to do was pour them into you."

His blunt confession and the loving stroke of his thumb over the tender bud of her nipple were her undoing. Longing coursed through her in dark waves. She rubbed her lips against his chest, tasting the salty spice of his skin, teasing the rigid nub of his own nipple beneath her tongue.

Justin was shaking almost as hard as Emily was, hardly

daring to believe his sweetest fantasy was unfolding like a dream before him.

To hold Emily naked in the moonlight, her smooth young body his domain to pleasure and possess. To slake her darkest and most secret desires with his fevered touch. To ease himself inside her scrumptious body and take her, each stroke as deep and measured as the tide against the shore. It was as if time had rolled back to that other windy night and he'd been given a precious gift he thought lost forever. Now that gift had been sweetened by the privilege of knowing her sparkling mischief, her tender wit, and her irrepressible spirit. She was no longer a mysterious nymph coughed up by the sea. She was his Emily, a shining thread of melody wound around his heart.

His deft fingers tugged at the knot of her bandeau. Before she could moan a protest, the fabric unfurled and slipped from his finger to the sand, baring her breasts in all their pagan splendor.

Emily could feel their dusky peaks pucker beneath the greedy mouth of the wind and the smoldering caress of Justin's gaze. She shivered, seized by a terrible vulnerability.

He wrapped his arms around her, crushing her against the unyielding warmth of his chest. "What is it? Have I frightened you?"

Beneath her ear his heart slammed like the distant thunder of drums. "Everything is happening so quickly."

"Quickly?" He tilted her chin up and gazed into her eyes. "I've waited a lifetime for this."

Her broken hiccup was half sob, half laugh. "So have I. If you only knew . . ." No longer caring if this was revenge or madness, she tangled her hands in his hair and drew his mouth down to hers, kissing him with a ravenous passion to match his own.

Groaning, Justin dropped to his knees in the sand, only too eager to worship at the altar of her pleasure. He stroked her rounded shoulders, the satiny hollow above her

collarbone, the plump underside of her breasts, utterly
captivated by the contrasts in their bodies. What had
seemed common with other women now seemed exotic,
shaded with mystery. Emily's body was ripe with secrets
just waiting to be unfolded and stroked and explored.

He reached beneath her skirt, running his hands up
the back of her calves and thighs to the bare curve of her
rump. His thumbs angled across her hipbones, marveling
at the cushion of flesh that softened her in all the places
bone and muscle tempered him to hardness.

She quivered at his touch but did not shrink from him,
not even when his thumbs curled around to graze the delicate fleece that sheltered the feminine heart of her. Not
yet, he warned himself. Too soon. He lay his burning
cheek between her breasts and let the sea breeze wash over
him, praying it might soothe the desperate tide of desire
in his groin. She had known enough of the hasty, selfish
fumbles of boys. Tonight she would go where only the
restraint of a man could take her.

His mouth captured her breast, sucking the tender
bud with a fierceness that made her arch against him and
whimper his name.

It was all the invitation he needed. He lifted her and
carried her to a sandy haven between two low-slung dunes.
As he laid her in the sugary bed, the endless throb of the
sea taunted him with the vain hope that this night might
last forever. Without a word he eased her skirt down over
her hips and cast it away.

He gazed down at her as he had on that first night,
enchanted by the hint of a dimple in her cheek, her luminous eyes. Tonight she seemed more angel than nymph.
Her nakedness stirred in him a fierce possessiveness centuries of civilized breeding should have exorcised. He had
blunted his emotions for too long. This rush of lust and
tenderness and primitive jealousy exhilarated him, making
him feel reckless and drunk.

Emily drew in a shaky breath as Justin's hungry gaze

raked her from head to toe, lingering at the nest of curls between her legs. "Justin?"

His gaze flew back to hers with a guilty haste she might have found amusing if she weren't petrified with fear. "Mmmm?" he said dreamily.

"Are you sure you haven't any Maori blood in you?"

His slow, wicked smile curled her toes. He reached down and popped open the first button of his dungarees in a gesture so totally out of character and so full of masculine swagger that she had to choke back a frantic giggle.

"Perhaps the Maori know something we don't. Why should I be denied the pleasures of your succulent flesh?"

His shadow blocked the moonlight as he came down over her, thrusting his tongue deep into her mouth. She could taste the salt of the sea on him. Her hands toyed with his hair, wrapping it around her fists as he moved lower to scrape his teeth against the peak of her breast and dip his tongue into the shy dimple of her navel. She moaned as he filled her, even as a void opened lower, making her clamp her thighs together against the blinding need.

As he slid his elegant fingers into the coarse silk between her legs, Emily felt the shock of it all the way to her soul. She knew it was wrong to let him touch her there—scandalous, forbidden. But he stroked her with agonizing tenderness and infinite patience, consuming her not in flesh, but in flame. Pleasure coursed hot and thick through her veins, drugging her, weighting her legs until they fell apart at the gentle insistence of his hands.

She had thought to use her body to enslave him, and here she lay, a chattel to his touch, writhing and begging for a fulfillment she couldn't even name. The stars blurred to glimmering shards before her eyes. Her fingers knotted over the sleek muscles of his shoulders.

Justin parted the slick petals of Emily's body as if she were the most fragile of tropical flowers. He rubbed his nose tenderly over her belly, basking in the intoxicating fragrance released by his exploration. Driven by the soft whimpers escaping her throat and the dig of her finger-nails into his back, he smeared her dew over the delicate bud nestled in her curls, then pressed his finger deep into the very heart of her bloom.

She cried out.

Her tautness was irresistible. Justin had never felt such a thing, not even in the woman he had once planned to wed. It made his whole body shudder in anticipation even as it birthed a terrible suspicion in his sluggish brain. Lifting his head so he could watch her face, he slipped his finger out of her, then gently eased it back in. She winced and bit her lip to muffle a cry.

His spirits hovered somewhere dangerously between plummeting and soaring. With lumbering reluctance he relinquished his prize and straddled her, crawling up until he could flatten his palms in the sand on both sides of her head.

"Emily?"

Her eyes flew open and she started to find his face only inches from hers. An enchanting mask of pleasure flushed her cheekbones. "Yes?"

"You're not nearly as bad a girl as you've led me to believe, are you?"

Her words tumbled out in nervous spurts. "Of course I am! All my teachers said I was horrid."

He sighed. "Let me phrase that a different way. That compromising position you were found in with the gar-dener's son—would you care to describe it?"

"Could we talk about this later?"

God, wouldn't he love to! he thought. Much later. While he was offering tender ministrations to her ravished body. "No. We have to talk about it now. What sort of position was it?"

She rolled her eyes in exasperation. "Oh, very well. He was lying on the ground all bloody and I was standing over him with a pitchfork." Groaning, Justin dropped his head to her breastbone. "He should never have stuck his tongue in my mouth. He was a most unpleasant boy. He had a tongue like a grubworm." She gave his hair a nervous pat. "I didn't kill him, you know. I only wounded him."

Justin feared his own wounds were mortal. He slowly lifted his head. "One more question, darling. How long have you been without a man?"

New patches of scarlet tinged her cheeks. The stubby silk of her lashes shuttered her eyes. "Eighteen years," she mumbled.

He threw himself off her with a yelp that was half laughter, half despair. The stars winked down at him, giggling behind their brittle shells.

He chose his next words with elaborate care. "Do you even know how a man and a woman make love?"

She sat up, hiding her breasts behind the indignant curl of her knees. "Of course I do. A man puts his—"

Justin clapped his hand over her mouth. An anatomy lesson taught in Emily's uncompromising terms was the last thing he needed. His fingers lingered against the softness of her lips. The shine in her eyes threatened to flow over into tears. How could he explain the agonized delight her sheepish confession of innocence was causing him?

All the masculine vanity and hypocrisy he despised welled up inside him, penetrating the haze of his desire and bringing the blurred visions of his heart into sharp focus: coaches rocking through the English countryside on a spring day, their lacquered roofs garlanded with flowers; bells ringing a joyful peal through the crisp air; Emily adrift in a cloud of white satin, her eyes dimmed not by tears but by the shimmering gauze of a veil.

Hope. Hope for the future.

He ran the backs of his fingers down her cheek. Life had finally handed him something pure and fine, and he could not bring himself to tarnish it.

Her tears spilled over his fingers. "What is it, Justin? Don't you want me?"

A groan escaped him in lieu of reassurances. If he dared take her in his arms, he'd never find the strength to let her go. He swung away from her, welcoming the gritty reality of the sand, praying it might dispel the heady enchantment of her nudity. He tried to focus his thoughts elsewhere—on the Fifth Symphony of Beethoven, on Bach's *Concerto in D Minor,* on Chopin's bloody *Funeral March,* but she was the only melody he could hear.

Emily stared at the bronze expanse of Justin's back, cringing inwardly at her own pathetic question. *Don't you want me?*

As his damning silence stretched on, the shrill malevolence of another voice hissed in her mind.

He don't want you. Nobody does.

Doreen had been right. He always turned his back on her. But somehow this was worse. It left her shivering, abandoned to the night wind, naked and raw, shamed in both body and soul. The darkness no longer enveloped her, but hovered like a murky cloud, the stars shards of ice in an uncaring void. A vast loneliness rose like bile in her throat.

She swiped at her nose with the back of her fist as the familiar anger slammed like a shield over her pain. "There's really no need to explain. My friend warned me most gentlemen find virgins a bore. They're clumsy and predictable and they always cry at the wrong times." She dashed a hot tear away. "Like now."

Justin swung around, shocked by the bitter tenor of her voice. How could she believe he would think her clumsy? Or predictable? She was as clumsy as a she-tiger, as predictable as a summer storm at sea. He watched, paralyzed with disbelief, as she scrambled to her feet, snatching up her skirt.

"We'll just forget this ever happened, won't we? If you like, I'll send your darling Rangimarie back to tend to you. I'm sure she's had scads of experience. Most of it with the almighty, all-potent Pakeha."

She backed away without even bothering to cloak her nakedness with the skirt. Moonlight bathed her luminous skin and tipped her breasts with silver. Justin's head reeled as he imagined her strutting into the Maori encampment in all her naked glory to deliver a scathing invitation to the unsuspecting Rangimarie. He eased himself to his heels.

She spread a hand as if to ward him off. "Don't bother getting up. I don't want to be any trouble. I never wished to be a burden to anyone. Especially not to you."

She spun around to flee. Justin dove for her, his strength and grace serving him well. He tackled her easily, bringing her down in a soft explosion of sand. He hadn't expected her to fight him, but she twisted in his arms like a wild thing, beating at his back with her fists, raking his neck with her fingernails. She swore at him through her tears, calling him names so vile they would have made even the worldly Nicholas blush.

Grunting with exertion, he caught her hands and pinned her beneath his weight. He kissed her damp lashes, the salty curve of her cheek, the corner of her trembling mouth. "Don't you know, angel? Don't you know how much I want you?"

A broken sob escaped her. He dragged one of her hands downward. She resisted him, but his greater strength, even in gentleness, bent her inexorably to his will. "Touch me," he commanded hoarsely. "Touch me and then tell me I don't want you."

He pressed her hand inside his dungarees, cupping it around the full, rigid length of him.

The fury in her eyes slowly faded and shy wonder dawned. "Oh, my," she whispered, her fingers enfolding him like velvety petals.

A spasm of exquisite agony made him shudder.

"Oh, my!" she repeated. He had finally succeeded in rendering her speechless.

The extent of her innocence washed over him like a spring rain. He pressed an adoring kiss to her freckled nose. "That, my dear, is by far the most gratifying response I've ever had from a woman."

"A woman? Not a child?" She stroked him, enslaving him with her artless touch, her dark, questioning eyes.

He shook his head. "Not a woman." He kissed away the clouds threatening to gather across her brow. "A goddess."

He plunged his tongue into her mouth and drove himself hard into the sheath of her palm, allowing himself one moment of shameless pleasure. Then, ignoring her dazed moan of protest, he pulled her hand away and brought it to his lips, kissing each fingertip in turn, then her palm.

He met her gaze over her hand. "I need a gift from you, my goddess."

"Anything," she whispered.

The enticing visions that one word provoked almost wreaked havoc on his determination. He laced his fingers around hers and squeezed her hand. "Time. I need time."

"Time?" Emily echoed. Her thoughts spiraled crazily. *Time?* How much time did this man require before he loved her? A decade? A lifetime? He'd already had seven years of her time. Time tucked away in a golden watch case. Time ticking away against his heart. Time frozen forever in a faded tintype of a happy child.

He stroked her hair away from her face. "I need time to get my life in order. I've been running from the past for far too long."

Emily had to close her eyes at the irony of that. What would he do if she blurted out that the past was lying naked and trembling beneath him?

She opened her eyes, praying they would not betray her. "And when you get your life in order?"

"You'll be the first to know. I promise you that."

He kissed her, his mouth moist and sweet against her own. She hooked an arm around his nape, pressing him into her as if it might be the last kiss they would ever share.

Groaning, Justin pulled away. He rolled to his back, dragging her snugly into his arms.

"For a man who doesn't like me, you're being terribly kind," she said.

He smoothed her curls and spoke without even a hint of humor. "I said I didn't like you. I never said I didn't love you."

Justin couldn't sleep. But this wasn't the dream-plagued insomnia of a tortured man. His body tingled with the edgy excitement of fresh hope. It was as if a door had been thrown open, showing him a sunlit world brimming with plans and possibilities. He watched the encroaching dawn absorb the darkness, bleaching the sky to a pale rose. The sea was a glassy jade, smooth and unmarred like a mirror that has yet to know an ugly reflection.

He drew Emily deeper into his arms, savoring the lush feel of her bare skin against his own. She looked so terribly young with her lips parted in sleep. He felt more than a little depraved, wanting her so desperately, but still he could not stem the swift tide of desire rising in him. He swore softly under his breath.

Soon, he promised himself. Soon he would awaken like this every morning, snuggled with Emily on the . . . floor. The floor? He would have to build a bed for the hut immediately. Hell, he'd have to build a new hut. One with a separate room for Penfeld at a discreet distance from their own. And another room, airy with sunlight and decorated in chintz and dolls.

He felt a reluctant grin touch his lips. What would Emily say when he informed her they would start their new life with a daughter? She had professed a gruff dislike for children, but he had seen how Kawiri and Dani adored her. She treated them like people, not dolls.

He traced her features with his loving gaze. She had taught him so much in so short a time. She had charged headlong into his life, meeting its challenges with verve and tenacity. He owed her nothing less.

He was done cowering from life. He was no longer going to hide from his family, his inheritance, or even from the child awaiting him in England. When they returned to the hut, he would pen a letter to his father, asking him to see to Claire Scarborough's well-being until he could send for her. A hint of bitterness touched him. His father would probably have an easier time understanding if the child had been gotten off some mistress rather than from a pledge to a dying friend.

Emily stirred, moving her lips in a seeking caress against his chest. His doubts melted at her touch. His spirits soared, unfettered by guilt or remorse. It was as if her innocence had somehow washed away his own dark sins.

His thoughts, though, were far from virginal as Emily stretched with feline grace, giving him an untrammeled view of her delectable body, all vanilla cream sprinkled with cinnamon.

He crooked an eyebrow. Surely even the most noble gentleman allowed himself a few liberties with the woman he intended to make his bride.

Someone was stroking Emily like a kitten. She was afraid to open her eyes for fear they would stop. Her drowsy contentment was melting to a quicksilver shimmer of joy. The touch was completely unselfish. It demanded nothing of her, but gave only pleasure—pure, feathery strokes of pleasure. She tried to catch her breath but couldn't.

Justin hadn't played the piano in years, but he played Emily like a master, using the full skill of his long, tan fingers to bring her to the shuddering brink of ecstasy.

His lips caught her cry as his touch splintered her into a thousand shards of pleasure.

Her eyes slowly fluttered open. Justin hung over her, breathing hard, his slanted grin both proud and endearing.

"What was that?" she asked, gulping for breath.

"A hurricane? An earthquake?" he offered.

She blinked in wonder. "Was it legal?"

"Probably not. Immoral, too. I fear I just took shameless advantage of you."

"Am I compromised?"

He laid his lips against hers in a lingering caress. "If I compromise you, you'll know it. I promise."

They rose with reluctance, hesitant to leave their sandy haven. Justin went in search of Emily's bandeau, leaving her sitting in the sand, her hands pressed shyly over her breasts. The morning wind ruffled her curls. She stared out to sea, fighting off the panic that threatened to claim her. How could she have been so foolish as to believe she could take Justin's soul without losing her own?

He reappeared, dangling her bandeau from his finger like a flag of surrender. He insisted on tying it himself, sneaking behind her to nuzzle the back of her neck. She moaned helplessly as his arousal nudged against her rump.

"A normal phenomenon of the morning?" she asked him.

He reached around to stroke her nipples beneath the thin calico. "That's right. It has nothing to do with you."

"Liar," she whispered, wiggling against him.

"Tease," he countered, nipping her ear.

Justin caught himself whistling as they strolled hand in hand down the gleaming strand of beach. Sunlight sparkled off crystals in the sand. A gull soared into the deepening blue of the sky.

"I've been thinking about building a house," he shyly confessed. "Not a hut, but a real house with polished wood floors and scads of sunlight. I don't want any shadows or gloom like the house I grew up in."

Emily was strangely silent although she gripped his hand so tightly he was in fear for his fingers. He attributed her pensive mood to a new shyness. He grinned at that. Shyness was the last trait he would have associated with Emily. He would soon break her of it. He fully intended to keep his private vow of celibacy, but that didn't mean he couldn't give her a taste of what they would share once they were wed. The weeks of waiting to hear from his father might be agony for him, but it would be a sweet agony indeed.

As they rounded the bend and came in sight of their own beach, Emily gave his hand a squeeze that made his knuckles crack.

He winced. "Careful, dear. I might want to play the piano again someday. Or—" He lowered his head to whisper a more enticing suggestion, but his voice faded as he saw the massive steamer anchored offshore.

The sun gleamed off the two words emblazoned on its mighty hull.

WINTHROP SHIPPING.

Chapter 13

· ❦ ·

I've always wanted the best for you. . . .

The steamer loomed offshore, squat, ugly, and incongruous against the crystalline sea. Even at rest its towering stacks belched out smoke as if some serpentine beast snored within its belly. The black wisps fouled the air with their stench. Justin clung to her hand, squeezing it as hard as she had squeezed his own just a moment before. An icy knot hardened in Emily's throat.

The Maori had fled back to their fortified *pa* at the approach of the foreign vessel, leaving only scattered clam shells and barren ashes to mark the site of their feast.

"Damnation," Justin muttered. "I should have been here to reassure them."

Down the beach a dinghy had been dragged up on the sand. Two sailors lounged beside it, smoking pipes and talking among themselves. If the steamer looked odd against the pristine background of sea and sky, the scene on the beach appeared positively ludicrous. Emily might have laughed if she could have choked any sound past the lump of dread in her throat.

A folding table draped in snowy linen and spread with gleaming china had been set up in the sand. Three men perched like black crows around it. In the middle of the table sat Penfeld's teapot, dripping a steady amber stream from its inverted spout. The valet jumped to his feet as they approached, pinkening as if he'd been caught with his pants around his ankles at a bawdy house.

A fat man in a towering stovepipe hat rose with him, but his companion remained seated, in no apparent haste to abandon his leisurely breakfast.

"Good morning!" he called out, spearing something with a silver fork. "Care for a kipper?"

"No, thank you," Justin replied. "May I help you gentlemen?"

"We certainly hope so," the plump man boomed out. He offered Justin his hand. "Thaddeus Goodstocking at your service."

Justin released her with obvious reluctance and allowed the man to pump his hand, but Emily noticed he did not offer his name. Wariness cut shallow grooves around his mouth.

"And I am Bentley Chalmers." The seated man dabbed his waxed mustache with his napkin. "Your charming valet was kind enough to offer us a spot of tea to wash down our breakfast."

Penfeld inched toward Justin as if sneaking out of an enemy camp. It was only too easy to understand how he'd been seduced by their creamy china, their salted kippers, their London gossip.

Both of the strangers looked hot and stifled in their quilted waistcoats. The leaner man had been smart enough to drape his heavy frock coat over the back of his chair. Emily pitied Mr. Goodstocking. Sweat dripped into his bushy whiskers, and the points of his starched collar cut into his heavy jowls.

"You must forgive our interruption," he said. "We do so hate to draw you away from your native delights." Her sympathy vanished as his piggish eyes raked her in leering curiosity.

She was suddenly and painfully aware of her appearance. Her curls were tangled, her feet bare and sandy. With her scant garb, tan skin, and sun-burnished freckles, she must appear to these proper English gentlemen as the basest of whores. Her first instinct was to shrink behind Justin, but she had too often endured shame and condemnation from forbidding figures dressed in black.

Justin was not oblivious to the exchange. He stepped in front of her, his jaw hardening with the glacial dignity she had glimpsed before. "You didn't come all the way to New Zealand for a good cup of tea."

Mr. Goodstocking retreated from Justin's frosty stare even as Chalmers rose with a placating smile, taking a thick leather packet from beside his plate. He refused to even acknowledge Emily, which was somehow more cutting than Goodstocking's leer.

"No," he admitted. "We didn't come for the tea. We came as agents acting on behalf of the Duchess of Winthrop to seek a man calling himself Justin Connor."

Justin hesitated; Emily could hear her heart pounding in her ears.

"I am that man," he finally replied, his New Zealand brogue as flat as she had ever heard it.

Goodstocking's gaze traveled from the ragged knees of Justin's dungarees to his bare feet. He cleared his throat and exchanged a long look with his companion.

Chalmers handed Justin the leather packet, then swept off his neat bowler in a deferent bow that might have belonged to another century. "Your Grace."

Penfeld gasped. Emily took a step backward without realizing it.

Justin stared down at the packet in his hands. Chalmers's benign address had conveyed a wealth of meaning. His father was dead. He was now the Duke of Winthrop.

He ran his fingers over the pitted leather, desperate to

feel something, anything at all. But all he felt was a vast emptiness. David Scarborough had been more father to him in six months than his own father had been in a lifetime. His grief was not the sharp pain of loss, but an overwhelming sense of regret for the moments they might have shared, moments lost forever to them now.

Chalmers gestured. "Within that packet you will find several letters from your mother. She would like you to return to London immediately to assist her in the matter of settling your father's estate. She needs you."

Those three words tightened the noose around his neck. For a terrible moment the old choking pressure returned. He was now the owner of that crude vessel anchored offshore and a fleet of sailing ships and steamers strewn from the English Channel to the Bering Strait.

Not this time, he thought. Things were different now. He was no longer a helpless child or even a rash, rebellious young man. He was lord of the manor now. There was no one to stop him from returning to New Zealand and running his empire from the sunny coast of the North Island. He could hire men to take care of the mundane details of the business while he used his wealth and influence as he chose. He slapped the packet against his palm, seeing it not as a warrant of execution, but as a golden ticket of opportunity for both him and Emily, his chance to make amends to his family and to David's daughter.

Chalmers droned on. "It would have taken us much longer to find you, but we had the good fortune to stumble upon a detective who had located you while employed by a Miss Amelia Winters."

Justin didn't even hear him. He was already dwelling on his first meeting with Claire Scarborough, praying he would have the courage to look her in the eye and tell her the truth about her father's death. His jaw tightened with resolve. With Emily by his side he could do anything.

He turned, eager to share his plans with her.

Emily was gone.

Chapter 14

·❦·

*If your mother taught me nothing else, it was that
wealth cannot buy joy. . . .*

Emily tossed the little blue journal on the stack of books
and bound them together with a leather strip. Her hands
worked separately from her brain, knotting and neatening,
tying and folding in a soothing stream designed to numb
both mind and heart. She bundled a pile of blankets into
two bedrolls and began to wrap what was left of Penfeld's
tea set in soft scraps of flannel. Her hands did not falter
until they ran across the box containing her father's watch.
Justin would have no need to send it to Miss Winters now.
He would soon discover that all the gold in the world
couldn't buy him Claire Scarborough.

She padded to the table and eased Justin's symphonies
from their hidden drawer. The embossed document she
had seen once before slid out with them, but she tossed it
aside. She had no more interest in grants or deeds or mysterious maps. The gold mine was as dead as her father's
dreams.

All that remained in the drawer were Justin's letters to

Claire. Emily drew them out, crumpling them in her clumsy fingers. Justin had never shared them willingly, but they still belonged to her. They might be all she ever had of him.

Justin's shadow fell across her like a caress.

Shoving the letters into the waistband of her skirt, she spoke without turning around. "I'm afraid you won't be able to take all the books. You'd sink the dinghy. Perhaps even the steamer."

"What do you think you're doing?" he asked.

"Packing," she replied, jamming the sugar bowl into a wicker basket. She folded the tablecloth, refusing to halt her frenetic activity long enough to look at him.

She heard the betraying shuffle of claws across the dirt floor. Fluffy had taken advantage of the open door to skitter in.

She picked up another teacup, praying her clumsy motions would not betray her. "You'd best leave the lizard with me. You'd look odd walking him on a leash in Kensington Gardens. I suggest you buy a nice English bulldog instead."

Justin's footfalls sounded behind her. The cup slipped from her hand and struck the edge of the table, shattering.

"You're going with me, Emily."

She crouched and gathered up the fragile bits of china. There would be no gumming them back together this time. The pieces were too jagged to fit.

"No," she said softly. "I'm not."

He caught her arm and pulled her around to face him. "Why not?"

She inclined her head, fearful of finding her own pain mirrored in his tawny eyes. "I can't go back to England with you."

He was silent for a long moment. She could almost hear the facile little wheels of his mind clicking. "If you're in trouble with the law, Emily, I can help you. I'm an influential man now. I'll have an army of barristers at my disposal."

She laughed weakly. "Probably a few judges as well."

His fingers bit into her arm. "What is this? Your brave attempt at gallows humor?"

Tilting her face to his, she flattened her quavering voice to dead calm. "Unless you care to tie me up and put me on that ship, I'm not going."

Justin was tempted to do just that. But as he gazed down at her, he didn't see her pale and drawn as she was now. He saw her pelting down the beach with the children, her curls dancing, her merry, freckled face turned to the sun. He saw her swaying in the firelight with sensual abandon, her skirt billowing around her ankles. Try as he might, he could not imagine her trapped in the winter chill of London, her glow fading to pallor beneath a gray sky dulled with soot.

Grief stabbed him, fresher than anything he'd felt at the news of his father's death. Emily was right. She didn't belong in London any more than he did. She belonged here, bathed by sunlight and sea, cloaked in the sweet melodies and loving grace of the Maori. Despite her tough veneer, she was a wild, fragile bloom that would surely wither if transplanted.

He paced away from her, raking a hand through his hair. If it weren't for David's child, he would stay. But he couldn't offer Emily a heart unfettered by the past until he'd repaid that old debt. "I have to go. I have no choice."

"I know."

Why didn't she cry? Why didn't she throw herself at his feet and beg him to stay? Her damnable pride was tearing him apart. A fierce regret touched him. He should have taken her last night, forged the bond between them that much stronger. What a joy it would have been to return to find her splashing through the waves, rosy and plump with his child!

"I shouldn't be gone for more than a few months. I'm leaving Penfeld with you."

"You can't. You'd break his heart. He'd never forgive you if he missed a shopping expedition to Fleet Street. Trini can look in on me if you'd like, but I'm really quite good at looking after myself."

He snorted. "This from a woman who fell off a boat in the middle of the Tasman Sea?"

She shrugged. "I tripped over my boot lace."

His shoulders slumped in helpless laughter. "Christ, Em, what am I going to do without you?" Aching with longing, he reached to fold her in his arms.

She backed away, her dark eyes aflame with the dangerous sparkle of tears. "Please, don't. I detest good-byes."

With those words she spun around and fled the hut, leaving him to gaze at the barren table and wonder how she could have swept his heart so empty with a single careless stroke.

Emily stood alone on the bluff, gazing out to sea. Her fingers trailed absently over the blunt peak of the wooden cross.

The sun's splintered rays bathed her face in warmth. She closed her eyes. The wind raked her with tender fingers, fresh and pure like a melody never to be heard by any ears but her own. Its beauty made her ache. But when she opened her eyes they felt as dry and barren as the withered husks of the flowers rustling at the base of the cross.

She was waiting for Justin. She knew he would come. She had seen him on the beach below saying his good-byes —embracing Trini, grasping the sun-browned hands of the solemn natives, lifting Dani to his shoulders for a last ride.

The Winthrop steamer loomed like a dark blot on the misty azure and jade of a wet painting. Justin didn't make a sound, but Emily knew he was behind her.

"I hate ships," she said. "They're always taking people away."

"But they bring them back too."

She turned to face him, hugging back a shiver as if the wind were cold instead of warm. A jolt of shock raced through her. She had never seen Justin in anything but his faded dungarees. Seeing him fully clothed now was somehow more erotic than his near nakedness. He wore no coat, but a handsome waistcoat covered a shirt pressed to crisp perfection. Her mouth went dry with unexpected longing.

The shirt hung loosely over his broad shoulders. Tenderness washed over her for the brawny young prospector who had come to New Zealand filled with dreams and hope. But she wouldn't have traded a single thread of silver from his temples to have that man back.

His lean form suited the elegance of his garb. Emily felt sorely lacking in her primitive skirt. She shuffled her feet in the sand, fighting a desperate shyness. "I've never seen you with shoes before."

He cast the polished leather a woeful glance. "They pinch like hell."

She drew in a breath, but instead of the laugh she had intended, a broken sob burst forth. Justin reached for her. She melted into him, throwing her arms around him like a bereft child.

He held her as if he would never let her go, kissing her nose, rubbing his stubbled chin against her cheek, mingling her tears into a salty balm against his seeking lips.

He buried his mouth in her hair. "I'll be back for you, Emily. I swear it."

Her slender shoulders convulsed beneath Justin's hands. Her small fists opened and closed against his back, and in the desperation of her grasp he realized something that cut him almost as deeply as leaving her.

She didn't believe him.

With staggering reluctance he dragged himself out of

her embrace. He reached in the inner pocket of his waist-coat and drew out a box.

"I have no ring to give you. All I have is this." His hands shook as he dropped the lid in the sand and drew out the shining rope of gold.

The watch dangled between them, casting shards of sunlight across Emily's tear-stained face. She sucked in a shuddering breath as he lowered the chain over her head. The watch fell between her breasts, golden bright against her tanned skin.

He cupped her face between his palms and gave her one last kiss, hot, sweet, and fierce with promise. Then he started down the hill, nearly stumbling in his haste to leave her before his will faltered.

"Justin Connor!"

The croaked bellow brought him to a sliding halt. He shaded his eyes against the sun and looked back at the bluff.

Emily was jumping up and down, waving her arms. "Show them you're the best damned duke England has ever seen! Better than Prince Albert. Better even than the Duke of Wellington. And tell Mr. Thaddeus Swinestocking his spit isn't fit to polish your shoes!"

He wouldn't have to. The hefty agent was standing beside the dinghy, his fat jowls drooping in consternation.

Justin touched his fingers to his lips, then spread them toward Emily in a silent salute.

"Buy Penfeld some china!" she shouted, cupping a hand around her mouth. "Wedgwood jasperware with a floral pattern."

The natives watched with solemn eyes as he climbed into the dinghy. The sailors used the long oars to shove them away from the shore. Penfeld perched awkwardly in the bow, clutching the sides of the boat with whitened fingers. Justin didn't dare look at him. If his valet's fat little chin quivered the tiniest bit, Justin feared he would throw himself overboard and swim back to Emily even if they were halfway to England.

"Don't forget that English bulldog! He'll need a spiked collar. Keep him away from poodles. They're not real dogs, you know, just rats with curly hair and you mustn't breed . . ." Her hoarse voice was fading.

The oars parted the water in long, rippling strokes, shoving away the shoreline. A plaintive melody filled the air, sonorous and sweet.

He had told Emily the truth. The Maori could do nothing without singing.

Not even say good-bye.

Chalmers's cool, questioning gaze touched his face, but Justin didn't even blink. He kept his gaze riveted on the slender figure standing on the shrinking bluff and let the salty breeze burn the tears from his eyes before they could fall.

It was twilight before Emily made her way down from the bluff. The last tawny rays of the sun bathed the beach. Her limbs, her eyelids, her throat, ached with a leaden heaviness like the weight of the watch against her breastbone, but her heart felt as drained as her eyes. She had watered her father's grave with her tears for the last time. The sand had absorbed them, sucking them away as if they had never fallen.

The packet of letters she had taken from the hut rustled against her skin. She had spent the past few hours poring over them. They were simple letters written to a child, filled with the warmth, wit, and charm she had come to expect from Justin. They were filled with the pleasures of his days, the beauty of the island, his friendships with the Maori, and humorous anecdotes about her father. He had shared all of himself in those letters, everything but the puzzling truth that had kept him from posting them.

Emily's steps faltered as she saw Trini sitting cross-legged in the sand. She didn't want to see him. She didn't want to see anyone. She just wanted to crawl back into the sea as she had come. She walked past him without a word.

He scrambled to his feet. "Where will you go?"

She forced back a groan. When Trini used words under five syllables, he was deadly serious. She turned to face him. "Away."

"What shall I tell the Pakeha when he returns?"

"He won't be back." The bitter words shot out before she could stop them.

"And if you are wrong?"

She squared her shoulders. "Then I'll be the one to leave this time."

A sad smile played around his lips. He drew a line in the sand with his toe. "Perhaps you are no wiser than we Maori. Seeking *utu*, your own personal revenge, for every slight."

"He slighted my whole life!" she cried.

Emily realized then that it wasn't about the gold. It never had been. She couldn't forgive him for breaking the heart of a child who had believed in him. And she couldn't afford to find out if he would do it again. Time had robbed her of her defenses. Her woman's heart wasn't as resilient as the child's had been. Another blow would surely shatter it. She felt the warning prick of tears behind her eyes. She blinked them away, not wanting Trini to see her cry. Not wanting anyone to ever see her cry again.

"It reminds me of something the Pakeha's mighty God once said—'Vengeance is mine.' "

"Not this time, Trini." She stabbed her chest with her finger, tapping the locket. "This time vengeance is *mine*." His solemn brown eyes surveyed her with maddening wisdom. She turned away with a dismissive wave. "How can I expect you to understand?"

"Perhaps I understand better than you know . . . Claire."

Emily froze in mid-stride, flinching as the name

sounded like a slap across her face. She turned slowly, remembering all the times she had seen him entranced by the shiny watch case. "How?"

Trini pointed. For the first time, Emily saw the children scattered among the dunes, their normal jubilance muted to pensive quiet.

"Dani," he said. "She recognized you from the watch. She told me you were the Pakeha's lost angel freed at last from a terrible spell."

Dani was wrong, Emily thought. She had only fallen under a more deadly spell. She opened the watch case with a trembling hand. The case was empty, the photograph gone. Once again Justin had taken the best part of her with him.

She cast Trini a pleading glance. "How could he not have known?"

The native's lips quirked in an enigmatic smile. "The Pakeha sees only what he chooses to see. It is his way."

As Emily stared blindly into the locket, a low chant rose from the dunes. The children were repeating one word over and over. *Claire.* They pelted out of the dunes, surrounding her. She sank to her knees, wrapping Dani's warm little body in her arms. She pressed her eyes shut, imagining how it would have felt to hold the child she would never have. She could almost see him—his silky dark hair falling in his eyes as he bent over the piano.

She opened her eyes. Trini helped her to her feet, his tattooed brow furrowed in a frown. "How will you go from here? You have no money, no means."

Her eyes burned with a fierce light. "Oh, yes, I do. Gold brought me here, and gold will take me away."

A yelp of dismay escaped him as she held the watch aloft and twisted, shattering the last chain that bound her to Justin Connor.

$\mathscr{P}$ART II

*Now cracks a noble heart. Good
night, sweet prince:
And flights of angels sing thee to
thy rest!*

*Angels are bright still, though the
brightest fell.*

—WILLIAM SHAKESPEARE

*C*hapter 15

· ❦ ·

*I would trade all the gold in New Zealand
to see your mama's smile one more time. . . .*

*A*melia Winters flinched as the thunderous crash of a
door and shouting masculine voices shattered the quiet of
her domain. Her fingers tightened into claws on the windowsill. Outside, sleet skittered from the pewter sky, coat-
ing the tiny garden within the walled courtyard in a shiny
layer of ice. Amelia stared absently at the dormant rose-
bushes. They needed to be pruned. She'd been forced to let
the gardener go with a tidy sum after he'd threatened to
summon the constable when the Scarborough girl had
stabbed his son.

The door behind her creaked open. Timid feet shuffled
on the worn carpet. "His Grace, the Duke of Winthrop, to
see you, ma'am."

"Show him in."

"Aye, mum."

Amelia smiled bitterly. Doreen always slipped back
into cockney in moments of travail. It was a habit Amelia
had bred out of herself after she had clawed her own way
out of a rookery crib to found this school.

Heavy footsteps shuddered the floorboards. They might have been the footsteps of her executioner. London had been abuzz with the young duke's return for over a week, and now she knew her brief reprieve was done.

The door slammed into the wall. Cold air from the foyer buffeted her. Amelia steeled her spine and swung around, somewhat relieved to finally come face-to-face with her most dreaded nightmare.

Her relief was short-lived. A man stood in the doorway, tall, gaunt, but undeniably striking. Drops of melted sleet beaded the cape of his greatcoat. He was scandalously hatless, and his eyes burned like twin flames beneath a sweeping fall of dark hair. His clenched jaw was shaded not with a proper beard, but by the stubble of a savage. She had heard rumors that he'd been living with cannibals for the past seven years. He looked more than eager to devour her frail bones.

His sheer masculine presence dwarfed the shabby parlor. The room seemed suddenly full of people. Doreen hovered at the door, her homely face more pinched and pale than usual. Barney stood behind their callers, eyeing them with ill-disguised hostility. The slender stranger at the duke's elbow tipped his bowler to her, his face a bland, affable mask that did not fool Amelia for an instant.

The duke moved toward her, his greatcoat swirling around his boots. She realized that despite the silver threads at his temples and the sun-etched lines around his eyes, Justin Connor was younger than she had expected. Much younger. And far more dangerous. She clutched at the high collar of her blouse.

"I have come for my ward," he announced, giving her a bow so brief as to be an insult. A volatile muscle twitched in his cheek. "Your Miss Dobbins has tried to tell me that she is not in residence at this school."

A sharp cough failed to unravel the knot in Amelia's throat. She was terrified his knowing eyes would burn away the layers of her deceit, exposing the ugly truth for all to see. "I fear she is correct."

"Then I demand an explanation. My partner David Scarborough left his only child, Claire, in your care seven years ago. I have written record of it."

"As do I. But as my staff tried to tell you, she is no longer here."

Justin raked a hand through his hair, thankful for Bentley Chalmers's unruffled presence at his elbow. This woman's cryptic explanations were maddening him to distraction. He had wasted a week working up the courage to come to this place. A week in which his old insomnia had returned with a vengeance. A week of driving past the school in his luxurious carriage, wondering which of the lighted windows might be Claire's. He had risked everything to come here. Even Emily.

A maid carrying a bucket of coal slipped into the parlor. Justin sighed, summoning his last ounce of self-control. "Then would you mind telling me where I might find Claire Scarborough?"

Was it a reflection of the fire, or did he see a flicker of malicious satisfaction in the old woman's eyes? "I haven't the faintest idea where the girl is. She ran away months ago."

Blood roared through Justin's ears. The room went dark, then red. Then he was moving forward, only dimly aware of hands tugging at him and a woman's terrified keening.

"Your Grace!" It was Chalmers's imperturbable voice, shaken to near hysteria, that finally reached him.

The room slowly lightened. Chalmers held his arm while the sullen lad with the big ears clung to his leg. Justin shook the boy off like a mongrel pup. The young teacher had pressed a handkerchief to her mouth to muffle a scream, her complexion as chalky as her mistress's. The maid was a vague white shape, open-mouthed and wide-eyed at the hearth.

Only Amelia Winters stood unmoving, almost as if she expected his blow, even welcomed it. Stricken to his soul, Justin lowered his arm.

Wringing her hands, the old woman began to babble. "I did everything in my power, but the child was always headstrong and wicked. I could not control her. I tried to guide her by the Christian principles of discipline and self-restraint, but she remained unrepentant and hopelessly ill behaved."

Justin gripped the spine of a rosewood armchair, sickened by how close he had come to striking this woman. He bowed his head. He was too late. The child was gone. He had come this close only to lose her, perhaps forever. His own cowardice had cost him the girl. What right did he have to berate this pathetic old woman?

Her voice soared on a note of hysteria. "Even with my limited means I gave her the best care and education I could afford. Why, I treated her like my very own child!"

"She's lying!"

The words burst out like a breath of wind in the stale air of the parlor. Justin jerked his head up. The coal bucket clattered to the hearth in a cloud of ashes. The young maid marched toward him, wiping her hands on her apron.

"Shut yer trap, Tansy, or I'll shut it for ya," the boy snarled, starting for her.

With one smooth motion Justin grabbed Chalmers's cane and slammed it down across a table, neatly blocking the boy's path. He ducked his head and shot Justin a glare of pure hatred.

Even in his agitation Justin couldn't help but notice how startlingly pretty the maid was. Silky tendrils of black hair escaped her drooping mobcap. Her drab, stained apron couldn't hide the bold curves beneath the limp ruffles.

Her brilliant blue eyes brimmed with angry tears. "The old witch is lyin'. She treated the girl like a bloody slave. Made 'er 'aul coal and work in the kitchens dawn to dusk. Made 'er teach the little ones so she wouldn't 'ave to pay no one else to do it. Fed 'er scraps just like she does me. Always throwin' it up in 'er proud little face she'd be on the streets fendin' fer 'erself if it weren't fer Miss Amelia Winters's bloody Christian charity."

She grabbed his hand, painting streaks of coal dust between his fingers. "The girl weren't wicked, sir. I swear she weren't. High-spirited maybe, but not truly wicked." She nodded toward Barney and Doreen. "Not like them there. Why, before 'er da died, she was a regular angel, and even after that she was the best mate I ever 'ad."

A fresh pain jolted Justin's heart. The girl tried to withdraw her hand as if shamed by her own boldness, but he held it fast. She gazed up at him, awestruck. She must have known so little kindness in her short life, he thought, but was kind enough herself to befriend an orphaned child.

"Did she leave any clue as to where she might be going?" he asked. "A letter? A note? Anything?"

The maid ducked her head. "I couldn't 'ave read it if she 'ad. She just up and disappeared one night when the wind was 'owling 'round the attic." Her accusing gaze flicked to Doreen. "About the same time those two—"

"Tansy!" Barney barked.

Justin thought he might have seen a flash of genuine fear in the girl's eyes. "Show me where she slept," he said gently but firmly. He was determined to find some clue as to why the maid's confession was making them all fidget.

"Take one step, Tansy, and you'll be dismissed." The headmistress's voice rang out like a steel bell, then softened to a wheedling tone. "Just think of all I've done for you."

The girl wavered for only an instant before lifting her round little chin in proud defiance. "I am, Miss Winters. By gawd, I am."

With a regal swish of her stained skirt she gestured for Justin to follow. Chalmers took two steps, but Justin stayed him with his hand. There were some things he would have to do alone.

He followed Tansy up the stairs, making rapid mental notes to stave off his panic. The carpet was faded, its floral pattern worn bare in the center of each tread. Several of the balusters were cracked, and only the newel post at the bottom of the stairs showed signs of being replaced in recent years. As they reached the upper landing, the patter of feet was followed by the slamming of a door. The sound echoed as if there were very few warm little bodies to absorb it.

Tansy took a candle from a hall table and led him to a rough-hewn door. Justin's dread swelled. As she opened the door, the flame quivered in a blast of cold wind. Narrow steps wound into utter darkness. He hesitated, knowing he did not want to see what awaited him. But the thought of Emily gave him courage. She would have charged headlong up those steps, banishing every shadow with her unrelenting light.

Wiping his clammy palms on his trousers, he started after Tansy. Chill, heavy air bore down on him. Before he was halfway up, his breath was billowing out in frigid clouds.

They reached a shadowy landing. Tansy pointed to a door. "That there is my room."

He understood her gentle prodding. There was only one other door.

He reached for it, his hand shaking. The battered knob felt like ice. He turned it and pushed, half hoping it would be locked. The door creaked open. Tansy hung back as if reluctant to finish what she'd started.

As Justin saw where Claire Scarborough's weary steps had led her each night, something inside of him curled up and died. It would have broken David's heart to know his daughter had come to this.

The room was cramped, barely more than a closet

tucked beneath the attic beams. As he ducked beneath the lintel, cobwebs brushed his hair.

A grimy window let in a thin sliver of winter light. Beyond the pigeons cooing on the sill he could see an endless ocean of chimneys and roofs, all dulled by a miasma of soot. A narrow bed sat in one corner, still rumpled as if someone had just climbed out of it. He ran his hand over the lumpy tick, knowing it madness to wish it might still be warm. He sat down on it, dropping his head into his hands.

Someone was watching him. Tiny prickles danced along his spine. He twisted his head to find stoic blue eyes gazing at him. A doll sat propped against the pillow. He picked her up and brushed his hand over golden curls matted with age, touched the jagged crack in her porcelain skull.

Tansy's voice startled him. "That there is Annabel. I used to 'ear 'er talkin' to the doll when she thought I weren't listenin'. Sometimes she'd cry." She shrugged apologetically. "The walls are thin."

The doll hung limp in his hands. Yes, the walls were thin, he thought. Even now he could hear within them the rustle of mice and other skittering creatures.

It shouldn't surprise him that the child had run away. It should only surprise him that she had stayed so long.

Icy fury poured through his veins, washing away the hopeless despair, sharpening his sense of purpose. His hands tightened on the doll. Damn Amelia Winters for condemning an orphaned child to this attic coffin! And damn himself most of all for letting it happen!

He rose and started down the stairs. Tansy followed, galloping behind him. As he strode into the parlor, still clutching the bedraggled doll, even Barney backed away, leaving the headmistress to face him alone.

The woman's name suited her, he thought maliciously. She was as gray and colorless as the peeling paint and faded carpet of her school. How could David have left his

precious Claire with this grim creature? Of course, he and
Nicky had convinced David he would be gone for only a
few months. Not forever.

His baleful stare fell on the old woman's gnarled
hands. They were trembling as if palsied. Her steely façade
was cracking just like the paint on the medallioned ceiling. For the first time Justin saw her for what she was. A
pitiful old woman whose school was crumbling around her
head.

His empathy did not soften the bite of pure contempt
in his voice. "My detectives are going to comb this city for
Claire Scarborough. If so much as one curl on her little
head has been harmed, I'll see you ruined. I'll tell all of
London about that attic prison you built for David Scarborough's daughter. I'll ensure that even the poorest mer-
chant wouldn't trust his dog to your care."

He spun on his heel, whipping his greatcoat around
him. He paused in front of the wide-eyed Tansy and pulled
a fat handful of pound notes from his pocket. Money
meant little to him. He had lived too long free of its
encumbrance.

He pressed the notes into her hand. "If you remember
anything else about the night Claire ran away, or if you
require any kind of assistance at all, come to Grymwilde
Mansion in Portland Square and ask for me."

"Gor blimey, sir! Ya really mustn't!" But she was already shoving the money into the bodice of her shirt.

"Lord Winthrop."

The voice raked down Justin's spine like a steely claw.

The headmistress's gray eyes bored into him. "I may
have failed with the child, Your Grace, but your own care
left much to be desired."

His jaw twitched. The clock on the mantel ticked in
the utter silence. Then he dipped at the waist in a gallant
bow. "I concede your point, madam. If I have the good
fortune to find her, I intend to spend the rest of my life
atoning for my neglect."

"Aye, that ya will. She'll see to it, I'll wager," Tansy muttered under her breath.

Chalmers cast her a curious look, but Justin hadn't heard her. The agent tipped his derby and gave his cane a jaunty toss. "A good afternoon to all of you," he wished them before following the duke's determined form into the winter afternoon.

Justin didn't think he would ever be warm again. The dawn sun shining through the carriage window shed pale light but little else. His clasped hands were numb beneath their white gloves. The cold sank deep into his joints, chilling him to utter exhaustion. He tried to let his mind drift away, but each passing day made it harder to hear the chanted song of the sea, the taunting whisper of a balmy breeze against his skin. His memories of Emily were his only warmth.

A month of searching had yielded nothing. Claire Scarborough had vanished into London's merciless jaws without a trace.

Neatly trimmed lawns and iron gates drifted past the carriage. Portland Square was a world away from the slums he had haunted through the long night. He had spent it as he had a dozen others—combing the narrow streets, shoving his way through taverns and gin mills, growling questions at anyone who would listen. Even the motliest of scoundrels gave him wide berth. Perhaps there was something to be said for the reliable web of society gossip. News of the wild-eyed duke had filtered down even to their ranks.

He sighed, almost wishing for Chalmers's dapper form to steady him. But he had sent his chief agent with an efficient army of detectives to search the orphanages and cottages in the countryside around London.

The carriage turned a corner and clip-clopped down a cobblestone drive. Justin's spirits plunged further, as they did every time he saw his father's house. No, his house, he reminded himself ruefully. Grymwilde was a veritable Gothic nightmare of pitched roofs, gables, and bay windows. A crenellated tower perched like a clumsy growth on one side. The house's only symmetry had been achieved by planting two leering gargoyles on matching turrets at each end of the roof. Justin swore under his breath, cursing Mortimer Connor, the first Duke of Winthrop, who had been so enamored of his newly bought title that he had built this vulgar monstrosity as a monument to his own bad taste.

Climbing down from the carriage, he commanded the droopy-eyed coachman to get some sleep. He slipped through the front door, thankful for the sleeping peace of the house.

His mother was more concerned with throwing a ball to introduce him to the eligible ladies of her acquaintance than with his vain search for his partner's child. His three sisters had all married vapid men who had promptly taken up residence at Grymwilde and had no discernible occupations other than wandering the house with the most current copy of the *Times* tucked under their arms. Justin was starved for privacy. He missed his simple hut and his native friends who had known when to speak and when to be silent.

Most of all he missed Emily. He missed her dimpled smile, the warmth of her golden skin beneath his palms, the intoxicating taste of her lips.

A hard ache curled deep inside of him. He peeled off his gloves and tossed them on a lacquered table, meeting his reflection in the mirrored panel above. He had avoided mirrors in the last few weeks, and now he remembered why. His eyes were red-rimmed with exhaustion, his hair wild as if raked too many times by desperate fingers. Against the incongruity of his finely cut evening clothes, he looked every inch the crazed savage half of society believed him to be.

He touched his cheek. His tan was fading as rapidly as

his hopes. His seven years on the North Island were melting before his eyes like a forgotten dream, unbearably
sweet in its poignancy. Only the daily letters he scribbled
to Emily kept him sane. He posted them half mad with
panic and frustration, knowing it might take weeks, even
months, for them to reach her.

Would she wait for him? he wondered. Or would the
greedy sea take her back to punish him for being fool
enough to leave her?

He shoved away from the table, too tired to do anything but stumble up the stairs and fall into the dubious
comfort of his cold, lonely bed.

Chapter 16

·❀·

*I hold dear to my heart the hope that someday,
in a better place than this, we will be reunited. . . .*

*E*mily's fingertips brushed something smooth and cold.
She stretched out her hand. The object rolled just out of
her reach. She swore softly under her breath and craned her
neck to peer over the edge of the cart. An apple, fat, shiny,
and red, taunted her from its perch, making her mouth
water and her stomach snarl.

The vendor swung away from the cart to hand a sack
to a gentleman in a tall beaver hat. Emily lunged, crook-
ing her fingernails into claws to snag the tender skin of the
apple.

The vendor would have been none the wiser if her
shawl hadn't caught on the handle of the cart. As she
broke into a run, the cart tipped, spilling apples in a
stream of scarlet into the dirty snow.

"Thief!" the vendor bellowed. "Come back 'ere, ya
bloody brat! Constable!"

She didn't dare look behind her. She could already hear
running feet, confused shouts, and the all-too-familiar

shrill of a constable's whistle. The thin soles of her boots slapped the snow as she sped down the narrow sidewalk, shoving her way through the crowds. A gray-haired matron screamed and dropped an armful of packages. Three grimy urchins joined in the chase, dogging her heels until they became bored.

The whistle sounded again, closer this time. She plunged into the busy street, darting between a hansom cab and an omnibus, narrowly missing the flailing hooves of the startled horses. A driver's jeering curse rang in her ears.

She rounded a corner into a narrow alley, then threw herself into a doorway and waited, her chest heaving as the slam of running feet passed and subsided. Without waiting to get her breath back, she sank to a crouch on the filthy stoop and dug her teeth into the crunchy apple. She knew she was behaving like a piglet, but she was beyond caring. Her empty stomach knotted around the food. The core dropped from her fingers. She hugged herself as a sharp cramp seized her.

It passed as quickly as it had come, leaving her shivering in its aftermath. The overhanging roofs above blocked even the meager winter sunlight. She pulled her threadbare shawl tight around her shoulders, fearing all the stolen apples in the world couldn't fill the yawning void inside her.

She squared her chin, determined to rally her flagging spirits. What did she have to whine and moan about? It had finally stopped snowing and she was free at last after being crammed in a steamer cabin for the past month with five other women, most of whom had never discovered the pleasures of daily bathing. It had taken the last of the money from the sale of her father's watch to book passage from Australia to England, but she was no longer reliant on the fickle charity of Amelia Winters. She was her own mistress now and London was hers.

She shoved herself to her feet and made her way toward

the street, stepping gingerly over a snoring drunk clutching a gin bottle. Her robbery had already been forgotten, replaced by the fresh scandal of a skinny ragamuffin caught stealing a gentleman's purse.

She wandered the streets, wondering how the city could have grown so much smaller and danker while she was away. Horse-drawn vehicles thronged the roadway, churning the snow into black slush. No one took any notice of her. She was just one of a sea of faces in this vast slum.

Before she realized it, she'd turned down a finer street with freshly salted cobblestones and broad sidewalks flanked by shops. Gas lamps flickered in shop windows, illuminating shining displays of goods nestled in fresh boughs of pine and holly. She paused at the window of a toy shop to watch a mechanical St. Nicholas beat a tiny green drum.

As she turned away, she came face-to-face with her own image tacked to a lamppost. A sigh caught in her throat. Was this one photograph to haunt her forever? She pulled down the notice, her hands trembling more in shock than cold. The sketch was a very good one, obviously done by a professional from her father's old tintype. Her eyes widened at the staggering amount of the reward. She hadn't a halfpenny to her name and she was worth more than any notorious criminal stalking the London alleys.

Two words seemed to leap out of the elaborate script—
LOST CHILD.

She leaned her forehead against the cold lamppost, no longer able to fight the despair. More lost than Justin could ever know, she thought. Her hatred for him had sustained her for years. Now that it was gone, she felt nothing. Nothing at all but a desperate yearning for warmth. He had shed his sunlight across her soul, then slammed the door, leaving her cold and alone. Would he return to New Zealand, seeking the woman he had known only as Emily Scarlet? By taking the coward's way out, she would never have to know if he didn't.

"Move along, girlie. We don't need your kind scaring the customers away." A fat shopkeeper shooed at her with his apron.

Emily gave him such an evil look that he began to bellow for a constable. She broke into a run, feeling as if she might run forever and never get anywhere. She had no intention of trading one kind of cell for another, although the jail might be warmer than the park had been last night. Dusk was nearing and the temperature was plunging rapidly. Warm tears blurred her vision.

She never saw the soft, immovable object in her path until she slammed into it. She went sprawling. A torrent of packages rained down on her head.

She glared upward, rubbing her brow and preparing to unleash a string of curses on the hapless shopper.

"Gor blimey, if it ain't Emily Claire Scarborough, as I live an' breathe!"

"Tansy?" Emily whispered in awe. She clambered to her feet, shoving boxes off her lap.

Surely this statuesque creature could not be her Tansy. A feathered hat perched jauntily on her nest of ebony curls. A dress of yellow satin sculpted her ample curves in scandalous relief, then tapered to scalloped ruffles piled high over a bustle. But surely no one else could possess eyes as big and blue as Dresden saucers.

"Tansy?" she repeated, her voice rising to a squeak.

"Oh, Em!"

All of her doubts flew away as Tansy threw her arms around her, enveloping her in a perfumed embrace. Time melted and suddenly they were just two frightened little girls clinging to each other in a lonely attic.

Emily drew back, still clutching Tansy's arms, loath to relinquish her familiar warmth. "What happened to you? Did you inherit a fortune? Rob a bank? Finally snare a rich gentleman for a husband?"

Tansy cocked her head, preening with guileless abandon. "Not yet, but I might very soon. I'm workin' fer Mrs. Rose now."

Emily frowned as the name struck a discordant note in her memory. "Mrs. Rose? She must pay you very well indeed. Are you her personal maid?"

"She don't pay me at all. It's 'er gentlemen callers that pays me."

Emily felt her mouth fall open in shock. Tansy gently pushed her chin up with the tip of her finger. Her finger was now smooth without a hint of a callus.

Emily swallowed hard. "You're working at a bordello?"

"That I am. Most of the gentlemen are very kind with gentle hands an' open purses. They luvs me, they do. They all tell me so. I'm one o' their favorites."

"I don't understand. What happened to Miss Winters?"

Tansy's full lips tightened in a pout. "She tossed me out, she did, after yer guardian plucked 'er nerves. Ya should 'ave been there. 'E tore into the old 'ag right and proper."

Emily's throat tightened. "You saw him?"

"Lordy, did I! And ain't 'e the prettiest fellow I ever did see!"

"Yes," Emily admitted softly. "He is that."

"Some of my gentlemen friends say 'e's rough and dangerous like, but I knows better. Gave me money, 'e did. Told me if I ever needed 'elp to march straight to Grymwilde Mansion in Portland Square an' ask for 'im. If I 'adn't been set on provin' I could stand on me own two feet, I might 'ave done it, too."

For a dazed moment Emily's pain was so intense she couldn't see straight. She barely felt Tansy's gentle touch on her arm.

"Where've ya been, girl? Why'd ya go and run off like that without tellin' me?"

"I didn't run off. Barney and Doreen carted me off on some mad scheme of Miss Winters's."

Tansy's full lips tightened. "I knew them bloomin' buggers was up to no good. I shoulda told that nice gentleman when 'e came lookin' fer ya. 'E'd 'ave cooked both their skinny gooses."

"No!" Besieged by sudden panic, Emily gripped her arm. "You must swear to me that if your paths should cross again, you won't tell him you saw me. He mustn't know I'm in London."

"What is it, Em? Are ya in some sort of trouble? 'E's a good man. I know 'e'd lend a 'elpin' 'and if ya'd let 'im."

Emily pressed her eyes shut, trying to banish the memory of Justin's graceful tan hands against her skin. When she opened them, they burned like raw flames. "He can't help me now. I've done something terrible. And if he finds out, he'll despise me forever."

"Come now, dearie. What could be that terrible?"

Falling in love with Justin. Making him fall in love with her while lying to him with every breath. Emily just shook her head, unable to choke a reply past the icy lump in her throat.

Tansy's blue eyes were painfully earnest. "Why don't ya come with me, then? Mrs. Rose'd be glad to 'ave ya and those fine gentlemen would gobble a pretty thing like you right up! You'd be able to earn yer own money right and proper with good honest work. You'd never 'ave to rely on anyone's charity again."

Emily almost shivered to hear her own thoughts echoed so clearly. For one shocking instant she was tempted. But the thought of a stranger's hands touching her the way Justin's had filled her with revulsion.

"I'm sorry, Tansy. I'm glad you're happy, but I simply can't."

They faced each other, awkward again, strangers on a busy street. The passing shoppers stared curiously. Emily caught a glimpse of her reflection in a darkened shop window—a small figure in a shabby black dress, torn stockings, and ragged shawl. Her bare fingers poked out the ends of her gloves. How dare she accost a fine lady on the street?

Her worst fears were founded as Tansy thrust a hand in her purse and pulled out a shilling. "I 'aven't any pound notes with me. Won't ya let me buy ya a nice meat pie?"

Emily stared at the gleaming coin. The warm, yeasty aroma of a nearby bakery wafted to her nostrils. She couldn't live on charity again. Not even Tansy's.

She put her hands behind her back to ease the temptation. "Oh, no. I'm quite full, thank you. I just ate at a friend's house, you see, and had a splendid helping of roast pheasant. And gravy. A whole tureen of gravy." She started to walk backward. "Tarts, too. Those charming ones you douse in brandy and set aflame. I ate half a tray of those, then polished them off with a pitcher of cream. You know how I love cream." She clasped her hands over her stomach. "Why, my little belly is so stuffed, I feel like a Christmas turkey!"

The jostling crowd was beginning to come between them. She caught a glimpse of Tansy perched like a bewildered canary among her scattered packages.

"Em, wait! Don't go!" she cried.

Emily lifted her hand in a cheery wave. "I'm glad you're happy in your new situation. Perhaps we can meet for tea soon."

A cloaked man tipped his hat to Tansy, offering his assistance in retrieving her packages. Emily took advantage of her divided attention to slip into a merry throng of carolers and be swept away on a tide of "God Rest Ye Merry Gentlemen."

As she dodged around a corner, the carolers went on, their laughter ringing on the crisp air. An emptiness worse than hunger seized her heart. She had learned all she needed to know of Christmas as Justin read to a circle of rapt Maori in his resonant voice.

Grymwilde Mansion in Portland Square.

The lamplighters had come out to coax the gas lamps to flickering life above her head. Her feet moved of their own accord, although even exertion wasn't enough to stave off the deepening chill. The bells of St. Paul's began to chime. She wondered if Penfeld was curled up somewhere before a cozy fire, savoring their sweet refrain and sipping a cup of hot tea.

Grymwilde Mansion in Portland Square.

The cacophony of the city streets faded to a muted hush. She stood in the falling darkness at the neck of a broad street lined by wrought-iron fences and towering oaks. Their naked branches brushed stark fingers against the sky. Even the snow was clean here, laid in a milky blanket over rolling lawns and terra-cotta fountains. Emily felt like an intruder from another land.

Grymwilde Mansion in Portland Square.

Did she really think she could abide in the same city, walk the same streets without even trying to steal a glimpse of him? Did he sit sad and alone in a deserted house with only his regrets for company? Did he wander a cold, snowy garden, dreaming of her?

There was only one way to find out.

The sky began to spit snow. Sighing, Emily pulled her shawl up over her hair and hastened through the deepening dusk.

*C*hapter *17*

· ❀ ·

Only the promise of a brighter tomorrow
for the both of us could have dragged me away
from you. . . .

*J*ustin stood at the window and watched the fat snow-flakes drift down to fur the lawn. Despite his longing for sunlight and sea, the snow still captivated him with its purity, its eternal promise of fresh hope.

"Justin, oh, Justin, my darling, where are you?"

He blew out a breath of frustration, fogging the cold windowpane. Even the heavy damask of the drapes wasn't enough to deter his mother. She swept them aside, smothering him in the cloying fog of her perfume.

"*There* you are! I was beginning to think you were hiding under the bed as you used to do when you were little."

"Fat lot of good that would have done me. You would have just sent the butler to drag me out by my heels."

She slapped his arm with her fan. "Don't be a bad boy. You promised to be civil to my guests, not spend the evening lurking behind the drapes. It was heartless of you to deny me my annual Christmas ball. The least you can do is grace my modest fête with your presence."

Justin sighed. The duchess's idea of a modest fête was cramming a hundred guests into the octagonal drawing room. "I warned you I wouldn't be good company, Mother. I have more pressing matters on my mind than playing Simile with a bevy of sotted swells."

"I suppose you mean that infernal child. You must stop this ridiculous fretting. You've got the finest men in the business on it. They'll find the little lad soon enough."

"It's a girl," he explained for the hundredth time. "A girl."

"Speaking of girls," his mother said, rescuing a perfumed handkerchief from the bodice of her dress, "there's that charming du Pardieu woman I told you about. You simply must meet her daughter. Quite a bewitching little creature. Fresh out of seminary." She fluttered the hanky in the air like a flag of surrender, calling out, "Over here, dear."

Justin jerked her arm down, cringing at her shrill titter. Now that she'd regained one rightful Winthrop heir, her primary mission in life seemed to be to ensure he produced another one. "I don't want to meet the charming du Pardieu woman and I don't want to meet her daughter. If Queen Victoria is here, I don't want to meet her either. I wish to be left alone."

The duchess's iron-gray ringlets quivered in indignation. "Very well, then. Perhaps I'll let them think you a savage."

She sailed away, her formidable bosom jutting out like the prow of some mighty ship. The staring guests milled in her wake. Justin shook his head, understanding for the first time why his father, in his own besotted youth, had ordered a figurehead carved in her honor.

He turned away from the window, tugging irritably at his starched collar. Perhaps he should make more of an effort to be pleasant. He might want to bring Emily back here someday after they were wed, and he didn't want her reputation besmirched by his.

He wandered through the crowd, managing a smile here, a friendly nod there. The diplomacy of his years with the Maori seemed to have deserted him. He felt stiff and awkward, beset by the painful shyness that had troubled him as a child.

His sister Edith was pounding out "Joy to the World" on the grand piano. He winced, his heart aching for the poor beleaguered instrument. Her husband Harold had thrown back his head and was baying along with her. Or was it Herbert? Justin frowned. He still could not keep his sisters' husbands straight.

He angled toward a punch bowl ringed with glossy leaves of holly, hoping to find a safe haven in its rum-soaked depths.

A gloved hand caught his arm in a velvety vise. "Hello, Justin. Haven't you a moment to spare for an old friend?" The familiar voice had the huskiness of mellow brandy ignited by flame.

"Suzanne," he said, turning to greet his former fiancée and lover.

The years had been kind to her, softening her nubile beauty to glowing maturity, betraying her only in the faint puffiness beneath her eyes. Sweeping wings of auburn framed her face. Justin knew he should feel something for her, some hint of affection, or even nostalgia, but he felt nothing. She might have been a stranger. She must have sensed his detachment, for her grip tightened.

"I thought perhaps you'd care to dance. I fear my husband is more interested in discussing the Bank Holidays Act with his friends than he is in dancing with me."

Justin glanced at the man she indicated—a dapper, gray-haired chap much older than she. And doubtlessly very wealthy.

His first instinct was to decline, but her possessive grip dissuaded him. "If you'll honor me . . . ?" he said, spreading his arms.

She stepped into them, smiling. Edith had switched to

a tinkling little waltz, and several of the guests had begun to dance.

"Do you still play?" Suzanne said, breaking the awkward silence.

"Only when everyone else is asleep."

She laughed briefly, but stopped when she realized he was serious. "Did you ever make it to Vienna to study?"

He swept her past the gleaming windows. "No. I took a . . . detour along the way."

"Dreams are like that sometimes. We give up what we really want to reach for something else. If we could only go back . . ." Her wistful voice trailed off.

She rested her head against his shoulder, and for a moment Justin was content to hold someone else who understood the terrible cost of hesitation. But as they spun in the arms of the music, his heart balked, remembering another night when he had waltzed beneath the merry twinkle of the stars. He had danced to the wrong music, held the wrong woman, but nothing in his life had ever felt so right.

He closed his eyes, breathing in not the delicate lavender of Suzanne's perfume, but the haunting aroma of vanilla warmed by sun-honeyed skin. His body responded to the dangerous provocation with a will of its own.

"Perhaps we could meet again. My husband travels frequently in his work. He's leaving for Belgium next week."

The breathless voice scattered his memories. He opened his eyes. Suzanne was gazing up at him, her lips parted in glistening invitation.

"Oh, God." He pushed her away, holding her at arm's length. "I'm terribly sorry."

"For what?"

His words echoed his despair. "We can't go back, Suzanne. We can't ever go back."

He drew away from her, frantic to escape her crushed bewilderment. He pressed his way through the crowd, snatching a full bottle of rum from the tray of a liveried footman.

"But, Your Grace, that's for the punch!"

"Not anymore, it isn't," he replied, escaping into the deserted peace of a darkened sitting room.

Tall windows framed the front lawn in a swirling vista of moonlight and snow. Justin leaned against the window frame and tilted the bottle to his lips. The familiar heat failed to warm him or soothe his temper. His fingers bit into the smooth glass.

In the drawing room Herbert or Harold was crooning some maudlin ballad about a man who searched the world over for his love, only to find her in the arms of another man. Groaning, Justin closed his eyes and rapped his forehead against the icy pane.

When he opened them, someone was standing just outside the gate.

Snowflakes danced in his vision. He blinked, thinking he might have imagined it. But the small figure clad in black was still there, clinging in eerie stillness to the wrought-iron gate.

It must be a beggar child, he thought.

He had spent much time in the past few weeks reacquainting himself with the orphans and urchins of the London streets. There were no hungry children among the Maori. What was planted by one was harvested by all. It had appalled him to see the children of London starving in the slums. Perhaps one of those he had helped had sent this bedraggled creature to his doorstep to beg for food.

A blast of wind rattled the windowpane. How very cold she must be! He would have Penfeld invite her into the kitchen for a hot meal.

As he turned from the window, a thought brushed him with icy fingers, an idea both so horrible and so magnificent, it chilled him to the bone.

He narrowed his eyes. The figure was still there. Motionless. Waiting.

He tore across the room, swearing under his breath as his knee slammed into a brass pedestal crowned by a glowering bust of Prince Albert. He burst into the drawing room and shoved his way through the crowd, ignoring the crash of a footman's tray and the startled cries of alarm.

"Good Lord, where's the lad off to now?"

"Careful there, Millicent, he trod all over my train."

"Where's the fire, son? Shall we call out the brigade?"

Justin flew across the entranceway and flung open the front door. Frigid air burned his lungs. Tears of cold stung his eyes. He blinked rapidly to dispel them.

Snowflakes tumbled and spun in a wind-driven waltz, frosting the world in white. Leaving the front door gaping, he ran, sliding across the icy lawn to the street.

He searched both ways. The street was empty. The iron gate swung in the wind, creaking an eerie refrain.

Justin sank down on the curb and rested his elbows on his knees. He stared blindly into the night, wondering if he was going mad and listening to the falling snowflakes whisper promises they could never keep.

Emily's long strides ate up the pavement. Her shoulder slammed into a passing chimney sweep, knocking his tools into the snow.

"Watch where you're goin', you little fool!" he growled.

She jerked up his metal broom and swung around to press the sharp bristles to his throat. "Why don't you watch who you're calling a fool, pudding head."

He recoiled and lifted his palms in surrender. She tossed him the broom.

"And a merry Christmas to you, too," he called after her as she marched on.

Emily was madder than hell.

She rushed on to nowhere, nursing the cold ashes of her bitterness to raging flame. She toyed with her anger, ripping the familiar comfort of the old scar wide open. She knew her anger well. It had been her friend, enabling her to hold her head high despite the giggles and slights. It had been her enemy, driving her to stomp toes and tie Cecille's braids in knots. And it had been her lover, sustaining her through cold, dark nights shivering in her attic bed by building a stone wall of fury against the despair.

Most of the shop windows were dark now, their owners gone home to sit in front of crackling fires. Emily heard the crunch of a footfall behind her. She glanced over her shoulder, expecting the chimney sweep's broom to slam into her head. A shadow vanished into a narrow alley. She almost laughed aloud. Anyone contemplating robbing her had to be desperate indeed.

She crossed a broad street where light and laughter spilled from a corner coffeehouse. A familiar scrap of paper on a lamppost caught her eye. A man stared as he passed, and Emily pulled her shawl up around her face. The likeness in the tintype was still there. Not everyone in London was as blindly stupid as Justin.

Poor, pathetic Justin.

Instead of finding him mooning for her in a deserted house, she had found him gliding past a shining expanse of glass, a beautiful stranger in his arms. He had slipped back into his life of noble decadence with alarming ease, leaving her once again on the outside, looking in.

Perhaps if she possessed the sophistication of his waltz partner, she would have known he was only toying with her on the island. Why shouldn't he? She was the only woman in miles except for the Maori, and he had already seduced his way through their ranks before she arrived. Justin wasn't the pathetic one. She was.

That night on the beach she had allowed him to touch the most tender part of her, both in body and soul. Yet tonight he had clasped another woman to his heart as he had once held her beneath a foggy pearl of a moon. He had been terribly handsome in his black evening garb, the rakish sweep of his hair over his starched collar oddly endearing. A wretched sense of betrayal closed her throat.

Her hands clenched into fists. She couldn't let the pain in. Not even for an instant. If she did, she would curl into a little ball right there in the street and they would find her in the morning, just another frozen casualty.

She marched on, achingly aware of her every misery. The soles of her boots were soaked through. Her naked fingers were numb. The blowing snow stung her cheeks like tiny shards of glass.

A well-dressed couple passed her. The woman tittered and the man raked her with a contemptuous glance. They knew she didn't belong there. She didn't belong anywhere.

A bakery door opened in a blast of warmth, sugaring the air with the tantalizing aroma of gingerbread. Emily stopped dead, as paralyzed and vulnerable as if she'd been caught naked on Piccadilly Circus. She crept nearer and pressed her nose to the icy window.

Fresh rows of pastries cooled on the shelves, swollen to bursting with red and amber fruit. Flat scones rolled in cinnamon dotted the gleaming counter. Emily's breath fogged the glass.

Suddenly she was hungry. Wickedly, savagely hungry.

Her father had once taken her to such a place. He had lifted her in his strong arms so she could see the steaming array of treasures, then allowed her to pick three of the most tempting. They had sat in the bakery the rest of that cold winter afternoon, gorging themselves on pie and pastries until they had both retired to bed that night with aching bellies.

The door swung open again. A plump woman with her hands jammed deep in a fur muff was ushered into the bakery by her towering escort. Without hesitation Emily slipped in behind them.

She lurked behind the man's cloak while they made their choices. As the baker turned to fill a sack with powdery crumpets, Emily saw her chance.

She reached over the counter and snatched a fat tart, burning her fingers with its delicious heat.

"Ho there, little lady, you can't do that."

It was not the baker, but the man who spoke, his jovial tones ringing in the silence. Emily fled for the door. She tripped over the threshold and stumbled into the snow.

"Constable! Stop this thief!"

The baker burst out behind her. She scrambled to her feet, but had barely taken two steps when she heard pounding footsteps coming from both directions. The blast of twin whistles deafened her. She spun around, not knowing which way to run. Her hesitation cost her dearly. The baker's genial customer caught her by the back of her dress and lifted her high.

"There now, little one, quit squirming. You mustn't be such a wicked gel. Wicked gels end up in jail, you know."

He lowered her, but before she could flee, a uniformed constable caught her arm and wrenched it behind her back. The tart slipped from her fingers and plopped into the dirty snow. A heartbroken wail escaped her.

Caught in an implacable tangle of arms and legs, she fought wildly. Her foot connected with the shin of one of the constables with a satisfying thud. The other one howled as her teeth sank into his wrist. The shawl slid from her hair.

"Stand back, lad!" one of them shouted. "We don't need no crowds. She's a rabid wench."

A hand caught in her curls and tugged her head straight back, stilling her struggles. Tears of pain stung her eyes.

"Aye, a rabid wench she is. But don't worry, gents. I'll muzzle her right and proper."

As Emily stared up into black, beady eyes glistening with lust and greed, she moaned in utter dread.

He jerked her hard against him and grinned at the

gaping constables. "Mr. Barney Dobbins, mates, at yer service."

Somewhere a child was laughing.

Justin sat bolt upright in bed. His heart pounded in his throat, deafening him for a long moment before the shift of the coals on the fire penetrated his panicked haze. The blankets bound his legs in tangled cords, as twisted as the dreams that haunted his waking hours, and made sleep a nightly torment.

There was something he should know. Something hovering at the edge of his nightmares, taunting him.

He threw back the heavy drapes of the bed and struggled out of the feather tick. Like everything else in this house, the bed was a monstrosity. Every inch of the dark mahogany had been carved with the serpentine vines and pronged leaves of miniature Venus's-flytraps. He dreaded climbing into it each night for fear the mattress would swallow him without a trace.

A thread of light shone beneath Penfeld's adjoining door. The valet never slept without his lamp lit. Justin pulled a dressing gown over his nakedness, wishing light were enough to keep his own demons at bay.

He marched down the long, curving staircase, raking his hair out of his eyes. No one would dare trouble him. The servants had grown accustomed to him prowling the house at all hours. They gave him wide berth, frightened of the gaunt shadows beneath his eyes. He was beginning to feel as mad as they must think him.

He was the Duke of Winthrop now. He could buy a dozen gold mines. He could travel to Vienna and study music, as he had always longed to do. He could rent an opera house to feature nothing but his own symphonies night after night. But all he craved was the warmth of sunlight on his face and the music of Emily's laughter.

His shin slammed into a wooden pedestal in the dark and he bit off an oath. There wasn't an inch of grace or simplicity to be found in this cramped house. He grabbed the teetering vase atop the pedestal and threw it. It shattered against the far wall with a satisfying crash. Somewhere in the house a door closed as a curious servant beat a wise retreat.

The moon-drenched drawing room beckoned him. He slid onto the piano bench and sat in brooding silence. The snow lay in a serene blanket beyond the tall windows. Midnight bells chimed in the distance, and he realized with a shock that it was Christmas Eve.

Christmas Eve. The night when hope had first entered the world. But not for him. Not while David's child was out there somewhere, shivering in the dark. To him, the echo of the bells sounded the death knell of his dreams.

He lifted his gaze to meet the impassive blue eyes of Claire Scarborough's doll. She reigned on the piano with the aplomb of a ragged little queen. No one had dared to do so much as dust her since Justin had placed her there. He glared at her now, almost hating her for the secrets she withheld. What would she say if she could speak? Would she curse him, reproach him for his terrible cowardice?

He crooked his fingers over the keys and began to play. He chose not his own music, but the melancholy strains of Beethoven's "Für Elise". Instead of losing himself in the music as he'd hoped, the notes flailed him like exquisite barbs.

What a fool he had been! He had let go of Emily to chase a phantom. Now he had neither.

He felt as if he were moldering in this mausoleum. He hungered to feel the powdery sand between his toes, to hear Trini's sonorous laughter and the welcoming song of the Maori shimmering on the balmy air. His hands flew over the keys, stroking, caressing the smooth ivory as he longed to caress the heated satin of Emily's skin. But how could he face her, knowing he had abandoned David's child to the merciless streets of London? Emily deserved more in life than a desolate man crippled by guilt.

His hands faltered. His fingers were stiff and callused, his left hand still inflexible from lack of practice. He struck the wrong note, then slammed his fist down on the keys in a burst of despair.

The discordant notes jarred the air. Justin dropped his face into his hands. Emily's features were already growing misty in his memory, blurring like a hazy watercolor into another face, a face he knew as well as his own.

A polite cough broke the silence. Justin's head flew up. A dark shape was silhouetted against the moonlight, and for one crazy moment he thought it was David's ghost.

Bentley Chalmers's clipped tones rang out. "They've found her, sir."

Justin blinked, fighting to clear the fog of confusion from his brain. His thoughts were so rife with Emily that for a weary moment he didn't know who the man was talking about—Emily or Claire?

Chalmers turned his bowler in his hands. "They've found the girl, sir. She's alive."

"Alive?" he whispered.

The piano keys blurred before his grateful eyes, and a chiming carol broke free in his head as if all the bells of London had started to ring at once.

Chapter 18

❦

It seems only yesterday you were toddling
after me, tugging at my coattails with your
chubby little hands. . . .

"Criminy, Penfeld, I asked to be shaved, not beheaded."
Justin bit back a yelp as the razor nicked his throat.

Penfeld dabbed at the welling dollop of blood with a
towel, his hands shaking visibly. The water in the ceramic
washbasin at his elbow was stained a pleasant shade of
pink. "I am frightfully sorry, sir. I must confess I'm a bit
nervous myself."

"*You're* nervous? What about me? I've never been a
father before." He ducked beneath the approaching blade
and bounded out of the chair to the mirror. Stroking the
foreign smoothness of his chin, he cocked his head sideways, studying his profile. "Do I look like a suitable
papa?"

Beaming proudly, Penfeld wiped the soap from the
gleaming blade with a flourish. "The very model of paternal decorum."

Justin flicked a stray hair from the shoulder of his coat,
then cast the ebony strands scattered around his chair a
rueful glance. "I hope this is worth it. I feel naked."

"But you look splendid."

Justin jerked his coat straight, then reached to his chest for a watch that wasn't there. He remembered the last time he had seen it, gleaming against the satin of Emily's skin. A smile touched his lips. If things went well today, he would retrieve it soon enough.

"What time is it, Penfeld?"

The valet checked his own watch. "Eleven-oh-two, sir, approximately three minutes since you last asked."

"Eleven-oh-two? Oh, dear God." He paced to the door, then stopped with his hand on the knob. "Is my tie crooked?"

It wasn't, but Penfeld dutifully straightened it. Justin marched to the door again, but faltered halfway there.

His massive bed was swimming in a frivolous sea of lace and velvet. Sweeping away a dainty chintz frock, he sank down on the edge of the mattress and hooked his heels beneath the tester to keep from being sucked into a whirlpool of tiny silk gloves and mink muffs.

"In a few minutes David's daughter is going to walk through that front door. The first thing I must do is tell her the truth about her father." He lifted his bleak gaze to Penfeld. "How will I find the courage?"

"Shall I tell her, sir?"

A rush of affection flooded Justin. Penfeld had been known to blanch with terror at the mere sight of a child. "No. But you are a treasure to offer."

Emboldened by Penfeld's devotion, he jumped to his feet. "One more thing."

"Yes, sir?"

Justin gave him his warmest smile. "Merry Christmas, Penfeld."

The valet snapped to attention. "And a merry Christmas to you, too, sir."

As Justin strode down the corridor, a cheery whistle rose unbidden to his lips.

"Good morning, Mary," he called out, startling a shocked maid into dropping her load. Little polished boots and kid slippers scattered across the plush carpet. As he tripped down the stairs, one of his brothers-in-law passed him, his long nose tucked into a newspaper. "And a good day to you, Harvey," Justin said.

"Harold," the man mumbled, turning the page.

Justin stopped, frowned, then bounced back up three steps and peered into the man's face. "Why, I'll be damned, it is Harold, isn't it!"

As he hit the bottom step, he grinned to discover the first floor of the mansion in utter chaos. Servants scurried from room to room, polishing gas lamps, scrubbing the baseboards, and draping the banisters with fragrant garlands of cedar.

A toothless cook thrust a tray of steaming biscuits under his nose. "Thirty dozen, Yer Grace, just as you asked for."

The delicious aroma filled his nostrils. "Mmmm. Superb, Gracie! Did you bake any with raisins? Children like raisins, don't they?"

"Mine allus did, sir."

He tweaked her plump cheek. "Twelve dozen more, then. Loaded with raisins."

"Aye, my lord. Right away." She bobbed a curtsy and scampered back toward the kitchen.

A disgruntled butler caught his elbow. "I really must protest, my lord. Someone has left a pony in the library."

Justin didn't even slow. "Imagine that. Take him into the ballroom. He'll have more room to frolic."

He came to a dead halt at the door of the drawing room, his eyes misting with wonder. Within the meager space of a day, the room had been transformed into a Christmas miracle. A towering tree crowned the corner, tickling his nose with the pungent scent of spruce. Edith perched on a ladder, lighting the tiny candles nestled in its boughs while his younger sisters, Lily and Millicent, giggled and offered her suggestions.

"What did you do, brother?" Lily called out. "Buy out every toy store in London?"

"Only the ones that would open on Christmas Eve."

The flash of his purse had opened more than one door, and there was hardly room to walk for all the toys. There were mechanical elephants and drum-beating bears, skipping ropes and miniature stoves, paints and charcoals, clockwork trains and even a cluttered dollhouse with a tiny grand piano. Two mechanical birds twittered from a golden cage hanging off one of the gasoliers.

Justin had no idea what a girl of ten would enjoy, so he had bought one of everything—including sacks of glass marbles and a handsome regiment of iron Napoleon soldiers. Propped against the sleek spokes of a velocipede was a shiny sled of just the sort he had always wanted as a boy. His father had denied him, but he would deny David's daughter nothing. He had already robbed her of too much in her life.

His mother swept in and gave the room a droll inspection. "I'm glad to see you're not planning on spoiling the child."

"Of course not. I shall rule her with a firm but gentle hand," Justin replied, kissing her perfumed cheek.

A grubby yardboy came pounding through the door, gasping for breath. "There's a carriage comin' this way, my lord. It looks to be the one."

Justin swallowed a jagged flare of panic. "Well done, lad." He tossed the boy a coin, then threw back his head and bellowed, "Penfeld!"

He took one last look around to reassure himself that everything was perfect. A dazzling array of dolls blanketed the top of the piano, pouting and simpering in yards of satin and lace. Out of their elegant depths protruded a grimy little porcelain nose. Seized by a strange compulsion, Justin rescued the doll he had found in Claire's stark attic and set her on the music stand, arranging her stained skirts with painstaking care. Her haughty gaze seemed to mock him.

Penfeld came bouncing into the room, pausing long enough to pick an invisible speck of lint from Justin's trousers. As a plain black carriage clattered up the drive, word flew through the mansion and the drawing room filled.

The servants lined up on one side, making last-second adjustments to their caps and aprons and trying not to crane their necks to look out the window. Justin's sisters whispered together on the other side, backed by their stalwart husbands and the indomitable duchess.

The air quivered with a nervous hush as Justin took his place at the foot of the handsome tree.

When Penfeld tried to slip away and join the servants, Justin clutched his arm. "Stay, please," he muttered out of the corner of his mouth. "You can catch me if I faint."

They all watched through the windows as the driver threw open the carriage door. A bony hand protruded and Justin stiffened as Amelia Winters climbed out. His only regret lay in having to pay her the reward he had offered. It was her perverse good fortune that the child had returned to the only home she had known, however lacking in care and comfort it might have been.

The driver cast the house a surly look, and Justin recognized him as the same lad he had met at the seminary. His steps were hampered by a definite limp, and even from this distance Justin could see the mottled bruise blacking one of his eyes.

Justin's breath froze in his throat as a diminutive figure in a simple navy frock and wide-brimmed bonnet climbed out of the carriage, disdaining the driver's assistance.

Penfeld leaned over and whispered, "A bit large for a ten-year-old, isn't she?"

Justin frowned.

The severe parade made its way up the walk with the driver lagging behind. As the butler ushered them in, Miss Winters's cane clicked on the marble tile. The girl appeared in the doorway.

Justin's heart tripped into double time. He locked his hands at the small of his back and forced a smile he feared was more grimace than grin.

She didn't even look up. Head bowed and hands shoved into a ratty muff, she marched past the somber column of servants and family, straight toward him. His frown deepened. There was something in the sway of her hips . . . a false submissiveness to her sullen stance that struck a disturbing chord of recognition. A bell of warning jangled in his head.

She stopped dead in front of him. He gazed at the top of her bonnet, holding his breath without realizing it. Even before she slowly tilted her face to his, he knew what he would see. Tumbled chestnut curls framed by the bonnet's brim. A mocking dimple slashed in a plump cheek. Coffee-brown eyes glittering not in merriment, but bitter triumph.

Her hand came out of the muff and crossed his face with a resounding crack. Someone in the room gasped. He stood there, paralyzed, feeling all the blood drain from his face except for the vivid burn of her handprint against his cheek.

Tilting her pert nose in the air, she dismissed him coolly and turned to Penfeld. "You may show me to my room now. The attic will do if you've nothing more suitable. I've grown quite fond of rats and pigeons over the years. They're far better company than most people."

Penfeld made a helpless gurgle, but Justin gave him a curt nod and he recovered enough to lead her past the gaping servants and white-faced family. She marched past the piles of toys and games without so much as a disdainful glance, but at the piano she paused.

A strange emotion flickered across her face, squeezing

Justin's heart like a vise. Ignoring all the elegantly garbed and coiffed dolls, Emily picked up the ragged doll on the music stand and hugged it to her breast. As Penfeld led her from the drawing room, the doll peered at Justin over her stiffened shoulder and he would have almost sworn he saw mocking amusement sparkle in her vapid blue eyes.

C*hapter* 19

·🐚·

I still long to think of you as a child. . . .

One by one the candle flames winked out, leaving the Christmas tree shrouded in darkness. Justin stood unmoving, hands in pockets, as the maid set down the brass snuffer and brushed past him, averting her eyes. Two footmen wheeled away the shiny velocipede, their voices lowered to somber whispers.

Outside the drawing room windows the sky faded from dull pewter to smoky black. Servants came and went, sweeping away the last traces of mistletoe and tinsel until Justin stood alone, the naked tree towering over him like the specter of his own folly. He reached up and plucked a stray holly leaf from the gilt cage where the mechanical birds now hung in silence.

Penfeld appeared in the doorway, clutching a stuffed bear nearly as big as himself. He cleared his throat before speaking. "Sir, there's still the matter of the pony."

Justin ran his thumb over the sharp points of the leaf, remembering how Trini had laid the sprig of greenery at

Emily's feet to welcome her into their lives. At least the native hadn't been foolish enough to lay his heart there.

"Have the groom stable it for tonight. It can be returned in the morning."

"Aye, sir. As you wish." The valet hesitated as if he would have liked to say something more, then hefted the bear to his shoulder and lumbered away.

How could he have been such a fool? Justin wondered. Emily had scattered clues like the crimson petals of the pohutukawas along every path he took, but his own obsessive desire had blinded him. Could he blame only himself, though, when she had deliberately and maliciously deceived him about her identity? As the full realization of her betrayal struck him, a new emotion ribboned through his self-contempt—anger, dark and compelling and dangerous. His gaze lifted to the ceiling above his head.

His terse interview with Miss Winters had provided some of the answers he sought, but he had some questions of his own for the elusive Miss Scarborough. Ignoring the prick of its points, he crumpled the shiny leaf in his hand and started for the stairs.

Justin scaled a mountain of pink taffeta and picked his way through a jungle of ribbons and sashes. Toys, books, and beribboned frocks littered the burgundy carpet of the corridor outside Emily's room as if someone had gathered careless armfuls and tossed them out the door.

He turned the knob, expecting the door to be locked. To his mingled regret and relief, it swung open soundlessly beneath his touch.

The only sounds in the room were the crackle of the flames on the grate and a slow, lazy creak.

Emily perched sidesaddle on the rocking horse he had ordered brought down from the attic that morning. She rocked idly, her pensive profile turned toward the dancing flames. The fresh shock of seeing her there buffeted Justin's senses, igniting a raw hunger to jerk her up and shake the answers out of her. Or did he just seek any pretense to drag her into his arms? A hint of white cotton stocking peeked out from beneath the navy wool of her skirt. He had seen her garbed in far less, yet the innocent sight made the blood roar in his ears.

He pushed the door shut and leaned against it, arms crossed. His puzzled family had witnessed enough of their private little war. This battle would be their own.

The moments creaked away beneath the rhythmic shift of Emily's thighs. Finally, she lifted her hand. A satin glove trimmed in tiny pearls dangled from her pinkie. "A bit small for me, don't you think?"

With agonizing effort Justin kept his face smooth and expressionless. "I thought you were just a baby when your father died. The only photograph I ever saw was the one in the watch. David used to tell me stories about you. About the time you ate the buttons off his coat. The time you crawled onto the window ledge and fell asleep in the flower box. Those were hardly the actions of a girl on the verge of womanhood."

Her winsome smile never reached her eyes. "No, but they were Daddy's favorite stories."

"How was I to know?"

The glove fluttered to the floor. "You might have tried the conventional ways. A visit. A letter."

The curtain between past and present seemed to blur. "I've written you every day since I've been in London."

"Writing letters was never a problem for you, was it? Posting them was always the challenge." Her legs swung in childish defiance.

"Why didn't you simply tell me you were David's daughter?"

"We all live by our expectations, don't we, Mr. Connor? You expected Claire Scarborough to be a little girl and I expected you to be an unfeeling monster who would steal his best friend's gold and abandon a child entrusted to his care."

Justin's jaw tightened, but he refused to quail before her taunts. "Forgive me if I disappointed you. If I'd have known you were coming, I'd have sharpened my horns. The truth of the matter is that the Maori took the gold mine during the uprising and I thought you well cared for. I had no idea Miss Winters was such an old b—"

"Battle ax," she supplied. "You really should police your language in front of your ward. Children can be so impressionable."

She climbed off the rocking horse, the roll of her hips beneath the ill-fitting wool a taunt of its own. She gazed up at him, her lips parted, her eyes darkened in smoky accusation. Would he ever again see them sparkle in merriment? he wondered. The winter months had faded her skin to a delicate peach and carved faint hollows beneath her cheekbones. What had she endured on the harsh voyage from New Zealand to England?

His heartbeat quickened at her nearness. "Miss Winters said they were bringing you to me. That you jumped off the boat and ran away rather than be delivered into my hands."

"And she accused *me* of having a vivid imagination! I didn't jump off the boat. When they couldn't find my wealthy guardian, they tossed me overboard like so much shark bait."

His hand shot out to grasp her wrist. "If that miserable wretch Barney ever laid a hand on you, I'll—" He left the threat unfinished, but the vision of the ruffian's stringy paws against Emily's skin tightened his grip.

"Surely you jest." Her low laugh hit an off-key note. "Miss Winters would never have allowed it. She wanted me given into the hands of my illustrious guardian, pure and undefiled."

Her words struck Justin like a blow. Reeling from its shock, he stared down at her wrist. The dusky hairs on the backs of his knuckles stood out in sharp relief against the pale silk of her skin. His hands were strong, graceful, from long hours at the piano, honed and callused by hard physical labor, and like any man's hands, capable of both gentleness and cruelty.

His fingers had stroked her until she cried out for his touch in a voice husky with passion. His hands, not Barney's, had defiled the child given into his care.

His thumb massaged the circlet of prints he had left in her tender flesh. "Ironic, isn't it? I'd kill any man who had touched you as I have."

She pulled her arm free and paced to the window, turning her back on him. "A pity dueling is out of fashion. You could challenge yourself. Penfeld would make a dapper second."

A ragged sigh escaped him. The flippant Miss Scarborough was beyond his reach. His only hope lay in coaxing out a glimpse of his Emily.

His voice softened. "Why didn't you wait in New Zealand? I was coming back for you."

"Too little, too late, Mr. Connor!" Emily spun around, her ruse of control snapping. Unshed tears polished her eyes to brilliance. "What did you want me to do? Sit at the hut window until the birds built nests in my hair? No, thank you! I've had my fill of waiting for the likes of you. Seven years of it. Dreaming, hoping, praying. Sitting with my fingers pressed to the window until I thought they'd crack and fall off from the cold. Even after I'd stopped hoping and started to hate you, I'd wake up crying in the middle of the night and think I heard your footsteps on the stairs."

Justin started for her. She recoiled violently, stumbling over a miniature railway laid before the window.

Her foot lashed out, sending the caboose slamming into the wall, marring the wallpaper with an ugly red gash. "Did you really think you could erase years of neglect with trains and dolls?"

Her arm raked across the marble-topped chiffonier. Tiny bottles of toilet water tumbled to the carpet, their crystal stoppers rolling away. The sickly sweet fragrance of lavender water stung Justin's eyes. "Did you hope to buy my forgiveness with baubles? Trinkets?" She hauled open the doors of the lacquered wardrobe, snatched out an armful of dresses, and hurled them toward him. "I fear you've misjudged me, sir. My affections can't be bought for a length of ribbon or a scrap of lace."

Justin stood unmoving beneath her assault, allowing Emily her anger. He owed her that much. She was finally giving vent to the pain she hid so well behind sarcasm and flippancy. She was magnificent in her fury, whirling through the bedroom like a cherubic demon of vengeance.

She wrapped her arms around a magnificent wedding doll complete with tiny trousseau and thrust it into his arms. "Why don't you send all of these charming things over to the seminary? I'm sure Miss Winters will waste no time finding some other poor beggar child to board in my attic."

Her fury spent, she folded her arm over her brow and leaned against the bedpost. Her slender throat convulsed, and it broke Justin's heart to know how hard she was fighting not to cry in front of him.

He set the doll gently on the bed, afraid Emily might crumple if he touched her. "I didn't know, Emily. I swear to God I didn't know."

She gazed at him over her shoulder, her eyes glistening with tears. "And if you had known? Would you have come?"

He yearned to offer her that pathetic scrap of reassurance. But even now he hadn't the courage to say the words that would freeze the contempt on her face forever. The words that would brand him as the monster she had believed him to be. She had every reason to hate him. Far more reason than she knew. He couldn't give her the truth. But he couldn't lie to her either.

"I would have made the necessary arrangements."

Her beautiful eyes darkened in bitter triumph. "And you thought me fool enough to wait for you again."

Justin's sense of helplessness nearly choked him. "I would have never left New Zealand if I hadn't had to comb this godforsaken city for David's daughter." He narrowed his eyes as realization dawned. "If I had gone back, you wouldn't have been there, would you? Because you were here, leading me on a merry chase for a child that didn't exist. I'd have gone back to a deserted beach and an empty hut. Was that to be your final revenge, *Claire*?"

She tossed back her head in proud defiance. "Don't call me that. You haven't the right."

With agonizing clarity Justin realized all of the other things he had no right to do. She was standing near enough for him to touch, but forever out of his reach. A wall of propriety had slid between them, as fragile as glass and as impenetrable as stone. Society had a name for men who seduced their wards. Their shocked whispers and stares might never touch him, but Emily had already lived half her life under the burden of their scorn. She deserved far better.

His oath to David bound his heart like chains of iron. He had robbed her of her father and it was his penance and duty to replace him. To atone for his own neglect, he could give her a home, an education, a place in society. He could even find her a husband who would cherish her as David had. Fate had ensured he could never be that man. She would despise him if she knew the truth about the night that had left her father's blood on his hands. All his noble intentions paled in comparison to what he could never give her—his love, his body, his children.

A white-hot anger blazed through him. Anger at her cunning, her blatant deceit, and the terrible unfairness of it all. His desire for her flared as brightly as ever. He wanted this defiant woman no less than he had wanted the angelic creature who had washed up on his beach garbed in nothing but sand and moondust.

He caught her arms and drove her back against the bedpost. His fingers pressed into her soft flesh, assuring himself she was real and not an illusion of his maddened desire. Her lips trembled, and he felt a bitter satisfaction to know she was not as immune to him as she was pretending to be.

He lowered his lips near enough to smell the tantalizing musk of fear and anticipation on her breath. "Are we even now? Have you punished me enough, Miss Scarborough? Are you satisfied with your revenge? To make me want you? To make me dream of you when you knew that once I discovered I was your guardian, I could never lay a hand on you?" She turned her face away, but he forced it back, capturing her chin between two fingers. "It was a terrible and wicked thing to do. Your father would be ashamed of you."

With those words Justin turned and left her, slamming the door behind him. He sank against the door, knowing his survival depended on pretending those stolen moments of passion and tenderness in New Zealand had never happened. But his bluff had not fooled him. Emily's revenge had just begun, and the punishing flames of hell couldn't lick any higher than his burning need for her.

Emily drifted in and out of sleep, her jumbled dreams as tortured as her waking thoughts. She threw back the suffocating weight of the comforter. An icy draft blasted her fevered skin, drying the sweat and rippling goose flesh over her body. Shivering, she burrowed back under the comforter and tried to pinch her down pillow into some semblance of comfort. It was too wet from her tears to be salvageable. She heaved it off the bed and threw herself back, rapping her head sharply against the carved headboard. Groaning, she rolled facefirst into the mattress.

She had taken to her bed after Justin had stormed out, and was contemplating spending the remainder of her life there.

She had lain unmoving, her sullen face turned to the wall when the maids had come to clear away the toys and sweep up the debris. She ignored the broth they brought, rising only to wiggle out of the binding wool and creep into the nightdress they left draped across the footboard of the bed. For hours people had tiptoed and whispered outside her door as if she were dying, but now, at last, even they had gone away.

She sat up, hugging her knees. One by one the tears slipped unbidden down her cheeks. Loneliness was no stranger to her. She had often tasted its bitter draft huddled in the attic with only Annabel for company. But that was a vague melancholy compared to this shuddering ache. All she wanted was someone to hold her. Annabel's porcelain limbs were a cold comfort at best.

How could she be so miserable in such luxury? Two nights ago, shivering on an icy park bench, she would have swooned to imagine being snuggled between a feather mattress and a fat down comforter. A brass warming pan had been tucked at the foot of the bed to toast her toes. A fire licked at the grate, but its serene glow only emphasized the unfamiliar shadows of the room. The half-tester loomed over her head like a black cloud.

The alien house creaked and sighed a mournful refrain. Emily shivered. This was worse than being alone—a thousand times worse. Justin was in this house somewhere, near enough to hear her cry out but separated from her by a jagged chasm of broken promises and lies.

Emily wiped her cheek with her ruffled sleeve, becoming slowly aware of a new sound—music seeping through the floorboards. The faint notes swept her heart, bittersweet and hauntingly familiar. They called out to her, compelling her to rise and seek their source.

Her fists knotted in the comforter. How could she face Justin again? Her first glimpse of him beneath the Christmas tree had wreaked havoc on her fragile control.

With his dark hair trimmed against his nape and his

face clean-shaven, he had looked ten years younger than she remembered—vulnerable but devastatingly handsome in a crisp suit tailored to the lean planes of his chest and thighs. He had offered his heart in that lopsided grin, looking as tempting and delectable as a present waiting to be unwrapped. Emily had felt like a dowdy wren in Doreen's borrowed dress and bonnet. Only her humiliated pride had given her the strength to spurn him.

It had been so easy to condemn him, but having him look at her as if he despised her, knowing he loathed what she had done, made her feel truly ashamed for the first time in her life.

The music played on, dancing over her nerves like silken fingers. She threw back the comforter and climbed down from the bed. A pair of velvet slippers warmed on the rug in front of the hearth. She shoved her feet into them, unable to resist a wiggle of her toes in their plush contours.

As she slipped out of her room, the music grew louder, a dark and fantastical lullaby in the sleeping hush of the house.

She crept down the long, curving staircase, realizing halfway down that the drawing room lay directly across the checkered tile of the foyer. Moonlight spilled through the wall of windows, varnishing the grand piano to an ebony gloss.

Justin's hair flew as he pounded the keys. He had abandoned his waistcoat, and his white shirt was half unbuttoned. The muscles in his shoulders rippled beneath the rich linen. Sweat glistened on the column of his throat.

Emily sank to a sitting position on the stairs, clasping the wooden balusters in her trembling hands. The melody poured over her in jarring shocks of recognition. It was the symphony he had written for her on the island. Hearing it rendered in these magnificent tones made her realize what pathetic justice her own reedy voice had done it.

Justin played the piano like a master. His hands flew

over the keys, making her purr and thunder beneath his skillful touch.

Emily's eyes fluttered shut. Her mouth felt dry, her breathing unsteady. It was as if Justin were ravishing not the piano, but her, taking her against her will with each crash of the chords. As the music climbed to a crescendo, a broken gasp escaped her. Her eyes flew open.

Justin looked up, and his gaze met hers across the gleaming expanse of tile. His eyes were dark and dangerous. His fingers never missed a stroke.

I've spent the last few nights pouring all of my passions into my music when all I really wanted to do was pour them into you.

Without warning his words came back to her, rough with promise.

Tearing her gaze away from his, she rose and flew back up the stairs. She slammed her door and locked it, her heart beating frantic wings in her throat. She jumped into the bed, slippers and all, and pulled the comforter over her head. But no matter how hard she pressed her hands to her ears, she still could not stop the music.

Chapter 20

· 🐚 ·

*Yet when we said good-bye, the shadow
of the woman you will become was in your eyes. . . .*

"Here's one, sir," Penfeld said, jabbing his finger at the newspaper spread on the dining room table. " 'Personal maid,' " he read over Justin's shoulder, " 'Companion. Expert dresser of hair. Fluent in French and Italian.' "

Something slammed into the ceiling above them. Tiny specks of plaster floated down to dust Justin's tea. A muffled oath that was neither French nor Italian burned their ears.

"Do you think we can find a maid fluent in bear wrestling?" Justin muttered.

"You might try the circus," Penfeld suggested.

Justin held the paper in front of his face, trying to ignore the alarmed cries, thumps, and howls coming from the second floor. He winced at the tinkling sound of glass shattering.

Penfeld lifted the teapot to pour him a fresh cup of tea.

"One. Two," Justin counted under his breath.

A door slammed. The valet gazed upward, pouring a

stream of amber over the ivory tablecloth. Footsteps thundered down the stairs accompanied by hysterical sobbing. *Click, click, click* went the shoes across the marble tiles of the foyer, then the front door slammed with a bang that echoed like a gunshot through the waiting house.

"Three," Justin dourly pronounced, massaging his aching brow with the palm of his hand.

Warm tea trickled into his lap.

"Oh dear, sir. I'm frightfully sorry." Penfeld snatched up a napkin and mopped his trousers.

The duchess entered the room at full sail, the flounces of her skirt following a good foot behind her. "That was the third maid in as many days. The girl can't sulk in her bedroom forever. If she refuses to be dressed, I insist you see to her."

Justin laid down the paper, biting back a groan. Dressing Emily was the last thing his frazzled nerves needed.

His mother droned on. "Your sisters and I have been planning an intimate gathering to introduce your young ward to society, followed by a splendid ball to launch her into the company of the more eligible young men." She sighed happily. "It will be such a joy having a young girl in the house again, won't it, dear?"

"A pure delight," Justin replied grimly.

He rose and slipped from the room before his mother could begin discussing the flower arrangements for Emily's wedding or sewing the christening gown for her first child.

He smoothed his waistcoat as he climbed the stairs, steeling himself behind his only shield—a cool paternal demeanor. His sharp knock received no answer. He opened the door to find his entire view captured by the charming sight of Emily's ruffled drawers upended in the window.

She was leaning halfway over the sill, shaking her fist. "Don't come back either! It'll take a lot more than a puny creature like you to shove me into one of those bloody contraptions."

She leaned out farther as a bonneted figure scampered

out of earshot. Her pantaloons hugged the sleek curves of her thighs. Justin wiped his mouth on the back of his hand before striding across the room and catching her by the waistband. He could just see her tumbling out the window in her white drawers and lacy camisole.

She wiggled in his grasp. "I won't wear it. I won't. You can't make me. And if you try, I'll . . ." She jabbed the air with a sinister-looking hat pin before realizing who had caught her.

He stepped back, dodging her easily. "You'll what? Deflate me?"

She straightened, muttering something about "hot air." A flush dusted her cheekbones. She crossed her arms over her breasts, then folded her hands casually at the juncture of her thighs, finally giving up all attempts at modesty by resting her hands on her hips and glaring at him.

"Is there a problem?" he asked, already knowing there was. Five feet three inches of problem, exuding a rumpled femininity that would have given a eunuch pause.

She stabbed an accusing finger at the chair. "*That* is the problem."

Justin picked up the object she indicated and ran his hands over the rigid whalebone. "What is it? A hat of some sort?"

Emily realized he was genuinely perplexed. She'd forgotten how long he'd been away from society. His innocence touched her until she remembered that lush native beauties like Rangimarie would never bother with such contrivances. All he had to do was reach his hands beneath her skirt and—

She jerked it away from him. "It's a torture device designed to fill out the shape of my rump."

Justin muttered something under *his* breath, then frowned. "That must be what Mother's wearing. I thought she had a bird cage under her dress."

Emily rested the cumbersome form on her hips and

struggled with the tapes. The bustle swayed like a gangly bell. Justin caught her before she crashed into a floor lamp.

"See what I mean?" she pleaded, clutching his arm. "There's no need for all this fuss. Couldn't I just wear a skirt like the one I wore in New Zealand?"

As he gazed down into her earnest brown eyes, memories pierced Justin's heart like beams of fragrant sunlight. Emily frolicking through the waves, her wet skirt plastered to her hips; Emily sitting in the sand, her palms pressed to her naked breasts, her hair ruffled by the morning wind and his stolen caresses.

He gently but firmly extracted his arm from her grasp. "We're in London now. Not New Zealand." His reminder was more for himself than for her, but it failed to dull his gnawing hunger.

He escaped her disappointed gaze by moving to the bed. A charming array of clothing had been laid out by the poor departed maid.

He caressed the softness of a silk stocking between thumb and forefinger. "You've been barricaded up here for three days. If I allow you to leave off this bustle thing, will you join us downstairs?"

Emily glared at the heap of feminine garments. "I'll not wear the gloves. They're ridiculous."

He rolled his eyes. "Very well. Forget the gloves." He tossed the stocking over her shoulder and turned away. "I'll be waiting for you."

"Now, that's a switch, isn't it?"

Justin stopped, his broad shoulders rigid. His exhaled breath echoed through the room. He left, pulling the door shut behind him with such pained gentleness that Emily knew he itched to slam it out of its frame.

Justin waited for Emily at the foot of the stairs. He had never seen so many people trying to look inconspicuous while milling around the foyer. Two maids dusted the tripod base of an occasional table while an underfootman polished the tinkling glass prisms dangling from a fringed lampshade. Their gazes kept wandering to the top of the stairs, craving a glimpse of the severe little creature who had dared to slap their master.

The long-case clock chimed the hour. Justin drummed his fingers on the banister. One of the husbands had parked himself on the bench of the cloak stand and was puffing away on a long-stemmed pipe. Justin wondered if even his sisters could tell them apart. They all had the same tepid brown hair and wore tweed jackets in lieu of more formal garments that might suggest they were going to leave the house in search of other pursuits—such as gainful employment. He supposed this one was Herbert, spouse of Millicent. His bushy eyebrows were in desperate need of a combing.

Justin suppressed a sigh as Edith and his mother strolled arm in arm from the drawing room, their heads inclined as if enjoying a profound conversation, something he knew to be impossible. The last thing Emily needed was an audience. She might take one look at their rabid faces and shy back to her room like a frightened doe.

His fears melted as an enchanting vision appeared on the landing above, taking his breath away. This girl bore no resemblance to the stern creature who had marched into the house. Her white dimity frock belled around her ankles, revealing a tantalizing hint of ruffled crinoline and kid slippers. Justin had chosen the short frock himself to remind him Emily was little more than a child. A blue velvet sash hugged her slender waist and a matching bow tamed her curls. The warmth of a new and unexpected emotion flowed through Justin's veins—pride.

Emily's fingers were poised lightly on the banister. Her lips curved in a smile so sweet it made him feel he was the only man in the room—or the universe.

Her smile never wavered as she hooked one leg over the banister, giving the entire foyer a healthy peek at the starched layers of her petticoats. The duchess gasped.

Cries of alarm rang out as she threw both arms in the air and shot down the polished banister like a ruffled cannonball. At the last possible second Justin stepped out of the way.

She crashed in a disgruntled heap, her dress sprawled all the way up to the little pink rosettes on her garters. When both his mother and the footman started forward, Justin waved them back.

Emily glared up at him through the curl flopped over her eyes. "You might have caught me."

He bit the inside of his cheek, afraid to do so much as smile. "You might have descended the staircase in a more conventional manner."

Groaning, she rubbed her bottom with both hands. Justin swallowed an offer of assistance. It was only too easy to remember the feel of her plush rear cupped in his palms.

"Perhaps you should reconsider that bustle," he said coolly, offering her a hand.

"Perhaps they shouldn't wax the banister quite so often. I thought I was going to sail clear across the Channel to Paris."

He pulled her to her feet. He had forgotten how fragile her small, warm hand felt in his own. He jerked his own hand away as if she had scorched him. "Breakfast is waiting for you in the dining room. Now, if you'll excuse me, I have business to attend to." He gave her a crisp bow and fled toward the study.

His mother's chiding tones rang after him. "I don't know what's gotten into that boy. You'd have thought I never taught him any manners at all."

Justin was spared Emily's murmured reply by the hastily erected barrier of the study door. He strode through the dusty gloom to the towering *secrétaire* and slammed open one of the doors. The glass panes rattled. Curse the girl! He would be damned if she would blunder into his life and create utter chaos yet again. Eyeing his father's well-aged Scotch with distaste, he pulled out the rum bottle he had stashed behind a leather-bound edition of *The Pickwick Papers* and uncorked it. Tipping it all the way back, he took a deep swig.

An image rose unbidden to his mind—Emily sailing off the banister and drifting across the English Channel, her starched petticoats swollen like the skin of a hot-air balloon.

He choked, spewing rum. Tears stung his eyes and seared his nostrils. He sank into a chair and clutched his aching sides as the laughter he'd been holding back rolled out in silent waves.

Justin spent the morning barricaded in the study, refusing to even look up from the Winthrop Shipping reports until Penfeld interrupted him for tea and sandwiches.

He took a sip of tea, then frowned. A frilly object was curled at the bottom of the cup. He crooked his pinkie and fished it out. Tea dripped from dainty pink rosettes.

"Penfeld," he said, pulling off his spectacles and glowering at the valet from beneath his brows. "May I ask what this is?"

Penfeld looked up from cutting the sandwiches into flawless squares. A flush blistered his cheeks. "Good Lord, sir. I believe it's a woman's garter."

"Would you care to explain how it got into my tea?"

"I haven't a clue." Penfeld lifted the lid off the teapot and peeped into it as if afraid an entire trousseau of women's underwear might leap out at him.

A timid knock sounded on the door.

"Come in," Justin barked.

A gardener crept in, holding a rake at arm's length with such trepidation that Justin expected to see a snake twirled around its prongs. It was not a serpent, but a rumpled crinoline that dangled in his face. "Sorry to trouble ye, master, but I found this stuffed into one of the flower pots in the shed. Shall I burn it?"

Justin's face was grim as he plucked the crinoline off the rake. "No, Will. I'll take care of it."

Breathing a sigh of relief to be rid of the offensive thing, the gardener left. Justin smoothed the rich linen over his palms. The pure, sweet fragrance of vanilla wafted to his nostrils.

He shook his head ruefully. "If Emily keeps shedding garments at this alarming rate, she'll be naked by nightfall." Groaning at his own words, he dropped his face into the soft folds of the garment. "Where is she?" he growled.

They found Emily wandering the gilt cavern of the ballroom, her hands tucked at the small of her back. A sparkling wall of French doors fronted the long room. Justin hovered behind the translucent panel of a lace curtain, his hunger to watch her smothering his flare of guilt for spying on her so blatantly.

"Looks a bit out of pocket, doesn't she?" Penfeld said.

Justin gave a noncommittal grunt. She did look tiny beneath the vaulted ceiling. How did she feel in this strange house, surrounded by strangers? he wondered. He remembered how desolate his own childhood had been. The enormous house had seemed a maze of endless doors, dusty corners, and gloomy attics. Every table and chair had rested on carved talons or claws, and he'd been half afraid to sit for fear they'd lurch into motion and carry him off. His mother and sisters had whispered their own language while his father remained safely cordoned behind the unrelenting oak of his study door. Just as he had done today.

"She might be bored, sir. Perhaps if you spent some time with her . . . ?"

Justin dug his fingers into the curtain, unable to hide his horror at that suggestion. He didn't trust himself enough to eat breakfast with her. How long would it take before he reached over to correct a wayward curl? Smooth a puckered ruffle? Lick the sugary muffin crumbs from her lips?

As they watched, Emily stood on tiptoe to run her curious fingers over the medallioned wall. Without the crinoline her skirt clung to the curve of her hips. He almost grinned to see her bare toes peeping out from beneath it. Gracie would be fortunate not to find one of her slippers floating in the soup tonight.

She cast the double doors at the end of the ballroom a furtive glance. What was she going to do now? Justin wondered. Peel off her dress and frolic like a wanton nymph beneath the gasoliers? His throat tightened.

Emily flung out her arms and spun around. The dimity skirt ballooned around her ankles. She danced in silence, but Justin heard another melody, marked by the stamp of Maori feet, beguiling in its wailing simplicity. He wanted to march in there and take her in his arms. To sweep her around the room until the swells and hollows of their bodies made music like the bow and strings of a finely tuned violin.

Groaning back his despair, he caught Penfeld by his starched lapels and shoved him against the nearest wall. An Oriental vase rattled in protest. "Take her, Penfeld. Take her out for the afternoon. She's your charge. Amuse her."

"B-b-but, sir," the valet sputtered. "I fear I'm not very amusing. The rest of the staff find me hopelessly dull. However shall I entertain her?"

"How the hell should I know? Take her to the zoo. Walk her in the park. Buy her a bloody puppy. Just get her out of my sight." He freed Penfeld and raked his hair into nervous spikes, forgetting it wasn't long anymore. "Just make sure she wears a cloak. And a hat. And shoes— two of them."

As Justin strode away, still muttering under his breath, Penfeld tugged thoughtfully at his whiskers. "A puppy. I do say, a splendid suggestion."

·   ·   ·

Eight hours later Justin was pacing the parlor, trying not to flinch at each incisive tick of the black marble clock on the mantel. His mother and Edith kept vigil with him, their ringleted heads inclined toward their embroidery. Lily and Millicent had retired at a respectable hour with all the dreary husbands, even Edith's, in tow.

The long-case clock in the foyer gonged. Once. Twice. Ten times. Justin's oath shattered its echo. Edith stabbed herself with her needle, but the duchess didn't even flinch.

He paced to the window and braced his weight on the sill with both hands. The night's chill seeped through the frosted panes. Was he going to have to hire a detective to return Emily from a simple shopping expedition? he wondered. He must have been mad to send her out with Penfeld. But these weren't the teeming streets of Auckland. London was Penfeld's orderly domain. Justin fought despair, refusing to give in to his fear that Emily might have taken this opportunity to flee from him yet again.

He should have taken her out himself. Even if it meant being trapped in the confines of a carriage with her ethereal scent. Even if it meant sitting for hours with her warm thigh pressed to his own. His torment was nothing compared to her safety.

He turned around and leaned against the windowsill. His mother was watching him beneath hooded lids, her eyes sharpened to a lively glint. Justin knew she hadn't always been stupid. Olivia Connor had chosen long ago to veil her intelligence behind insipid vaguery, but at times he still caught a glimpse of the Fleet Street shopgirl who had memorized Debrett's *Peerage* to land not one of the many impoverished dukes haunting London, but the only peer of the realm with a thriving shipping empire. To hold the affections of her rigid husband, she had learned to betray everything else she held dear—even her son. Especially her son.

She stabbed the thick linen with the needle. "You care for the girl, don't you?"

"Of course I care for her. She's my ward. Her father was a dear friend."

"Yet you've never laid eyes on her in all these years?"

His gaze was caught by the hypnotic flick of her needle. She sewed the way he played the piano, all grace and no hesitation. Justin wondered what she would do if he told her he'd laid far more than his eyes on Emily.

He was spared from answering by the discordant clang of bells. His mother's hands froze in their motion. Edith jerked her head up to meet Justin's puzzled gaze. Hooves clattered on the drive, adding to the ear-shattering cacophony of the bells.

As Justin sprinted through the foyer, Herbert, Harold, and Harvey came flying down the stairs in their long nightgowns and caps. Lily and Millicent trailed behind, their candles casting wavering shadows on the wallpaper.

Harold rubbed his eyes. "I do say, can't a chap get a decent night's sleep in this mausoleum?"

"What the devil is it?" Herbert bellowed, tripping over Harvey's hem. "Is the house afire?"

They spilled onto the lawn as a closed police wagon rolled to a halt in the drive. Rusty bars blocked the windows. The Winthrop carriage clattered to a halt behind the wagon, the driver hanging his head in sheepish defeat.

Justin stared as a uniformed bobby climbed off the driver's seat, tipped his tall hat in a crisp greeting, and moved to swing open the barred door at the back of the wagon.

A demure, white-gloved hand emerged. At least Emily had worn her gloves, Justin thought crazily. The bobby took her hand with obvious deference and Emily descended, favoring him with a regal smile. Justin started for her, determined to wring an explanation from her charming little neck.

Before he could reach her, a snarling, fanged monster exploded from the back of the wagon and lunged straight for his throat.

Chapter 21

· 🐚 ·

*(You should thank God you were blessed
with your mama's eyes; it more than makes up
for being cursed with my hair.)*

*J*ustin backed away from the slavering beast, instinctively
drawing it away from Emily. The deafening shrill of his
sisters' screams was almost drowned out by its bass-
throated rumble. Something had come flying out of the
wagon behind the creature. It stumbled along for a few
steps before Justin realized it was Penfeld, and he was
attached to the monster by Emily's blue velvet sash. The
dog's massive spiked collar might as well have been
around the valet's neck. The beast dragged him across the
slick lawn, eyeing Justin hungrily. The horses whinnied
and tossed their heads in terror.

"What is the meaning of this, Penfeld?" Justin said,
his voice soft enough not to spook the animal but lethal
enough to be heard by them all.

Penfeld dug his heels into the ground and strained
against the dog's squat weight. His whiskers stuck out in
matted tufts. His immaculate jacket was torn and his
white shirt smeared with mud.

His brown eyes were entreating. "You told me to buy her a puppy, sir."

Justin eyed the thing. White foam dripped from its bared fangs. "That's not a puppy. It's a bull."

As if offended by his words, the dog lunged again, dragging Penfeld flat. The monster's snapping teeth missed Justin's crotch by half an inch.

"A bull*dog* to be precise," Emily said, waltzing between Penfeld and the dog. She patted the creature's massive head and scratched behind his ears. "There, now. That's a nice Pudding. Down, boy."

The dog sank to its stocky haunches at her feet, drooling adoringly on her slippers. Justin was surprised it didn't purr.

"Pudding?" he echoed ominously.

"What did you want me to call him? Fluffy?" Her smile was angelic. Justin's stomach spasmed a warning.

The bobby stepped between them, pulling off his hat. Another policeman lurked in his shadow.

He twirled his bushy mustache. "I'm turribly sorry for the disturbance, sir, but I thought it best if we escorted the young lady home. After we arrested her the first time—"

"The first time?" Justin bit off, glowering at Emily.

"It weren't really her fault, Your Grace. The dog got away from your man and the door to the crystal shop was open." He brightened visibly. "Once she assured the shopkeeper the Duke of Winthrop would pay for all the damages, he turned out to be quite a reasonable chap."

Behind him, one of the husbands moaned. Justin closed his eyes and counted slowly under his breath.

"And the second time, sir . . ."

His eyes flew open.

The other policeman chimed in helpfully. "That would have been the elephant, wouldn't it, Clarence?"

Justin swallowed. "She let an elephant run through the crystal shop?"

"Oh, no, sir," the bobby reassured him. "The elephant ran through the zoo. After she slipped the latch on its cage."

Justin narrowed his eyes. He would like to see her caged. And chained. Preferably to his bed.

Her smile faded an inkling beneath his glare. "I was simply trying to feed him a peanut. I couldn't reach his trunk."

The second policeman chuckled. "I didn't know those old nannies could move so fast. You should have seen the perambulators flying!"

The bobby rubbed the back of his neck. Justin could have sworn he was blushing. "Of course, the last time we were more concerned with her own health. Hyde Park's a bit cold to be swimming this time of year, especially without—" He stopped dead and looked over his shoulder, aware for the first time of the women's avid gazes and the heated puffs of fog emerging from the men's lips. He leaned over and whispered something in Justin's ear.

Justin dropped his gaze to Emily as if seeing her for the first time. Her curls glistened with damp. Her dress— the charming girlish confection he had chosen in order to keep himself at bay—clung to her skin in all the wrong places, the pristine white going almost sheer over the dusky hint of her nipples. Her lips quirked in an apologetic smile.

He took one step toward her. Then another. Her smile faltered. "What are you going to do?"

He smiled pleasantly. "Murder you."

"Oh dear," Herbert murmured.

Moaning, Lily pressed a scented handkerchief to her lips. The bobbies exchanged a nervous glance, wondering if the rumors they'd heard about the savage young duke were true.

The dog growled. Justin gave it one look and it buried its head beneath its paws, whimpering. Justin stretched out a hand toward Penfeld. "Give me the sash."

"Whatever for, sir?"

"I'm going to strangle her with it."

"Very good, sir. Right away." He began to tug at the knot around the dog's collar.

"Penfeld!" Emily wailed. As she backed away from Justin, her feet slid on the dead grass.

He stalked her, grinning like a vengeful demon. "Why make these poor policemen come all the way out here for nothing? They can use their wagon to cart me off to jail. Think what a nice, peaceful place prison will be after living with you for a day. I can while away the hours with thieves, ruffians, and other killers."

Her voice trembled. "This isn't very sporting. You can't murder me in front of all these witnesses."

She came up against the trunk of an oak. His fingers closed ever so gently around her throat, his broad thumbs seeking and caressing her throbbing pulse points. "Why not? They can testify before the House of Lords that I was provoked. They won't hang me. They might even give me a medal of valor."

The pads of his fingertips combed through the delicate fleece at her nape. Her shiver vibrated through his taut body like the stroke of fingers against harp strings. A shiver of what? Justin wondered. Cold? Fear? Reaction to the heat blasting like a furnace from his body? A glint of triumph sharpened in her smoky eyes. The tip of her pink tongue moistened her lips. Taunting him. Tempting him.

Her husky whisper was meant only for his ears. "What do you really want to do, Justin? Kill me . . . or kiss me?"

He wanted to kiss her, all right, long and hard and rough. He wanted to mate her mouth with his teeth and tongue until he'd wiped away her teasing smirk. He wanted to carry her upstairs to his bedroom and lock the door against them all. He wanted to peel off her damp clothes and drown her beneath the unrelenting weight of his body until neither of them could think or walk straight.

Then he'd kill her.

She'd done it again, he realized. With barely a flutter of her silky lashes she'd committed the unpardonable sin of shattering his composure and making him feel alive again. More alive than he'd felt since he buried her father.

His hands dropped from her throat. He unbuttoned his coat and with a sweeping motion laid it over her shoulders.

"I must apologize for the inconvenience, gentlemen," he told the bobbies. "I fear my ward is a bit high-spirited."

"Nothing a good beating wouldn't cure," Harold muttered, still sulky from being rousted from his bed. His bluster wilted beneath Justin's glacial stare. He slipped behind Edith's skirts.

Justin linked his hands over his waistcoat, every inch the affable lord of the manor. "I'm sure you know how trying children can be."

The bobby ducked his head. "That we do, Your Grace. Got eight of 'em between us, don't we, Ned?"

"Aye, Clarence. And a feisty lot they are."

Justin divided a wad of pound notes between the two men. "Buy yourselves a round of ale when you get off duty. For your trouble."

As the men climbed onto the wagon, still singing the praises of the generous duke, Justin commanded his own driver to take the dog to the stables. Penfeld mopped his brow with Emily's sash, thankful to be relieved of his monstrous burden. Justin refused to look behind him.

"Mother, would you please escort Emily to her room?"

"That won't be necessary." Emily's words rang out in the crisp air.

He pivoted to face her. She hugged his coat closed at her throat like a queen's mantle. She wore her dignity well, but not well enough to disguise the stricken look in her eyes—eyes darkened by his casual betrayal.

"Thank you, but I'm not so young I can't toddle up the stairs unassisted." As she brushed past him, a whiff of vanilla tickled his nostrils.

"If you want to be treated like an adult," he said softly, "you might try behaving like one."

She hesitated, then moved up the shallow stairs into the house, her shoulders set at proud angles.

"Coming, dear?" his mother crooned as the others filed after Emily, the husbands grumbling and the wives murmuring soothing lullabies.

Justin jammed his hands deep into his pockets. "Later."

Penfeld stood before him, his face folded in miserable lines of defeat. "If you wish to dismiss me, sir, I understand. I'd appreciate a reference, but if you don't feel I deserve it . . ."

Justin sighed as sudden exhaustion overtook him. He felt as if he'd been master of this house for centuries instead of months. "Go ring for a bath, Penfeld."

"You wish to bathe at this hour?"

He straightened the valet's crooked tie. "Not for me. For you."

"Aye, sir! As you wish." Penfeld bowed his thanks and went scurrying for the house.

Justin stood alone on the barren stretch of lawn, staring up at Emily's window until the light fluttered and went out, leaving the glazed pane a square of black. He shivered as from somewhere behind the house came the mournful baying of a dog.

In the next few days Justin was to regret his cool rebuke. With the stubborn conviction of a woman wronged, Emily became exactly what he had requested.

She seldom smiled, and if she did, it was a watery imitation of her infectious grin. Lily used an iron to tame her wayward curls to rigid ringlets. The stench of scorched hair hung in the musty air of the house. Millicent taught her to embroider and Edith to bang out Beethoven's "Minuet in G" on the piano with military precision. She practiced each evening for hours until Justin's head throbbed from gritting his teeth. Penfeld became her unofficial lady's maid, pressing her childish pinafores to starched perfection. Her crinolines appeared so stiff that Justin found it a marvel she could sit without them flying up over her face.

When Justin entered a room she'd make some snippet of conversation about the weather or the dinner party his mother was planning at the end of the week. His sisters would chime in about the upcoming New Year's ball and he'd be left gazing at the smooth cap of Emily's head as she bent back to stitching the family crest on his handkerchiefs with slavish devotion.

She was a perfect lady.

Justin hated her.

He couldn't decide who he despised more—this new Emily or himself. Unable to bear this pale shadow of his vibrant Emily, he shut himself in the study, immersing himself in Winthrop Shipping business with an enthusiasm that made his father seem a rakish wastrel. He glared at reports until his vision blurred. His insomnia returned with savage force, but even pounding the piano until dawn did not ease it. His temper flared without provocation, and the servants scurried to avoid him. They whispered among themselves that it was as if the gruff ghost of Frank Connor had returned to stalk the halls of Grymwilde.

Armed with a tumbler of his father's Scotch, Justin emerged from the study one evening. He veered away from the smoking room where the men had retired for brandy and cigars. Last night he had severed himself from their company and reduced poor Harvey to nervous snivels by snapping that he ought to consider seeking a job instead of living off his wife's dowry like a spineless slug.

As he passed the parlor, the siren song of badly struck piano keys and feminine chatter lured him in. He knew his brooding presence made his sisters nervous. Edith and his mother lapsed to whispers. Millicent hummed under her breath while Lily's trembling fingers dropped stitches all over the place. Only Emily seemed undisturbed by his crude intrusion. She continued her graceless thumping on the spinet.

Even Emily's bulldog seemed drained of spirit. He lolled on the rug at Emily's feet, his massive head stretched out on his paws and his spiked collar replaced by a garish pink bow. As Justin sank into the chair beside the piano, the dog rose and slunk out the door.

Justin leaned back in the chair, nursing his Scotch and eyeing Emily through narrowed eyes. She sat in a luminous halo of lamplight, her skirts spread in a perfect bell around the piano bench. Her piquant face glowed with serenity. Justin shifted his weight and rolled the amber liquid in the bottom of his glass. He had done in one careless night what Miss Winters had failed to do in seven years—made a lady out of Emily Claire Scarborough. So why did he want to yank her up by her ridiculous ringlets and demand some show of spirit?

Emily could feel Justin's smoldering gaze on her, but she willed her fingers to continue their mechanical pounding, knowing she was slowly driving him insane. The fact that she'd just ripped out his initials and sewn *Homer* onto all of his handkerchiefs inspired her to continue.

She stole a look at him from beneath the shelter of her lashes. Her heart skipped in her throat. In the mere space of days he had descended from mildly rakish to barbarous. His jaw was shadowed, his thick hair tousled. His waistcoat was rumpled and his white shirt lay open at the throat. Emily remembered only too well the feel of him beneath her fingers. With his long legs stretched out before him and his eyes glittering beneath the ebony silk of his lashes, he didn't look the sort of gentleman to seduce his ward. He looked the sort to ravish her.

Emily experimented by striking an off-key chord. A muscle in his jaw twitched dangerously. She hid her smile behind a frown of concentration. As she finished the min-uet, his shoulders slumped and he tossed back the rest of the Scotch in a relieved swig. Shooting him a sly glance, she hooked her fingers and started at the beginning again.

Justin choked. He shot out of the chair, his face dark-ened with emotion. "For God's sake, woman! You're not some wind-up monkey beating a drum. Must you play like one?"

Emily froze, her fingers poised over the keys.

His sisters gaped at him in open-mouthed shock. They had seen their brother frustrated, morose, angry, elated, and white-faced with shame beneath his father's taunts, but they'd never seen him show deliberate cruelty to any-one.

His breath seared the back of her neck as he folded his hands over hers, forcing them out of their rigid stance.

"Loosen your fingers," he commanded. "Stop clawing the keys like a bloody cat."

He massaged each of her knuckles until her hands went limp in his rough embrace. "There. Can you feel the difference?"

"Yes," she murmured. "I can feel it."

She could feel other things as well. The press of his muscled thigh against her back. The whisper of his breath against her cheek, its Scotch-warmed fragrance as intoxi-cating as fresh sin. She gazed down at their linked hands. His knuckles had yet to lose their island tan.

She could also feel his fingers on top of hers, stroking them toward the waiting keys. A shimmering chord vi-brated on the air.

"That's it," he said, his voice softening to husky vel-vet. "Don't attack the keys. Stroke them. Possess them. Make them your own."

He reversed their positions, slipping his hands beneath hers until they rested lightly in the cup of her palms. Her hands looked pale and delicate against the swarthiness of his own. He began the piece, not merely playing the keys but seducing them with his touch. She could feel the music reverberating through his powerful tendons. She turned her head to watch his face, captivated by the play of emotions over his handsome features.

"Music isn't like sewing, Emily. It's feeling and not skill that separates mastery from mechanics. Listen to this piece. It's deceptively simple. But hear it as Mozart did. See the dancers twirling around the ballroom. See two lovers meet and touch hands."

The final note chimed with the crystalline purity of a bell. Their gazes locked in its echo.

Justin felt his breath quicken. Emily smelled like burnt vanilla and her ringlets made her look like a forlorn cocker spaniel, but all he wanted to do was graze his lips against the creamy flesh of her throat and sink his teeth into the inviting fullness of her lower lip.

She gazed up at him, her eyes wide and guileless. "Like this?"

She slipped her hands beneath his and played the piece with the flawless accuracy of any schoolgirl accustomed to a music teacher rapping her knuckles for each error.

Justin straightened. His voice sounded tight, as if something were caught in his throat. "Yes. That will do very nicely."

As he spun on his heel and marched out of the room, Olivia Connor buried her face in her embroidery, her plump ringlets dancing with amusement.

The next day Emily ducked into the kitchen, seeking an escape from Lily. Justin's sister had devised some gruesome new coiffure for that night's dinner party, and had been trailing her for hours, brandishing an iron and some alarming tongs that looked better suited for shoeing horses. She doubted if any of Justin's sisters even knew the kitchen had been moved out of the basement in recent years. They seemed to be caught in a web of perpetual girlhood. Emily thought Justin ought to boot both them and their shiftless husbands out of Grymwilde to start homes and families of their own.

The kitchen was in an uproar. Cooks and maids scurried from oven to table, their aprons streaked with flour and their faces flushed from heat and exertion. Damp tendrils of hair escaped their crooked caps. Gracie, the toothless old cook, hovered over an enameled caldron, stirring and muttering under her breath like one of Macbeth's witches. The salty tang of mussel chowder hung in the air.

As Emily sidled around the coal box, Gracie cocked her bulbous nose and sniffed the air. "Check the buns, Sally. I smell somethin' burnin'."

Emily sighed and blew a singed ringlet out of her eyes.

Gracie's pink gums cracked in a smile. "Never mind, Sal. It's only Miss Emily. And how are ya today, my dear? Come to pilfer another o' my raisin buns, have ya?"

"Not today, Gracie. I just came in to . . . warm myself."

It was true there was little enough warmth in the drafty old house. The fire in Justin's eyes had been banked to an unnatural coolness that made her shiver.

One of the maids burst into tears over a pan of clotted-cream sauce and Gracie bustled over to comfort her. Emily wandered down the long galley, hoping to alleviate her boredom by peering into this pan or that one. At the sight on one of the tables she let out a cry of dismay.

"Can't cook those till it's time to serve 'em," one of the maids explained, brushing past with a tray of steaming buns. "The duchess likes 'em nice and fresh."

Emily knelt and rested her folded arms on the table, bringing herself eye to eye with a glass tank of live lobsters. Pity touched her at the sight of their shiny claws bound by thick twine. They looked helpless and trapped.

Just like her. She imagined her own arms hobbled by ruffles, her legs by crinolines.

She cocked her head sideways, studying the lobsters. Did they dream of the sea as she did? Did they hear its haunting rhythms? Taste its pungent tang?

At least the lobsters did not wake in the night, dreaming of a man garbed not in a crisp waistcoat and trousers, but a pair of faded dungarees. They never ached to remember his dark hair tousled by the wind, his stern features softened by laughter. She reached into the water and stroked a sleek head, surprised by the burn of tears in her eyes.

"There you are, Em!" Lily's shrill tones grated down her spine. "I've found the most enchanting coif in this magazine. Do you think Gracie might give us some egg whites to stiffen your curls?"

Groaning, Emily dropped her head. The lobsters' stalked eyes seemed to glint with sympathy.

"I won't go. I'm not hungry," Emily repeated, digging her nails into the polished oak of the door frame.

"Of course you'll go," Lily chirped, prying her free and dragging her another ten feet. "Mama wouldn't tolerate your not making an appearance. She's hoping you'll make some friends among girls of your own sort."

"Girls with birds' nests on their heads?"

"Don't be ridiculous. Your hair looks charming."

Emily caught her reflection in a console glass as they passed. Her ringlets had been swept up and stiffened with an alarming mixture of egg white and starch. She ducked under a gasolier, afraid her hair might ignite if touched.

She dug her heels into the carpet, but Lily jerked her onward. The frail-looking creature must have inherited her mother's muscle tone if not her fortitude, Emily thought. "Do hurry," she commanded. "Mama will be cranky if we're late."

Emily entered the long dining room in dread. An awkward silence fell over the gathering. She could see only a blur of seated guests, all of them staring fixedly at her head. She jerked her hand out of Lily's, wanting desperately to slither beneath the Brussels carpet.

At the far head of the table sat Justin, riveting in his black tailcoat and silk revers. The startling white of his shirt and bow tie drew out the bronze lingering in his skin. His gaze flicked to her for the briefest moment, and she lowered her eyes, fearful of revealing a hunger that had little to do with the succulent aromas wafting from the serving dishes.

A silvery peal of laughter broke the silence. Emily jerked her head up as a helpless shudder of remembered distaste rippled down her spine.

Seated next to Justin, her icy blond hair the perfect complement to his dark head, was the former toast of Foxworth Seminary and the bane of Emily's existence—Cecille du Pardieu.

Chapter 22

· ✾ ·

*Too soon, the day will come when you take your
heart away from your daddy and give
it to another. . . .*

Emily slunk to her chair beneath the curious stares of
Harvey and Herbert. Harold was too busy slurping his
chowder to notice her. As she sank down, she stole a look
at her old nemesis. Cecille looked as prim and elegant as a
Dresden statuette in a froth of silver-gray silk trimmed in
tiny blue roses. Her hair was knotted in a stark chignon.
Loose tendrils softened the heart-shaped angles of her face.

Emily smoothed the stiff ruffles of her bodice, wondering if anyone would notice if she sawed them off with her
knife. Compared to Cecille's polished sophistication, she
felt like an overgrown six-year-old. As Cecille draped her
graceful fingers over Justin's arm, Emily's hand tightened
around the ivory hilt of her spoon.

A test. She must simply think of this as her trial by
fire. She had practically bitten off her tongue in the past
week to maintain the image of the perfect young lady. If
she survived tonight, Justin would be forced to see her as a
woman, not a child.

"So nice of you to join us, Emily," the duchess brayed. "I should like to introduce you to the Comtesse Guermond and her charming daughter—"

"We've met," Emily mumbled into her chowder.

"I'm sure I don't remember," the countess said. She was a tiny creature swathed in lace who chirped rather than talked.

"Mama," Cecille drawled in the French fashion, "Miss Scarborough is that poor dear creature they were discussing at Baroness Gutwild's last week. The one who spent all of those dreary years working at Foxworth's."

Justin laid down his spoon and pushed back his chowder bowl.

Even Harold stopped slurping as she continued, her blue eyes sparkling with malice. "Quite an industrious little thing, too. You used to give my boots a good polish, didn't you, darling?"

Emily swallowed, remembering Cecille's shrieks at finding a dead mouse stuffed in the patent leather toe of her brand new jemimas.

She grinned sweetly. "Every chance I got."

Cecille's eyes narrowed, but she recovered by fixing Justin with an adoring gaze. Emily's stomach churned.

"You must realize, Your Grace, that you are the gossip of every salon in London. It was so benevolent of you to open your heart and home to an unfortunate orphan in this Christmas season. There's even talk of organizing a society in your name to help rescue other"—she cast Emily a sly glance—"urchins."

Justin met Emily's gaze, his eyes somber beneath the muted glow of the gasoliers. "It was the least I could do."

"Yes, it was," Emily replied, tilting her goblet to her lips. "The very least."

She almost choked as the rich, sweet liquid flowed down her throat. Milk, she realized. Crystalline droplets of wine sparkled on Cecille's pink lips. Emily wiped her upper lip with her napkin, praying she didn't have a foamy mustache to rival Herbert's.

Justin had given her milk just like some babe. She set down the goblet with a deceptively mild thump and fixed Cecille with her most innocent gaze. "My guardian has been the very soul of benevolence." She shifted her gaze to Justin. "Haven't you, *Daddy*?"

Justin's head snapped up. His eyes darkened in warning.

"So what do you all think about those pesky Zulus?" Herbert offered, obviously hoping to steer the conversation in a safer direction.

"Shut up, Herbert," Millicent and Edith snapped in unison.

Emily dipped her spoon in her chowder. Justin's gaze dropped to her lips. "His Grace likes it when I call him *daddy*," she announced.

Cecille's smile waned. "Does he now?"

Emily swirled the spoon around her mouth, then slowly slid it out, licking away the stray drops of chowder with feline satisfaction. Herbert gaped, the pesky Zulus forgotten. Justin lifted his goblet and began to drink in long, convulsive swallows.

"Especially after dinner each night." Emily lowered her voice to a sultry whisper. The little countess bobbed forward so far that her lacy fichu sank into her chowder. "That's when he makes me sit on his lap for my bedtime story."

Justin choked, spewing wine all over Harold. Cecille's elegant mouth dropped open. Edith and Millicent gasped and Herbert went scarlet. As Justin disappeared behind his napkin, Harvey jumped up and began pounding him on the back.

"If you'll excuse me for a moment," Emily murmured. She slipped her knife up her sleeve as she rose, thankful for once for the voluminous ruffles.

When she returned, the second course had been served

and they were eating their shrimp in chill silence. The countess's fichu drooped and Harold's silk waistcoat was speckled with wine. Justin watched her take her seat, his golden eyes glittering with banked fury.

Cecille's laugh sounded more inclined to shatter than tinkle. "I'm not surprised our Emily has ingratiated herself into your affections, Your Grace. She was the darling of every delivery boy and chimney sweep in our neighborhood. She was always so generous with her . . . person."

Justin slammed down his fork. "I've had enough." His voice was low but laced with warning. "My ward's past is of no concern to anyone but me. I'll not have her maligned at her own table. Anyone who cares to do so is not welcome in my house."

As Emily met his possessive gaze, a strange warmth spread in the pit of her stomach.

Cecille threw down her napkin. "The other girls were right, Mama. The man is a beast. I won't marry him! I simply won't!"

"That's a relief, since I never bloody asked you," Justin shouted.

Cecille and her mama rose.

"Now, Comtesse," the duchess said hastily, "I really must apologize for the behavior of my son. I'm sure he meant no—"

Before she could finish, Gracie trotted in from the kitchen, twisting her apron in her hands. Her normally ruddy cheeks had gone as pale as a wraith's. She whispered something to her mistress. The duchess's eyes widened. She cast a furtive glance at the floor. Emily casually tucked her feet up in her chair.

Cecille screamed.

Her shrill howls shook bits of plaster from the ceiling. They all gaped as she leaped onto the brocaded seat of her chair, then onto the table. As she lifted her skirts and shook them wildly, the cause of her distress became evident. Hanging off the thigh of her pantaloons was a live lobster, his jagged claws entangled in her charming white ruffles.

Emily bit into a succulent shrimp and watched with mild interest as Cecille danced a merry reel among the rattling plates. The husbands groped beneath her skirts, trying to dislodge the stubborn creature. Lily and Millicent jumped into a chair, clutching each other while Edith and the duchess tried to soothe the hysterical countess. A bevy of servants rushed into the dining room, crawling around on hands and knees to capture the rest of the lobsters skittering around on the Brussels carpet.

It was Justin who finally disentangled the hapless fellow from Cecille's underwear. He tossed the lobster to Gracie, who thrust it into her apron and raced for the kitchen. As the last of the lobsters were rounded up, Cecille collapsed sniveling into her mother's arms.

The countess drew herself up to her full four feet eight inches. Her voice quavered in righteous indignation. "I must say, I've never seen such a scandalous display."

Emily popped another shrimp into her mouth. "I concur heartily. Those little pink bows on Cecille's drawers shocked the bloody hell out of me."

Every eye turned to her. She stopped chewing. Perhaps now would be a good time to retire, she thought. She rose, slipping a bowl of shrimp under her arm, suddenly ravenous.

"Emily." The single word was spoken in a tone of velvet command.

She paused, then kept walking. Only three more steps to the door. She counted them in her head. One. Two.

"Emily Claire Scarborough!" Justin thundered.

The silver rattled. The crystal drops of the chandelier tinkled like tiny bells. No one even dared to breathe.

Emily pivoted slowly on her heel. "Yes, sir?"

He pointed a finger at her, his face livid. "You little . . ." He looked at Cecille, then back at her. His hand started to shake. A furious snort escaped him, then another.

Suddenly he threw back his head and roared with laughter. They all gaped at him. One by one the maids came peeping around the dining room door frame, their white caps bobbing. Gracie stood aside so they could see what they'd never seen before—the brooding master of Grymwilde Mansion howling with laughter. Justin sank into his chair, clutching his stomach, then rolled from the chair to the floor, still guffawing.

As her only son disappeared beneath the tablecloth, the duchess rose. "Perhaps we should retire to the drawing room for dessert," she announced as if it were the end of any flawless dinner party and the heir to the Winthrop title and fortune wasn't a raving lunatic.

"I've lost my appetite," the countess snapped, dragging Cecille toward the door in the wake of her icy wrath. "Come, darling. We're going home. And we shan't come back until we are offered a formal apology."

The rest of the family filed out, Harold and Herbert grumbling over being deprived of their after-dinner brandy and cigars. The door to the kitchen swung shut. Emily set the bowl on the sideboard and crept toward the end of the table as if approaching a mad boar. Justin was snuffling rather like one.

She stood on tiptoe and peeped over the edge of the table. Justin was doubled up against his chair, shuddering with laughter. He wiped tears from his sparkling eyes and sucked in a wheezing breath. "Every time I think . . . dancing a jig on the table . . . those ridiculous pantaloons . . . I just can't . . ." Wheezing for breath, he made pinching motions against her ankles with his long fingers. Emily giggled.

Soon her giggles deepened to chortles. Her knees folded and she dropped to the carpet beside him, hugging her own stomach as the dam of hilarity she'd stemmed all week burst with a vengeance.

Justin pounded his fist against the floor, struggling for control.

Emily gasped for breath. "I haven't seen Cecille move that fast since I waxed the soles of her ballet shoes."

He collapsed against her shoulder. "I shudder to think of it. God, you must have been awful."

"Incorrigible," she admitted modestly.

They relaxed against each other, knowing one would fall without the other. The stilted conversations and awkward silences of the past week melted in the warmth of their nearness. It seemed only natural that Emily would reach up and brush a strand of hair from his eyes. Only natural that he would capture her hand in his own and caress her palm with his eloquent thumb.

His smile softened. "Whatever am I to do with you?"

Suddenly their faces were very close. Close enough for her to see the spark that lit his eyes. Danger scented the air, as sharp and acrid as the smell of lightning on a summer day.

"Come here, you wicked girl," he whispered. "Sit on my lap and I'll tell you a bedtime story."

Emily moaned softly as he drew her into his lap and touched his mouth to hers. It was like touching flame to hot wax. Her lips melted beneath his, deepening his tender kiss to the ravenous flick and thrust of his tongue against her own. A sweet, interminable ache licked through her. She tangled her hands in the hair at his nape, marveling at the silky fineness of the new growth against his starched collar. The heady scent of his bay rum intoxicated her. She wiggled against him in an artless attempt to press herself closer, to somehow absorb all his textures and scents, both new and remembered.

Justin groaned. "You're going to be the death of me, woman," he muttered against her lips. Then his tongue filled her mouth again, plunging deep in a blatant act of possession.

Justin wasn't sure how she managed it, but Emily was

just as enticing in her silly garments as she had been naked on a moonlit beach. Each scrap of lace, pearl button, and hook and eyelet was a provocative challenge to his desire. She was dressed like a ruffled cake and he wanted nothing more than to lick off all her icing. Her untamed response to his touch shattered his inhibitions. He rained a delicate shower of kisses down her throat.

Not even the starched layers of her petticoats were enough to shield Emily from the rigid evidence of Justin's desire. He nudged against her, his hard, hungry heat making her shudder.

With a hoarse oath Justin reached beneath her skirt and shoved aside the crinolines until only the sheer cotton of her pantaloons and the crisp linen of his trousers separated them. She gasped against his lips as he moved against her, coaxing, enticing, until she could feel every inch of him pressed to the damp valley between her legs. A helpless whimper, half fear, half need, caught in her throat.

"Sweet Christ, this is madness!" he exploded, dumping her out of his lap.

He rose and strode to the sideboard, raking a hand through his hair. As he sloshed wine into a glass, filling it to the rim, Emily could see his hand was shaking violently.

She climbed to her feet, smoothing her skirts with her own trembling hands. "Why?" she said softly. "Why must it be madness?"

He cocked the glass up and drained it. "Aside from the fact that we were writhing around on the dining room floor with a kitchen of gossiping servants only a careless moan away?"

She nodded, refusing to make this easy for him. "Aside from that."

Justin slammed down the glass. He knew it wasn't enough to put physical distance between them. She could bridge that with just one yearning look. He had to put emotional distance between them as well. He had to build walls so high she could never tear them down. Even if they imprisoned his heart forever.

"You're too young for me," he said.

Emily flinched at Justin's emotionless tone. "What of Cecille? Is she too young for you as well? Isn't she just the sort of wife your mother would choose for you?"

He swung around to face her. "Cecille is neither my ward nor my responsibility. You are. If I had an ounce of brains, I'd have declared for her tonight."

She tapped her pursed lips thoughtfully. "Now, would that make her my auntie or my stepmother?"

He caught her shoulders in a frantic grip, pulling her hard against him. "This isn't a game. Do you think this is why David entrusted you to my care? So I could compromise you like some aging lech without a thought for your reputation or future? Is that what your father would have wanted?"

She met his gaze squarely. "My father is dead. You should know that better than anyone."

His hands went limp. He laughed shakily. "Yes, I should, shouldn't I?"

"Justin!" she called after him, frightened by the glimpse of hopeless despair she'd seen in his eyes.

He walked out on her, his gait oddly uneven, like that of a wounded man. Emily sank down among the ruins of the dinner party and buried her head in her arms.

Emily Claire Scarborough was a very bad girl. She had heard it whispered for years, and in some small corner of her heart she had come to believe it. So when Justin again shut himself away from her behind a wall of cool reserve, she set out to do the one thing she did best. Misbehave.

She swaggered around in an old pair of Justin's trousers and a discarded jacket from one of Edith's riding habits, her curls an uncombed tangle.

But Justin's calm was imperturbable. When she began

to sprinkle her speech with careless profanities, he blithely retaliated by hiring a tutor, an art teacher, and a dancing master, all of whom resigned in hysterics within the week. When she shortened the legs of all of his trousers, he summoned a tailor and ordered new ones. When she stuffed the chimney in the study with her discarded petticoats, layering the room in coal dust and soot, he moved his work to the library until the room could be aired.

To both servants and family Justin was no longer caustic, but only distant. Music stopped flowing through the darkened rooms at night. The grand piano in the drawing room gathered a thin layer of dust. The servants attributed his brief burst of good cheer and subsequent mood change to a brain fever he had suffered during his exotic travels. No one knew what to attribute Miss Emily's behavior to, although Jimmie the stablemaster, a devout Roman Catholic, was the first to whisper of demon possession. He swore he had glanced up at her lighted window at night and seen objects flying about, spurred on by curses so uproarious, they made even his worldly ears burn.

The formal apology the duchess sent Cecille and her mama after the disastrous dinner party bought their stilted forgiveness but not their silence. Gossip spread through London that the Duke of Winthrop had a madwoman on his hands, a wild creature he'd do well to shuffle off to Bedlam before she harmed someone. People scrambled for invitations to the ball the duchess was throwing to introduce Emily to society, hoping to catch even a glimpse of the duke's eccentric ward.

It was a bitterly cold January morning when the door of the study burst open and Emily marched in on him and Penfeld, trailed by a shouting contingent of servants.

Justin barely glanced up from his ledger. "Good morning, Emily." His deep voice carried over the cacophony.

"Good morning, sir," she replied evenly.

Penfeld busied himself with straightening a perfectly aligned stack of papers. Emily stood stiffly, danger smoldering in her dark eyes as her domestic captors mobbed the desk.

"Sir, I must insist on a moment of your time—"

"—cannot be tolerated, Your Grace, not for another day—"

"Ye must take action, my lord, afor she burns the 'ouse down 'round our bloomin' heads!"

Justin lifted a hand in a plea for silence. "One at a time, please."

It was Gracie who stepped forward. The other servants subsided to murmurs in deference to her age and years of loyal service to the Connors. "I'm not one to be stickin' me nose into family affairs, Yer Grace. I know the child has a good heart an' all, but . . ."

"Get on with it, Gracie. I'm listening."

The cook honked into her apron. "I left the pie on the windowsill only for a minute, sir, and now we've no rhubarb for lunch a'tall."

A horse-faced maid poked her long nose over Gracie's shoulder. "There won't be no need for the rhubarb, sir, for 'twas the curate who was to partake of it and the girl sent him packin' by tellin' him he could take his prayer book and put it—"

At a titter from one of the younger groomsmen, she cupped her hands around Justin's ear and whispered something that made his eyes widen with interest.

"Mmm. I didn't know that was possible."

Emily rolled her eyes and tapped her toe in obvious boredom.

The valet shared by Harold, Herbert, and Harvey shoved past her. "That's nothing, Your Grace, look what she did to the hat my master bought for the ball next week."

He thrust the top hat into Justin's hand. An odd squeaking and mewling rose from its silk confines. When Justin lifted his head, he was smiling. "She had a litter of kittens in it?"

The valet sputtered. "Of course she didn't have a litter of kittens. She hid it in the stable, where the mama cat would be sure to find it. Why, Master Harold will be livid!"

Justin's smile spread. "Master Harold, you say?" He handed the hat back. "Return it to the stable for now. Perhaps when Master Harold finds a suitable position, he can buy a new one. As for now, you're all dismissed."

"But, sir—"

"Your Grace, there's no time. With the ball next Friday!"

"My lord—"

"Good day," Justin said with utter finality.

Emily stood in sullen silence as her disappointed accusers filed out. Penfeld slipped out behind them, shaking his head and muttering under his breath.

The door whispered shut, leaving them alone. Justin drew off his spectacles, leaned back in his chair, and surveyed his young charge from boots to crown. If she was trying to look boyish, she had failed dismally. The trousers only emphasized her slender waist and hugged the ample curve of her rump. Edith's jacket had not been tailored for a bosom as generous as Emily's. Unhindered by corset or chemise, her breasts strained against the worn fabric.

Only a hint of color in her cheeks betrayed her response to his casual perusal. Her spine was stiff with that terrible pride that made her seem so fragile yet so unreachable.

He steepled his fingers beneath his chin. "Have you anything to say for yourself?"

She crossed her arms over her chest and blew a stray curl out of her eyes. "Damnable liars, every one of them."

"You didn't swear at the curate?"

"Hell, no."

His lips twitched. "You didn't eat the entire rhubarb pie?"

"Of course not. I gave it to Pudding. Bulldogs love rhubarb."

"And you didn't allow the stable cat to birth in Harold's new hat?"

"Cats are notoriously stubborn. They birth where they please."

Sighing, he slipped on his spectacles and went back to scrawling in the ledger. "Very well. You may go."

Emily slammed her palms on the desk. "Aren't you even going to punish me?"

"Punish you?" He nibbled on the end of his pen. "If it pleases you, you may take supper in your room."

She spoke through gritted teeth. "I take all my meals in my room."

"Then you may take supper in the dining room." He flipped a page of the ledger.

"Damn you," she whispered, her voice husky with thwarted emotion. He didn't even look up.

She spun around and marched for the door.

"Emily?"

She turned, her hand on the doorknob.

The pen kept up its even scratch. "Nothing you do, no matter how horrendous, is going to change the way I feel about you." His hand stilled. He slanted her a look over the rim of his spectacles. "Nor the fact that I am not free to act on those feelings."

Emily threw open the door, horrified by the betraying sting in her eyes. She closed the door and slumped against it, pressing them shut against the burning pressure. When she opened them, a black mountain blocked her vision.

She blinked the tears away and found herself face-to-face with Penfeld's starched lapels. "Penfeld? What the devil—"

She was totally unprepared when the valet fastened his meaty fingers around her earlobe in a pinch that would have made Doreen Dobbins swoon with envy. Emily's mouth fell open, more from shock than pain.

Penfeld thrust his face into Emily's. "March, little missy," he hissed, "or I'll give you something to cry about."

"How dare you—!"

Emily's cry of protest was cut off by a vicious yank that almost dragged her off her feet. Needles of pain shot through her skull. Wherever Penfeld was going, he was obviously intent on taking her ear with him, whether it was attached or not. Emily's feet slid on the polished wood floor, but he never faltered. A grinning footman swept open the door to the foyer.

A mobcapped head appeared around the corner, then another. Doors flew open. Grubby faces popped up in the windows. The servants gaped as their master's mild-mannered valet dragged a howling Emily across the foyer and up the stairs.

When Justin emerged from the study to investigate the distant smattering of applause, he found nothing but a bevy of servants industriously polishing the gleaming banister.

Chapter 23

· 🐚 ·

I pray the man you choose is worthy
of such a prize. . . .

𝒫enfeld gave her a less than genteel shove into her bedroom. Emily groped for her ear, surprised to find it still in place, then stood with fists clenched.

The valet planted his bulk between the bed and the door. "I had seven younger brothers, all bigger and meaner than you, dear. Think about it."

Emily did. Penfeld's hands hung like creased hams from his immaculate sleeves. She sank down on the edge of the bed and gave him a sullen glare.

Returning a sweet smile, he locked the door and slipped the key into the pocket of his waistcoat.

She rubbed her throbbing ear. "What are you going to do? Beat me?"

"It would be a bit overdue, don't you think? Someone should have cared enough to yank your ear and blister your little bum a long time ago. But no one did, did they?"

It wasn't the shocking language, but the complete absence of pity in his tone that made it so compelling. He scraped over the chair from the hearth, turned it backward, and straddled it.

"Why, Penfeld, I hardly know you," Emily breathed in amazement.

"No, you don't," he said briskly. "And I think it high time to remedy that. I was born on Tenant Street, the second oldest of fifteen, three of whom died at birth. My father was a tanner, my mother a drunk. I was commonly known by the undignified sobriquet of Penny. My older sister died of typhoid at the age of fifteen. Before her corpse could cool, I snatched her job at a Bond Street haberdashery, where I met my first master."

Emily nodded, cautious but empathetic. Ambition. Level-headed thinking. A yearning for independence. These were all traits she respected.

"I discovered that by serving as a valet, a 'gentleman's gentleman' so to speak, I could partake of the finer and more civilized aspects of life and earn wages for doing so."

"Don't you ever tire of being on the outside? Don't you ever want to *be* that gentleman?"

"A gentleman has many responsibilities. I have only one. Ensuring the happiness of my master."

She traced the gold leaf pattern on the rug with the toe of her boot. "I see. Is that why you dragged me up here? Because I am interfering with that task?"

"Precisely."

Emily swallowed, bracing herself to hear she was unwanted yet again. Somehow the words would hurt more coming from the gentle valet. Penfeld had never so much as rebuked her. "What would you have me do? Shall I disappear from his life again? For good this time?"

"Would that make him happy?"

She searched his earnest face. "I honestly don't know."

Penfeld folded his arms on the back of the chair. "Why don't we give him exactly what he's asked for? First, you must stop this infernal misbehaving."

"I already tried acting like a lady. It made us both miserable."

A triumphant smile wreathed the valet's round face. "Ah, but that's because my master doesn't need a lady. My master needs a woman."

Justin had gone stone deaf. He masked it behind a polite smile as he wound his way through the guests in the ballroom. He felt them touch his sleeve, saw them smile in greeting, but only gibberish spilled from their lips. The music of the orchestra seated on the low dais skittered off his ears like rain off oilcloth. Bows sawed madly away at violin strings. Fingers plucked the gleaming strands of the harp. Yet Justin could hear nothing but the terrible silence in his head. Not only had he lost the ability to write music; he had lost the ability to hear it. He wondered how Beethoven in his deafness had kept from going mad.

"Your Grace?" From the footman's patient tone Justin knew he had repeated the words more than once. "Would you care for some champagne?"

"Thank you, Sims." His own voice sounded muffled, as if it came from beneath a roaring sea.

He took a fluted glass from the tray and brought it to his lips. The tart bubbles tickled his nostrils.

He had thought this ball an ill-conceived idea from the start, but his mother had pouted until he relented. At any moment he expected Emily to swing past on one of the chandeliers or ride Pudding through the glass doors. She had been sulking in her room all week, doubtlessly planning some horrific revenge for his dispassionate treatment of her. What better place to execute it than at the ball given in her honor? Someone bumped him in passing and he jumped, sloshing champagne on his white-gloved hand. He swore softly, cursing his raw nerves.

He drained the glass. If she only knew the terrible cost of his apathy.

He caught a glimpse of his reflection in a looking glass

hung between two columns. He could almost see his father's whiskers superimposed over his unsmiling face. Unable to bear the oppressive silence of his head, he had actually gone to the Winthrop Shipping offices yesterday and spent hours in a dusty alcove, poring over meaningless figures.

Amid a flurry of greetings at the door he saw Cecille du Pardieu and her mama enter, arms linked as if fearful some wayward crustacean might come dashing out at them. Apparently, both their fear and their wounded feelings had been bested by curiosity and a deeper fear of missing the social event of the holiday season. The room swirled around Justin, awash in a tapestry of gaiety and celebration. He heard nothing but the muffled thump of his own faltering heart.

He had set off in search of more champagne when a slight figure slipped through the glass doors into the ballroom. There was no fanfare, no sudden stillness or rustle of movement to herald her arrival, but Justin's heart dulled to a whisper and Mendelssohn's *On Wings of Song* began to beat wildly in his brain.

Emily.

Emily gentled, but not tamed, her milky skin aglow, her dark eyes vibrant with laughter and curiosity. A dress of cream silk trimmed in roses hugged her slender figure. Flounces of lace draped a modest bustle, flowing down to a short train adorned with three simple bows. A circlet of silk roses crowned her hair. Her curls haloed her face as they had on the island, no longer stiff and singed, but soft and loose and perfect for a man to bury his hands in.

Justin drifted toward her like a traveler who has spotted a breath of spring on a frozen tundra.

"More champagne, sir?"

Justin recoiled from the tray thrust in front of him. "Christ, Sims, must you bellow in that manner?"

Curious stares assailed them, and Justin realized he had shouted at the hapless man. Before he could apologize, he became aware of other sounds—the nervous rattle of the footman's tray, the shrill notes of Cecille's voice, Harold's inane bray of laughter. The women seemed to be clumping around in their dainty slippers like dancing bears. He would almost swear he could hear the tinkle of a hairpin sliding from a dancer's neat chignon and striking the floor.

Justin gripped the footman's sleeve. "Did you hear that?"

"Of course, sir. As you say, sir." Sims gently disengaged himself and fled for the kitchen, obviously fearing his master was in the grip of some new and dreadful brain fever.

Justin's gaze flew to the doors. His mother had taken her place at Emily's side. His eyes moved to the line of gilt chairs against the wall where Emily sat, folding her gloved hands demurely in her lap. As an unmarried woman she would be expected to remain at her chaperone's side until she was asked to dance and to be returned there after each twirl about the floor.

As others in the room became aware of their presence, the murmurs and whispers swelled, making Justin's ears tingle with their newly found acuity. A couple danced past him.

"She must be the one, darling," the man said. "Look at the way the duchess is fussing over her."

"Not quite the drooling madwoman the countess described, is she?"

His reply was lost in the maddening rustle of his wife's taffeta petticoats. Justin started forward, determined to reach Emily this time. Just as he did, a bewhiskered young man swept her away, and he was left staring stupidly at her empty chair.

His mother tapped her feet to the music; her fat ringlets bobbed. "Hello, darling. Enjoying yourself?"

"Immensely," he lied.

He slipped behind Emily's chair and leaned against the wall, determined to be there when she returned. His gaze wasn't the only one locked on her. Heads craned as she spun around the room in an enchanting swirl of cream and rose. Justin's breath quickened. He wanted to dance with her as he had in New Zealand. He wanted to splay his hand over the delicate expanse of her ribs, and damn the consequences. As he watched her, his heart lurched into reckless song. His fingers drummed on the back of the chair, itching for a smooth scrap of paper on which to record his melody.

At last the interminable tune was done and Emily and her escort made their way back toward the chair. Justin picked a minuscule speck of lint off his sleeve and stepped forward. Penfeld chose that moment to lean over and offer his mother an hors d'oeuvre from a silver tray. Before Justin could maneuver around them, Emily was gone again, whisked off by another young swain. He swore under his breath.

The orchestra launched into a waltz by Brahms that captured perfectly the floating sway of Emily's skirt.

His mother popped a little sausage into her mouth. "Hungry, dear?"

Emily's smooth cheek dimpled as she smiled up at her partner. Justin's nails dug into the back of the chair. "Ravenous."

Penfeld beamed at the dance floor. "They make a charming couple, don't they?"

Justin grunted, refusing to commit himself. The man's golden hair shimmered as he inclined his head to Emily.

"Young Peter just graduated from Oxford," the duchess said. "He's level-headed, bright, and very interested in his father's mining business. A simply marvelous prospect."

"A prospect for what?" Justin snapped. If the level-headed Peter didn't keep his gloved hands still on Emily's back, he was going to be a marvelous prospect for getting his head dunked in the punch bowl.

His mother only made a mysterious noise.

Justin leaned over her shoulder, craning his neck as another couple blocked his view. "That fuzz on his chin makes him look a little like an overgrown rat, don't you think?" He smugly stroked his own jaw, where a day's growth was already pricking the skin.

She tittered. "Don't be so harsh on the boy. Has it been so long that you've forgotten your first whiskers?"

Justin's hand froze in its motion, then fell limp at his side. He resisted the urge to check the looking glass, afraid he might discover his hair had gone snow white.

This time he didn't wait for the last note of the waltz to sound. As soon as Penfeld started to shift his bulk, he flung himself over the valet's legs and plunged through the crowd.

He took Emily's arm firmly and forced himself to make a genteel bow. "Would you be kind enough to grant me the pleasure of your company for a dance?"

She opened the card affixed to her wrist by a golden thread and studied it. A charming line of concentration furrowed her brow. "I'm afraid not. My dance card is full." She patted his sleeve. "Perhaps another time."

Stung by her careless rejection, Justin's grip on her arm tightened, but before he could protest, a familiar voice chimed between them. "Why, good evening, Your Grace. Charming ball, is it not?" Cecille du Pardieu bobbed him a schoolroom curtsy that made him feel at least eighty. "Come along, Emily dear. There's a young gentleman who's simply dying to meet you."

He had to admire Cecille's opportunism. Emily was the obvious belle of the ball, and claiming her now could only enhance Cecille's own reputation. Hooking her arm in Emily's, she dragged her away, chattering as if they had always been the best of friends. They disappeared in a crowd of laughing, jostling young people.

He dragged his creaking bones back to Emily's chair and sank into it. When Sims, standing back at a discreet distance, offered him another glass of champagne, Justin took the entire tray and balanced it on his knees, leaving the perspiring footman empty-handed.

"Dry, sweeting?" his mother chirped.

"Parched," he replied. As he tossed back a glass, his hungry gaze combed the crowd for a hint of chestnut curls garlanded with roses.

Justin rolled the fluted stem of the champagne glass between his fingers. The ballroom was nearly as empty as the tray sitting at his feet. His head gave a warning throb.

It was well after midnight. A crowd had gathered at the door where the duchess and Millicent were bidding farewell to the last of their guests. He ought to be with them. But doubting his ability to stand, much less converse socially, he remained sprawled in his chair.

He didn't relish the prospect of climbing the winding stairs to his big, lonely bed. Penfeld sat beside him, humming tunelessly under his breath. Justin was surprised the valet hadn't fainted dead away from mortification. He had long ago clawed away the tie Penfeld had knotted with such painstaking care, and draped it around his collar.

He narrowed his eyes as Emily untangled herself from the last knot of her admirers and started across the ballroom, her kid slippers whispering on the polished tile. Her silk roses might have wilted a bit under the strain, but she still looked as fresh as a spring rain in the desert.

She approached, smothering a yawn into her glove.

"Tired?" Justin gave his knee a pat of invitation and quirked a devilish eyebrow.

Her cheek dimpled in reproach. She brushed past him, leaned over, and kissed Penfeld's cheek. "G'night, Penny."

"Penny?" he muttered. She was already turning away. "What about me?"

She stopped, the curve of her bare shoulders alabaster in the fading light. Justin crossed his arms over his chest and stared straight ahead, regretting the childish challenge the instant it left his lips.

Emily turned in a swirl of silk. The scent of rosewater and vanilla jolted his senses. She bent to give his cheek a peck, but before he even realized he was going to do it, Justin turned his head, grazing her mouth with his own. The contact was brief, warm, and sweet. He knew it wasn't fair, but he was unable to deny himself a fleeting taste of her lips.

"Come, my dear." The duchess appeared at Emily's elbow. "Won't you escort an old lady to her room?"

As his mother drew her away, Emily looked over her shoulder at him. He leaned the back of his head against the wall, oddly sobered by the rebuke in her eyes.

The clock on the landing below chimed twice. Emily turned over in her bed as the hollow bongs rolled through the house. Why should sleep elude her now? The night had been a smashing success. She ought to be savoring her triumph, dreaming of the hectic days to come as she accepted the invitations Penfeld had assured her would come pouring in tomorrow.

Instead, she lay staring wide-eyed into the shadows, unable to erase from her mind her last glimpse of Justin as he sat alone in the dimming gaslights, surrounded by a sea of limp confetti.

His own behavior at the ball had caused quite a stir. He had appeared the height of rakish splendor with his tie unknotted and his long legs sprawled before him in disreputable indolence. Whispers about his roguish past had flown through the staid crowd on wings of fascination. Oddly enough, while such innuendo would have been the ruin of a woman, it only enhanced his reputation and made him all the more desirable to the eligible girls and their mamas. Emily wondered what they would think if they could have seen him sweating in the fields like a common farmer or reading the Bible to a tribe of rapt natives.

His rakish pose did not fool her. She had seen the hollowness in his eyes as he watched her go. She touched her lower lip, remembering the jarring brush of his lips against her own.

She rolled over. Champagne glasses had littered the floor around Justin's chair. Had Penfeld remained to help him to bed? What if he stumbled over something in the dark and fell? Lord knew, there was plenty to stumble over in this cluttered museum. Her father had once lost a friend who, after imbibing too much gin, took a tumble down the stairs and cracked his head. Emily sat straight up, beset by a vivid image of Justin's body sprawled on the first-floor landing, his white shirt stained with blood.

She climbed out of bed and drew a robe of woolly cashmere over her nightdress. As the toys and fairy-tale books had disappeared from her room, other things had appeared—an olivewood stationery case lined in velvet, a delicate box of rose-leaf face powder, a handsome leather diary inscribed with her initials. Gifts not for a child, but for a woman, all placed by magical, unseen hands.

Leaving Pudding drowsing in front of the fire, she padded down the stairs. Silence enveloped her in its dark cloak, making her realize how badly she missed Justin's music.

She pushed open the door to the ballroom. A pale splinter of a moon shone through the oriel windows, bathing the long, empty room in a silver wash. She felt foolish. Of course, Penfeld would have rescued his master by now. She shivered as the chill of the marble tile crept into her bare feet.

She was turning to go when a voice came out of the shadows, as husky and intimate as a touch. "You still owe me a dance, Emily Scarborough."

Chapter 24

·❀·

I have hesitated to speak of things
that might trouble you. . . .

Justin stepped away from the dais into a shallow arc of moonlight. His hands were shoved into his pockets, his head inclined at a sheepish angle.

Emily's breath tightened in her throat. She smoothed back her curls and hugged the robe tighter around her. "How can we dance? There isn't any music."

His eyes searched the reaches of the vaulted ceiling. "Don't you hear it?" He lowered his gaze to her face. "The angels sing every time you walk into a room."

She laughed nervously. "It's more likely a chorus of demons."

Justin's laugh never came. He walked toward her, his steps measured, his eyes glowing with an odd light. Emily resisted the urge to fly back up the stairs to the safe cocoon of her bed.

He stopped in front of her and bowed with no trace of a drunken falter. "May I have this dance, Miss Scarborough?"

He opened his arms to her, and just as she had in New Zealand, Emily stepped into them, powerless to do otherwise. Justin held her with perfect propriety, sweeping her around the floor in eerie silence. Emily didn't dare look at his face, so she looked at his chest instead, painfully aware of the shift of his powerful muscles, his flawless rhythm, the off-key cadence of his breathing.

Each faint brush of their bodies in the darkness made her feel as if she were suspended over a dangerous chasm, too high to drop without shattering. The peaks of her breasts ached against the soft cotton of her nightdress.

His breath touched her ear, warm and tart with the scent of champagne. "Can you hear it now?" he whispered. "The thundering chords? The sigh of the harp? The moan of the oboe?"

"All I can hear are drums."

"Drums?"

"My heart."

Laughing softly, he gave her a gentle squeeze. His steps slowed, and he released her reluctantly, as if hearing the music come to an end. Emily could still hear its bittersweet echo lingering on the air.

She took a step away from him. "I'd best go. I wanted to make sure you were all right, but I should be getting back upstairs now. It's late."

"Too late." She might have imagined his whispered words. As she turned to go, he called her name.

She stopped. Their eyes met across the polished expanse of moonlight and marble.

"You were magnificent tonight. I wish David could have seen you. You made me"—he balled his hands and shoved them back in his pockets—"proud."

Swallowing around the knot in her throat, Emily fled the ballroom, leaving Justin as she had found him. Alone.

When Emily slipped into her chair at breakfast the next morning, Justin greeted her with a polite nod. He and

Harold were engaged in a heated debate pitting the efficiency of clipper ships against steamers. She stole a look at him over her milk glass. His black coat was impeccable, his gray tie knotted in sleek folds. He bore no resemblance to the rumpled roué who had swept her around a deserted ballroom.

She glanced up at the gasolier, but heard no choir of angels announcing her entrance. This Justin did not look the sort of man inclined to such romantic folly. Although he bore no visible scars from last night's debauchery, she wondered if he had been too drunk to even remember their stolen interlude.

A serving maid leaned over his shoulder with a silver platter. "Kippers, Your Grace?"

Emily might have imagined the faint paling around his mouth as he replied, "No, thank you, Libby."

He stared as his mother took the fork the maid offered and heaped kippers on her own plate, filling the dining room with the pungent aroma of herring. Justin pushed away his plate and Emily thrust a hot scone into her mouth to hide her smile.

"Will you be going out today, Emily?"

His question caught her off guard, and she swallowed quickly, licking away the stray crumbs. "Lily and I might go shopping this afternoon." She held her breath, waiting for him to forbid her her freedom as he had done on the island.

He pulled his napkin out of his lap and dabbed his lips. "You may take the brougham if you like. I'll tell the coachman to make it ready. If you wish to purchase anything, charge it to my name."

"Why, thank you . . . sir."

At her added note of respect he cast her an unreadable glance that might have been displeasure.

"Will you be going to the office today, dear?" the duchess inquired, her booming voice an octave lower than usual.

Justin flinched and touched his fingertips to his temple. "I might. There is a surfeit of accounting to be done."

She bit into a kipper with unmistakable relish. "Don't we have men hired for that?"

He shot her a dark glance. "Of course we do. But even the best of men require supervision."

As Harold launched into a soliloquy pronouncing steam engines instruments of the devil and predicting a return to sailing ships by all right-thinking men, Emily murmured her excuses and slipped out.

When she returned to her room at midmorning, the fairies had visited again. A plum-colored cloak of luxuriant wool was fanned across her bed. Among its folds lay a mother-of-pearl calling-card case polished to a lustrous gleam. She touched her fingertips to the cool inlay, remembering Justin's words.

You made me proud.

She had made people many things since her father's death—ashamed, infuriated, embarrassed, frustrated, murderous—but she couldn't remember making anyone proud. She rubbed the prickly softness of the cloak against her cheek, knowing she could not have imagined the hint of bay rum that clung to it.

"What's she doing now, Penfeld?" Justin whispered.

Penfeld lowered his newspaper a fraction of an inch and peered over the top. "Ribbons, sir. She's finished with the brooches and gone on to the ribbons."

Justin stole a glance around the edge of his own paper, squinting against the glare of the setting sun striking the frosted shop window. Emily stood at the counter inside, studying a display of ribbons proffered by a fawning shopgirl. She tapped her lips in indecision, then plucked up a burgundy ribbon and held it against her dimpled cheek for Lily to admire. The gesture was so girlish and free of care that it made his heart catch. He watched mesmerized as the velvet length trailed her skin. His fingers itched to follow its path.

Without warning Emily dropped the ribbon and glanced at the window. Justin jerked up the paper, burying his nose in it.

Penfeld stamped his feet on the pavement and adjusted the collar of his greatcoat. "My toes are going numb again."

"Wiggle them," Justin snapped, daring another peep around the paper.

The clatter of a passing omnibus drowned out the warning tinkle of the shop bells. Emily and Lily were headed out the door, their arms loaded with packages. Justin grabbed Penfeld and hurled him around the corner into the waiting carriage.

He slammed his walking stick into the roof of the carriage and yelled, "Follow that brougham!"

"Aye, sir." At the driver's urging the horses clip-clopped into motion and Justin settled back in the plush seat.

Penfeld hunkered down into the lap blankets until all but the reddened bulb of his nose disappeared. "I'd be the last to suggest a flaw in your character, Your Grace," he said, his voice muffled, "but don't you think you're being a bit overzealous?"

Justin slid open the window and craned his neck for a glimpse of Emily's plum-hooded head in the graceful brougham in front of them. "Nonsense, Penfeld. You know Emily has a penchant for getting into mischief. London is full of dangerous sorts who might take advantage of that. I simply want to ensure her safety."

Penfeld suspected his master's motives had more to do with Emily's transformation than London's dangers. Now that his little caterpillar had sprouted wings, he didn't want to risk her flying away. "But we've been following her all day, and she has been the very model of propriety."

"That doesn't alter my responsibility to her. It's no more than any other guardian would do."

The valet rolled his eyes and muttered, "In a pig's eye."

Justin drew back his head. "Pardon me?"

Penfeld cleared his throat. "Impeccable, sir. I said your devotion to your ward was impeccable."

"Hmm." Justin leaned back in the seat, smirking. "I thought that was what you said."

Emily poked her head out the brougham window for the sheer pleasure of watching Justin's handsome, dark head disappear again. She threw herself back in the seat, biting her lip to keep from laughing. With a frame as rugged and masculine as Justin's, he was hardly unobtrusive lurking behind lampposts and skulking outside ladies' dress shops. Why, she could hear the chattering of Penfeld's teeth through the window of the last haberdashery!

Lily shot her a curious look. "Why are you looking so pleased with yourself? Have you tacked a note saying 'Pinch me' to my bustle?"

"Would I do such a thing?" She leaned forward and whispered, "Actually I stuffed a dead hedgehog in your muff."

Lily jerked off her ermine muff and shook it in horror.

"For heaven's sake, I was only joking!" Emily assured her.

She hung out the window again, checking the progress of Justin's carriage. A hansom cab had come between them, and the coachman was frantically searching for a way past. She could well imagine the shouted instructions he was receiving from his master.

Lily squealed, startling her into bumping her head. "Good Lord, what was that for? Did you see a mouse?"

"No. I saw a house."

Emily blinked. Lily was even more unintelligible than her mother at times.

Lily caught the collar of her cloak and dragged her to the opposite window. "Look!" She clapped her hands over Emily's eyes. "No, wait. Don't look. Someone might see you. All right, you may look now."

All Emily saw was a rather ordinary-looking gray town house, fronted by a wrought-iron fence and a neatly trimmed lawn.

Lily lowered her voice to a theatrical whisper. "Mrs. Rose lives there with all of her little blooms."

"Mrs. Rose," Emily echoed softly, pushing back her hood.

She stared up at a lighted window on the second floor, thinking of Tansy. A sharp pang of nostalgia touched her. She wondered if her friend was still warmed by her fancy gentlemen with their gentle hands and generous purses?

Lily threw herself back in the seat, sighing in content. "Harvey will have a Hereford if he knows we took this route." She giggled slyly. "Sometimes I wish he'd take this way himself. I try to lie very still and endure his attentions as Mama taught me, but I shouldn't mind so much if he snuck off to fertilize someone else's bloom."

Lily began to sing under her breath, some ditty about the bees buzzing around Mrs. Rose's garden. Emily sank back, fingering the soft wool of her cloak. She was hard pressed to imagine lying still beneath the tender stroke of Justin's hands. The image brought warmth stinging to her cheeks.

How familiar was Justin with this street? Had his carriage ever been parked outside the pretty gray town house with the curtained windows? She frowned. If he was so determined to follow her, why shouldn't she lead him on a merry chase?

The carriage slowed at the corner. Emily reached for the door handle.

Lily recognized the sparkle of mischief in her eyes only too well. Her gloved hand closed over Emily's. "Oh, no, you don't. What are you up to? Going to jab the horses with a hairpin and send me careening into the Thames?"

"This joke isn't on you. I promise." She pried away Lily's clinging fingers. "Have the driver circle the block a few times, then pick me up in the park."

Ignoring Lily's protests, she opened the door a crack and eased out of the carriage. The driver clucked the horses into motion, unaware that he had lost a passenger.

As the brougham rolled away, Lily hung out the window and hissed, "Take care, silly. The moon is already out. It'll be full dark soon."

Emily strolled across the road to the park, swinging her embroidered purse as if she hadn't a care in the world. From behind her she heard a frantic cry of "Whoa!" a horse's whinny, and the clatter of someone spilling out of a carriage in great haste. Pretending to brush a stray hair from her shoulder, she looked back just as Justin ducked behind the mottled trunk of a sycamore.

Pulling her hood up over her hair, she darted into a thicket of trees. The air was much colder here. A lacy web of branches blocked out all but the most tenacious rays of light. She followed a cobbled path around a frozen pond and past a terra-cotta cupid. Icicles dangled from his pouting lips. Dusk was falling fast.

She swung around a fragrant spruce, fully intending to circle back to the brougham by another path and leave Justin combing the park for her. The deepening shadows rendered the tangled shrubs a maze. She took one path, then another, only to find herself at the fountain again. Cupid smirked at her. She stuck her tongue out at him.

Hugging herself against the chill, she chose the only path she had not taken. It was much narrower than the others. Dead weeds sprouted through the cracked cobblestones. She was beginning to wish she were sitting in the parlor at Grymwilde, sipping hot spiced cider and listening to Edith drone on about a new embroidery pattern.

The bushes rustled behind her. Emily hesitated, regretting her folly. A woman walking unchaperoned in a park was fair game for any scoundrel. A shiver crept down her spine. She swung around to face the looming shadows.

For a long moment there was only silence, then came the reassuring click of a walking stick against the cobblestones. She pressed a fist to her thundering heart in relief. Perhaps Justin had decided to play the game along with her.

She started to sing softly in Maori, a child's tune Dani had taught her, hoping to entice him to show himself.

A match flared in the darkness, followed by the unmistakable sizzle of flame against paper and the stringent tang of smoke. Emily's voice trailed to silence. She'd seen Justin partake of a pipe on occasion after dinner, but she'd never known him to smoke a cigarette.

She took two steps backward. "Justin?" she whispered to the encroaching twilight.

The shadows held their silence. Emily spun around to flee and crashed into something so warm and solid it could only be a man's chest. Her purse fell to the ground, spilling out her card case and an ivory array of calling cards.

The man knelt to retrieve them.

She gave his shiny top hat an aggravated thump. "You scared me half to death! Didn't you hear me calling you? I almost . . ."

Her voice faded as he lifted his head. The rising moon shone through the trees, and she found herself gazing into the molten brown eyes of a man more beautiful than Satan himself.

Chapter 25

· ❀ ·

*I am torn between wanting to shelter you and
wanting you to face this fickle world with those
bright eyes of yours wide open. . . .*

The moon caressed a face of pure masculine beauty. Not a
single whisker marred the purity of its narrow planes. Except for Justin, he was the first clean-shaven man Emily
had seen in London. An ivory cigarette holder hung from
his lips. His dark eyes seemed not opaque, but translucent,
lit from within by a diabolical fire.

With a flick of his elegant fingers he held up one of her
calling cards. "Miss Scarborough, I presume?"

She could not help staring at his hand. His nails were
trimmed to precise points, their beds as pink and smooth
as a baby's. He cleared his throat and Emily realized she
was behaving like a churl.

"Why, thank you. I'll just take that." She reached for
the card, but he slipped it into his breast pocket with the
deftness of a magician.

"Allow me." He handed her the purse and straightened, looming over her in the growing darkness. An opera
cloak rippled in ebony folds from his narrow shoulders.

"Have you come calling today, Miss Scarborough?" His voice held the faintest trace of a continental accent.

"Not quite. I'm afraid I'm lost," she said lamely.

He tapped the ash from his long, slender cigarette. "A condition my soul is quite familiar with."

The dark humor in his voice was irresistible. Emily laughed, then wished she hadn't.

He flicked the cigarette from the holder. The polished heel of his boot ground it to pulp. "Will you allow me to escort you to a safer haven?"

He smiled, his canine teeth gleaming in the moonlight. Whoever filed his nails ought to take a crack at his teeth, Emily thought uncharitably. She hesitated, feeling a bit like Red Riding Hood being invited to picnic with the wolf.

He read her mind with eerie accuracy. "I fear you're safe with me. I've already gobbled up three lost young ladies this evening. I'm quite sated at the moment."

She flushed. Mayfair *was* a genteel neighborhood. He was probably some nice gent, whose wife didn't allow him to smoke in the house, eager to get home to his cozy fire and three chubby babes.

Feeling sheepish, she tucked her hand in the curve of his arm. "I'd be honored."

The new moon shone through the naked branches, casting a silver latticework across their path.

"I couldn't help but hear your charming little song," he said. "Was it Swahili?"

"No. Maori."

"Ah, the Maori. Natives of"—he hesitated as if searching his brain—"New Guinea?"

"New Zealand."

"My goodness, you are lost, aren't you? Did your boat capsize?"

Emily thought of the tangled chain of events that had returned her to London. "In a manner of speaking, yes."

They emerged from the trees onto the gaslit street to

find the brougham silhouetted against the darkening sky. An unbidden sigh of relief escaped Emily. In this light the whiteness of the stranger's shirtfront was dazzling. She was tempted to shield her eyes from its brilliance.

She bobbed an awkward curtsy. "I can find my way from here."

His response was interrupted by Lily, who came running up, her bustle listing to starboard. "There you are! My head is positively spinning from circling this block. Harvey is going to slay me for coming home after dark. If he forbids me the opera next week, I'll die a thousand gruesome deaths. Oh."

Her rebuke died as she realized they had an audience. Her hazel eyes widened to mesmerized splendor as she gazed up at the stranger's compelling face.

He inclined his head and brought Lily's gloved fingers to his lips. "Good evening, madam."

He turned to Emily. "Perhaps another time, Miss Scarborough." He lifted her hand to his lips, but instead of kissing her fingers, he brought his moist lips to bear against the naked flesh of her inner wrist. Emily would have sworn his teeth grazed her skin.

"Thank you for your kindness," she said, withdrawing her hand.

"My pleasure, *cara mia.*"

He tipped his hat to them both, revealing a sleek, dark cap of hair, then strode off into the night, his opera cloak swirling around his ankles.

"Oh, my." Lily rubbed the tips of her fingers absently against her lips. "Wasn't he the most gorgeous creature you've ever seen? Like some sort of archangel."

"Look again, dear. Your angel has fallen from grace."

Lily's mouth fell open as they watched him saunter across the street and up the stairs to Mrs. Rose's establishment. The stained-glass door swung open. A burst of music and laughter tarnished the winter stillness. Then he was gone, so quickly they might have imagined him.

"Can you believe his boldness?" Lily said. "Most of the gentlemen have the decency to use the back entrance from the alley. He just strolls up to the front door as if he owns the place. Who does he think he is?"

"I wish I knew," Emily murmured.

He had not offered his name. She remembered her calling card disappearing into his breast pocket. He knew who she was, though. A faint shudder rippled down her spine.

Lily patted her shoulder. "You poor dear. You must be chilled to the marrow."

"I dare say she is."

The voice came out of the shadows behind them, as cool and lethal as pistol fire. Emily started as if she'd been shot. Justin stalked out of the trees like a hungry wolf who has spotted a helpless fawn.

His tie was no longer knotted. His greatcoat was littered with twigs and smudged with dirt. His hair was wild, as if it had wrestled with more than one tree and lost. But even a fresh limp did not mar the murderous grace of his intent.

"Good evening . . . sir," she said weakly.

"A little late for a stroll in the park, isn't it, dear?" he bit off.

Lily wisely drifted toward the brougham.

Emily stared straight ahead. "I find the air invigorating this time of night."

His eyes narrowed to amber slits. "So do all sorts of dangerous characters."

Emily found it laughable that only minutes before she had found a suave stranger so menacing. No man was more dangerous to her than this one. She lived daily with the mortal risk of falling to her knees at his feet and begging him to love her.

He circled her, then stopped so close behind her that she could feel the angry heat emanating from his lean form. His lips touched her ear, bringing the tiny hairs along her lobe to tingling life. "How would you like to be robbed or murdered . . . or raped?"

"Are those my only choices?" His sigh scorched the back of her neck. She turned to face him. "Why were you following me anyway? Don't you trust me?"

He rubbed the back of his neck. "I wasn't following you. I just happened to be passing by."

At that moment his carriage rumbled around the corner at a full gallop with Penfeld hanging out the window, waving his handkerchief. "Thank the Lord, sir!" he cried as the carriage clattered to a halt. "You found her. If anything had happened to her, I would have blamed myself. . . ."

He trailed off beneath Justin's glower, realizing that Emily was grinning like a Cheshire cat.

"You might be a bit more inconspicuous if the Winthrop crest weren't emblazoned on your carriage door," she said, brushing a stray twig from the shoulder of Justin's greatcoat. "I'd suggest you pay Bentley Chalmers whatever it takes to keep him in your employ. The two of you make rotten detectives."

With those words she marched away, disappearing into the brougham with a twitch of her sassy little bustle.

Justin muttered, "I'd like to put my foot—"

The coachman twisted on his bench, craning his neck.

Shaking his head in disgust, Justin threw himself into the carriage. As they drove into the night, the dark figure at the window of the house across the street lifted his glass in a mocking toast.

Emily's behavior in the next week was beyond reproach. Each expedition she made was chaperoned by the duchess or one of Justin's sisters. When her newfound popularity showed no sign of abating, even Cecille and her diminutive mama deigned to woo her affections. Justin heard not even a whisper of impropriety as she became the toast of London. He heard other things, though. How she had leaped out of a moving carriage to rescue a terrified puppy darting among the congested traffic of the Strand. How she had tossed the silk purse containing her entire allowance to a shivering beggar child on the street. How she had shamed Cecille and her fast set out of going to Bedlam to poke fun at the lunatics.

Justin could find no fault with her. To complain would have been the worst sort of hypocrisy. She was the kind of daughter every father dreamed of having. But Justin wasn't a father. And he suspected the ways he dreamed of having her were not only immoral, but possibly illegal.

The whirl of activity left little time for him. At each soiree and ball her dance card was filled minutes after arriving. At each luncheon and card party the seat next to hers was taken by some fawning young toff who hung on her every word as if it might be her last. Justin was relegated to the position of watchful uncle even though he knew none of the eager young men were the threat to her virtue that he was.

He tripped down the stairs late one afternoon, struggling to knot his tie for the opera that evening. Penfeld had a way of disappearing whenever Emily was preparing for a night out, leaving Justin to struggle with the damnable scrap of silk alone.

Two strange young men were hovering in the foyer.

"Excuse me," he said, brushing past them.

"Your Grace, may I have a word with you?" The one with the flaming red hair trotted after him. Justin took the freckled hand he offered and he pumped eagerly. "Claiborne, sir. Richard Claiborne. My friends call me Dick."

Justin looked him up and down from his yellow boots to his checkered jacket. "I dare say they do."

The other man rushed forward, clutching a stovepipe hat. His slicked-back hair reeked of bear's grease. "Henry Simpkins, Your Grace. At your humble service."

"Yes, well, that's very nice," Justin said vaguely. His tie curled like a serpent around his Adam's apple. He tugged at it and started to walk away. "If the two of you are seeking employment, I suggest you make an appointment with my offices."

Dick Claiborne flushed to the roots of his hair. "I wish to speak to you about a very private matter."

"Bite your tongue, Dick. That's not fair. I was here first!" Henry cried.

Claiborne whirled around and stabbed Henry's chest with his forefinger. "Sod off, Henry. I *saw* her first."

A horrified suspicion grew in Justin's mind. Leaving the irate young gentlemen nose to nose, he lifted a lace curtain and peered out the window. Two more carriages had drawn up to block the drive. One of their occupants was hanging out his window, shouting insults at the man emerging from the other carriage. As Justin watched, the young swell thrust up his shirt-sleeves and launched himself past a stoic footman into the window of his taunter's brougham. The brougham rocked wildly. The driver grabbed the lamp to keep his seat.

Justin groaned to find his mansion under siege. The snarls from behind him were becoming more rabid. He marched back to Simpkins and Claiborne, dragged them apart by their collars, and shook them like limp puppies.

"Cease this nonsense," he snapped. "I'll tolerate blood on my grass, but I won't tolerate it on my marble tiles."

He shoved them toward the door without loosening his grip.

Claiborne dragged his heels. "But, sir, I'd make a very good husband. Truly I would!"

"Thank you, *Dick,* but you're not my sort. Simpkins is looking for a mate. Perhaps the two of you can come to an arrangement."

He thrust them out the door. As they went tumbling down the shallow steps, a dead silence fell over the waiting carriages.

Justin waved cheerfully. "Do call again. I'd love to tell you more about my years with the cannibals. Charming tribe, the Maori. They've been known to pluck out the eyes of any man who offends them and eat them whole."

Dusting off his hands, he marched back into the house. The frantic jingle of harnesses and bridles was followed by the gratifying clatter of galloping hooves. Justin leaned his back against the door, blowing out a slow breath.

"A pity we're not living in the days when maidens were locked in stone towers."

Justin slowly lifted his eyes to find Emily sitting like an elf on the balcony above, her stockinged legs dangling through the balusters. It was obvious she had witnessed the entire spectacle.

His gaze traced the curve of her thighs as they straddled the thick post. A hoarse note touched his voice. "It wouldn't do me any good. I'd still have a key."

At that moment Lily and Millicent entered from the parlor, chattering about their opera dresses. When Justin looked up again, the balcony was empty.

For those seeking the drama of the bards, the Theatre Royal in Drury Lane was the favored choice, but those craving the loftier charms of opera flocked to the Theatre Royal in Covent Garden. The theater had been a glowing jewel in the crown of London since the first majestic strains of Handel's *Rinaldo* had graced its stage over a century before. As a small boy clinging to his father's trouser leg, Justin had believed its elegance a taste of heaven itself, and the busty diva one of God's own angels.

A touch of the old magic brushed him as he ushered Lily and Millicent into the Winthrop box. They settled into the red plush seats behind him as the orchestra began to tune their instruments. Penfeld hovered in the narrow aisle beside them, holding Justin's perfectly draped opera cloak over his arm. Knowing how the valet loved fine music, Justin had invited him as a guest, but he was obviously more comfortable in his role as human cloak stand.

An expectant murmur raced through the audience, accompanied by the rustle of satin and broadcloth. The private boxes and seats below started to fill. Justin's own awe was dampened by apprehension. Naturally, Emily had been too busy to attend with the family. Against his better judgment he had allowed her to accompany Cecille, leaving only the delicate countess to chaperone them.

He leaned forward and scanned the rows of boxes with his opera glasses. The gaslight from the crystal chandeliers shimmered off diamond chokers and gold Albert watch chains. The women clustered like multicolored blooms planted in window boxes next to their black-garbed escorts. Their fans fluttered like delicate petals in the wind.

Justin finally spotted Emily in a box on the tier below. She was on the same side as they were, but much farther from the stage. His worst fears were founded. The box was packed to overflowing with rowdy young swells and milling girls. He glimpsed the countess dozing in her ruffles in the back of the box.

"Sir," Penfeld said, tugging on his coat. "The performance is beginning."

Justin lowered the opera glasses and settled irritably back in his seat. There were two empty seats beside him, since his mother and Edith had begged off with throbbing megrims, refusing to admit they both detested the opera.

"Why don't you sit down, man?" he asked Penfeld, indicating the vacant chairs.

"Oh, no, sir." The valet stared stoically ahead as if even glancing at the stage might be considered a breach of duty. "It wouldn't be proper."

The first notes of the overture began, and the massive curtain rose. Lily tapped his shoulder. "May I borrow your opera glasses?"

"No," he snapped.

She leaned back in her seat with a wounded sniff.

The chandeliers dimmed and stage arcs flooded the brilliant backdrop with light. Justin was deaf to the musical charms of Bizet's *La Jolie Fille de Perth.* He was too obsessed by another *jolie fille.*

Using the opera glasses, he turned his gaze away from the stage and back to Emily. She was wearing the soft shade of rose so complimentary to her coloring; her curls had been caught up in a loose topknot.

Justin adjusted the glasses. A furious breath escaped him as a blazing shock of red hair came into focus. Who else could that be but Richard "Dick" Claiborne slobbering all over her bared shoulder? Someone passed in front of them. He leaned over the balcony, craning his neck. A fat eyeball filled his vision.

He slowly lowered the glasses. The gentleman in the next box was glaring at him. "The stage is that way," he said gruffly, pointing.

Nodding a curt apology, Justin ducked back into his seat. The door to the box opened, sweeping in the unmistakable scent of lavender.

Suzanne's husky whisper raked over him. "Do you mind if my husband and I share your box? It seems ours has been seized by my visiting cousin and his family."

Without waiting for an invitation, his ex-fiancée claimed the seat next to his while her husband settled in the back of the box. "Deplorable stuff, opera," he grumbled. "Don't know what the women see in it."

Justin grunted an agreement, too distracted to defend his fondest passion. Within minutes the dapper little man was snoring. Justin cast Suzanne a wry glance, wondering if she was remembering their last disastrous night at the opera when she'd called him a foolish bastard for turning his back on his inheritance.

He shifted in his seat. Studied his program. Drummed his fingernails against the balcony railing. When he could no longer resist, he jerked up the opera glasses and trained them on Emily's box. Suzanne leaned curiously over his shoulder, enveloping him in her perfume. Justin found himself staring down the twin barrels of another pair of opera glasses.

He started. Emily was watching him. As she realized she'd been caught, she dropped the glasses in her lap and stared fixedly at the stage as if entranced by the trilling vibrato of the plump prima donna. Justin lowered his own glasses, feeling a slow smile spread across his face. He leaned back and dropped a casual arm over the back of Suzanne's chair.

"I can't see," Millicent whined.

"It's opera, Millie," he said. "You don't have to see. Just listen."

He dared a glance from the corner of his eye. Emily was watching them again. He tilted his head toward Suzanne as if sharing the most intimate of confidences.

As act one approached its majestic climax, there was a stir in Emily's box. Justin snatched up the glasses. Several of the young people were sneaking past the drowsing countess, probably off to seek the more invigorating and forbidden entertainment of the music halls. Emily and Claiborne were left quite alone in the front row.

Justin stood, ignoring his sisters' protests. The soprano's aria soared, rattling the crystal drops of the chandeliers. Justin's fingers bit into the pearl casing of the glasses as he watched Claiborne loom over Emily. She whacked him with her fan. Undaunted, he grabbed her around her slender waist and planted a sloppy kiss on her neck.

The soprano drew in a breath, and in that perfect lull of silence between one note and the next, Justin slammed down the opera glasses and shouted, "Dammit to bloody hell! I've had enough!"

*C*hapter 26

· 🐚 ·

But if these words to you should be my last, I dare
not soften them with platitudes
and half-truths. . . .

*E*very eye in the opera house turned to Justin, even the shocked prima donna's. Her plump chin quivered. The tenor quickly cut in, his magnificent voice wavering as he sped through the music to bring the rattled company to the haven of intermission. The audience was more fascinated by the scandalous performance of the Duke of Winthrop.

The curtain began to unfurl. Penfeld lunged for the tails of his master's coat too late as Justin vaulted over the rail and swung into the box below. The audience gasped, then began to pour out of their own seats, not wanting to miss a moment of the delightful spectacle.

Justin sped down the wide marble steps that led to the lobby, ignoring the crowds streaming around him. Towering columns limited his vision, but his gaze found Emily as unerringly as if she'd been the only woman in the room.

His voice rang out, echoing back from the vaulted ceiling. "Emily!"

The excited chatter faded to a breathless murmur.

Emily kept walking, her delicate slippers and narrow train forcing her into tiny, mincing steps. The crowd cleared a wide swath between them, recoiling from Justin's long, dangerous strides. He caught up with her easily.

He fell into step behind her. "Get your cape. We're going home."

"You're insane. I'm not going anywhere with you."

"I said, *get your cape,*" he thundered.

The crowd fell into dead silence.

Emily whirled around, her dark eyes flashing. "And what if I don't?" Her tongue darted out to moisten her parted lips. "What are you going to do? Spank me?"

Swishing her skirt defiantly, she turned and marched away. Justin stood unmoving for a moment, then closed the distance between them in two furious strides. He grabbed her arm and pulled her around, jerking her against him.

A shadow of his New Zealand accent touched his speech, his low, flat words meant only for her. "We're going home. Now, you can walk or I can throw you over my shoulder and carry you. It makes no difference to me."

Emily went dead white except for the furious splotches of color in her cheeks. Her bosom heaved with impotent rage, but something in his eyes must have warned her he wasn't bluffing. She lowered her gaze to his buttons, her lips tightened in mutinous rebellion.

"Sir, your cloak!" Penfeld tossed the garment.

Justin caught it in one hand and threw it over Emily's shoulders. Two footmen swept open the double gilt doors, letting in a blast of bitter cold. As the duke ushered his young charge into the night, the lobby of the opera house erupted in a scandalized roar.

A light snow had begun to fall. It dusted Justin's hair as he handed Emily into the waiting carriage. She threw herself into the broad seat opposite him and slumped into a sullen knot. She shoved his opera cloak from her shoulders, finding its rugged warmth offensive. It smelled warm and spicy, like Justin's bay rum. Like his bare skin heated by an island sun. A stray tendril of hair flopped out of her topknot; she irritably raked it away.

The carriage lurched into motion. They rode in dead silence. Emily stared at the curtained window. Justin stared at her. She could feel the condemning heat of his gaze.

The confines of the carriage seemed to grow smaller with each turn of the wheels. They were cordoned off from the winter night by the cozy glow of the lantern and the warmth wafting from the coal footstove. Justin seemed bigger somehow, more overwhelming. His arms were crossed over his chest, his long legs relaxed in an arrogant sprawl. Her senses were enveloped by the sound of his breathing, his heat, his masculine scent. An arc of tension sizzled between them.

When she could no longer bear the silence, she said, "Doesn't it concern you that half of London thinks you a madman?"

His eyes flicked over her like tawny flames. "Better than having them think you a shameless trollop."

She gasped, stinging from the unfair cut. "What's wrong, Justin? Does it gall you because a man found me attractive? Because he dared to treat me as a woman, not a child?"

He snorted. "I'd hardly call that freckled toad a man."

"As avidly as you were watching us, you probably counted every one of those freckles. Wasn't your own trollop holding your interest, or are you one of those debauched men who gets his thrills by spying on others?"

His eyes darkened. "What are they teaching at Foxworth's these days—de Sade? Your education has been quite extensive, my dear."

"Not as extensive as yours, I'm sure."

He spoke through gritted teeth. "When we get to the

house, you will go directly to your room. I will no longer tolerate your insolence."

Her voice rose to a shout. "You can't tell me what to do. You're not my father!"

Her words hung in the air. Justin went utterly still. A thoughtful glint appeared in his eyes. Then a smile of profound wonder slanted his lips. "Why, I'll be damned. I'm not, am I?"

Then he was on her. He came across the carriage with the grace of a lunging tiger, bearing her back into the plush cushion. His mouth came down on hers in an unholy surrender to a dark and sweet temptation. His tongue savaged her mouth even as his hand reached up with cool calculation to extinguish the lamp, leaving Emily to drown in his taste, his fragrance, the feel of his hands hot and rough against the bare skin of her shoulders. The darkness rendered him a dangerous stranger. His touch consumed her in flame. She couldn't fight him. She could only cling to him, bunching the fine broadcloth of his coat in her helpless fists.

Not only did she no longer know him. She no longer knew herself. Who was this wanton who moaned and tugged at the dusky silk of his hair, drawing him deeper into her kiss? Their bodies slid against the lush velvet, gliding downward, ever downward, into forbidden delight.

He muttered soft, rough words against her lips. His hands reached for her skirt, too fervent in their need to be anything but clumsy. She lifted her hips to help him until she lay beneath him, her dress bunched around her waist, thighs parted, garters and stockings sprawled in wanton abandon. A word that might have been either prayer or oath escaped him as he molded the damp cambric of her drawers to the silky mound beneath.

When his beautiful, strong fingers slipped beneath the fabric to touch her, Emily, who had so long prided herself on her fierce independence, hid her face in his shirt, unable to face the terrifying knowledge that there was nothing she wouldn't let this man do to her. Nothing.

Pleasure ribboned through her in dark cascades as he gently fingered her throbbing flesh, all of his haste and clumsiness vanquished by wonder and grace. Too soon she felt the first shiver of ecstasy approaching through the darkness. A soft cry escaped her as he brought her to a sweet, fierce climax that shattered them both.

For an eternity there was no sound within the carriage but the hoarse rasp of their breathing in the darkness. Slowly, other sensations came into play: the rocking motion of the carriage, the clatter of the wheels against cobblestones, the jingle of the harness ringing like a bell in the crisp winter air.

The bitter wine of guilt poured through Justin. Emily nestled into his chest like some small, fragile creature, kneading his waistcoat between her fingers. He had never meant to humble her, but to exalt her with his touch. A latent tremor rocked her, and he cupped his arm around her, beset by a fierce desire to protect what was his.

Take care of my little angel, Justin. Swear you will.

Even the memory of David's charge wasn't enough to stanch the fire flaming in his belly. She was as trusting as a kitten in his arms. How easy it would be to slide her drawers down over her knees. To part her gartered thighs and undo the buttons of his trousers, freeing that part of him that ached to take her like the most common of whores on the seat of his carriage. He sensed that she wouldn't stop him until he'd plunged them both into the abyss of their own erotic destruction.

Emily's eyes fluttered open. Even in the darkness they had a luminous shine. "Was that in lieu of a spanking, or are you going to spank me later?"

A choked laugh escaped him. He raked a desperate hand through his hair. "Was I so harsh on you?"

"Monstrous," she whispered. "I shall take care to misbehave with far greater regularity."

"I don't believe my poor heart could stand it."

It wasn't his heart stiffening in protest as he reached down with shaking hands and drew his cloak over her. He didn't trust himself to smooth her stockings, tighten her lacy garters, or draw her skirt down to cover the pliant sprawl of her thighs. He didn't even trust himself to look at her.

He sank back into his seat and whipped back the window curtain to stare into the wintry night. A row of elegant shops glided past. A frail finger of moonlight pierced the snow clouds.

Emily sat up, hugging his cloak around her. Her topknot of curls drooped over her brow. She blew them out of her eyes. "Perhaps Tansy was remiss in the more sordid aspects of my education, but I was under the impression that there was more." Her shy gaze flicked to his lap, then back to his face. "Much more."

Justin realized then that the walls he might build between them with propriety or excuses were flimsy structures, easily torn by his selfish passions. If he stayed, he would be forced to erect the one barrier he could never scale—Emily's hatred. And he would rather never see her again than to see her look at him with loathing for the terrible act he had once committed in a moment of desperation.

He knew of no other way to say the words than harshly and cleanly. "It was a mistake to stay here. I should have returned to New Zealand as soon as I found you."

A tremulous cry of joy broke from her lips. "We were very happy there, weren't we? I know we can be happy again. I can't wait to see Trini's face when he sees we've come back together. And Dani—"

"I'm going back alone."

The carriage slowed as they reached the congested traffic of Oxford Street. Justin heard the driver spit out a foul oath as he vied with a crowded omnibus for a space in the narrow lanes.

"Why?" she whispered.

"The natives need me." The words sounded hollow, even to him.

She knelt on the floor between his legs. The cloak slid from her shoulders, baring their alabaster smoothness. Her imploring gaze searched his face. "But what do you need, Justin?"

Driven to desperation by her nearness, he cupped her buttocks in his hands and pulled her up against him, molding her ruthlessly to his arousal. "This," he said hoarsely. "This is what I need."

She refused to be daunted by his crudity. A sad, sweet smile touched her lips. "For a handful of coins you can find that in the arms of any stranger." She gently drew her fingers along his cheek. "What of tenderness, Justin? What of love?"

A groan caught in his throat. Her passion and courage stunned him. As badly as he wanted her, he couldn't allow her to give him what he would never be worthy of.

He gently fastened the cloak beneath her trembling chin. "You once said it better than I ever could. *I have no right.*"

"No right to what, Justin? No right to happiness?"

He turned back to the window, despising the cold man he saw reflected in the thick glass.

Emily sat back in her seat, her eyes sparkling dangerously. "So you're going back to New Zealand. And I'm to stay at Grymwilde and live off your charity."

"It's not charity. I owe you."

"For what? For killing my father?"

His gut spasmed as if she'd plunged a red-hot knife into it. He stared at her.

"I know you blame yourself," she said. "It *was* you and your smooth friend Nicky who talked him into investing my mother's inheritance in your little venture. But Daddy was always a bit of a dreamer. He was convinced his rainbow was right around the next corner. If it hadn't been gold, it would have been African diamonds or Indian rubber seeds. It's not your fault he went and got his fool self killed."

Justin closed his eyes, regretting that she could never give him the one thing he truly needed—absolution.

Sarcasm ripened in her voice. "I have a bright future ahead of me, don't I? Moldering in that house with Lily, Millie, and Edith. Marrying some insipid boob named Horatio or Humphrey who wears a tasseled nightcap to bed."

He forced his voice into a low and passionless tone. "Shall I paint another portrait of your future for you? Shall I take you home right now and bed you? Of course, you'd have to be up by dawn to pack your things because it wouldn't do to have my mistress lodged in the same house with reputable women like my mother and sisters." He steeled himself as she blanched. "Is that what you want? To live as I have? As an outcast? Shall I ruin you tonight for any other man?"

"You already have," she cried. She bowed her head, struggling for composure. Tears trembled on her silky lashes, betraying the terrible cost of her whispered words. "You don't have to make me your mistress. You could make me your wife."

Justin knew she would choke on that tender plea if she knew the truth. His silence damned them both. Watching the darkness cloud her eyes was like watching his own dreams wither in a poisonous blast of gunpowder.

"Damn your charity to hell, Justin Connor. I won't be left behind again. If anyone leaves this time, it'll be me."

Before he realized what she was going to do, she threw his cloak in his face and lunged for the door handle. He shoved away the enveloping folds, but it was too late. A blast of icy air struck his face. Emily spilled from the moving carriage in a pool of rose, then took off, running, darting between the hansom cabs and carriages with the feline grace of a street urchin.

Justin jumped from the carriage after her, hearing behind him a startled "Whoa!" from his driver. He lunged in front of a public coach, fighting to keep Emily in his sight among the churning chaos. The theaters and opera houses were just letting out, and lacquered carriages were pouring onto the thoroughfare in a steady stream.

"Watch yer step, guv'nor! Comin' through!" boomed a hearty voice. Warning given, the burly omnibus driver raised his whip and gave his straining team a brutal lick.

The horses lurched forward. The iron-shod hooves bore down on Justin. He leaped backward to avoid being crushed. As the vehicle thundered past, the conductor mockingly tipped his hat to the cursing drivers of a hansom cab and brougham struggling to calm their frenzied horses.

Justin's gaze frantically searched the fray. Emily was nowhere to be seen. He swore. Emily was a bigger fool than he if she thought he was going to let her disappear from his life again. Icy flecks of snow cut his cheeks. Dodging hacks and carriages, he loped to the end of the street. Drawn by a smudge of pink against the cobblestones, he slowed and bent to examine it.

It was a single rose-colored slipper, crushed flat by the massive wheels of the omnibus.

Mrs. Rose's parlor on a snowy winter night was a warm and congenial place to be. The satisfying of men was both her livelihood and her pleasure. Her parlor resembled less a bordello than a cheery home, for the crafty madam wisely realized the gentlemen who frequented her establishment came for both much more and much less than the easing of their physical needs.

They came to loosen their ties, pull off their heavy coats, and recline in overstuffed chairs. They came to prop their stockinged feet on ottomans and smoke the pipes and cigars their wives would allow them only in the most obscure corners of their own homes. Most of all, they came to hear the pretty girls laugh at their jokes and make them feel young and handsome again.

The peaceful lull that had descended over the parlor this Friday night didn't concern Mrs. Rose or any of her girls. They knew both the parlor and the bedrooms upstairs would fill to overflowing after the gentlemen of the theater crowd escorted their wives home for the night.

A haze of smoke hung over the room. A portly gentleman rested before the fire, reading the *Times* while Mrs. Rose massaged his toes. A swarthy man reclined on the settee, nursing a cognac and absently fondling the woman on his lap. A girl in a diaphanous robe sat alone at the piano, lazily picking out the notes of *Beautiful Dreamer.*

The front door flew open. A blast of icy wind and swirling snow rushed into the parlor.

"Shut the bloomin' door. It's bloody freezin' out there," yelled the girl at the piano.

When the door didn't close, they all looked up to find a bedraggled creature standing on the stoop, barefoot and shivering in a thin silk evening gown. She wore no cloak or cape. Snow frosted her tangled hair.

"Good Lord, what happened to the poor child?" shouted the portly gentleman.

"Has she been attacked?" cried out the girl on the piano bench. To Mrs. Rose's girls, no crime was more heinous than that of rape. Why would any man take from the unwilling what they so willingly provided?

"Somebody fetch a blanket," Mrs. Rose commanded.

The dark-eyed man on the settee extracted his elegant fingers from beneath his companion's skirt and pushed her off his lap. "Why, look what the cat dragged in!"

"What, darling?"

"Never mind. You just run along." He softened his command by giving the whore's rump a fond pinch.

He rose and started forward, pulling off his immaculate jacket, but before he could reach the trembling girl, another woman came down the stairs, twined around a skinny stripling whose face was flushed with a sated glow.

As she unpeeled herself from her most recent customer, her round blue eyes widened. "Holy Christ, Em?" she breathed. "Is that you?"

"Oh, Tansy," came the answering wail as the pathetic creature flung herself across the room into the whore's arms.

The man melted back into the shadows. A sneer touched his lips as he watched the tender reunion. He shook a cigarette out of his gold case and lit it. He inhaled deeply, savoring the lazy furl of the smoke through his lungs. There was no need for careless haste to spoil his plans, he reminded himself. Dead men had all the time they needed.

Chapter 27

· ❧ ·

*I have always striven to search
for the best in any man. . . .*

Justin stood on the deserted street, staring up at the stone edifice of the school. Why did his weary steps always lead him here? In the gray light of dawn the old building looked sad, its polished edges dulled by bleak neglect. Some things remained the same since his last visit—the paint peeling from the shutters, the rust caking the wrought-iron balusters. But other things had changed. The downstairs windows had been boarded shut, giving the house an abandoned air. The darkened squares of the upstairs windows surveyed him with drowsy indifference. Against his will his gaze flicked upward to the attic windows. They were all broken now, and as he watched, a pigeon hopped out and winged its way into the morning sky.

Justin climbed the stairs to the front door, his boots breaking the thin crust of snow. The snow had stopped near midnight, leaving London frosted in a brittle cloak swirled by icy gusts. Justin had long ago gone too numb to feel its bite.

He pulled his hands out of his pockets and pounded on the door. The sound reverberated with a hollow ring that only fueled his despair. Still, he didn't stop.

"Jesus bloody Christ!" came the bellow from the connecting house. "Quit your banging, ya fool. Can't a God-fearin' man get a decent night's rest?"

Justin ignored it. He pounded until his raw knuckles began to bleed. His arms fell limp at his sides. He turned his collar up and started to turn away.

The door slowly creaked open. A gaunt face appeared in the darkened crack. A chill shot down Justin's spine. At first he thought it was Miss Winters beneath the dingy ruffles of the mobcap, but then he realized it was her young teacher, Doreen. The girl had aged twenty• years since he had seen her last.

"Where is your mistress?" he asked hoarsely. "I must speak with her."

"She's gone. Gone like all the rest." Doreen's voice was as flat as a wraith's. She tried to close the door, but Justin jammed his foot in it. She stared up at his face, then her eyes came to life in a blaze of spirit. "Ye're the one, ain't ya? Ye're the golden-eyed devil wot drove 'em all away!"

Ignoring the protesting rasp of his throat, Justin deepened his voice, hoping he might break her with the sheer force of his will. "I must see your mistress. It's imperative. Where might I find her?"

"She's gone to an 'ome fer other broken-down old women. She didn't even fight 'em when they come to take 'er away. Ya took all the fight out of 'er with yer bloody rumors and insinuations. Ain't a decent family in London would 'ave trusted their brat to 'er care after ya poisoned their minds against 'er." Her pinched nose reddened. "Miss Amelia always took care 'o me, even to the end. Left me this fine 'ouse, she did."

Justin knew the house had seen the end of its finer days. It would be nothing but a crumbling albatross around its owner's neck. He raked a hand through his hair, torn between pity and frustration. "Perhaps you can help me. Have you seen Emily Scarborough?"

Doreen's face twisted. Justin was tempted to recoil from its pure malevolence. "Emily Scarborough!" she spat out. "She's the one wot started all this. I always knew she'd be the death of us all. The only place I 'opes to see the little bitch is burnin' in 'ell!"

She tried to slam the door in his face. Justin caught her shoulders and pulled her out, pinning her against the iron railing of the stoop. Her nightdress whipped in the wind. "You're the one who threw her off the boat, aren't you? Yes, I see you are. She told me all about it. So unless you want me to fetch the police and bring you up on charges of attempted murder, I suggest you answer my questions."

Doreen's freckles stood out in sharp relief against her pallor. Justin could smell the fetid odor of sleep and fear on her breath. Exhaustion was making him reckless. He gave her a hard shake, eliciting a sullen whimper.

"I ain't seen the wench. Not since the day we give 'er to you."

Even though he had expected it, the disappointment was grueling. His mind raced. Who in London would Emily turn to? "What of the other girl? The maid you called Tansy? Do you know what's become of her?"

Doreen licked her thin lips with lascivious malice. "That I do. She's gone on to her natural callin'. Servicin' the young swells for some highfalutin madam."

"What house?"

"I don't know."

Justin's spirits plunged further. Could his own rejection have caused Emily to rush headlong into the arms of another man? His grip loosened.

Doreen took advantage of his divided attention to twist away and dart back into the house. The door slammed, and he heard the sharp crack of the bolt being rammed home.

Certain she was lying, he lifted his fist, determined to

break the door down if he had to. His hand slowly fell. He would be of no good to Emily if he ended up in jail for murder.

Turning his collar up against the cold, he started down the street, his steps driven by desperate purpose.

"Well, wot do ya think of it? It does ya real fine, don't it?"

Emily ran a tentative finger beneath her eye, smearing the thick kohl. "I look like one of those American raccoons."

Sighing, Tansy spit on a handkerchief and dabbed at her cheek. Emily squirmed away, but Tansy grabbed a fat ringlet and held her still. "There now. Keep yer 'ands away from yer face or we'll 'ave to do it all again."

Emily gazed dourly at herself in the mirror. "I hate ruffles." She cast Tansy's reflection a pleading look. "Couldn't I be something more exotic? A Nubian princess? Or perhaps a harem girl?"

"Ye're a trifle light fer a Nubian, and Peggy's been promised the 'arem costume this week." Tansy gave her cheek a fond tweak. "Stop frettin'. Mrs. Rose says a ruffled little schoolgirl is every gent's dream."

Every gent but one, Emily thought grimly. She swallowed hard. "Who am I to argue with Mrs. Rose?"

Who was she, indeed? Last night the buxom mistress of the establishment had welcomed her in from the storm as if she were a long lost daughter. She had dried her tears, tucked her into Tansy's bed, smothered her under a thick quilt, and coddled her with a devotion that made even Penfeld seem the soul of cold neglect.

Tansy smoothed circles of rouge on her cheeks. When a door slammed in the next room, Emily started, shooting a streak of pink up to her temples. A female giggle was followed by a throaty grunt and then by a rhythmic creaking that made the far wall shudder. Their gazes met in the mirror.

"Oh, no," Tansy groaned. "There ye go again. I keep puttin' pink in yer cheeks and it just keeps drainin' away."

She rested her hands lightly on Emily's shoulders. "Are ya sure this is what ya want, Em? It ain't too late to turn back."

Was it what she wanted? To be finally free? To pay her rent and board to Mrs. Rose out of her own pocket and not be dependent on someone else's charity? To never be beholden to any man—especially not Justin Connor? Even Penfeld had done what he had to do to win his independence from a life he no longer found tolerable. Surely she could find within her that much courage. Tansy was wrong. It had been too late to turn back from the first moment she had laid eyes on her guardian.

From the next room came a guttural groan, then silence. The wall stopped rocking. Emily pressed her eyes shut. When she opened them, they had darkened to bitter sable. "I'm ready."

A fist slammed into the closed door. Emily jumped so high, she almost fell off the stool.

"Gor blimey, keep yer bloomin' drawers on," Tansy called out, pulling a ceramic chamber pot from a cupboard.

As she swung open the door, a disgruntled male voice rang out. "'Ell, Tansy, not again. Why can't ya use the water closet like everybody else? Or are ya flat on yer back in bed too much?"

The open door blocked Emily's view, but she would have known that raspy voice anywhere. She lifted the skirts of the dressing table, searching for a place to hide.

Tansy cocked back the pot. "Empty it or wear it, Barney."

A wiry arm shot out to relieve her of her burden. "Damned uppity whore," he muttered. "Costs me a week's wages to get what I used to get fer free in the linen closet at Foxworth's."

Taunting him with a smile that would have melted an

ice sculpture, Tansy lifted her shapely leg and rubbed it along the door facing. "But ya still pay, don't ya?"

Her provocative action sent the door swinging open, and Emily found herself staring into Barney Dobbins's greedy little pig eyes.

His mouth dropped open. The chamber pot tilted dangerously. "Hey! Wot's she doin' 'ere?"

Tansy gave his bony chest a shove. "Don't worry about it. It'd cost more than you've got."

He wiped his moist lips with the back of his hand. Emily shuddered. "Don't count on it," he said. "I'll start savin' me pennies now. I've wanted a taste o' that fer a long, long time."

Tansy slammed the door in his leering face.

Emily clapped a hand over her mouth. The enormity of what she was about to do rolled over her in dull waves of panic. But it was too late. Tansy was already powdering her nose, guiding her out the door, shoving something into her hand.

Dazed, she looked down to discover she was holding a sugared pink lollipop. "What am I supposed to do with this?" she asked, baffled.

Tansy gave her a gentle push toward the stairs. "Why lick it, of course!"

When Justin returned to Grymwilde late that night, all the lamps except for those in the parlor had been extinguished. He turned instinctively toward the gentle glow, knowing his family's comfort was better than none.

None of them dared to speak as he threw himself into an upholstered chair and rubbed his bristled jaw.

His mother's needle flicked calmly through the flowered fire screen she was embroidering. "Unless you acquired some peculiar tastes in cologne in New Zealand, son, I would venture to say you smell like a house of ill repute."

"As would you if you'd visited every brothel in London in the past twelve hours."

"My goodness," she said dryly. "Such stamina."

Lily and Millicent blushed like twin roses. Edith buried her nose deeper in her novel.

Justin shot her a dark look. "Perhaps we should discuss this in private."

The duchess only smiled benignly. "Your sisters are married, aren't they? If they don't wish to hear what I have to say, they can join their husbands in their respective beds." She laid her embroidery across her knees and looked at Justin squarely. "I'm more interested in why you think your ward might have taken up such an unsavory occupation. Did she perhaps have a little nudge in that direction?"

Justin was shocked by his mother's frankness. All the spirit and fire she had banked for years flickered in her gray eyes. They must have been startlingly pretty in their day, he realized, like misty bits of smoked glass. His guilty soul could not bear their scrutiny.

He rose and paced to the hearth. A rumpled, hollow-eyed stranger stared back at him from the chimney glass. "I didn't touch her." He dropped his head, despising the lie. "I didn't compromise her," he amended.

"Perhaps you should have," his mother pronounced. "Then she might not have run away."

Justin swung around, wide-eyed, but his mother had returned to her embroidery. In the awkward silence Lily began to sing under her breath, some ridiculous tune about bees flitting from bloom to bloom.

Justin's raw temper snapped. He turned on her. "Would you stop that infernal squawking!"

Lily flinched. "So sorry. All of this talk of lewd pursuits put me in mind of Mrs. Rose's garden in Mayfair."

Justin failed to see how lewd pursuits related to some matron's garden in the fashionable district of Mayfair.

His mother nodded sagely. "Quite an establishment.

Caters only to the carriage set—the crème de la crème of society."

Realization slowly dawned on Justin. "There's a bordello in Mayfair? How would you know of it?"

His mother blinked up at him. "Why, your father frequented it. Only on Fridays, of course. Saturdays he saved for me."

A wild song of hope sang through Justin's heart. He snatched up Lily and kissed her full on the mouth. "Thank you, you witless little darling. If I find her, I swear I'll make Herbert secretary-general of Winthrop's." He dropped her back in her chair and dashed for the door.

"That's all very nice for Millicent," Lily called after him. "But what about my Harvey?"

Emily's fingers bit into the slick wood of the banister as she crept downstairs behind Tansy. Mrs. Rose's drawing room appeared far more crowded than it had last night. Masculine laughter mingled with the rich ripple of female conversation. A girl garbed in a canary-yellow ballet costume was twirling around the piano to the improbable strains of a Bach aria. Emily's eyes watered from the thin haze of smoke that veiled the room. Cutting through the smoke was the sickly sweet aroma of too many perfumes. A kissing couple on their way up the stairs brushed past them.

Two burly footmen flanked the front door, their battered, scarred visages looking incongruous beneath their powdered wigs. Tansy had assured her Mrs. Rose never dealt in "rough trade." With those two bulldogs guarding her gate, Emily could see why.

Emily froze as her gaze fell on a dark-eyed man leaning against the black marble mantel. She tugged the back of Tansy's skirt, bringing her to an abrupt halt. "I know that man. I met him in the park. Who is he?"

Tansy whispered. "'E's fabulous rich, that one. Some say a millionaire." Her pretty features took on a hard set, giving Emily a frightening glimpse of what she might look like after a few years of this life. "But I can tell ya from experience 'e's got lots o' clever uses fer them pretty silk ties 'e wears—none of 'em decent. Stay away from 'im. 'E's more than ya can 'andle right now."

Emily suspected the grizzled old man dozing in Mrs. Rose's lap was more than she could handle. Her spirits plummeted as Tansy gave her a comforting wink and slipped away, leaving her to fend for herself.

She sank onto a settee in the shadow of the stairs and gave her lollipop a nervous lick. The virginal white of her skirt floated around her ankles in a diaphanous cloud so sheer she could see the shadow of her lace garters holding up her silk stockings. Flat white slippers adorned her feet. Dear Lord, what would her daddy say if he could see her now? Perhaps if she sat very still, no one would notice her.

Her hopes died as a portly gentleman sauntered over. He peered at her through an antique quizzing glass, his gaze lingering at her ruffled bosom. "My, my, what a precious little gel you are," he boomed out. "Would you like to sit on Uncle George's lap?"

Emily sucked noisily on her lollipop to keep from replying. She realized that was a mistake as his rapt gaze traced the shape of her lips cradling the hard, sugary candy. "Shy, are you? How delightful! Your uncle George loves shy little gels." Tittering, he tried to shove his bulk onto the settee beside her. "Scoot over and make room, won't you? I shouldn't wish to spank you for being ill mannered."

"Sorry, Uncle, this seat is taken." The voice was smooth and cold, like velvet ice. Emily looked up as the shadow of the dark-eyed stranger she had met in the park fell over them.

Uncle George drew himself to his full height, huffing and puffing in protest. With taunting grace the stranger reached out and struck a match off the brass button of George's waistcoat. As he touched it to the tip of his cigarette, the dancing flame caressed the ruthless planes of his face.

"Well, I never . . ." Obviously deciding a hasty retreat might be in order, Uncle George trailed after a girl dressed as Queen Victoria, muttering something about his crown jewels.

The stranger propped his foot on the settee. The impeccable cut of his trousers hugged his long, elegant leg. Cocking an eyebrow, he offered Emily the cigarette. Shaken by her narrow escape from the jovial George, she snatched it and took a deep drag.

A paroxysm of coughing seized her. The man slapped her on the back. "Sorry. Turkish tobacco. Strong stuff. I should have warned you." He pried the cigarette from her shaking fingers, brought it to his lips, and inhaled deeply.

Emily blinked away the burning tears, still wheezing. "You seem destined to rescue me, sir."

A smile played around his thin lips as if he were savoring some small, private joke. "I do, don't I?" His eyes flicked over her like hypnotic flames. "It seems you've become a bit more lost since our last encounter, *cara mia.*"

Her faint shiver at his endearment was not lost on him. "I fear you are correct," she agreed glumly.

The woman at the piano lurched into a new tune. The man dropped his cigarette and stubbed it out on the Oriental carpet with his heel. "I despise Chopin. Why don't we retire upstairs, where we can talk without the burden of his tiresome romanticism?"

Emily eyed the silk folds of his tie nervously, remembering Tansy's warning. She had no intention of being led to her ruin by this urbane stranger. She searched the crowd for Tansy, but found no glimpse of her. The brawny men at the door looked more menacing now. Were they planted there to protect Mrs. Rose's blossoms, or to pluck them if they threatened to wilt before blooming? Her safest bet would be to escape without an obvious scuffle.

Her hesitation cost her dearly. The man pulled her to

her feet, his grip around her wrist as resolute as a silken snare. Perhaps she should just tell him the truth.

She searched his face earnestly. "I can't go upstairs with you, sir. I'm afraid I've made a dreadful mistake."

His eyes glowed with an unholy light. "So have I, my dear. But I intend to remedy it very shortly."

Twisting out of his grasp, Emily broke away and darted down the nearest dim hallway. Before she could go more than a few feet, Barney Dobbins stepped out of a shadowy doorway, blocking her only avenue of escape.

He bared his yellowed teeth in a leer. "Ye'd best run back to yer fine fellow, Em. I 'eard 'e 'as a nasty temper if crossed." He lowered his voice to a taunting whisper. "I know ye're eager, but I can wait. I ain't too proud to mop up the leftovers from them fine gents. My turn'll come soon enough."

Trapped, Emily backed away, as near to swooning as she had ever been in her life. God only knew what lurid things they might do to her if she fainted.

She backed into the stranger's arms. His elegant fingers closed around her throat, pressing gently against her throbbing pulse.

"Come with me, *cara mia,*" he commanded. "You won't be sorry."

Emily was already sorry. She bowed her head, sorry she had shamed her father. Sorry Justin didn't love her enough to marry her. Sorry she'd been such a fool as to believe selling her body wouldn't cost her her soul.

A sinister swirl of music, light, and laughter enveloped her as he drew her inexorably toward the stairs. Suddenly, the frenzied gaiety was marred by shouts and the sounds of struggle. Emily jerked her head up just in time to see one of the guards go flying into a walnut occasional table, splintering it. He sat up, eyes crossed and wig hanging askew over one ear, then slumped back over, out cold.

Women screamed and several of the gentlemen tried to climb over each other in a rush for the back door, fearing a constable's raid. She saw lascivious Uncle George crawling around on hands and knees, searching for his precious quizzing glass. It rolled under Emily's foot, and she gave it an unkind stomp.

Shouts rang out near the door. "Grab him!"

"Careful, he might be an opium user."

"He's quite mad! A bloody savage!"

A cold rush of air behind her warned Emily her debonair captor had fled. She lifted her skirts and peered around wildly, planning to take advantage of the chaos to make her own escape.

At that moment a path parted through the jostling crowd, revealing the golden-eyed tiger clawing his way through their midst.

Emily's heart leaped in her throat, and she went flying across the room to fling herself into the mad savage's arms.

Chapter 28

❦

*I hesitate to shatter Justin's faith
in his friend. . . .*

Emily snuffled into Justin's rumpled waistcoat. "Oh, Justin, it was awful!" she wailed. "Tansy made me wear this ridiculous dress, and there was this horrid man with the whitest, sharpest teeth you've ever seen just like the Big Bad Wolf's and the most cleverly knotted tie. Better than Penfeld's even. And then there was Barney lurking in doorways, waiting to jump out at me just like he did at Foxworth's, and he said the most awful things."

Emily was too intent on gulping in the musky spice of Justin's scent to realize how strangely stiff he stood in her embrace. Clutching his sleeves, she tilted her head and peered up at his face. It was set in lines of polished granite. She dropped her arms and backed away from him, more afraid than she'd been in the entire terrible night.

In grim silence he reached down, pried her lollipop off his sleeve, and thrust the fuzzy offender into her hand. He wouldn't even look at her. His eyes were all for the buxom woman who came sauntering out of the crowd.

Gone was the grandmotherly creature who had spooned warm broth down Emily's throat and bussed her cheek good night. Mrs. Rose's ample curves undulated beneath the blush satin sheath of her dress. "You're that renegade duke, aren't you?" she drawled.

"Those damn ruffians have scuffled with a duke. Bloody hell, we're done for now," breathed one of the women.

The guard who was still conscious awkwardly tried to brush off Justin's cloak. Justin shoved his hand away.

"Justin Marcus Homer Lloyd Farnsworth Connor . . . the third," he added, bowing and bringing Mrs. Rose's hand to his lips. "At your service."

"I should be so lucky." She looked him up and down with the approving eye of a woman who has developed an appreciation for raw male beauty in all of its forms. "I once knew a Farnsworth Connor. But he always let me call him Frank. Among other things." She planted a hand on her hip. "I'm not averse to a bit of brawling on a Saturday night, Your Grace, but perhaps I could interest you in some of our more . . . delicate pleasures."

Justin finally looked at her then, but Emily wished he hadn't. She hardly recognized the man who swaggered toward her. The crowd melted back, leaving her to face him alone. He circled her leisurely, his cloak swirling around his ankles. His hungry gaze devoured every inch of her. Her traitorous nipples tightened against the sheer material of her bodice, and a flush shot up her throat. She stared at the carpet, mortified. His blunt masculine scrutiny made her feel more like a whore than any of Barney's slurs.

He stroked the backs of his fingers down her cheek. Emily shivered at the deft touch, but resisted the lure of his stormy gaze.

His hand dropped to his side. "Little Bo Peep here will do just fine," he announced, all business again.

Her flush turned to one of anger. It was bad enough to

be publicly humiliated. He didn't have to poke fun at her silly costume.

Emily would never know if it was concern for her customer's satisfaction or a latent qualm of maternal conscience that forbade the throwing of lambs to lions, but Mrs. Rose bustled forward, clucking her disapproval. "Oh, no, she won't do at all. Far too young and raw for your seasoned palate, I'm sure. Perhaps one of my more refined lovelies . . ."

She dragged forward a girl draped in the gauzy veil of the harem and thrust her at him. The hapless Peggy shrank back against her mistress, and Emily couldn't blame her. With his jaw unshaven, his hair tousled, and his eyes burning with contemptuous fire, Justin looked like the sort of heathen to debauch maidens with one hand while swilling down a tankard of virgin's blood with the other.

He looked Emily dead in the eye. "I want her."

Emily's knees quivered. Mrs. Rose harrumphed nervously and went in search of more tempting bait. "Why, here's my Solange, quite skilled in the Far Eastern art of—"

A fat purse of Persian leather clinked to the carpet at her feet. The madam bent and retrieved it, obviously intrigued by its rustle.

"A hundred pounds," Justin said coolly.

A gasp traveled around the parlor. Emily's suspicion that Mrs. Rose would sell her own daughter for a hundred pounds was strengthened as an avaricious smile curved the woman's lips.

She gave Emily an apologetic shrug. "Why don't you accompany His Grace upstairs, my dear? I do believe he's just the man to help you find your lost sheep."

Justin wasted no time. He swept her up and tossed her over his shoulder.

"Is the carriage outside? Are we going home now?" Emily asked hopefully, bobbing with each of his pur-

poseful strides. But those strides were carrying them not
toward the door, but the stairs. She kicked and squirmed,
but his muscular arm only tightened across her rump,
holding her fast. "I don't want to go back up there, Justin.
Really I don't."

To her embarrassment, as they started up the stairs the
crowd began to cheer and shout encouragement. Barney
emerged from his rat hole and hooted, "Poke 'er once fer
me, mate!"

Howling in outrage, Emily reached over the banister
and slapped the lollipop in his greasy hair.

Emily bounced on Justin's back like a sack of meal. The
muscled ridge of his shoulder cut off her breath with each
long stride.

"You . . . might . . . consider . . . putting . . .
me . . . down," she gasped.

He ignored her. He paused at the first door they en-
countered and kicked it open, jarring Emily's entire body.

She heard an angry cry and a muffled squeak of protest.

"Sorry," he said, but his tone was unrepentant.

He swung away from the door without bothering to
close it, treating Emily to a most sordid sight. She twisted
her head to the left, then to the right, before slapping her
hands over her eyes. "My goodness! She must be frightfully agile, mustn't she? I saw something like that once in
the circus."

Justin maintained his stony silence. His foot slammed
into the next door. To Emily's distress, the room was unoc-
cupied.

"I should really like to go home now," she said in a
small voice.

He tossed her on the bed and strode back to bolt the
door. She sat up and hugged her knees, curling into a
timid knot among the rumpled sheets. Stale perfume rose
from their folds, and she tried not to think about what

might have transpired there only moments earlier. A dank chill hung in the fireless room.

Justin whipped off his cloak and threw it over a chair, then turned to face her. Emily realized she had seen him angry before, but never so coldly furious.

He raked a hand through his hair. "I haven't slept for over thirty-six hours. I've spent the last twelve of those combing every lice-infested claphouse in London for you." A single word shot from his lips. "Why?"

She bowed her head, struggling to gather the threads of her pride, sensing she might need them. When she lifted her head, her eyes were dry, her voice calm. "I no longer wished to be a burden to you. I wanted my freedom."

"Freedom?" His voice cracked on a disbelieving note. He crossed to the bed and snatched her up by the shoulders. "Is this what you call freedom? Spreading your legs for any man willing to lay down his coin?" His eyes blazed, giving her a harrowing glimpse of the raw hurt fueling his anger.

An uncontrollable shaking seized her. She couldn't look him in the eye.

He lowered her. "Fine," he said with glacial calm. "I've paid my coin."

He dragged off his tie and began to unbutton his waistcoat.

Emily scrambled back against the headboard. "Not you?" she whispered, horror-struck.

He stood with legs planted firmly apart, his fists resting on his narrow hips. "Any man but me, eh? How gratifying. Didn't Mrs. Rose teach you to flatter your clients, not unman them?"

Emily could tell by the precise cut of Justin's broadcloth trousers that he was in no danger of being unmanned.

He strode to the bed and cupped her head in his palm. His long fingers tangled in her curls in a travesty of tenderness. "Sorry, darling, but whores don't have the privilege of picking and choosing their liaisons. For a hundred pounds I'll expect a little enthusiasm." His lips came down on hers in a silken whisper. "Fake it if you must."

Emily expected his kiss to be brutal, only to find it utterly ruthless in its gentleness. His mouth played over hers with merciless skill, teasing, tugging with his teeth, then laving her parted lips with his tongue, priming her for its deeper invasion. His was the kiss of the concubine, enslaving with its promise of erotic pleasures to come. It was a kiss to steal not only her body, but her soul as well. The first tear slipped from her lashes before he could pause to draw a breath.

He blew softly on her moistened lips. "Emily, sweet Emily," he whispered hoarsely. "You were made for this, weren't you? Made to pleasure a man."

Not just any man, her heart cried. Only him.

He slid his tongue between her lips, taking her mouth in deep possessive strokes as he eased her back on the bed. She felt herself sliding irrevocably beneath the lean, hard planes of his body. His hands glided down her sides, grazing the swell of her breasts, the slender dip of her waist. His palms cupped her rear, molding her for his pleasure, the sheer dress a gossamer web between them.

Emily felt herself losing to the consummate seduction of this cool, practiced stranger. Losing everything she had fought so hard to win. Her pride. Her independence. Even the anger that had kept the world at bay until she had washed up into Justin's waiting arms. She had outwitted the sea, only to find herself drowning in a deeper pool. She had leaned over to find her reflection in its still, cool depths and been dragged into a whirling maelstrom of passion. If she couldn't kick her way to the surface, she knew she would die a thousand shuddering deaths beneath his artful touch.

She tugged her mouth away from his. She was crying

in earnest now, small convulsive sobs that wouldn't stop. "Please, Justin. Not like this."

"Shhh," he whispered. He gently stroked her breast, soothing her puckered nipple beneath his thumb. His other hand wandered lower. "That's it, darling, open your legs for me. You're so sweet, Em. So sweet and hot . . . and wet."

Her sob broke on a moan.

Justin smothered it with his lips, further beyond her reach than she realized. He had intended only to frighten her, to teach her a lesson. To show her she couldn't persist in her madcap schemes without suffering the consequences.

He had expected resistance to his crude assault. But when her soft, trembling lips had parted beneath his, he had become more lost than she. The lesson was out of his hands now. A primal lust overpowered him. He had wanted her for so long . . . forever, it seemed.

Maddened by the promise of heaven cupped in his palm, he pressed his fingers deep inside of her, shamelessly ravishing her quivering warmth.

It was then that he realized how still she was lying beneath him. He lifted his head. She lay shivering, her eyes shut, tears sparkling like gilt on her lashes. Dear God, she was going to allow him to do it, he thought. To take her in the punishing heat of anger. Her abject surrender was so alien to her proud nature that he felt something inside of him twist in anguish.

Was it any wonder she was confused? One minute he was berating her like a child, the next fondling her like a whore. He hadn't the courage to treat her like a woman because that might mean losing her forever.

Blood pounded through his groin in a primal protest, but he knew to take her now would somehow be as cruel or crueler than rape.

She kept her eyes pressed shut as he wrapped his cloak around her and lifted her. Her arms crept around his neck with a lingering trust that reopened a raw wound in his heart. As Justin strode through the parlor with his burden, Mrs. Rose's clientele fell into an awed hush. Emily burrowed her face into his chest and he eased a fold of the cloak over her, shielding her from their stares and whispers. The footmen hastily stepped out of his way. Not a soul dared protest as he carried her into the sheltering darkness of the night.

Penfeld, God bless his proper English soul, didn't utter a word of reproach when his wild-eyed master came pounding on his bedroom door near midnight.

"Please," Justin said, holding out a warm, sleepy bundle. "Take her."

The dire consequences of his refusal were clearly implied in Justin's gaze. Penfeld adjusted his nightcap, set his chimneyed candle on his washstand, and gently removed Emily from his arms. A corner of the cloak fell back to reveal an angelic countenance, marred by grubby tear stains.

As they disappeared down the shadowy corridor, Penfeld waddling in his long nightshirt, Justin sank into the nearest chair and buried his face in his hands. When the valet returned after tucking Emily into her bed, Justin was gone and the wild, wistful strains of Chopin's "Fantaisie-Impromptu" were pouring through the silent house.

Justin slammed the chord home, ignoring the unharmonious groan of the piano. His fingers tore over the keys, no longer content to coax or cajole. They plundered each note, driving the music into the air with the force of a blow. The fine bones in his hands ached. Sweat trickled from his temples. But still he played on, fighting to drown his own wild despair in the crashing magnificence of the music.

He had thrown open a window, hoping the icy air might cool his fevered senses. The night was moonless. A single candle flickered on top of the piano, bathing him in a pool of fragile light. His battered fingers struck yet another blow, clumsy in their thwarted passion. The many faces of the women he had seen in that long day floated past him. Once he might have been the sort of man who could drown his desires in the perfumed arms of a stranger, but instinct warned him he needed far more than a shuddering spasm of relief to ease his longing for Emily. The music thundered to a crescendo. The shadows danced around him in macabre relief. In that half-beat of peace between one note and the next, he heard it—the faintest whisper of a sigh.

He was not alone.

His hands froze above the keys. Who in this household would be mad enough to approach him now? The candle guttered in a gust of wind, and the shadows closed in with the silence. The harsh rasp of his breathing was the only sound.

He swung around on the bench.

Emily stood like a ghost in her long white nightdress, clutching her ragged old doll. Her feet were bare and her cheeks still streaked with tear stains. A lump hardened in Justin's throat. She looked very young, like a child creeping downstairs in the night for a drink of water. But there was no denying her eyes were the eyes of a woman, darkened in some unspeakable plea.

His emotions choked him. Why couldn't he hold her? Why couldn't he draw her into his lap and gently cradle her head to his chest? Why couldn't he dry her tears on his shirt and promise her everything would be all right?

Because it would be a lie. And he hadn't paid the price for his silence all these lonely years to start lying to her now.

If he laid his hands on her, he wouldn't stop. The same hand that drew her into his lap would ease her nightdress up over her hips. The same lips that murmured soothing reassurances would cover hers as he laid her back on the piano, parted her ivory thighs, and drove himself home in her honeyed depths. He didn't dare touch her. He didn't dare even look at her.

He turned his face away, feeling his jaw stiffen as if it were set in granite. "Go back to bed, Emily," he commanded, hardly recognizing the hoarse voice as his own. "Now."

He felt her hesitancy, heard the soft shuffle of her bare feet on the rug. Damn her. Why couldn't she ever do anything the first time she was asked?

Knowing he had no choice, he swallowed the ruins of his pride and leveled the full force of his raw gaze at her. "Go to your room and lock your door. Please."

Her lips trembled. A glistening tear slipped down her cheek, then another. The doll thumped to the carpet as she turned and fled. The blackness of the house swallowed her without a trace.

"I'm sorry, Em. I'm so damned sorry," he whispered to the silent shadows.

His words were more heartfelt than she would ever know. He was sorry he had made her cry. Sorry David hadn't lived to introduce him to his spirited daughter. David had adored them both. Perhaps it wouldn't have been such a stretch to imagine him blessing their love.

But David had died, forever taking his blessing with him.

Justin picked up the doll and set her on the music stand. He smoothed her matted curls. "We're old friends, you and I, aren't we?"

The opaque blue eyes surveyed him without expression. He touched the piano, stroking first one key, then another, but the music had gone, leaving him in utter silence.

He rose and climbed the stairs, his tread heavy. His steps slowed outside of Emily's door. He heard nothing from within her room, no sniffing or broken weeping, only a whisper of silence more taunting than an invitation. He braced his brow against the door, choking back a groan. How long would it be before even locks would fail to keep him out? A week? A month? A year? Was he to betray David yet again by seducing his daughter? His hand clenched into a fist against the thick mahogany.

As he splayed his fingers to ease their tension, the door swung open without a sound.

*C*hapter 29

· 🐚 ·

*Please do not begrudge me the peace I have bought
with my silence. . . .*

*H*ardly daring to breathe, Emily lay back on her pillows
and watched the crack between door and frame slowly
widen. A man appeared, his lean form silhouetted against
the light from the corridor candles. Time swung back to a
barren attic room and a thousand other lonely nights. Her
heart thundered. Her shadow lover had finally come to her
as she had always known he would.

He closed the door behind him and twisted the key in
the lock. The click of the tumbler echoed in the silence.
He came toward the bed, measuring his steps as if drawn
into a web he no longer had the will to resist.

He braced his hands on each side of her head. His eyes
asked the question her unlocked door had already answered. "I've waited so long for you."

"Not nearly so long as I've waited for you," she said
fiercely, entangling her fingers at his nape and pulling him
down to her.

Their lips met and mingled in sweet communion,

soothed not by the salty balm of the sea, but by her tears. Justin traced the curves of her cheekbones with his thumbs. "No tears, angel. No tears tonight."

His mouth came down on hers to seal their vow. She clung to him as they rolled across the feather mattress, entangling the sheets around their limbs. A hoarse groan escaped Justin as he realized she was naked beneath him, just as she had been that night on the beach. They had wasted so much precious time getting here from there. But this was no time for regrets.

Tonight he would bury his dark secrets in her tender body until there existed for them no past and no tomorrow. Only tonight. Only he and Emily, destined to love not in sunlight, but in the ebony cloak of night. His tongue flicked softly across her dimpled cheek. His lips grazed the curve of her jaw, then glided downward to the milky smoothness of her throat.

Emily clawed open his buttons and ran her hands over his chest, marveling at the masculine mesh of bone and muscle. She felt the flat disks of his nipples harden in response. Justin had breathed life into the phantom who had once haunted her girlish dreams. She couldn't get enough of him. She wanted to feel the weight of him crushing her. She wanted to drink him in through her fingertips. She felt greedy and selfish and fierce like a mewling baby tiger, blinded by the explosive light of its first sunrise. The walls of her pride were crumbling beneath its heat.

She tugged at his hair, bringing his face to hers. Her voice broke on a whimper as she said the words she'd bitten back for so long. "Love me, Justin. Please."

He touched two fingers to her bottom lip. "You never have to beg me, Emily. Never."

Then he was sliding down on her into a darkness that heightened every sensation. His warm hands cupped her bottom, lifting and coaxing. A sudden burst of shyness made her clamp her thighs together.

He brushed his lips against her silky triangle of curls, then blew softly against the wet spot his mouth had made. His voice was a husky whisper, half command, half prayer. "Trust me."

He'd never before asked that of her. How could she deny him now? Her head fell back against the pillow and her legs went limp, giving him dominion over far more than her body. Moaning, she bunched the back of his shirt in her fists. He was her lover, both demon and angel, giving her ecstasy untold, burying his tongue in her velvety folds, flicking and stroking until her womb convulsed in an agony of pleasure. Before she could shatter the silence of the sleeping house with her cry, his lips were there, both shocking and intoxicating her with the taste of her own forbidden nectar.

The tiny hairs on the back of his hand tickled her naked belly as he tore open the buttons of his trousers. His intensity both excited and frightened her. She shuddered, realizing she was about to learn the full measure of this man's passion.

But her sweet torment at his hands had just begun. He slid his arm around her rump and lifted her to a half-sitting position against the headboard. His hands eased her thighs as far apart as they would go, exposing her fully. She felt terribly vulnerable and sinfully decadent. Even in the sheltering darkness she could feel her cheeks burn.

"Did I ever mention to you how very shy I am?" she whispered.

He touched her there, softly, eliciting a moan. "It was one of the first things I noticed about you."

"Really?"

She could hear the grin in his voice. "No."

A shudder of pleasure banished her shyness as he slid a finger from each hand up into her folds until they found the silky little bud nestled beneath. At the same time, his thumbs began to circle the taut, distended satin of her flesh below, laving her, pearling the hot, thick honey around her melting core. Her world narrowed to pure sensation. An emptiness more gaping than any she had known yawned within her. Wild with need, she arched against him, pressing against his thumbs, wanting more, so much more.

Justin was half crazed from wanting her, but still he continued his exquisite torture. His eyes had adjusted to the darkness, and he watched her face, entranced by the flickers of pleasure dancing across her features. She whimpered his name. Her teeth cut into the tender bud of her lower lip. Fighting for control, he clenched his jaw against the hoarse rasp of his own breathing. When he got to where he was going, he wanted her already there, waiting for him.

His deft fingers never ceased their maddening dance, not even when he rubbed the hard length of himself where his thumbs had been.

Emily gasped at the shock of it. Her eyes flew open. Justin's face, darkened by passion, was very near to hers. His eyes sparkled as he pressed against her, sliding the very tip of himself into her, then withdrawing, taunting her with its promise. Both wonder and fear shook her as she realized his intent. When her first dark shiver of ecstasy came, this man was going to make her his own.

The flames of his fingertips licked her higher. His rigid manhood breached her again, probing gently, then pulling back, maddening her into a frenzy with its deliberate teasing. She writhed against him. Her hands tangled in his hair. When he bent his head and took her breast into his mouth, first gently sucking, then tugging at her nipple with his teeth, Emily broke. Pleasure raked her in shuddering waves and Justin thrust up into her, hard.

Emily muffled her scream against his shoulder. The pain was no less phenomenal than the pleasure. As her untried body clamped down in protest, Justin threw back his head in masculine ecstasy and gritted his teeth, pressing into her inch by unrelenting inch. Sweat sheened his chest.

She felt her tender flesh stretching to sheath him. Shamed by her inadequacy, her voice broke on a groan. "I can't, Justin. Oh, God, you're too much. I can't take all of you."

Shifting her hips with his hands, he proved her wrong, driving upward until every throbbing inch of him was cloaked in the taut, velvety folds of her body. His lips caught her cry, drowning it in his own.

This wasn't the way Justin had planned it—panting, half undressed, pinioning Emily against the headboard, but when had life with Emily ever gone as planned? He fought the urge to move within her, wanting to give her body time to adjust to his invasion. His tongue soothed her swollen lips, sworled in tender apology through her mouth even as his body exulted in her exquisite gloving. A tear trickled from beneath her dark lashes.

He caught it on his tongue before it could reach her dimple. Her luminous eyes opened.

"No tears," he said softly. "You promised."

She kissed him gently, a smile trembling on her lips. "No tears," she repeated. As proof of her pledge she braced her palm against his chest and arched her back, taking him both higher and deeper than he would have ever dreamed possible.

A guttural groan escaped him, but even through his haze of ecstasy he saw her flinch. He caught her hips in his hands and eased her flat beneath him, determined to banish all memories of pain from her mind or die a glorious death trying.

As Justin began to move deep within her, Emily felt her body surrendering to his sweet sorcery. He braced his weight on his hands and ground his hips against her, both consuming her and making her whole with each silken stroke. She clung to him, unable to remember a time when he had not been a part of her. Her hips rose to meet each of his bewitching thrusts. This sensation was different from the earlier ecstasy he had given her, fuller, darker somehow, and fraught with all the perils of surrender. Small, helpless noises escaped her throat until finally, drugged with pleasure, she could do nothing but lie beneath his powerful body, spread for the slaking of his desire.

"Emily," he muttered in evocation against her lips. "My sweet, sweet Emily."

He reached between them and touched her then. The gentlest touch of his fingertips set off a quaking tremor. Just when she thought he couldn't get any bigger or harder, he did, and the tremor became a shuddering explosion. Their lips crashed, fusing in the desperate need to silence their screams as all the passion he'd kept locked inside came roaring from his loins, spilling hot within her.

Groaning, Justin collapsed against her and buried his face in her curls, breathing hard. She rubbed her lips against his stubbled cheek, tasting the salty wetness, and knew that this night they had both broken their vow.

Tingling ribbons of sunlight caressed the exhausted muscles of Justin's back. He was drowsing in the warm sand beneath a cobalt sky, lulled by the whisper of the waves against the shore. The sand was powder-fine and soft, so soft he could feel himself sinking painlessly into its feathery depths. He drew in a lungful of its fragrance—a musky vanilla like the purest and most potent of aphrodisiacs.

He rolled to his back and stretched, savoring the ache of his sated muscles. He didn't want to open his eyes. He wanted to sleep for another week. Warmth bathed his face.

Where was he? he wondered. Where were the heavy bed curtains that smothered the light and kept the fresh air at bay? He forced his eyes open to find himself gazing up at the scalloped half-tester over Emily's bed.

He sat up abruptly, pulling the sheet to his waist. It wasn't the waves he had heard but the soft shuffle of Emily's hands as she folded her undergarments into a carpeted valise. Her back was to him, and she wore nothing but his discarded shirt. The dawn light cast a buttery halo around her curls.

"What are you doing?" he said. His untried voice sounded gruff, even to him.

"Pudding is very fond of your stables," she said calmly. "I believe I shall leave him to Jimmie's care. Do you think I might have a cat at my new lodgings? Miss Winters always detested them. I don't require a lot of room, you know. Daddy and I were always happiest in our more modest apartments. My fondest memories are of our little cottage at Brighton." Her hands faltered. "I've never been a mistress before. I hope I shall be a good one."

It took Justin's bleary mind a moment to sort out her ramblings. When he had, he rose, leaving the sheet behind, and padded up behind her. He slipped his arms around her waist and drew her back against him. She couldn't meet his eyes, not even in the full-length looking glass fixed between her wardrobe doors.

Touched by her unexpected shyness, he rubbed his bristled cheek against her temple. "And where do you think you're going?"

Emily felt her gaze drawn inexorably upward, captivated by the spell cast by their reflection. The contrast was stunning. Justin's dark hair next to her burnished curls. His feral, naked grace against the rumpled folds of the shirt. She watched in fascination as his bronze hands glided over the white linen, unable to forget the feel of those hands on her . . . and in her.

She drew in a shaky breath. "Your mother . . . your sisters . . . we mustn't expose them to my tarnished reputation."

He cupped her breasts in his reverent palms. "Is that how I made you feel last night? Tarnished?"

Emily thought of all the times she'd been made to feel less than she was. She met his gaze boldly in the mirror. "No. Not tarnished. Cherished." She laced her fingers around his. "Did you know you have the most amazing hands?"

His slow, lazy grin melted her bones. "I always knew practicing those infernal scales would pay off someday." He nuzzled her throat, sending a shiver of delight down her spine. "You're not going anywhere, angel, except back to bed."

She lay her head against his shoulder, baring her throat for his sweet plundering. "There's no time. What if Penfeld comes looking for you?"

He nudged his hips against her rump and began to gently ease the shirt upward. "I assure you, this won't take nearly as long as I'd like."

Peace reigned at Grymwilde Mansion for the first time since its master's return. The only explanation Justin offered for Emily's brief disappearance was that she had become "lost." Only he and Emily knew how close she had come to being eternally lost. His family was too wise to press for more. They were all reaping the benefits of his sunny disposition.

The parlor rang with laughter and music at all hours of the day. Justin and Emily played endless rounds of cards with Lily, sang warbling duets with Edith, and helped Millicent pick out the tangled threads of her embroidery. Each morning Herbert and Harvey marched off to their new offices at Winthrop Shipping, proudly displaying the handsome leather writing cases given them by their brother-in-law. Finally, bored and grumbling, Harold even took himself off to apply for a position at the Exchange.

If this was yet another manifestation of His Grace's mysterious brain fever, whispered the servants as they counted their generous bonuses, it was a pleasant one indeed. Only Justin knew he had been possessed by a different sort of fever altogether.

Penfeld was gazing out the bay window overlooking

the garden one afternoon when the duchess came sailing up.

The two of them stood in silence, watching Justin and Emily romp around a frozen fountain, Pudding hard at their heels. Their antics brought such a breath of spring to the dead garden that the duchess wouldn't have been surprised to see a blush of green come creeping over the trellises before their very eyes.

As they watched, Emily darted behind the naked spines of a hawthorn bush, her cheeks flushed with laughter and cold. Her escape was cut short when Justin caught a handful of her hood in his fist and dragged her back over his arm. The laughter faded from Emily's eyes and she went still. He inclined his head, his lips hovering so close over hers that the mist from their mouths mingled.

The duchess sucked in an audible breath.

At that moment a jealous Pudding stood on his hind legs and thrust his pug nose between them. Penfeld pulled a handkerchief from his pocket and dabbed at his brow.

They must have seen the flash of white, because both of them looked guiltily to the window. Emily broke away from Justin's arms and waved cheerily before kneeling to bury her face in Pudding's brindle coat.

Penfeld tilted his nose in the air and sniffed. "Heartwarming, is it not, to see a man taking such an active interest in his responsibilities?"

The duchess eyed the portly valet through narrowed eyes. "Oh, deeply affecting. Deeply."

The game was on. Justin and Emily played it with relish. By day they appeared the very model of propriety with no one the wiser if her foot climbed up his calf beneath the shelter of the tablecloth, or if he slipped her an extra card beneath the loo table. The interminable moments ticked away, measured not by the swing of the pendulum in the long-case clock, but by longing looks and stolen kisses until finally the hour came when Emily might politely smother a yawn into her handkerchief and climb the long, curving stairs to bed.

She would lie trembling on tenterhooks of anticipation until the house fell silent. Then the telltale creak of the unlocked door would come and Justin would slip into her bed and arms.

With the pleasure of Emily's company by day and the delight of her lithe young body by night, Justin felt he had died and gone to heaven. He was in thrall to her tender possession of his heart and body. He had never in his life imagined such sweetness and passion at his fingertips. She was a miracle, a marvel who brought the same enthusiasm and adventurous spirit to her lovemaking as she had brought to his life.

Late one night the drowsing peace of the house was fractured by the crash of heavy furniture and breaking glass. A herd of feet stampeded to Emily's door.

Harold's fist rattled the mahogany panels. "Hullo there, gel. Open up! What's going on in there? Are you all right?"

Emily swung open the door, her cheeks burning, to face a nightcapped mob that included Penfeld, Justin's entire family, and a few of the bolder servants.

She brushed back her tousled curls, laughing nervously. "I'm my clumsy old self, I fear. I must have been having a nightmare. I seem to have fallen out of bed and overturned the nightstand." She reached up to smooth the ribbons of her nightdress, then realized in horror they were trailing down her back because her nightdress was on backward.

One of the wide-eyed housemaids tried to peer around her at the carnage. "I'll fetch a broom, miss, straightaway, and clean up the mess."

"Oh, no," said Emily hastily, narrowing the crack between door and wall. "That won't be necessary. I'm really quite exhausted. You may clean up in the morning."

Justin's mother rested her fists on her ample hips.

With her iron-gray ringlets wrapped in rags, she resembled a matronly Medusa. Emily lowered her eyes, fearing the duchess's accusing gaze might turn her to something worse than stone.

"Where's my son?" she demanded. "I would have thought a crash like that would have brought the dead running."

Penfeld quickly piped up with "My master is a very sound sleeper."

They all stared at him. Emily couldn't stop her own mouth from falling open at that preposterous falsehood. But even in his tasseled nightcap and long nightshirt, Penfeld's dignity was so profound that no one dared challenge him.

"Harrumph," pronounced the duchess skeptically.

She charted a course for her chambers, the skirts of her brocaded dressing gown frothing in her wake. One by one the others trailed away.

Penfeld was the last to go. He gallantly tipped his nightcap to Emily and gave her a knowing wink.

She closed her door and twisted the key. "Why, that pompous little scoundrel. He's known all along." She clapped a hand over her mouth to smother her giggle.

The door of her wardrobe swung open and Justin emerged, her satin dressing gown wrapped around his waist. He plucked a stray ostrich feather out of his hair.

"Don't look at me like that," she said. "I didn't lie. I *did* fall out of bed."

He wagged the feather at her. "Like you fell off that boat in New Zealand?"

"Oh, no. That wasn't the same at all."

"Thank God." He bent to graze her lips. He trailed the feather down the curve of her back and she moaned softly. "I despise this need for silence. I wish we were in New Zealand now, lying on the beach with nothing but the moon and stars to hear us." His voice lowered to a husky whisper. "I'd like to spend all night making you scream."

She buried her mouth in his chest. "What did you have in mind? A complete recitation of Penfeld's tea collection?"

"Why don't I just show you?" He gently guided her around until she was kneeling in the plush cushions of the window seat. The curtains of Brussels lace tickled the tip of her nose.

Her voice caught on a tremulous note. "Justin?"

"Mmm?" he answered, kneeling behind her and pushing the backward nightdress up.

"If we fall out the window, I'm going to leave the explanations to you."

"My pleasure, darling."

As the dressing gown fell in a shimmering satin pool around their knees, Emily arched against him, knowing the pleasure was all hers.

Justin wrapped a gossamer curl around his finger, then freed it, watching it spring back against Emily's cheek. She mumbled something in her sleep and wiggled deeper into the pillows.

The watery light of dawn crept across the tangled sheets. Justin despised its arrival. He hated dragging himself out of the warm cocoon of blankets and sneaking through the drafty old house to his own barren bed. A pain seized his heart. Emily looked so sweet and warm with her cheeks rosy with sleep and her curls rumpled. He didn't want to leave her. He realized with a shock that he never wanted to leave her.

He wanted the right to spend all night and all day in bed with her if he chose. He wanted to escort her to the countess's fête that afternoon and show the whole world that she belonged to him.

"Oh, David," he whispered. "What have I done?"

David had once given her to him. After all those years

of self-imposed exile, would he still find him worthy of such a prize? Justin knew if his friend were alive today, he would have gone to him on hands and knees if necessary to beg for her hand.

He smoothed back her curls and tenderly kissed her brow before climbing out of the bed. When she moaned a protest, he slid a pillow into the hollow his body had left. She pulled it into her embrace and tucked it under her chin, sighing in content.

Stepping over the carnage from the previous night's mishap, he dressed quickly, fearful his resolve to go might weaken. He wondered what his ever-so-proper servants would do if he simply jerked the tasseled cord hanging from the ceiling and ordered eggs and kippers in bed for him and his ward. He grinned at the thought.

His smile faded as he opened the door to find his mother leaning with arms crossed against the opposite wall.

*C*hapter *30*

· 🐚 ·

But I fear we have a serpent in our paradise,
poised and ready to strike. . . .

*O*livia Connor was no less intimidating in dressing gown
and slippers than she was armored in a full ball gown and
bustle. Justin reached behind him and pulled Emily's door
shut.

He faced his mother squarely, trying to ignore the
flush he could feel creeping up over his cheekbones. He
forced a wry smile. "Why do I feel like I'm six years old
and I've been caught dipping into Gracie's cookie jar?"

Her steely gaze raked him, taking in his unbuttoned
shirt, the rumpled folds of his trousers. "It seems you've
been caught dipping into much more than that."

Summoning the remnants of his grace, he leaned
against the door and crossed his arms, mirroring her posture deliberately. "Guilty as charged. So what are you going to do? Disinherit me again?"

"Have you forgotten? You're the duke now. I can't
disinherit you. But you may pack me off to a dower house
if you desire."

"Ah, but that would imply there was another duchess waiting in the wings."

She nodded toward the door. "Isn't there?"

Justin raked a hand through his hair, suddenly feeling less six than sixty. "I'm afraid not."

"More's the pity. The two of you would make pretty children together." She lifted an eyebrow. "That is, if you haven't already."

A muffled oath exploded from his lips. He strode a few paces away and stood with hands on hips, his back to her. A bitterness he'd pushed deep down clawed its way to the surface. "You were never there for me before, Mother. What makes you think I'd confide in you now?"

Her voice was devoid of self-pity. "I don't think you will. I know what I was. A good wife and a wretched mother."

Justin swung around, surprised by her blunt confession.

"Did you ever ask yourself why your father resented you so much?" she asked.

He stared at the carpet. "Every day. And I always came up with the same answer. There was something wrong with me."

She shook her head. "There was something *right* with you. Something so shining and bright that it blinded him with jealousy." He stared at her disbelievingly. "Frank Connor wasn't always the man you knew. He didn't want the business or the title any more than you did. It was like a lead anchor around his neck, dragging him down. He longed to sail one of those graceful clippers right over the horizon and explore the world. But he didn't have your guts. He didn't have the courage to simply walk away."

Justin stood awash in conflicting emotions as she moved toward him.

"Denying himself his dreams made your father a bitter, mean-spirited old man." She stood on tiptoe and kissed his cheek, filling his nostrils with the long-forgotten comfort of lilac and camphor. "Don't make the same mistake, son."

Justin stood alone, staring at nothing, after his mother had gone. Perhaps she was right. Perhaps it was time to bury the old ghosts and let David rest in peace at last. Perhaps the time had come for him and Emily to seize not only the day, but the morrow as well.

Emily handed the waiting footman her cloak as she and Lily entered the foyer of the Comtesse Guermond's sumptuous apartments. The drawing room beyond had been decorated in the Greek Revival style favored over a century ago. Graceful Doric columns mushroomed from polished bases. A lethargic quartet was playing in the corner. Emily's scalloped train swept the marble floor as they were ushered into the chattering fray.

The chandeliers sparkled beneath the kiss of winter sunlight streaming through the casement windows. After being smothered in the Gothic gloom of Grymwilde for so long, Emily found the effect dazzling.

As Lily wandered off with a friend, Emily stole a glance behind her, hoping to catch a glimpse of Justin entering. He had ridden alongside their carriage on a handsome bay—a striking sight in his top hat and greatcoat. He had seemed strangely excited all day, his golden eyes warmed by more than their usual glow. The afternoon would be sweet torment indeed. They didn't dare even dance together for fear of revealing themselves. But later, Emily thought, in the still, sweet hours of the night, while the rest of the world slept, their patience would be rewarded. Her cheeks warmed at the thought. Who would have ever dreamed she would make such a pudding of herself over a man? Especially that man.

"Emily, oh, Emily darling, is that you?" She cringed at the sound of Cecille's voice. Her old nemesis caught her in a girlish embrace. "I promised Henry you'd be here. He's simply drooling for a dance."

Emily tried to wiggle free. "I don't think so. I'm afraid my card is full."

"How can it be full? You just got here. Don't move an inch and I'll go fetch him."

As soon as Cecille trotted out of sight, Emily ducked into a safe corner and began to madly scribble fictional names on her dance card.

"I say, gel, haven't we met?"

She jerked her head around to find a bloodshot eye studying her through a cracked quizzing glass. A silent sigh of dread escaped her.

"I fear you are mistaken, sir." She edged away from the portly fellow.

"I'd stake my life on it," he boomed out. "You look frightfully familiar." His lascivious gaze lowered to the ruched silk of her bodice. "Perhaps we met at the earl's card party last week?"

"I think not." To her relief, Emily saw Justin approaching through the crowd. An impish smile transformed her face as she threw her arms around the gentleman's neck. "Why, Uncle George!" She beckoned to Justin and called out in a voice that carried through the entire room, "Look, Your Grace, it's one of my father's oldest friends—my dear old uncle George! You remember him, don't you? He used to so love to dandle me on his knee."

Justin may not have remembered, but Uncle George was beginning to. He went pale in her choke hold as the Duke of Winthrop parted the crowd with deadly grace. Several people were beginning to stare.

"No, no, gel," he stammered. "I'm sorry. You've got it all wrong. I don't know anyone named George. My name is Harry. I mean Alfred."

"Surely you jest!" Emily cried as Justin stopped in front of them. "Why, the resemblance is uncanny." She grasped his fat cheeks, turning his face for Justin's perusal. "He's the very image of George, isn't he, Your Grace?"

Only too aware of her adventures in the bordello, Justin stroked his chin. "Positively eerie. Are you sure you don't have a twin somewhere, my good man?"

"Yes. No. I don't know. Perhaps I do. My mum was never too clear on the matter. Now, if you'll excuse me, I really must be going." Uncle George-Harry-Alfred awkwardly extracted himself from Emily's embrace and fled toward the foyer, racing past the puzzled footman holding out his greatcoat and cane.

Laughter bubbled from Emily's throat. The heat of Justin's gaze warmed her like a touch. Her heart did a clumsy somersault.

"You look lovely," he said.

She inclined her head, suddenly shy. It was hard to equate this staid, elegant gentleman with the playful satyr who loved her until dawn each night. "So do you."

"Will you dance with me?" he asked, his eyes somber.

"What will they think?" For the first time in her life Emily feared the opinions of others. She had Justin's reputation to consider now.

"They'll think the rich, mad duke has finally found a woman daft enough to marry him."

Emily turned away from him, choking on emotion. Justin wanted her. Not just for a few hours of stolen pleasure in the night. For always. "But the scandal," she whispered. "You're my guardian. I've been living beneath your roof for over a month. They'll never accept us."

"Then they can all go to hell and I can take my bride to New Zealand for a Maori wedding." He waited for a long beat of silence. "What do you say? Will Cecille forgive us if we announce our engagement at her fête?"

Emily swung around, smiling through a blur of tears. "She forgave me for stuffing the dead mouse in her boot, didn't she?"

Justin folded her into his arms, ignoring the curious stares. "Stop that, now. Penfeld would never forgive you for soaking all the starch out of my lapels." He held his handkerchief to her nose. "There now. Blow. That's a good girl. Feel better?" At her nod, he said, "Come on, then. You've faced down cannibals and dragons. Surely a few matrons and snobbish swells don't scare you." Emily nodded again, this time more violently. "Well, if you must know, they scare me too, but there's no help for it. If they get mean, I'll send for my mother to defend us."

As he led her toward the open floor where people were dancing, Emily shyly clutched his sleeve. No one appeared to notice them. All eyes had turned to a new arrival from the foyer. A curious murmur rippled through the drawing room.

As the crowd parted to reveal the object of their fascination, Emily groaned aloud. "Not again. Do the countess and Mrs. Rose always travel in the same social circles?"

Justin's arm went rigid beneath her hand. She looked up. His face had gone stark white, drained of the last vestiges of tan.

She squeezed his arm, alarmed. "What's wrong? You look as if you've seen a ghost."

He shook her hand away and stood in utter stillness, his face drawn into a wary mask over his bones. Emily searched the room for a clue, but all she saw was the debonair stranger she had met in the park and the bordello charming his way through the guests. Impeccably attired as always, he drifted from group to group, tossing off a smile here, a witty remark there. A fluted champagne glass dangled from his elegant fingers as if he'd been born with it. Admiring glances followed his path.

"Why, he's as handsome as everyone says, isn't he?" Emily jumped as Cecille popped up behind them. Her stage whisper would have startled a deaf person. "All the girls are in a swoon over him. He's Italian, and you know what they say about Italian men." She giggled slyly. "And a millionaire at that. They say he made his fortune in gold."

As he paused near them to kiss a simpering beauty's

hand, Cecille saw her chance. She darted out, grabbed his arm, and dragged him over. Justin and the stranger stood eye to eye.

Cecille began, "Your Grace and Emily, I should love to introduce you to—"

"Hello, Justin," the stranger interrupted. His voice was as smooth as cognac and lightly accented, as Emily had remembered. Smiling, he lifted his glass and took a lazy swallow of champagne.

"Hello, Nicky," Justin replied. Then he drew back his fist and smashed it into the stranger's smug face, sending him reeling into the column behind him.

Spattered by champagne, Cecille finished in a daze. "—Mama's new and dear friend, Mr. Nicholas Saleri."

Chapter 31

. ❀ .

There may come a time when you must face life
without my love. . . .

Emily swayed. Cecille caught her before she could fall.
The crowd stood in silent shock.

Nicholas sat up, bracing his back against the column.
Blood spattered his immaculate shirtfront and trickled
from a corner of his mouth. A lank strand of ebony hair
dangled over his eyes. He smoothed it back, regaining his
composure quickly.

Waving away the footmen who rushed to assist him,
he struggled to his feet. "It's a pleasure to see you again,
too, Justin."

Weaving slightly, he bowed and brought Emily's limp
hand to his lips. "Always a delight, Miss Scarborough. You
have the look of your father about your eyes."

Emily stared at her hand, dazed. His blood smeared
her knuckles. She tried vainly to wipe it away on her skirt,
leaving an ugly stain.

"Keep your filthy hands off her," Justin snarled, taking
a step toward him.

The footmen backed away, more than a little leery of the duke's reputation for unpredictable savagery.

Nicholas drew a pristine handkerchief from his pocket and dabbed his lip. He eyed the results distastefully, then tossed it to a trembling maid.

He favored Emily with a patronizing smile. "You'll have to forgive my old friend, Miss Scarborough. I should have expected such a welcome. Guilt can have an odd effect on the human brain. I dare say he's been quite unhinged ever since he murdered your father."

A gasp traveled through the crowd.

"What are you talking about?" Emily cried. "Are you completely mad?" She grabbed Justin by the lapels. They were still damp from her tears of joy. Her frantic gaze searched his face. "What is this man saying? It's ridiculous. Tell him to stop making these absurd accusations."

Justin stared straight ahead.

She gave him a hard shake. Her voice rose on a hysterical note, ringing through the silent room. "Tell him, Justin. Tell him now. Tell them all you didn't kill my daddy!"

He looked down at her then, his gaze so fraught with pity that she wanted to die right there in his arms. He reached down to gently disengage her fingers from his coat, then turned and walked away. The murmurs and cries of shock swelled, but Emily could hear nothing but the merciless roaring of the sea.

She found him in the conservatory at Grymwilde. The late afternoon sun slanted through the west wall of frosted glass, staining the flagstones amber. A low, pebbled fountain sprang from the exotic tangle of flowers and vines. Justin sat on its edge, slowly plucking the petals from a fat winter rose. A puddle of scarlet surrounded his boots.

The damp heat of the winter garden had molded his shirt to his shoulders and tightened the hair at his nape to boyish curls. Emily realized with a shock how much it had grown since he had cut it.

She sank down on the pebbled ledge behind him, smoothing her bloodstained frock. A petal fluttered from his fingers. Emily stared, transfixed by the grace of his beautiful hands. A murderer's hands.

He lifted his head and she knew his gaze was fixed not on the shiny leaves of the aspidistra twining around the miniature trellis, but on a moonlit beach. His ears, like hers, were tuned not to the trickle of the fountain but to the primeval roar of the sea.

His voice was strangely flat. "Nicky had been missing for almost a week before I went to search for him. At first we thought nothing of it. It wouldn't be the first time he'd disappeared without explanation. But then the rumors started trickling in—rumors of conflict between the Maori and the whites.

"All I found of Nicky was the bloody rag that had been his coat. The Maori ambushed me less than a mile from our encampment. I fled for my life. They weren't like the Maori you met on the North Island. These were Hauhaus—a fanatical cult who despised all whites. They did things to their captives in the name of their religion—unspeakable things."

Emily knotted her fingers in her skirt to keep from touching him.

"I'd emptied my pistol of all but one bullet." A black laugh escaped him. "I was saving that for myself in case they caught me.

"By the time I reached the beach, I couldn't hear them anymore. I could see the lantern burning in the tent and I knew David was waiting for me. If we could just launch the boat, we had a chance of escaping with our lives. God knows, the Hauhaus had left us little else." He bowed his head. "I crouched in the bush for the longest time, afraid to brave that open stretch of sand. But then I thought about you."

Emily trailed her fingers through the cool water of the fountain.

"I thought of how David had traded his precious kid gloves for a piece of polished amber to send you. Somehow that thought gave me the courage I needed. I sprinted down the beach and stumbled up to the tent. David caught me as I fell."

My God, boy, what is it? Where's Nick? Is it worse than we feared?

"At first I couldn't convince him. He was dazed. He couldn't believe it was all gone—Nicky, the gold, your inheritance. I had to shake him, curse him."

Goddammit, David! There's no time for this. We've got to launch the curricle. It's our only chance.

A tear rolled off the tip of Emily's nose and plopped into the water, disappearing without a trace.

"I dragged him down the beach toward the boat. But he broke away from me and ran back to the tent. I've never felt as alone as I did at that moment. Standing on that beach, I felt as if I were the only man alive. The only white man.

"Then I heard them. They swarmed out of the rain forest and over the tent like tattooed spiders. I screamed a warning and ran toward the tent.

"Before I could reach it they dragged him out by his arms and legs. He was fighting them with every ounce of his strength. Then he started to yell something at me, but they were all screaming and I couldn't understand what he was saying."

Emily stared at Justin's profile, mesmerized by its bleak purity.

"I waved the pistol wildly, not knowing whom to fire at. There were too many of them, and I had only one bullet. Then I realized what he was saying. What he was begging me to do."

Shoot me! For God's sake, Justin, shoot me!

"He cursed and howled and begged. And I just stood

there, crying so hard I couldn't even aim. They were dragging him into the bush." His head dropped. "So I shot him."

Emily closed her eyes, flinching at the echo of the explosion. Her nostrils twitched at the acrid stench of gunpowder. Then, in the conservatory as on the beach, there was nothing but silence. Silence forever binding them together. Silence forever tearing them apart.

"When he slumped in their arms, the Hauhaus got very quiet. They just stared at me. I knew they'd come for me then. I taunted them."

Come get me! Come on, you miserable sons of bitches! What the bloody hell are you waiting for?

"Then they just dropped him and melted back into the forest." His shoulders slumped. "That was the worst of it, you know. When they didn't come back and kill me.

"When I lifted David in my arms, the chain was still dangling from his fingers. He'd never let go, not even in all his struggles. I knew then why he'd gone back to the tent. To get the watch—the watch with your photograph in it."

Emily rose, unable to bear any more.

Justin waited until she was at the door, her hand on the crystal knob. "Emily?"

He looked her straight in the eye, his golden gaze more searing than the sun. "Always remember one thing. I never lied to you."

She stiffened her chin to still its quiver. "Nor," she said softly, "did you tell me the truth."

As she pulled the door shut, the last thing she saw was the crumpled bloom falling from his limp fingers.

Justin slipped through the darkened house in absolute silence. He knew which creaking boards to step over, which occasional table to dodge so as not to rattle the silver-framed photographs clustered on its top. The thick carpet muffled his footsteps. The clock on the landing below bonged twice.

He felt as if he'd tumbled into one of his own nightmares. The endless corridor rolled out before him, a corridor with a door that grew farther away with each measured step. He feared he might walk forever and never reach it.

But, at last, there it was before him. He wiped his damp palms on his trousers before touching the knob. He'd never before noticed how cold it was. The chill seemed to shoot up his arm to his thundering heart. He forced his rigid fingers to close and slowly turned it. It moved a quarter of a turn, then stopped. He twisted harder. Nothing.

"Emily?" he whispered hoarsely. "Emily, please . . ."

His other hand clenched into a fist. For one crazy moment he wanted to slam his shoulder against the door, to splinter it beneath his weight. But he knew he'd only find another door behind it—a door thick and impenetrable with suspicion and betrayal.

His hand fell away. Despair washed over him in inky waves. He had hoped, foolishly, even wildly perhaps, that the darkness might lower the terrible cost of his silence. That Emily might relent and allow him to spin his regrets in the tender, forgiving cocoon of her embrace. He should have known he couldn't steal with his body what the truth should have bought him. Images from the past night assailed him with fresh grief. Could he have loved her any better if he had known it was their last night together?

He would have held her, just held her in his arms all night long, memorizing the tilt of her snub nose, the ethereal softness of her curls beneath his fingertips, savoring the warm aroma of her skin for all the cold, lonely nights to come.

"Good-bye, my love," he whispered. He pressed his open palm to the polished mahogany of the door, his hand lingering in reluctant farewell.

·   ·   ·

Emily huddled against the door, her knees drawn up to her chest, and listened to Justin's footsteps fade into silence. She shoved her hair away from her face with shaking hands, pressing hard against her temples as if she could somehow muffle the agonizing whispers of the ghosts in her head.

He don't want you. Nobody wants you.

I said I didn't like you. I never said I didn't love you.

. . . since he murdered your father.

I'll be back for you. I swear it.

Trust me.

Shoot me.

She rocked back and forth in a knot of aching misery. Tears rolled silently down her cheeks. One by one the ghosts reared their heads in visions seared like photographs onto the blank plate of her memory. Doreen thrust a coal bucket in her hand, taunting her. Nicholas's elegant lips curled in a sneer. Justin emerged from the waves, his dark hair whipping in the wind, his bronze skin misted with sea drops. Her daddy folded his tall frame to kneel before her so he could button her coat and straighten her bonnet before sending her out in the snow to play.

Yet, even those spirits were tolerable. The ghost who haunted her now was a child. A child dancing with sweet abandon through the darkened room, her petticoats layered with moonlight. She paused in her dance and bent to peer into Emily's face, her dark eyes softened with empathy as if she couldn't quite comprehend that anyone could hurt so much.

Emily recognized her then. She was the child she might have been had her father not died at the hand of her lover. Trusting, loving, convinced the world was a bright place filled with . people of good heart. Believing that someday a man would come, a man as fine and handsome as her daddy, who would love her forever.

It was that child Justin had touched with his love, that child Justin had wounded with his silence. The woman she might have become could have found it in her heart to forgive him. That woman would have been free of rancor and cynicism, free of the bitterness that raged within Emily now, burning their love to crashing ruins.

She reached out a trembling hand toward the child's luminous face. She vanished without even a good-bye, leaving Emily in utter darkness.

Chapter 32

❦

If you should ever pause to look back, I pray you won't think too harshly of me. . . .

It was midmorning the next day when Penfeld knocked on Emily's door. "His Grace requests your presence in the study," he announced.

Did the valet's voice sound strangely thick, or was it her own overwrought imagination? she wondered.

"Tell His Highness I shall hasten to answer his summons," she replied.

She stole a look out the window as she dressed. The same underfootman who had been lurking in the shrubs all morning was still there, whistling under his breath and studying the slumbering foliage as if his life depended on it. Emily took her brimming pitcher from its basin, eased up the sash, and poured a stream of wash water down on his unsuspecting head.

"Damn it all!" he sputtered, shaking himself like a sheepdog. "What in the deuced hell—"

"Hello, Jason," Emily called out. "I'm terribly sorry. I didn't realize you were down there."

His gaze shot up to the window; a sheepish smile transformed his freckled countenance. "Quite all right, Miss Emily. I was just inspecting the roses for—"

"Blight?" she suggested.

"Aye, blight!" he quickly agreed. "Been a bad year for it."

"Let's be thankful I discovered you before I emptied my night convenience," she said airily, slamming the window shut.

When she glanced out again, the dripping Jason was watching her window from the safer distance of the drive. She opened the door to find Penfeld still standing stiffly outside of it.

"I waited to escort you, miss," he explained.

She gave his starched collar a brittle flip. "They're dressing the prison guard with a bit more flair these days."

Refusing to rise to her bait, he accompanied her down the stairs to the study, where she marched in and stood in military posture before Justin's massive pedestal desk. He glanced at her over his spectacles, then went back to his scrawling.

His pen scratched across a ledger bound in cloth. "I hope after our talk yesterday, you better understand why I couldn't face you sooner."

"I understand quite clearly. You preferred to stay in New Zealand, wallowing in self-pity and flaying yourself alive with guilt. Far be it for me to deny you your pathetic entertainments."

Justin brought his pen to a grating halt and looked up. The feminine allure of Emily's cream wool frock and ribboned curls was belied by the steely angles of her shoulders.

He laid the pen down with a deliberate motion. "I realize I have no right to ask anything of you, but I need your assistance."

She bent over the desk. "Mending, perhaps? Does your hair shirt have a tear in it?"

He shot to his feet and slammed his palms on the desk. "No. My whip for self-flagellation is too short to reach my back. Although that shouldn't be a problem as long as your venomous tongue is available to lash me."

He was close enough to count every freckle on her pert little nose. The wicked sparkle of her eyes made his breath come at odds with itself. The last thing he had expected to feel toward her was anger. He was stunned by how invigorating it felt. Driving his fingers through his hair, he sank back into the chair.

"I need your help nailing Nicky. There's only one way he could have known I killed your father. The bastard was there. He saw the whole thing. He turned the natives on us, believing we'd both be killed, then took the mine for himself."

Emily propped her hip on the edge of the desk and picked up a glass paperweight, toying with it. "Charming fellow. And you thought there were no snakes in New Zealand."

"Perhaps I should have chosen my friends with more care."

She set the paperweight down with a gentle thump. "Perhaps my father should have as well."

He let that one pass with only a dark glance. "The more I think about it, the more I'm convinced it was Nicky's plan from the beginning. He was the one who spotted David coming into the music hall. He was the one who asked around until he found out David had an inheritance to invest." Justin leaned back in the chair and propped his boots on the desk. "I've made several inquiries this morning. It seems our debonair friend has been dividing his time between a gold-mining empire on the South Island of New Zealand and the Continent—Italy, France, Spain—wherever men of his ilk go to spend their ill-gotten wealth."

"But why would he return to England now?"

Justin leveled his gaze on her. "For the same reason I did. You."

Her eyes clouded. "Me?"

He nodded. "Like myself, Nicky thought you only a baby when your father died. I believe he's been biding his time, waiting for David's daughter to become old enough to start asking questions. I think he returned to England to protect his investment."

Emily shivered. Now that Nicholas realized she was not a child, but a woman grown, she presented that much more of a threat to him. She was not only old enough to ask questions; she was old enough to inherit. What might have happened to her that night at Mrs. Rose's if Justin hadn't intervened?

"What about you?" she asked. "Why didn't he kill you in New Zealand when he had the chance?"

Justin's throat tightened as he remembered all those lost years spent grieving over Nicky and David, all those regrets. "For all intents and purposes, he did. I'm sure it was only his perverse sense of humor that stopped him from burying me. He didn't have that much mercy in his black soul." A mocking smile touched his lips. "It must have been quite a shock for him to realize I'd returned to England, and an even worse blow to discover David's *grown* daughter was now part of the equation."

"He handled it with admirable aplomb."

Justin snorted. "Nicky would. Even when we hadn't a shilling to split between us, he'd spend his money on clothes instead of food. I've yet to see his elegant feathers ruffled."

"You'd like to ruffle them, wouldn't you?"

"I'd like to see him plucked, skinned, and thrown in the pot. That's why I've invited him to call this afternoon."

Emily straightened. "Have you gone mad?"

"Quite." He lowered his feet and rose. "At least that's what I want Nicholas to believe. We must force him to let down his guard by convincing him neither of us is any threat. I can capitalize on my reputation as a lunatic, which, I might add, seems to burgeon with any public appearance you and I make together. So far he's seen me wrestling with the trained bears at a bordello, carrying you off on my shoulder like a barbarian, and smashing his pretty face over champagne at a countess's fête."

Justin would have sworn it was a sparkle of mirth that warmed Emily's eyes. "What would you have me do?" she asked.

He could have answered that a thousand ways, but he choked them all back. Instead, he mustered his courage and folded her hands in his own. "You must portray the naive innocent seeking the truth about her father's death."

She gazed down at their entwined hands. A wry smile quirked her lips. "Innocent, eh? That'll be a bit of a stretch."

Justin dropped her hands and bent to shuffle a pile of meaningless papers. "You must promise me one thing. You're never to see him outside of this house."

"Why not? Are you afraid he'll compromise my virtue?"

Justin's hands spasmed. The papers scattered. Emily drifted to the window as if realizing she'd pushed him too far.

"You can't afford to forget that this man is very dangerous." He came around the desk, softening his voice with effort. "I'm still his legal partner, and you, my dear, are your father's only heir. We're all that stands between him and his precious fortune, and we both know to what lengths he'll go to protect it."

Her translucent skin seemed to absorb what little sunlight penetrated the narrow window. Justin stood behind her, aching to brush aside her curls, to lay his lips against the fleece at her nape. He clenched his hands to keep from touching her.

"I'm not asking you for love, or even friendship," he

said softly. "I'm asking you for justice." She stood as silent and unreadable as that damned doll she insisted on keeping on her nightstand. Once again he felt that dangerous flare of anger and passion. The deliberate lightness of his tone belied his turmoil. "Think of it this way. If we succeed in proving his guilt, you'll be a millionairess. You won't need me anymore."

She pivoted on her heel, her smile as bright and cutting as a blade. "I'll do it."

Her ruffled sleeve brushed his arm as she walked around him. Before she could reach the door, it opened from the other side to reveal a stalwart Penfeld.

She turned in a graceful swirl of wool. "It's safe to call off your dogs. I've no intention of running this time."

"Nor do I," Justin replied, jamming his hands into his pockets and rocking back on his heels. "It's also safe to leave your bedroom door unlocked. I've no intention of going where I'm not wanted."

Color brightened her cheeks. Penfeld cleared his throat, choked, and doubled over, wheezing. Emily ushered him out, slamming the door behind them so hard that the glass panes of the *secrétaire* rattled in protest.

Justin sank back against the windowsill, a thoughtful smile playing around his mouth. Only time would tell if he'd just earned himself a partner or an adversary.

Later that afternoon Emily paused at a gilt-framed mirror to smooth her skirt and pinch a smidgen of color into her ashen cheeks. Her hands felt like ice as she braced herself to meet again the third actor in the grim drama of friendship and betrayal that had begun over seven years before. Justin had chosen the smoking room in the east wing tower for their reunion, and as Emily entered, it was easy to see why.

The gloomy room was a study in masculine opulence. Decorated in the Turkish style, it boasted luxuriant Oriental rugs and fat leather chairs studded in brass. The day was already warm and the fire crackling on the hearth made it nearly unbearable. The palm plants scattered throughout the room drooped in the sweltering heat. Emily had barely taken two steps before she felt beads of sweat pop out on her brow.

Nicholas Saleri hovered near the door, his white-gloved hands clasped around the ivory claw of an elegant walking stick. Emily barely noticed him. She was too amazed at Justin's transformation.

He sat hunched in a spidery wheelchair by the fire, wearing nothing but a silk dressing gown and a pair of woolen stockings. His dark hair was rumpled, his brows drawn together in a fierce scowl. Penfeld fussed over him, smoothing a blanket over his legs.

Emily almost started when Nicky bowed and brought her hand to his lips. "Good afternoon, Miss Scarborough. I must admit your summons gave me a bit of a shock. I would have called on you sooner, but I feared you wouldn't consent to see me after our little misunderstanding."

"Misunderstanding?"

He ducked his handsome head and gave her a sheepish look from beneath the obscene length of his lashes. "At the house in Mayfair. Knowing you a lady of quality, I sensed you'd become embroiled in circumstances beyond your control. I knew of a back exit, but I'm afraid you misread my intentions when I sought to lead you to it."

Her gaze flicked involuntarily to the snowy folds of his tie. If Justin hadn't intervened that night, she wondered how long it would have taken before they found her strangled corpse.

She inclined her head, hoping he'd mistake her flush of anger for shyness. "An unfortunate incident, to be sure. I fear it was a result of a rather unpleasant quarrel with my guardian. Let's speak of it no more, shall we?" Emily offered no more of an explanation, allowing him to speculate on the sordid circumstances that might have led a lady of quality to seek shelter in a notorious bordello.

He cast Justin a nervous glance and lowered his voice to a whisper. "His Grace's attendant suggested I not approach him until you arrived. He said you had a calming effect on him."

Recovering her composure, Emily smiled sadly. "Only on his good days, I fear. Yesterday was one of those. We don't dare take him out too often." She forced her fingertips up to graze Nicky's swollen lip. "I'm sure you understand why."

A feral growl came from the other side of the room. Emily snatched her hand back.

"Dammit, man," Justin snarled, knocking away the box of cigars Penfeld was offering. "I don't want a cigar. I want my soldiers." His eyes narrowed as he peered through the gloom. "Who goes there? Do I know you?"

As Penfeld scrambled for the fallen cigars, Emily cast Nicky an apologetic look and rushed to Justin's side. She patted his hand soothingly. "There now. You mustn't fuss so. Your Emily is here now."

Justin wrapped his long fingers around her wrist and jerked her down to study her face. "Who the devil are you?" His voice rose an octave. "Mother, is that you?"

The devilish sparkle in his golden eyes was almost her undoing. She choked back a frantic giggle. "You remember me, don't you? It's Emily. David's Emily."

His face lit up with boyish pleasure. "Of course I remember you. Emily, my darling child."

He pressed a fervent kiss to her palm. She tried to pull away, but he refused to free her until she reached beneath the blanket and gave his thigh a sly pinch.

Throwing him a warning look, she crooked a finger at Nicky. "Look who's come to see you this fine afternoon, Your Grace. A very dear old friend."

Nicky approached, twisting his hat in his hands, but Justin ignored him. He tugged at the back of her skirt instead. "Why don't you sit for a while, love? Perhaps we can play at soldiers together." His smile slanted to a tri-

umphant leer. "My Napoleon came very close to mastering
your Wellington last night."

She reached behind her and slapped his hand, all the
while keeping her smile pasted on. He just tugged harder.
Her seams groaned and she was forced to sit on the rug at
his feet or risk losing her skirt altogether.

His fingers threaded gently through her hair; her scalp
tingled a warning.

Nicholas cleared his throat. "Perhaps this isn't a good
time . . ."

"Balderdash!" Justin bellowed, startling them all. Beneath the shelter of her hair his hand found her sensitive
nape. His broad fingers pressed, working their soothing
magic on her tense muscles. Her skin burned beneath his
livid touch, and her breath came fast and shallow.

He glowered up at Nicky. "Who the hell let you in?"
He drew back fearfully in his chair. "Are you a native?
Penfeld! Check the brush. It's crawling with savages, you
know. I can scent them."

Penfeld dutifully parted the fronds of a palm plant.
His face emerged like a broad moon on the other side. He
gave Nicky a conspiratorial wink. "No savages, sir.
They're all locked in the water closet, just as I promised."

With Justin's hand stroking her so possessively, it was
no challenge for Emily to summon an embarrassed blush.
"Perhaps you're right, Mr. Saleri. Perhaps this isn't a good
time." She rose. "If you'll keep an eye on His Grace,
Penfeld, I believe I shall accompany Mr. Saleri for a walk
in the garden."

"That's my girl." Justin grinned. "Run along now and
play like a good child." Emily choked back a yelp as he
gave her bottom a fond pat, his hand lingering an instant
too long on its rounded curve.

As she escorted their guest from the room, her cheeks
burning from more than the stifling heat, Justin's querulous voice rose to a shout. "I don't want a frigging cup of

tea, Penfeld. I want my soldiers. Fetch them for me post-haste, or it's off with your heads for the bloody lot of you!"

Emily chose a muslin shawl from the coat rack and accompanied Nicholas Saleri into the garden. After the stifling gloom of the smoking room, the cool, sunlit air sparkled with iridescence. A gentle breeze blew from the south and the plain little wrens hopped and twittered across the softening earth in a poignant reminder that winter would not last forever.

They strolled in companionable silence for several moments before Nicky sighed heavily. "He's much worse than I feared. How do you bear it?"

She lifted her shoulders in a delicate shrug. "On his good days he flirts with amnesia. On his bad days, insanity itself. I fear the shock of seeing you yesterday put a terrible strain on his mind."

His voice oozed polite sympathy. "I'd heard rumors about his more bizarre incidents, but I didn't suspect the worst of it. Did he really threaten to eat one of your suitors?"

Emily bit her lip to keep from laughing. "I'm afraid so. But that wasn't nearly as devastating as the night he tried to end his life by throwing himself out of our opera box."

Saleri shook his head. "Tragic. Simply tragic. He was such a talented young man. It breaks my heart to see so much promise wasted. It's astounding what guilt can do to a mind of such fragile, artistic bent."

Emily sank down on a rustic garden bench, hugging her shawl about her in a protective gesture. "Perhaps we shouldn't speak of him so, Mr. Saleri. He did take me in and give me a home. I feel disloyal."

"You, disloyal?" He folded himself beside her, propped his walking stick against the bench, and cupped her hands in one of his own. "Surely you must be the most forgiving of creatures."

He tilted back his hat with one finger. Emily forced herself to meet his dark, hypnotic gaze. "Forgiving? How could I not forgive him? He explained everything to me in one of his brief moments of clarity."

Frowning as if deep in thought, Nicholas freed her hands and withdrew his cigarette case from his pocket. "I'm afraid my encounter with your guardian has shaken me deeply. May I?"

She inclined her head demurely. "By all means."

He lit the cigarette, his hands steady, and took a deep draw. His lips puckered to blow out a flawless smoke ring. "I suppose Justin told you that ridiculous story about shooting your father to spare him a gruesome death at the hands of the natives."

"Ridiculous?" Emily echoed, trying to ignore the icy pounding of her heart.

"A charming fiction, I assure you, although perhaps he's grown to believe it himself over the years. I always told him he should have been a novelist instead of a pianist." He slanted her a look as if to assure himself of her full attention. "Justin's ambitions unbalanced him long before he shot your father. David suspected him of cheating us both and, sadly enough, chose to confront him while I was visiting with the natives."

"The Maori," she said softly. "I know of them. I spent some time with my guardian on the North Island."

"A kind and gentle people, as I'm sure you discovered. Hardly the devils with long forked tails of Justin's absurd tale." Trini's beaming face floated in Emily's vision. Saleri tapped away a cylinder of ash before continuing. "I heard Justin and your father quarreling when I approached from the bush that night. From what I could gather, David had caught Justin altering our land grant, erasing our names in favor of his own, all the better to cover the mysterious disappearance he'd planned for us." Emily remembered the ornate sheet of paper she'd found in Justin's cubbyhole. The sheet of paper she'd never bothered to examine.

"David was threatening to expose him to the governor general. Justin panicked and shot him. I had no choice but to flee for my own life."

"How terrible for you!"

"It was. After the murder Justin fled and I sought shelter with the Maori until I could be sure he wouldn't return. Then and only then did I dare to claim the gold mine. But I spent years looking over my shoulder, knowing Justin still had in his possession that altered land grant and a motive for murder. You can imagine my shock to discover he was once again living in London."

"And what brought *you* to London again after all these years, Mr. Saleri?" she asked, fearful she was treading on dangerous ground.

"You."

His answer so closely mirrored Justin's that it shook her to the core. "Me?" she whispered.

"I've been holding David's share of the gold mine in trust for you all these years. I would have returned much sooner, but I feared my very presence might put you in jeopardy. I had no way of knowing you were already living with the man who had gone unpunished for your father's murder."

Emily wrung her hands. "Perhaps the price he has paid for his treachery is worse than imprisonment."

"Perhaps," he said, skepticism thick in his voice. He dropped the cigarette and ground it into the sparse grass. His gaze floated over her like silken fingers. "He could still be dangerous, you know. I hate to think of a sweet, fragile creature like yourself living under his influence."

Emily stood abruptly, as if his bold look had shied her. "Your concern touches me."

He stood, his big, masculine shadow dwarfing her. "I've arranged for my solicitor to call on you to discuss your inheritance. I cannot help but feel somewhat responsible for your present situation. Perhaps if I had not waited so long to return . . ." He cupped her chin in his hands.

His smooth thumb grazed her lower lip. "May I call on you again as well, Miss Scarborough?"

She gazed up at him, softening her lips with the hint of a provocative pout. "I should be wounded if you did not, Mr. Saleri."

He snatched up her hand and pressed it to his lips. "I would rather destroy myself than wound you."

With that passionate declaration he gathered his walking stick and started toward the drive, pausing only once to look back and doff his hat to her in gallant farewell.

She stood alone after he had gone, the fringe of her shawl whipping in the wind. One question haunted her: Why was Nicholas Saleri offering to hand over her father's share of the gold mine without so much as a murmur of protest? Could Justin have been wrong about the man? And if he was, was he wrong about other things as well? The cold finger of a lengthening shadow touched her, making her shiver. She glanced toward the house. The sinking sun had set the windows of the west wing ablaze, but there was no mistaking the watchful stance of the dark figure framed in an upstairs window. Tucking the shawl around her, Emily bowed her head and strode quickly toward the house.

Shadowy shapes cavorted in the firelight, their bronze bodies sheened with sweat. They leaped and twirled in a feral frenzy, rolling eyes and thrusting hips to the hypnotic chant of the sea and the thundering rhythm of Emily's heart. She stood in their midst, her sheer nightdress dancing in the balmy wind.

The natives parted ranks and that's when she saw him—a dark figure emerging from the bush, a panama hat tilted low to hide his eyes. She tried to move, tried to run, but the sand sucked at her ankles. It was too deep, too thick.

Toying with her, the man drew a cigarette case out of his pocket and slipped the thin cylinder between his chiseled lips. He struck a match, and in that brief flare of glowing ash Emily saw his eyes—not the molten brown of Nicky's eyes, but ruthless gold. Justin's eyes.

He advanced on her, stalking her with the lean, deadly grace of a tiger. As he passed through the shadows cast by the feathery branches of a punga tree, he became a tiger, padding toward her on all fours. His powerful muscles shifted in lethal synchronicity as he crouched for the kill. Then he was Justin again, flicking the burning cigarette into the night.

Emily stood frozen. She couldn't move, couldn't breathe. Bewitched by his approach, she realized she didn't want to move. Tears of shame trickled down her cheeks as she realized she was willing to pay any price to feel his embrace one last time. He slipped behind her and wrapped his strong arms around her waist. He had the eyes of a tiger but the hands of a man. They were so warm, she could feel her flesh melting beneath their heat. Her head fell back in surrender.

The heat from the flames climbed as he bent his leg between hers, dipping low to mold the muscular planes of his body to her own. His palm drifted down to cup the damp fabric of her nightdress to her breasts, then to the throbbing flesh between her legs. She could feel the dark, watchful eyes of the natives on them, but was helpless to stop his sensual mastery of her body and soul.

Through a haze of dark pleasure she felt a new weight, heavy and cold, against her belly. Her gaze drifted down to see the pistol gripped in his beautiful hand. With exquisite tenderness he trailed the barrel between the aching fullness of her breasts and up until she felt the icy press of the muzzle against her temple. She writhed against him.

At the exact second his artful fingertips pressed her into ecstasy, his mouth sought and found hers, his kiss so sweet and fraught with tender promise that it made her sob . . .

. . . then he pulled the trigger.

Emily sat bolt upright in bed, gasping for breath. The flames of her dream were gone now, leaving her drenched with sweat and shivering among the twisted bedclothes. Her bedroom was dark, the fire almost out. She kicked the sheets off her ankles, remembering how the sand in the dream had held her fast. Her body still tingled as if from a lover's touch. She glanced at the door, half wishing the knob would turn, the door would swing open.

Justin's mocking words came back to her: *I have no intention of going where I'm not wanted.*

Justin was wrong. She wanted him badly. She wanted him to cradle her in his arms, to reassure her that Nicky was lying about her father's death, to chase away her doubts and nightmares with his tender kisses. But he'd kissed her in the dream, hadn't he . . . ?

Shuddering, Emily threw back the covers and padded restlessly to the hearth. Justin obviously had every intention of keeping his word. They'd barely spoken after Nicky's departure. Supper had been a stilted affair with the duchess and Justin's sisters casting puzzled glances between their guarded faces.

She stabbed at the glowing embers with the poker, hoping to stir the dying fire into flame. Beneath her clumsy probing, the last burning coal crumbled to ash. She dropped the poker and hugged herself, shivering. The sweat was drying on her skin and her bare feet felt like ice. Glaring at the door, she made her decision. Without bothering to grab her robe, she threw open the door and plunged into the black corridor.

Emily quickly realized it must be very late. The candles left burning at bedtime had all guttered in their sconces. The darkness enveloped her in its unrelenting folds. As she navigated the corridor, her toes slammed into the taloned base of an occasional table. Swearing under her breath, she caught a teetering china figurine before it could fall.

She continued on, hugging the center of the corridor. A loose board groaned beneath her weight. She froze, foot poised over the next board, waiting for a bevy of servants to come rushing up the stairs or for Harold to pop out of his bedroom and hit her over the head with something, believing her a burglar. The silence held its breath along with her.

She dared to move on, wandering the long corridors until she stood before the door to the master suite. Its carved mahogany splendor dwarfed her. She lifted a hand to knock, then drew it back. Was this how Justin had felt at her door—like a desperate pauper come to beg?

She brushed back her curls, then lifted her hand again. She still could not find the courage to shatter the fragile silence. So she folded her trembling fingers around the brass handle and gently eased the door open.

Chapter 33

❧

*Everything I did, even the wrong things, were done
out of love for you. . . .*

As Emily peeped into Justin's room, an unbidden rush of
fondness flooded her. She should have known he wouldn't
be sleeping at this late hour. He sat propped against the
pillows, reading by the flickering light of a single candle.
The heavy curtains of the four-poster had been drawn back
and tied with incongruous lengths of hemp.

The downy comforter rode low on his abdomen. His
chest was bare, his hair tousled. The candlelight danced off
his gold spectacles. There was something so compelling
about eyeglasses on a handsome man—such a teasing hint
of leashed potential that Emily felt her breath catch with
desire.

He looked up then to find her peering in at him. His
eyes darkened with surprise, then displeasure.

Seeing no chance of honorable retreat, she crept into
the room and stood shivering in the middle of his Aubusson carpet. A fire stoked by fresh coal crackled on the
grate. Justin laid aside the book, then drew off his specta-

cles and folded them on the nightstand. Emily approached the bed. It loomed over her, sumptuous, warm, and inviting. Unlike its occupant.

"I . . . um . . . I wanted . . ." She stammered, unable to find her words beneath his harsh gaze.

He threw back the comforter and bounded out of the bed, dragging the sheet around his waist. Emily realized he was nude beneath it.

He paced the bedroom in long strides. "So this is what it's come to between us. You think you can waltz in here after you've made it clear what you think of me." He paused in his pacing to glower at her. "Do you think me so desperate I'd take any scrap you'd care to throw my way?"

Dumbfounded by his impassioned speech, Emily felt her mouth fall open.

He raked a hand through his hair and circled her. "How could you expect me to face myself in the mirror tomorrow if I compromise my honor for a few fleeting seconds of ecstasy?" He caught her by the shoulders and gave her a hard little shake. "Do you think you're so charming in that silly little nightdress that I can't resist tumbling you? Do you think I have no pride when it comes to you?"

"B-b-but I—"

"Well, you're right," he shouted. "I don't!"

With that, his lips came down on hers. Emily tilted her head back, giving the full measure of her mouth to his possession. His tongue plundered her with warm, rough abandon. She answered his desperate plea with a soft swirl of her own.

He swung her around to the bed and laid her beneath him. His hands tore at her drawers, shoving them away with none of the artful preliminaries he excelled in. It was as if he were afraid any hesitation might give the lonely night cause to take her back. He pressed himself into her, groaning when he found her as ready for him as he was for her.

Emily wrapped her arms around him, shivering at his rough urgency. She had been cold before, but now a molten fire was spreading through her blood. His tongue invaded her mouth, taking her there just as his hips were taking her lower. There was a savage edge to Justin's lovemaking she'd never experienced before. Both shock and pleasure rippled through her as he dragged her hips to the edge of the bed and stood between her legs, spreading and molding her until she could feel each of his fierce strokes pounding at the mouth of her womb. She wanted to scream beneath the force of it. She bit her lip, tasting blood. She felt her eyes roll back as her body threatened to succumb to that dark netherworld between pleasure and swooning.

He cupped her face in his hands. "Look at me, Emily," he commanded her hoarsely. "Look at me now."

She met his devouring gaze, seeing the beautiful face of the man she loved strained in an agony of pleasure. Still holding her gaze in his golden vise, he pinned her shoulders to the bed, forcing her writhing body still for an even deeper possession.

Without warning, spasms of ecstasy wracked them both, and not even Justin's mouth on hers could completely muffle her broken wail.

Emily awoke with her mouth pressed against Justin's chest. Their bodies lay in a sleepy tangle, her leg thrown over his, his arm cupping her rump. The fire cast fingers of flame against the shadows. Caught in the cradle of Justin's arms, she found the massive bed warmer and cozier than she ever could have dreamed.

She rubbed her cheek against his chest, utterly sated. He had made love to her again after the first time, extinguishing the candle and taking her with such reverent gentleness it had made her weep. His hands had stroked and soothed her tender flesh as if to ease away the rough edges of their desperate coupling.

She sighed. If only the past were so easily vanquished.

Pulling the blanket over him, she sat up and delicately untangled herself from his embrace. As she crept out of the bed, every muscle ached in protest. She was surprised she could walk at all.

She had almost reached the door when Justin sat up. His bitter voice cut the shadows like a blade. "Leaving so soon? Did you get what you came for?"

Emily bit her lip, unable to stifle an odd little giggle. "No. Actually, I came to borrow some coal for my fire."

She eased open the door and slipped out, missing Justin's flabbergasted expression as he spread his arms and flopped back among the pillows.

When Emily entered the parlor the following day, the tension was thick enough to cut with a knife. The servants hastened in and out with their feather dusters, shooting Justin nervous glances. Word of his relapse, hastened by the bizarre accusation made by the wealthy Italian at the Comtesse Guermond's fête, had flown through their ranks. Emily had to admire his sisters' composure. They sat poking at their embroidery as if it were completely normal for their brother to be accused of murder, then to appear at midday garbed in nothing but his dressing gown and stockings. Although Justin was unable to explain the reason for his bizarre dress, he seemed to be maintaining a semblance of sanity while in their company.

Justin glanced up from his book as Emily claimed the balloon-backed chair opposite him. She was not completely able to hide her wince of pain as she sat. His gaze shifted quickly away.

The duchess beamed and held out an embroidered pillow. "Pillow, dear? Those unupholstered chairs can be so uncomfortable."

"No, thank you," Emily mumbled.

Could his mother possibly have heard their uninhibited cries in the night? Justin wondered. He was saved from further speculation by the arrival of Penfeld, who tilted his disapproving nose in the air and announced, "A Mr. Saleri is here to call upon Miss Scarborough."

The color drained from Emily's cheeks. She exchanged a look of dread with Justin. Neither of them had expected Nicky to take the bait so quickly.

"Tell him I shall receive him in the garden," she said, rising.

Edith rose along with her, laying her embroidery ring aside.

"Down, Edith," Justin commanded. "Emily's a big girl. She doesn't need a watchdog."

Bewilderment touched Edith's eyes. "But I thought . . . surely a chaperone . . ."

The duchess rose and took her daughter by the arm. "I do believe I need a chaperone, dear. Shall we stroll to the conservatory and check the roses?" As she led Edith from the room, she cast both Emily and her son a speculative glance over one shoulder.

Nicholas was waiting for her by a terra-cotta fountain, resplendent in a gray-striped morning suit. The day was much cooler. As Emily approached him, she pulled the woolen hood of her cloak over her hair to hide her expression.

He squeezed her hands and favored her with a melting smile. "Miss Scarborough, ever a delight. I believe you are fresher than even the morning dew."

"Why, Mr. Saleri, you flatter me." He certainly did. There had been little time for rest between her nightmares and bouts of Justin's loving and she knew the bags beneath her eyes must be roomier than portmanteaus.

He drew her hands to his lips and Emily braced herself to be licked. The first haunting notes of Chopin's "Waltz in C-Sharp Minor" floated into the garden. Nicky paled and glanced toward the opaque plates of the drawing room windows. It was the first time she had ever seen him shaken.

"He still plays?"

She nodded. "At times. It's one of the few comforts left to him."

Recovering his composure, Nicky tucked her hand in the crook of his elbow and led her down a cobbled path. "I could hardly sleep last night for thinking of our conversation. I fear you must think me the most despicable of liars."

The timeless strains of music drifted on the wind. Emily imagined Justin's strong, graceful fingers striking each key, sending her the strength to murmur, "I could never think ill of you, sir."

"Ah, but after all, it is my word against your guardian's. If only I could show you that land grant for the mine . . . do you think he has it in his possession here?"

Emily thought of the morass of papers and books moldering away on the North Island. "I doubt it. He was planning only a brief sojourn to England. He left all his papers in New Zealand."

Nicky shook his head. "How unfortunate. It's all I have to prove my story."

And all Justin has to prove his innocence, she thought grimly. "Even without proof I find you very convincing, Mr. Saleri."

He swung around to face her. Emily forced her expression to remain wide-eyed and ingenuous, hoping she didn't resemble a besotted rabbit.

He eased her hood back from her curls. "Please call me Nicholas, dear. Or even Nicky, if you would forgive my boldness."

His thumb stroked her cheek. He slowly lowered his head. Emily closed her eyes, praying God would give her the strength not to be ill. Before his lips could touch hers, a cacophonous banging shattered the moment. A raucous male voice broke into song:

> *Naughty Maud, the Shrewsbury bawd,*
> *She'll steal yer purse an' tickle yer rod,*
> *And still leave ya yellin' fer more, by gawd!*

Nicky snatched his hand back, wincing. Emily hoped her choking noise would be construed as one of humiliation rather than laughter. She jerked up her hood and took a few hasty steps away.

Nicky dogged her, obviously eager to try a new tactic. "His behavior must be a constant source of embarrassment to you. Has he ever harmed you in any way?"

"Oh, no. I believe he's quite fond of me"—she hesitated for the necessary heartbeat—"in his way."

As they walked on, Nicky took the bait and began to weave his serpentine twists of logic like a web around Justin's story. Each irrefutable strand was sticky-sweet with his charm. He dropped constant hints about the missing land grant until she wanted to clap her hands over her ears and run screaming from his presence. Oddly enough, it was Penfeld who rescued her when he appeared in the garden and engaged their elegant guest in a conversation about the competing merits of Indian and Chinese tea. Shooting him a thankful glance, Emily excused herself to summon a maidservant to serve refreshments in the salon.

As she marched through the drawing room, wiping her mouth with the back of her hand, a hand shot out and dragged her into a curtained window alcove. "Are you all right?" Justin asked.

"Yes. No." She clutched the lapels of his dressing gown. "I can't bear it. We have to end this soon."

His eyes hardened; their grim determination chilled her. "We'll end it right now if you like."

"No! We mustn't. He hasn't revealed anything yet. We have to push him somehow."

The click of Nicky's boots sounded on the parquet floor. They stood paralyzed until Emily reached up and frantically rumpled Justin's hair.

"What in the hell are you doing?" he whispered.

A heartrending sob caught in her voice. "No, please, Your Grace, I've begged you not to do this."

Justin quickly caught on to her scheme. He ripped a scrap of lace from her collar and shouted, "Come on, little girl, just one kiss for your new daddy."

They both heard the approaching footsteps pause. Emily emerged from the alcove, clutching her torn collar. She pretended not to see Nicholas tiptoeing toward the doorway behind them.

"Oh, please, sir, you promised not to do it again."

Justin grabbed her around the waist with a leer a bit too convincing for Emily's taste. "Don't fight me, child. You know you enjoy it!"

Nicholas peeped around the door frame.

"Hit me," Emily mouthed.

Justin jerked her close, genuine desperation in his grasp. "Don't ask that of me," he hissed.

Pretending to struggle, she dug her fingernails into his arms and pressed her mouth to his ear. "Hit me, dammit!"

His voice rang out. "You little brat, I'll teach you to disobey me." His eyes darkened in agonized apology as he drew back his hand and slapped her across the face.

His elbow bore the brunt of the blow. Emily barely felt a sting, but the shock of it still brought genuine tears to her eyes. At the flood of answering remorse in Justin's eyes, she would have done anything to summon them back. Justin hadn't the flare for playacting that she had. If Nicky took one glance at his face, the game would be up. The true enormity of what she must do struck her harder than his blow. Pressing her knuckles to her mouth, she whirled around to flee, only to find Nicholas standing rapt in the doorway.

It took him a second too long to veil the cruel, excited twist of his lips with righteous anger. "I say, man, what's the meaning of this?"

Justin shoved past him without a word. Emily flung herself across the room and crumpled into Nicky's arms. Clucking his sympathy, he led her to a settee beneath the window, where she made a valiant show of getting a grip on her emotions, all the while snuffling into his pristine shirtfront. He pried her off him and fished out a handkerchief, poorly hiding his moue of distaste.

"Please forgive me," she said, blowing her nose daintily into his handkerchief. "I never meant you to witness such a disgraceful spectacle."

"It only confirmed my worst suspicions," he said, his face set in noble lines. "I had hoped this wouldn't be necessary, but I fear your guardian's behavior has made it so."

He reached into his coat pocket and pulled out a tiny derringer. Emily's hands began to tremble in earnest. He opened her icy fingers and laid the weapon on her palm.

"I want you to take this, *cara mia*. To use it if need be to protect yourself from that madman. There's not a court in this land that would convict you for killing him."

Emily stared down at the charming little pistol, knowing it was no less lethal for its size. It was plated in polished mother-of-pearl and fit her palm as if it had been made for it.

He folded her fingers around the gun. "Go on. Take it. Your father would have wanted you to have it."

She gazed up at him, hypnotized by the glow of sincerity in his eyes. A blustering shout sounded from the nether reaches of the house.

Nicky hastily stood. "I think it best if I go now. I shall call again tomorrow. Don't forget what I said."

"I won't," she said, rising like a zombie. "Oh, Nicholas," she called as he turned to go.

He pivoted expectantly.

She waved the crumpled rag. "You forgot your handkerchief."

Smiling wanly, he took it between two fingers. She watched him juggle it all the way to the door before he finally stuffed it into a potted palm on the cloak rack.

When he had gone, Emily stood staring at the small gun. Seven years ago a weapon such as this had ended her father's life. A footstep sounded behind her, and she hastily dropped it into the pocket of her skirt.

She turned to find Justin watching her.

"What did he say to you?"

"Nothing." She averted her gaze. "Nothing of any import."

She started to walk past him. He caught her shoulders; his gaze searched her face. "You're lying to me. Why?"

Unable to bear the pain crystallizing in his eyes, she pulled away. "Please. I'd like to be alone now. I'm tired."

She brushed past him, knowing the most dangerous role in her charade had just begun. As she fled up the stairs, the derringer lay like a cold weight against her thigh.

Emily was slipping away from him. Moment by moment. Day by day. The knowledge tore at Justin's soul like jagged claws. Nicky's daily visits continued, but she no longer confided in him. He would enter a room to find them sitting with heads together, laughing and whispering. They would fall into silence at the sight of him, and Emily's beautiful eyes would turn dark and cold with suspicion. Was she so eager to believe ill of him that she'd allow even Nicky to spread his poison through her mind? He continued to play the invalid lunatic, at times querulous, at others fiercely jovial, each day feeling more like the madman he was pretending to be.

Both family and servants gave him wide berth. Not even the wounded bafflement in his mother's eyes was enough to make him lay down his pride and break his silence. It hurt too damned much to believe Emily would turn on him so easily. She made no more visits to his room, and he spent his nights pacing the spacious suite like a caged tiger. As his panic grew, he began to make his own inquiries into Nicholas's business ventures.

He returned from one of those sojourns late one evening, shaken to learn Nicky had booked two passages on a tramp steamer sailing for New Zealand within the week. Discovering Emily had gone out to attend the opera with her *dear friend* Mr. Saleri only fueled his panic.

"You did what?" he roared at the bewildered Edith. "You allowed her to go out unchaperoned?"

"You never wanted her chaperoned before in his company," she protested, her lower lip trembling. "You said he was an old friend of her father's. How was I to know?"

"If you'd use that porcelain head of yours for something besides hanging your ringlets on, you would have known," he shouted.

Edith dropped her embroidery and burst into noisy sobs. Lily and Millicent closed ranks around her, patting her heaving shoulders and giving Justin looks that would have shamed the devil himself.

He paced away from them, running a hand over his weary eyes.

His mother shoved her bulk out of her chair. "You were always a good boy, Justin. Your father never even had to take the cane to you. I'm beginning to think that was a terrible mistake."

Justin spun around. "What did Father need a cane for? He had his sarcastic wit and his demeaning remarks for weapons. I wish he'd had the common decency to give me a beating with his fists."

Emily's dulcet tones cut through the chaos. "Here now. What's all this fuss about?"

They all froze, staring at her. She stood in the doorway of the parlor, dripping sophistication. A cream-blue dress of ruched satin hugged her hips, falling to scalloped ruffles draped to reveal an ivory underskirt. She wore matching gloves studded with pearl buttons, and her hair had been swept back at the temples by mother-of-pearl combs. Combs he had bought for her, Justin realized, fighting blind rage.

Her skirts rustled as she swept in and knelt beside Edith, handing her a handkerchief from her satin reticule. "There now. You mustn't cry so. You're getting your lovely embroidery all soggy." She straightened and looked at him, her gaze free of reproach, or any feeling at all. "Didn't they tell you? I just went to the opera. *La Traviata.* It was marvelous. I do so love all things Italian."

Justin bit back the obvious retort. What was she trying to do? he wondered. Provoke him to murder right there in the parlor. "I need to talk to you."

She smothered a yawn into her gloved little hand. "In the morning perhaps. I'm off to bed now."

She strolled out, her bustled rump swaying beneath its satin sheath. There was dead silence for three long, lazy sweeps of the mantel clock's pendulum. Edith didn't dare even to sniffle. Then somewhere in the house a door closed. And locked.

That muffled turn of the key was Justin's downfall. He slammed out of the room and climbed the stairs two at a time, not caring anymore who heard him traverse the darkened corridors to Emily's room. His thigh struck a table, overturning it. The photographs toppled and struck the floor in an explosion of shattering glass. His long strides devoured the carpet until he stood outside her door once again. Sometimes he felt he'd spent half his life there.

Justin didn't waste time knocking or toying with the knob. And he definitely wasn't in the mood to beg. So he simply lifted his leg, and in one powerful motion, kicked the door down.

Chapter 34

· 🐚 ·

*Someday you'll hear my voice whispering
on the wind. . . .*

*E*mily pressed her palm to her thundering heart. Justin
stood in the doorway, the splintered door lying like an
altar of pagan sacrifice at his feet. The shattered lock dangled from its mooring. He stretched out his arms and
braced his weight on either side of the door frame. His lazy
grin never reached his eyes.

"Hello, darling. I thought you might need some coal
for your fire. Or has someone else been stoking your flames
these days?"

His clothes were rumpled. His untrimmed hair hung
in shaggy disarray. His eyes were red-rimmed and wild
from desperation and lack of sleep. He was everything the
polished and urbane Nicholas Saleri could never be.

She broke away from his compelling gaze, forcing herself to remain cool, knowing there was only one way to
earn any peace for either of the men she had loved.

She slipped an airy note into her voice. "If you must
know, Nicholas has asked me to marry him."

The wild look in Justin's eyes deepened. "What a tidy way to wrap up your inheritance! He marries you, takes you back to his mansion in New Zealand. And how long do you think it will be before the new Mrs. Saleri suffers a tragic accident? A week? A month? I know Nicky. Once he has your money, he'll have no further need for you. You'll only be an encumbrance to him. He'll dispose of you just as he did David and me." Justin crossed to her. "Have you forgotten what a monster he is? My God, he plotted your own father's death."

She lowered her lashes before he could see his own agony mirrored in her eyes. She had to use all of her wiles and passion to convince this man she hated him. She closed her eyes, summoning back all those feelings of anger and abandonment she'd fought so hard to vanquish.

When she opened them, she knew they sparkled with furious contempt. "He wasn't the one who pulled the trigger though, was he? Or the one who lied about it for seven years."

Justin ran a hand through his hair. A cynical laugh escaped him. "Nicky always was a randy little bastard. He'll probably let you live for a little while. At least until he tires of your skills in bed." He lifted a mocking eyebrow. "And we both know how considerable those are."

Emily drew back her hand and slapped him. He stared at her, giving her a harrowing glimpse of his utter helplessness before his eyes hardened to polished amber.

With one smooth motion he shoved her back against the wall. His powerful hands cupped her throat and his voice lowered to a husky growl. "If you think I'm capable of murder, you're bloody right. Because as God is my witness, I'll kill you myself before I'll let him have you."

He ground his lips against hers in a brief, raging kiss, then he was gone, leaving her heart as splintered as her door.

She slid down the wall to a sitting position and pressed her mouth to her knee to muffle her anguished sobs.

• • •

"Sir, sir! Please! You must wake up."

Someone was shaking him. Groaning, Justin batted the persistent hands away and rolled to his side. His fingers struck something cool. He pried his bleary eyes open to discover it was the taloned foot of the settee. He vaguely remembered collapsing in the study in the wild hope of silencing the torment in his head long enough to let him sleep. But it was stupor, not sleep, that had finally claimed him.

David's face had danced through his restless slumber. In his dreams he had reached for him, but David had vanished, just like Emily.

"Sir, please! You don't understand. You have to get up!"

The genteel hands lost their patience. They fastened on Justin's lapels and jerked him up, shaking him like a rag doll. The round moon of Penfeld's face finally penetrated the shrouded gloom of the library. The valet looked dangerously near tears and that fact, more than any other, stirred Justin to consciousness.

"Penfeld? My God, what is it, man? What's wrong?"

The valet's plump lip quivered. "She's gone, sir. For good this time, I fear."

Emily stood on the deck of the steamer and watched the coast of England melt into the dawn mist. Every rhythmic chug of the engine's pistons, every wave riding against the iron hull, carried her farther away from Justin. She pulled up her hood, drawing it like a cool veil over her seething emotions. As Nicky rested his hands on her shoulders, her gloved hands clenched on the rail.

"It's only a matter of time now, *cara mia*. Once we find that land grant he tampered with, we'll have the evidence we need. We can take it to the authorities and, with your testimony, have him put away for life. He'll never harm either of us again." He gave her shoulders a reassuring squeeze. Emily shuddered. "Don't be afraid, love. I'll take care of you now. Once we've put this ugly business of the past behind us, we can discuss our future. But first we must bring your father's murderer to justice."

Emily faced him. "Yes, Nicky," she said, standing on her tiptoes to kiss his cheek. "That's really all I ever wanted. Justice."

As her bedroom door flew open, Olivia Connor, the Duchess of Winthrop, rolled over and sat up in her modest tent bed.

"Opening the door instead of going through it? How dreadfully conventional. You disappoint me, son."

Justin strode across the room and flung himself to his knees beside the bed. He wrung her hands in his desperate grasp. "Please, Mother. I need your help."

Her rag-wrapped curls bobbed knowingly. "It's the girl, isn't it?"

"Isn't it always?" His beseeching eyes searched her face. "Father's fastest ship. I have to know. What is it? Is it a steamer? A sailing ship? Think hard, Mother. Emily's very life may depend on it."

She absently twirled a ringlet around her finger. A slow smile dawned on her face. "I should have thought of that sooner." She beamed up at him. "Why, the fastest ship would be the *Olivia*, of course!"

Sailors scurried like ants over the polished deck of the graceful clipper known as the *Olivia*. They scrambled up and down ramps, staggering beneath the crates and barrels of supplies for the long journey ahead. They shimmied up the towering masts to secure the sails, all the while casting their new master some very uneasy looks. Even the most grizzled and salt-beaten of them was aware that London gossip reputed him to be a madman. Should they bid a tearful farewell to their mistresses and wives? Was he about to send them all on a dark voyage of destruction?

They found it even more perplexing that their young captain stood straddle-legged on the deck, bellowing instructions as if he'd been born to command.

Justin was well aware of their trepidation, but there was damn little he could do about it now. He was determined to have the ship outfitted and asail by nightfall if it took every sailor in London to do it. The sea had brought him Emily, and he was more than willing to harness the sea to keep her.

As he stalked to the prow of the ship, the cool moist air filled his lungs. A blanket of fog had hung over the harbor all day. The slender spars rose like ghostly fingers into the darkening sky. The massive bosom of the clipper's figurehead jutted over the water.

Justin reached up and ran his fingers over her carved cheek. "Wish me luck, Duchess," he whispered. "I'm going to need it."

"Sir?"

Justin swung around to see a figure emerging from the fog. A carpeted satchel swung from his hand. A heavy woolen pea coat had replaced his frock coat, and a parrot-green bandanna hung at a jaunty angle around his neck. But even those things did not shock Justin as much as the dangerous-looking rifle slung across his back.

"Penfeld?"

The valet clicked his heels and gave him a snappy salute. "Aye, Cap'n, reporting for duty."

A rush of helpless affection blurred Justin's vision. God seemed to have dedicated himself to making amends for giving him Frank Connor for a father.

"Ah, Penfeld, I can't ask you to follow me halfway across the world, searching for a woman who may not even want me to find her."

"Pish posh, sir, if I may be so bold as to say so. I've discovered civilization isn't to my taste. I've come to believe a bit of adventure, like a cup of hot tea, warms the blood and keeps a man's heart thumping." He reached into the deep pocket of his coat. "Forgive my presumption, but I stopped at a shop on my way to the harbor. I thought you might have need of this."

Justin almost ducked as a long-barreled pistol came sailing at his head. He caught it between two fingers and ran his hands over the sleek metal. It was the first time he had held a pistol in his hands since he had killed his best friend with one.

The valet's eyes sparkled with a determination to match his own. Justin gave him a roguish grin and tucked the pistol into his waistband.

He strode down the deck and threw an arm around Penfeld's shoulders. "Come on, you old tar, there'll be no slackers among this crew. There's work to be done and bonnie fair maidens to be rescued."

Emily sat in a chair on the deck of the small steamer they had booked in Melbourne, watching Nicholas shave. He insisted on shaving outdoors, where the light was better. A white towel was slung around his neck and his shirt was half unbuttoned to reveal the smooth muscles of his chest. He leaned over the round mirror clipped to the railing and puckered his sensual lips.

Nicholas was talking. He was always talking. He talked incessantly, always about himself. She wondered why he'd bothered to rid himself of her father and Justin in such a clumsy manner. If they had remained his partners, it would have taken him only a few years to bore them to death. At least she'd been spared fending off any romantic advances. She understood now why he was satisfied with only chaste pecks on the cheek. No man that much in love with himself could have any desire for another. He seemed content to satisfy his own selfish pleasures with the mirror.

Her fingers dug pale cresents into the page of her book as she fought the temptation to plant her boot in the middle of his tight derriere and shove him over the side.

Perhaps he wouldn't be as fortunate with the sharks as Barney had been. She'd gladly cut off her entire hand and toss it after him if it would whet their appetites. She caught him watching her in the mirror's shiny surface and hoped her expression didn't reflect her bloodthirsty musings.

"What should I wear to dinner tonight, pet?" he asked. "The silk jacket or the paisley?"

"Oh, the silk," she said mildly. "It so complements your complexion."

He swore in Italian. "I'm not tanning, am I?" He tilted his chin for a critical perusal. "The sun always draws out the olive in my complexion." He slipped a tie around his neck and knotted it in crisp folds.

Emily fantasized about pulling the ends tight and drawing out the purple in his complexion.

A faint shudder raked him. "Too much sun is lethal for the skin. I should hate to look as old as Justin does."

Emily closed her eyes. Justin's bronze complexion floated in her memory. She imagined seeing the tiny lines around his eyes crinkle in laughter, tracing the chiseled grooves around his mouth with her tongue, running her fingers through the sun-streaked silver in his dark hair. A wave of longing, more potent than the sea, rushed over her.

She opened her eyes. "Don't fret, Nicky. Looking old is one thing you'll never have to worry about." With that cryptic reassurance she buried her nose in her book and went back to basking in the warm rays of the sun.

The clipper's sleek bow sliced through the jade-colored waves, scattering whitecaps in its path. Justin stood at the prow, his foot braced on a coil of hemp. He leaned forward as if his very posture could somehow hasten the magnificent ship's speed through the endless vista of sky and sea. Her sails rippled and snapped above his head, capturing the wind in billowing canvas clouds. The ship's navigator had assured him they were making excellent time and should reach the North Island by nightfall.

In the weeks they'd been at sea the sun had bronzed his skin and gilded his hair with a net of silver. He wore no shirt, and his worn dungarees hugged his hips and thighs like a second skin.

With the gold hoop once again dangling from one ear and the pistol wedged in his waistband, he knew he looked like the worst sort of pirate.

The primitive spirit of adventure that had sent him to New Zealand the first time roared through his veins. It had taken Emily to bring it to life, to pull him out of the emotional coffin he'd buried himself in. He had to find her. He'd promised David he'd take care of his daughter, and he intended to do just that, at the expense of his pride, or even his life.

All that mattered to him now was that she was still alive. He had tracked her and Nicky to Melbourne, where they'd switched steamers. He still had no idea why Nicky had veered off for the North Island instead of taking Emily to the palatial kingdom he'd built for himself on the South.

The balmy wind whipped his hair around his shoulders. Closing his eyes, he breathed deeply, savoring its salty tang. Its heat and scent had haunted him through the long, cold nights in London, nights softened only by that too-brief idyll when Emily had loved him.

As he opened his eyes, hope stirred within him like the faintest curl of a child's fingers reaching toward the sun.

The breaking waves slapped at the hull as Justin and Penfeld rowed the wooden dinghy toward the shore. Justin's men had already boarded the modest steamer anchored off the western coast of the North Island only to be told a man and woman had gone ashore at sunset.

They followed the curve of the shoreline, not wanting to warn anyone of their approach. Justin's restless gaze raked the shadowy forest. Was Emily there somewhere? Waiting for him?

He pressed a finger to his lips, silencing Penfeld's oars. The dinghy drifted around a narrow finger of sand. A chill touched him to see the familiar bluff and David's cross silhouetted against the violet sky. Penfeld removed his hat in a gesture of respect and clutched it to his chest.

The bottom of the boat scraped against land. In silent accord they climbed out and dragged it up the sandy slope, hiding it between two towering dunes. Penfeld reached around and drew his rifle from its sheath, handling it with surprising grace.

"Stay put," Justin commanded. "No matter what you hear, I want you to stay put. You've got to be ready to take her away from here if something goes wrong. Do you understand?"

"But, sir—"

Justin shook a stern finger at him. "That's an order, Penfeld. Disobey it and I'll . . . I'll . . . dismiss you."

"Aye, sir," he replied with obvious reluctance. He settled down with his back against a dune and the rifle cradled in his folded arms.

Justin picked his way along the shadows of the dunes until he came to the rim of the open beach. He squatted in the sand, remembering another night, another beach. There was no sign of the natives now. The glittering carpet of beach rolled out before him. A primitive fear knotted his gut as he braced himself to step onto that shimmering stretch of sand and sea, naked to any eyes that might be watching from the forest.

Then he saw it, a light shining through the trees from the hut just as the light had once shone from David's tent. This time he would not be too late. His hesitation wouldn't cost him the life of someone he loved.

He burst from the cover of the dunes and pounded down the beach, sending chunks of wet sand flying in his wake. Cold sea spray battered him. The beach unfurled in a sparkling ribbon, mocking him with the serene beauty of the rising moon silvering the indigo swells.

A ghost stepped out from the shadows. Nicky, luminous in a white linen suit and a wide-brimmed panama hat. Justin stumbled to a halt.

He stared, mesmerized, at the graceful flick of Nicky's fingers as he struck a match and touched the flame to the end of his cigarette. The sickly sweet aroma of burning hemp filled the air, and Justin knew it wasn't tobacco he was smoking.

Nicky held out a gold case and raised one mocking eyebrow. "Cigarette? As I recall, you sometimes indulged."

"Why couldn't you have left us alone, Nicky? We were happy together. Why couldn't you just walk away when you found us?"

A beatific smile curved his lips. "And give up the sheer pleasure of watching you destroy each other? You've always misread my intentions. I never wanted to kill you, Justin. I just wanted to watch you bleed."

"Where is she? What have you done with her?"

"Nothing." Nicky took a deep draw from the cigarette; his eyes glittered. "Yet."

With one smooth motion Justin drew the pistol from his waistband and pointed it at his old friend, his hands oddly steady. "I want to see her."

Nicky slid the cigarette case into his pocket and held up both hands. "Please don't shoot me. I'd never get the bloodstains out of this suit, and you know how expensive Egyptian linen is."

"Take me to her."

He dropped his hands, giving Justin a beleaguered smile. "I've always found your singleminded sense of purpose quite dull. I told you. She's safe for now. At least until I tire of her."

Justin started for him. "You ruthless bastard."

Nicky's low laugh rippled. "Ah, so that's the way of it.

I thought so. I wonder what your precious David would say if he knew you'd been tumbling his sweet little Claire between the sheets. I don't think that's quite what he had in mind when he asked you to take care of her. But I do hope you rode her hard and broke her in well for me."

Blinded by rage at the full extent of Nicholas's betrayal, Justin rammed the pistol back in his waistband and rushed him, coming in low and hard. His shoulder slammed into Nicky's stomach. The cigarette flew from his elegant lips. They rolled to the powdery sand in an explosion of flailing arms and legs.

Justin's right hook connected with a solid crack, rocking back Nicky's head. He wanted to pound his face to a bloody pulp, but all he got in was one more blow before he realized Nicky hadn't lifted his fists to fight back, but had balled them in front of his face to protect it. A keening whimper escaped him.

Grabbing his lapels, Justin slammed him to his back and straddled him. He shook him with each anguished word. "How could you do it, you son of a bitch? You were my friend!"

Nicky slowly lowered his hands, and Justin realized with horror that he was crying. Tears streaked the grit on his cheeks but didn't dim the virulent hatred in his eyes. "You don't know what it was like," he screamed. "You always had it all. You never had to scrounge in the sewers of Rome for food or pennies, selling whatever you could to stay alive—even yourself."

Justin sat back on his haunches, stunned.

"We could have had it all, you and I, but you gave up your inheritance! You just threw it away like it was nothing. And why shouldn't you? You never had to let some fat Sicilian pig maul you with his sweaty hands in the hopes he might give you a loaf of bread afterward for your trouble!"

Justin turned his face away. "I never knew," he whispered. "I swear I never knew."

He was completely unprepared when the sharp heel of Nicky's boot slammed into his jaw, knocking him backward. Before he could react, Nicky rolled up. Striking with the speed and cunning of a serpent, he snatched the pistol from Justin's waistband and leveled it at him.

Justin stood, backing away. Nicholas followed, scooping up his hat as he rose and tilting it back on his head at a rakish angle. His grip on the gun wavered wildly. "You ruined everything, you rich brat. Together we could have had the world."

There was a sigh then, softer than the wind, and they both turned to find Emily standing in the sand, the moonlight pearling off the barrel of the derringer cradled in her palm.

*C*hapter 35

· 🦪 ·

*Know in that moment that I'd cheat even death
for one last glimpse of my little girl. . . .*

*E*mily looked so beautiful with her skirts blowing in the
wind and her hair tousled by its fingers that Justin wanted
to weep. He was surprised she couldn't hear the crack of
his heart breaking.

Nicky slowly lowered his pistol.

She moved toward Justin, the gun never wavering in
her grip. The moonlight polished her skin to porcelain and
shaded her piquant features to an inscrutable mask. Only
her eyes were alive, sparkling with an inner flame that
burned bright and hot.

"I was hoping you'd leave me the pleasure of shooting
the bastard," she said.

A grin spread across Nicky's face. He tossed Justin's
pistol aside, pulled out a handkerchief, and scrubbed at his
palm as if the weapon had defiled it. "The pleasure is all
mine, *cara mia.*"

Justin faced her as he should have seven years earlier—
with his arms spread wide and his heart in his hands. "It's

all right, darling. Killing me won't stop me from loving you."

She took another step toward him. A single tear slipped from her lashes and tumbled down her cheek. Her thumb toyed with the hammer; her voice was as soft and lethal as a caress. "Now you'll know what it's like to die a thousand miles from home at the hand of someone you love."

"Ah, but that's where you're wrong. I am home. And I'd much rather die by your hand than his."

"Go on. Shoot him," Nicky urged. "Before he kills the both of us like he killed your father. Oh, they were a fine pair, those two. Always had their heads together, laughing about something, shutting me out like I wasn't good enough for the likes of them. What really happened the night he died, Justin?" he taunted. "Was it truly an act of mercy, or perhaps a lover's quarrel?"

With no warning Emily swung the gun around and aimed it at Nicky's head. "Nobody talks that way about my daddy."

The derringer exploded in a smoky blur.

Nicky's hat flew off. He rubbed his head, his expression of bewilderment almost comical. "Do you know how much that hat cost, you stupid little bitch?"

"More than your coat?" she queried politely, cocking the derringer and firing again. She winged his coat, tearing a blackened hole through the armpit. When she steadied her arm, the pistol was pointing straight at his heart.

"You don't have to do this, Emily," Justin said very softly, inching toward her. "We can have him put away for a very long time."

Tears were streaming down her face in earnest now. "Not long enough," she said, raking back the hammer.

Nicky's eyes rolled wildly, but his attention was not on her. It was as if he could hear something they could not. They froze, listening. It was the silence. There was something wrong with the silence. In that instant of Emily's hesitation it had become a living, breathing thing. The shimmering leaves of the rain forest quivered and sighed, alive with knowing eyes. Justin's skin crawled.

The brush exploded in a screeching mass of lithe bronze bodies. Justin dove for Emily, pressing her to her knees, forcing her face into his chest, wanting to spare her the sight of the familiar tattooed faces contorted into demonic masks of fury. Their ear-shattering cries for revenge drowned out the roar of the sea. Hordes of sun-browned feet stampeded around them in a beat more primitive than drums or thunder. Someone was screaming. It might have been Emily or it might have been him.

Nicky's hysterical wail rose above it all. "For God's sake, you savages. Not the suit. Don't tear the bloody suit!"

Justin lifted his face from Emily's trembling throat. A writhing mass of natives had Nicky by the arms and legs. Justin stared mesmerized as they dragged him howling and bucking into the forest, leaving only his panama hat flattened in the sand.

The screams and howls slowly died. For a wavering moment the silence was broken only by the whisper of the waves and the shrill cry of a kiwi.

Someone was watching them. The hair on Justin's nape stood erect. He turned his head to find a lean figure squatting beneath the shadow of a punga tree. Their gazes met across the moonlit stretch of beach, man to man, friend to friend. Then the native lifted his hand and melted into the arms of the brush without so much as a rustle of his flaxen skirt.

Chapter 36

· ❦ ·

Eternity will find me still watching over you. . . .

"Never underestimate the resourcefulness of an English valet left to his own devices," Justin murmured into Emily's hair.

She nuzzled against his chest, loath to surrender the comfort of his strong arms around her. He tasted so good —salty and gritty and real, as a man should taste. Her convulsive shivers slowly abated. She tilted her face to his, laughing and crying at the same time.

"Oh, Justin!" she exclaimed, throwing her arms around his neck.

It took her a moment to realize something was wrong. He knelt rigid in her embrace. She drew back fearfully. "You didn't really think I was going to shoot you, did you?"

"The thought did occur to me."

"But you were so wonderful, so gallant about it." She gazed up at him through a puddle of besotted tears. "Why, you smiled at me like an angel."

He pried her arms off his neck and stood, brushing the sand from his knees. "My manners at gunpoint have always been impeccable."

He walked to the edge of the waves and stared out to sea.

Emily trailed after him. "I had to do it, you know." She waded out in front of him, heedless of the foam washing over her skirt. "It was your face." Reaching up, she cupped his cheeks in her hands. "Your beautiful face. It's so expressive. I had no choice. You could have never maintained the charade. Nicky would have seen right through you. To make him believe I hated you, I had to make you believe it, too."

The planes of his face were cold and stony now. Only his eyes revealed the depths of his stormy thoughts. "You did an admirable job."

Emily dropped her hands. She paced back and forth through the waves, frantic to make him understand. "Saleri started harping about this land grant he claimed you altered to cheat him and Daddy out of their shares of the mine. He was going to use it to have you put away for life. I was afraid if he came here alone and got his hands on it, he would destroy it, or, even worse, doctor it himself to have you brought to trial for my father's murder."

Justin's voice was chillingly devoid of emotion. "Are you sure that's why you came with him?"

She wheeled to face him. "What do you mean?"

His eyes narrowed. "Maybe somewhere in your mind was just the tiniest smidgen of doubt. Maybe you wanted to see that land grant for yourself and find out if I really did murder your father."

"No!" She lifted her sodden hem and stumbled toward him. "I believed in you. I swear it. You're all I ever believed in."

Snorting in disbelief, Justin scooped up a shell, then drew back his arm to toss it into the sea. "What were you going to do after he took you to the land grant? Shoot him in cold blood?"

She grabbed his arm, not even realizing herself the full import of her words. "I didn't even think about what would happen next. I knew you'd come for me."

The shell slipped from his fingers. He slowly swung around to face her. "And if I hadn't come?" he asked brutally. "If I had decided a woman like you was hardly worth chasing halfway across the world?"

She bowed her head, wondering if he would ever understand or be able to forgive her for her own dark passions. She lifted her head, her heart in her eyes. "I would have done what I had to do. He killed my father."

A strange expression passed over Justin's face, then was gone, leaving it as impassive as before.

He ran his thumb over her cheek to flick away a tear. "Then you'll understand when I do what I have to do." With those words he gently disengaged her hand, turned, and walked away.

Emily's hands hung limply at her sides. "Where are you going?"

His stride did not slow. Desolation overwhelmed her with abandonment nipping close at its heels. All she could see was Justin Connor walking away from her one more time.

She trotted after him, pausing to hop up and down on one foot to peel off her sodden slipper. "Go on, you coward!" she yelled. "Run away from me. It's what you do best, isn't it?"

She hurled the slipper. It struck him solidly between the shoulder blades. He hesitated for a heartbeat, then kept going.

Her voice rose. "I don't need you. I never needed you. The day Emily Claire Scarborough needs anybody will be the day they grow tulips in hell!" She took a few more stumbling steps, then sank to her knees in the sand. "I

don't need you, you bastard." Tears blinded her. Her voice
faded to a mumble. "I don't need anyone."

Emily sat on the bluff where her father was buried, hugging her knees to her chest. She watched as Justin's clipper
unfurled its sails and set for open sea. The same warm
wind that tossed her curls around her face filled its billowing sails, sending it slicing for the horizon. It was a magnificent sight, silhouetted against the pagan moon like a
ghost of days long gone. Its beauty would have broken her
heart if it hadn't already been broken.

The lights of the ship slowly faded over the horizon,
leaving her alone with the brilliant glitter of the stars. She
tangled her bare toes in the tussock grass and laid her
damp cheek against her knee.

An unearthly sound filled the night. Emily lifted her
head, stiffening. She was afraid to turn around, afraid she
might have imagined the hymn brightening the darkness,
afraid it might be only the stars rubbing points or the
melodic wanderings of a lost choir of angels. The music
rose on magical wings, drifting through the wind to her
ears.

Her hands clenched into fists. She stood and dared to
turn, only to find a shimmering line of torches winding
their way down the beach toward the bluff. Her breath
caught in her throat.

The procession topped the bluff. Among their well-
loved faces stood Trini in full ceremonial garb, running his
hands down the lapels of a rumpled coat of the finest
Egyptian linen; Dani and Kawiri, their lithe naked bodies
draped with shells and fragments of polished amber; the
stern *ariki*, his mouth folded in what might have been a
smile on a more expressive face.

But Emily had eyes only for the man at the head of
their procession. A barefoot king in a pair of ragged dungarees.

The silence rustled expectantly around them.

"You're late again," she said, swallowing around the knot in her throat.

"Not too late, I hope," Justin replied. "It's bad form to be late for your own wedding."

Emily pressed her fingers to her trembling lips. She understood that he was offering her his life as bravely and as gallantly as he had on the beach. Not to end it in a flash of smoking gunpowder, but to cup its fragile moments in her palm, to nourish it and protect it as she would her own through all the sweet years to come.

She opened her mouth to give him her answer.

A silver tray popped into her vision, crowned by a conch shell brimming with amber liquid. Penfeld bowed. "A spot of tea, perhaps, my dear? To celebrate this momentous occasion."

He didn't utter a protest when she shoved the tray aside and flew across the bluff into Justin's waiting arms. Trini's deep-throated laughter pealed out as Justin rocked her in his hard embrace.

He swept out an arm toward the wind-battered cross. "I wanted David to share the moment with us."

"Oh, he is," Emily breathed in wonder. "Look."

They both stared at the base of the cross to discover a single fragile pohutukawa bloom had pushed its way up through the sandy soil, its tender petals unfurling in a fresh promise of new life.

Their lips met in a melting caress, making promises and vows they would gladly spend their lifetimes keeping. As the natives danced around them, Justin stroked her hair and pressed his lips to her ear, whispering the words she'd once thought never to hear again except on the distant wings of the wind—

"Stay with me always, my sweet, my love . . . my Claire."

ABOUT THE AUTHOR

USA Today and *Publishers Weekly* bestselling author Teresa Medeiros was recently chosen one of the Top Ten Favorite Romance Authors by *Affaire de Coeur* magazine and won the *Romantic Times* Reviewer's Choice Award for Best Historical Love and Laughter. A former Army brat and registered nurse, she wrote her first novel at the age of twenty-one and has since gone on to win the hearts of critics and readers alike. The author of thirteen novels, Teresa makes her home in Kentucky with her husband and two cats. Readers can visit her website at www.teresamedeiros.com.

If you loved ONCE AN ANGEL, don't miss

A Kiss to Remember

a bewitching romance
from the superb
Teresa Medeiros.
Available from
Bantam Books.

Read on for a preview....

My darling son, my hands are shaking as I pen this letter. . . .

The devil had come to Devonbrooke Hall.

He hadn't come in a coach drawn by four black horses, nor in a blast of brimstone, but in the honey-gold hair and angelic countenance of Sterling Harlow, the seventh duke of Devonbrooke. He strode through the marble corridors of the palatial mansion he had called home for the past twenty-one years, two brindle mastiffs padding at his heels with a leonine grace that matched his own.

He stayed the dogs with a negligent flick of one hand, then pushed open the study door and leaned against the frame, wondering just how long his cousin would pretend not to notice that he was there.

Her pen continued to scratch its way across the ledger for several minutes until a particularly violent *t*-crossing left an ugly splotch of ink on the page. Sighing with defeat, she glared at him over the top of her wire-rimmed spectacles. "I can see that Napoleon failed to teach you any manners at all."

"On the contrary," Sterling replied with a lazy smile. "I taught him a thing or two. They're saying that he abdicated after Waterloo just to get away from me."

"Now that you're back in London, I might consider joining him in exile."

As Sterling crossed the room, his cousin held herself as rigid as a dressmaker's dummy. Oddly enough, Diana was probably the only woman in London who did not seem out of place behind the leather-and-mahogany-appointed splendor of the desk. As always, she eschewed the pale pastels and virginal whites favored by the current crop of belles for the stately hues of forest green and wine. Her dark hair was drawn back in a simple chignon that accentuated the elegance of her widow's peak.

"Please don't sulk, cousin dear," he murmured, leaning down to kiss her cheek. "I can bear the world's censure, but yours cuts me to the heart."

"It might if you had one." She tilted her face to receive his kiss, her stern mouth softening. "I heard you came back over a week ago. I suppose you've been staying with that rascal Thane again."

Ignoring the leather wing chair in front of the desk, Sterling came around and propped one hip on the corner nearest his cousin. "He's never quite forgiven you for swearing off your engagement, you know. He claims you broke his heart and cast cruel aspersions upon his character."

Although Diana took care to keep her voice carefully neutral, a hint of color rose in her cheeks. "My problem wasn't with your friend's character. It was his lack of it."

"Yet in all these years, neither one of you has ever married. I've always found that rather . . . curious."

Diana drew off her spectacles, leveling a frosty gaze at him. "I'd rather live without a man than marry a boy." As if realizing she'd revealed too much, she slipped her spectacles back on and busied herself with wiping the excess ink from the nib of her pen. "I'm certain that even Thane's escapades must pale in comparison with your own. I hear you've been back in London long enough to have fought four duels, added the family fortunes of three unfortunate young bucks to your winnings, and broken an assortment of hearts."

Sterling gave her a reproachful look. "When will you learn not to listen to unkind gossip? I only winged two fellows, won the ancestral home of another, and bruised a single heart, which turned out to be far less innocent than I'd been led to believe."

Diana shook her head. "Any woman foolish enough to entrust her heart into your hands gets no more than she deserves."

"You may mock me if you like, but now that the war is over, I've every intention of beginning my search for a bride in earnest."

"That bit of news will warm the heart of every ambitious belle and matchmaking mama in the city. So tell me, what brought on this sudden yearning for home and hearth?"

"I'll soon be requiring an heir, and unlike dear old Uncle Granville, God rest his black soul, I've no intention of purchasing one."

A bone-chilling growl swelled through the room, almost as if Sterling's mention of his uncle had invoked some unearthly presence. He peered over the top of the desk to find the mastiffs peering beneath it, their tails quivering at attention.

Diana slowly leaned back in her chair to reveal the dainty white cat curled in her lap.

Sterling scowled. "Shouldn't that be in the barns? You know I can't abide the creatures."

Giving Sterling a feline smile of her own, Diana stroked the cat beneath its fluffy chin. "Yes, I know."

Sterling sighed. "Down, Caliban. Down, Cerberus." As the dogs slunk over to the hearth rug to pout, he gave his cousin an exasperated look. "I don't know why I bothered going off to war to fight the French when I could have stayed here and fought with you."

In truth, they both knew why he'd gone.

It hadn't taken Sterling long to discover why his uncle wasn't averse to a show of spirit in a lad. It was because the old wretch took such brutal pleasure in caning it out of him. Sterling had stoically endured his uncle's attempts to mold him into the next duke until he'd reached the age of seventeen and, like his father before him, shot up eight inches in as many months.

Sterling would never forget the cold winter night he had turned and ripped the cane from his uncle's gnarled hands. The old man had quailed before him, waiting for the blows to begin falling.

He still couldn't say whether it was contempt for his uncle or for himself that had driven him to snap the cane in two, hurl it at his uncle's feet, and walk away. The old man had never laid a hand on him again. A few short months later, Sterling had left Devonbrooke Hall, rejecting the grand tour his uncle had planned in favor of a ten-year tour of Napoleon's battlefields. His stellar military career was punctuated by frequent visits to London, during which he played as hard as he had fought.

"You might consider coming home to stay," Diana said. "My father's been dead for over six years now."

Sterling shook his head, his smile laced with regret. "Some ghosts can never be laid to rest."

"As well I know," she replied, her eyes distant.

His uncle had never once caned her. As a female, she wasn't worthy of even that much of his attention.

Sterling reached for her hand, but she was already drawing a folded, cream-colored piece of stationery from beneath the blotter. "This came in the post over four months ago. I would have had it forwarded to your regiment, but . . ." Her graceful shrug spoke volumes.

Proving her judgment sound, Sterling slid open a drawer and prepared to toss the missive onto a thick stack of identical letters—all addressed to Sterling Harlow, Lord Devonbrooke, and all unopened. But something stilled his hand. Although the fragrance of orange blossoms still clung to the stationery, the handwriting was not the gently looping script he had come to expect. A strange frisson, as subtle as a woman's breath, lifted the hairs on his nape.

"Open it," he commanded, pressing the letter back into Diana's hand.

Diana swallowed. "Are you certain?"

He nodded curtly.

Her hand trembled as she slid an ivory-handled letter opener beneath the wax seal and unfolded the missive. " 'Dear Lord Devonbrooke,' " she read softly. " 'I regret to inform you that your mother has passed from this world to a much kinder one.' " Diana hesitated, then continued with obvious reluctance. " 'Although you chose to ignore her repeated pleas for reconciliation over the past few years, she died with your name on her lips. I trust the news will not cause you any undue distress. Ever your humble servant, Miss Laura Fairleigh.' "

Diana slowly lowered the letter to the desk and drew off her spectacles. "Oh, Sterling, I'm so sorry."

A muscle in his jaw twitched once, then was still. Without a word, he took the letter from Diana's hands, dropped it in the drawer, and slid the drawer shut, leaving the fragrance of orange blossoms lingering in the air.

A smile curved his lips, deepening the dimple in his right cheek that always struck dread in his opponents, whether gazing at him across the gaming tables or the battlefield. "This Miss Fairleigh sounds less than humble to me. Just who is this cheeky chit who dares to reproach the all-powerful duke of Devonbrooke?"

He waited while Diana consulted a leather-bound ledger. His cousin kept meticulous records on all the properties that had once belonged to her father but now belonged to him.

"She's a rector's daughter. An orphan, I believe. Your mother took her in, along with her young brother and sister, seven years ago, after their parents were killed in an unfortunate fire that destroyed the estate's rectory."

"How very charitable of her." Sterling shook his head wryly. "A rector's daughter. I should have known. There's nothing quite like the righteous indignation of some poor deluded fool who fancies she has God fighting on her side." He whipped a sheet of stationery from a teakwood tray and slid it in front of Diana. "Pen a missive at once. Inform this Miss Fairleigh that the duke of Devonbrooke will be arriving in Hertfordshire in a month's time to take full possession of his property."

Diana gaped at him, letting the ledger fall shut. "You can't be serious."

"And why not? Both my parents are dead now. That would make Arden Manor mine, would it not?"

"And just what do you plan to do with the orphans? Cast them into the street?"

He stroked his chin. "I'll have my solicitor seek out situations for them. They'll probably thank me for my largesse. After all, three children left too long to their own devices can only arrive at mischief."

"Miss Fairleigh is no longer a child," Diana reminded him. "She's a woman grown."

Sterling shrugged. "Then I'll find her a husband—some enlisted man or law clerk who won't mind taking a cheeky chit to bride to curry my favor."

Diana clapped a hand to her breast, glaring at him. "You're such a romantic. It warms my heart."

"And you're an incorrigible scold," Sterling retorted, tweaking her patrician nose.

He rose, the casual motion bringing the mastiffs to attention. Diana waited until he'd crossed to the door, the dogs at his heels, before saying softly, "I still don't understand, Sterling. Arden is nothing but a humble country manor, little more than a cottage. Why would you wish to claim it for your own when you have a dozen vast estates you've never even bothered to visit?"

He hesitated, his eyes touched by bleak humor. "My parents sold my soul to obtain the deed to it. Perhaps I just want to decide for myself if it was worth the cost."

After sketching her a flawless bow, he closed the door behind him, leaving her to stroke the cat in her lap, her brow furrowed in a pensive frown.

"Soulless devil! Odious toad! Truffle-snorting man-pig! Oh, the wretched nerve of him!"

George and Lottie watched Laura storm back and forth across the drawing room in slack-jawed amazement. They'd never before seen their even-tempered sister in such an impressive rage. Even the rich brown hair that had been gathered in a tidy knot at the crown of her head quivered with indignation.

Laura spun around, waving the letter in her hand. The expensive stationery was woefully crumpled from having been wadded up in her fist numerous times since it had arrived in the morning post. "He didn't even have the common decency to pen the letter himself. He had his cousin write it! I can just see the heartless ogre now. He's probably rubbing his fat little hands together in greedy glee as he contemplates snatching the very roof from over our heads. It's no wonder they call him the Devil of Devonbrooke!"

"But Lady Eleanor died over five months ago," George said. "Why did he wait so long to contact us?"

"According to this letter, he's been abroad for the last several months," Laura replied. "Probably off on some Continental tour, no doubt, gorging himself on the shameless pleasures of any overindulged libertine."

"I'll bet he's a dwarf," Lottie ventured.

"Or a humpbacked troll with broken teeth and an insatiable appetite for ten-year-old brats." George curled his hands into claws and went lurching at Lottie, eliciting a squeal shrill enough to send the kittens napping beneath her petticoats scattering across the threadbare rug. Lottie never went anywhere without a herd of kittens trailing behind her. There were times when Laura would have sworn her little sister was spawning them herself.

Laura was forced to make an awkward hop to keep from tripping over one of them. Rather than darting for safety, the yellow tabby plopped down on its hindquarters and began to lick one paw with disdain, as if their near collision was solely Laura's fault.

"You needn't look so smug," she informed the little cat. "If we get evicted, you'll soon be gobbling down barn mice instead of those nice juicy kippers you fancy."

Sobering, George sank down beside Lottie on the settee. "Can he really evict us? And if he does, what's to become of us?"

Laura's laugh held little amusement. "Oh, we've nothing to worry about. Listen to this: 'Lord Devonbrooke begs your forgiveness,' " she read with contempt. " 'He sincerely regrets having been lax in his duties for so long. As the new master of Arden Manor, he will gladly shoulder the responsibility of finding new situations for you.' " She crumpled the letter again. "Situations indeed! He probably plans to cast us into the workhouse."

"I've never cared much for work. I do believe I'd prefer to be cast into the streets," Lottie said thoughtfully. "I'd make a rather fetching beggar, don't you think? Can't you just see me standing on a snowy street corner clutching a tin cup in my frostbitten fingers?" She heaved a sigh, her imagination feeding her love of drama. "I'd grow paler and thinner with each passing day, until I finally expired of consumption in the arms of some handsome but aloof stranger." She illustrated her words by swooning onto the settee and pressing the back of one plump little hand to her brow.

"The only thing you're likely to expire of," George muttered, "is eating too many of Cookie's teacakes."

Reviving herself, Lottie stuck out her tongue at him.

George sprang to his feet, raking his sandy hair out of his hazel eyes. "I know! I'll challenge the blackguard to a duel! He won't dare refuse me. Why, I'll be thirteen in December—nearly a man."

"Having no roof over my head *and* a dead brother isn't going to make me feel one whit better," Laura said grimly, shoving him back down.

"We could murder him," Lottie suggested cheerfully. A precocious reader of Gothic novels, she'd been dying to murder someone ever since she'd finished Mrs. Radcliffe's *The Mysteries of Udolpho*.

Laura snorted. "Given the unfeeling way he ignored his mother's letters for all these years, it would probably take a silver bullet or a stake through the heart."

"I don't understand," George said. "How can he toss us out on our arses"—catching Laura's warning glare, he cleared his throat—"on our *ears* when Lady Eleanor promised us that Arden Manor would always be our home?"

Laura moved to the window and drew back one of the lace curtains, avoiding her brother's shrewd gaze. "I never told you this before because I didn't want either of you to worry, but Lady Eleanor's promise possessed certain . . . *stipulations*."

George and Lottie exchanged an apprehensive glance before saying in unison, "Such as?"

Laura faced them, the truth coming out in a rush. "To inherit Arden Manor, I must marry before I reach my twenty-first birthday."

Lottie gasped while George groaned and buried his face in his hands

"You needn't look so appalled," Laura said with a sniff. "It's rather insulting."

"But you've already turned down a dozen proposals from every unmarried man in the village," George pointed out. "You knew Lady Eleanor didn't approve of your being so persnickety. That's probably why she tried to force your hand."

"Tooley Grantham's given to gluttony," Lottie said, ticking off Laura's reservations about her potential suitors on her pudgy little fingers. "Wesley Trumble's too hairy. Huey Kleef slurps when he eats. And Tom Dillmore always has little creases of dirt in the folds of his neck and behind his ears."

Laura shuddered. "I suppose you want me to spend the rest of my life with some hulking bear of a man with no table manners and an abhorrence of bathing."

"It might be better than spending the rest of your life waiting for a man who doesn't exist," George said darkly.

"But you know I've always dreamed of marrying a man who could carry on Papa's work in the parish. Most of the men in the village can't even read. Nor do they care to learn."

Lottie twined one long golden curl around her

finger. "It's a pity I'm not the older sister. 'Twould be a great sacrifice, of course, but I'd be perfectly willing to marry for money instead of love. Then I could take care of you and George forever. And I wouldn't have any trouble catching a rich husband. I'm going to be quite the incomparable beauty, you know. Everyone says so."

"You're already an incomparable bore," George muttered. He turned his accusing gaze on Laura. "You might have mentioned needing a husband sooner, you know. While there was still time to find you one who meets your exacting standards."

Laura plopped down on a creaky ottoman and rested her chin in her hand. "How was I to know that anyone but us would even want this run-down old place? I suppose I thought we could simply go on living here as long as we liked, with no one ever the wiser."

Unshed tears stung her eyes. The sunlight pouring through the east windows only served to underscore the genteel shabbiness of the drawing room. The petit-point roses embroidered on the settee cushions had long ago faded to a watery pink. An unsightly mildew stain marred the plaster frieze over the door, while a moldy stack of leather-bound books was being used to prop up one of the broken legs of the rosewood pianoforte. Arden Manor might be a humble country house that reflected only a shadow of its former glory, but to them it was home.

The only home any of them had known since they'd lost their parents over seven years ago.

Slowly becoming aware that her brother's and sister's dejected faces mirrored her own, Laura rose, forcing a smile. "There's no need for such long faces. We've an entire month before this Lord Devil arrives."

"But we've only a little over three weeks before your birthday," George reminded her.

Laura nodded. "I realize the situation seems hopeless, but we must always remember what Papa taught us—through prayer and persistence, the good Lord will provide."

"What should we tell Him to send us?" Lottie asked eagerly, bouncing to her knees.

Laura pondered her answer for a long moment, her pious demeanor at odds with the determined gleam in her eye. "A man."